WE HAVE YESTERDAY

BY

RICHARD THOMAS MAGNOTTI

Writing As

Richard Carmine Rose

"WE HAVE YESTERDAY"
BY
RICHARD THOMAS MAGNOTTI

PAGES:

INTRODUCTION

Ft. LAUDERDALE

1965

Ft. LAUDERDALE is a tropical mecca, an ocean front city of
very wealthy inhabitants whose names are listed on the social registry and whose forebears built this once swampy "Fort" into a burgeoning metropolis.

The privileged live in their waterfront villas and enjoy all
the accoutrements of a First Class city. They have their country clubs
and yacht clubs. They throw lavish parties for their fellow elites
and all their whims and wants are at their fingertips. There is a
heavy preponderance of the extremely wealthy concentrated here, with
a small middle class citizenry, many of whom are employed in the service of the affluent classes, or as skilled tradesmen, who will build
this small sea-side burg into a sprawling urban center for the bank-
ers, financiers and developers.

In the ensuing decade Ft. Lauderdale and the surrounding county of Broward, as well as Dade Co. to the south and Palm Beach Co. to
the north, will explode, the growth rate so rapid it will be unequal-
ed in the country. It will be paved over in its entirety from the
Atlantic shore westward to the very edge of the Everglades.

Land that is $10.00 an acre will balloon to 10 times that
amount per square foot. The rich will grow richer still, their holds
on the reins of power, political as well as financial, becoming absolute.

Nowhere will the maxim of, "Absolute power corrupts absolutely," be truer than here in S. Florida, the very spawning ground of greed.

Nothing will be spared, the selfish holding nothing sacred. Honor is but a mythic ideal and no more. Truth is to be bartered for lies, the ends justifying any means, any-, including death.

The sentiment of, "Do as I say, and not as I do," is the prevalent theme, more pronounced here where wealth and poverty reside in such close proximity.

There is benign racism. it's the first half of the 1960's. More blatant and commonplace is prejudice towards the have-nots, the poor.

Yankees are still much hated 100 years after Appomatox. Much is hidden, its not all overt or readily apparent. You'd have to look, to dig beneath the thin veneer of respectability and honesty. How much respectability is needed? How much honesty can you afford?

The affluent inhabitants of the East-side communities of Los Olas isles, Victoria Park, Coral Ridge, et. al., do not face the hardships that the inhabitants of the West-side neighborhoods must.

The draft is culling young men every year for military service, to cite just one example.

The short geographical separation between East and West, 10 miles perhaps, may just as well be the void, the chasm, between Valhalla and the river Styx.

If you by misfortune or birth reside on the West-side, and you are very determined, very brave or very foolish, perhaps both, and possibly luck and good fortune happen to smile down on you, at just the right moment, then maybe, maybe-, you'd cross the impenetrable void.

This is the age-old story of good versus evil- possibly - life's lines are never so clearly marked, are they?

PART I

BEAUTIFUL GIRLS

CHAPTER ONE
September 1965

"I'm in love for the first time."
Don't Let Me Down/ The Beatles

TRAFFIC is light at 7;00 A.M. this first day of the new school year, and James Carosa and his father, Angelo, are comfortable with each other and the silence in the car. The two are very close, young Jimmy often accompanying Angelo wherever he went.

The 5 years Angelo was absent from his family, "in the Army," being a terrible ordeal for all. Jimmy, the youngest, felt it worst.

But that is long past now, a distant memory, the family has been reunited almost the same amount of time they were separated, 5 years. The family is whole again, together, except for Angelo's oldest child Joseph, his 19 year old son, who is beginning his second full year at the United States Military Academy at West Point.

His daughter the middle child is 15 year old Christine, and then Jimmy the baby of the family at 13, who looks just like his mother Antoinette, Nettie.

Angelo loves all three of his children but Jimmy, who looks exactly like his mother though in every other aspect is his fathers son, truly a "chip off the old block," is Angelo's favorite. His youngest child takes every opportunity he can to be with him, he's making up for the lost years in New York.

Looking across the car seat now at his son he pinches Jimmy's cheek and asks, "You got enough money? Your mother give you any?" Jimmy says, "Only $5.00- Can you give me a little more?", feigning abject dejection with such exaggeration that Angelo can't help but laugh, and says, "Your such an actor, fachime!" He pinches his face again and peels off a $20.00 and gives it to him.

For such a young boy Jimmy can and does convey a wide variety of emotions with just a single gesture, its uncanny. Nettie has often told her youngest child, "You could sell ice-cubes to eskimos," and she means it.

Jimmy's whole demeanor changes and he says, "Thanks Dad! Now I can go to Wolfies with the rich kids-," and both father and son get a good laugh out of that.

You'll never see two people closer than Angelo and his young son, Jimmy is the apple of Angelo's eye, truly. And Angelo without question is a giant to Jimmy, he worships his father.

The irony of young Jimmy hob-nobbing with the off-spring of Ft. Lauderdale societies elite, considering Angelo's past, his background, and present occupation isn't lost on either of them, they find it very amusing indeed. Its their own private joke.

Angelo's sacrifice and subsequent absence from the family did not go uncompensated. How much is 5 years of a man's life, especially one with a family, worth? He didn't have much choice, he had shut his mouth, took the hit and went and did the time, refusing to cooperate with the prosecution. The D.A. had sought the maximum 10 year sentence and that's what Angelo had received.

Angelo has been a part of, or employed by, the Mob, in one capacity or another, since he was 11 years old and running numbers on the lower East-side of Manhattan for Guido. At the ripe old age of 15 he had encumbered the ungodly sum of $6,000 in gambling debts. Quite a fortune in the year 1928. The big boss, GeJo, had told every book in New York, "The kid Angelo don't owe you nothin," and every book in New York City had replied, "Yes sir, Mr. GeJo."

GeJo liked the gutsy young Napolitano Angelo, "The kids got balls," he had laughed. From then on Angelo worked directly for Mr.

GeJo, a relationship that would span close to 40 years, the final ones after GeJo's own death.

GeJo is Napolitano, Charles "Lucky" Luciano is Napolitano, the trouble between the two camps of the Mafia, the Siciliano and Napolitano has yet to begin, but its right around the corner from 1928.

In 1955 Angelo would finally have the opportunity to repay GeJo for saving his life 27 years previous, as well as everything else, he did so without hesitation.

By his guilty plea Angelo had closed the entire investigation, it stopped right there, with him, and him alone.

GeJo made sure Angelo knew Antoinette and his three children would be taken care of, and when Angelo was released in 1960 he'd have a job and a new start for him and his family in Florida, Miami, with GeJo's family down there, one Eddie Coco, the Boss of all Miami.

GeJo was 62 years old, Angelo 42, GeJo made sure he knew this would be his and his families ticket out of the New York rackets.

Whatever Florida entailed it would never be the razor's edge that New York is, and on this warm and sunny morning Angelo and his son have not one thought of the past.

They've lived here almost 5 years now, Angelo is "working", albeit not even close to the frenzied pace of before but that's just fine, its quiet here. The small neat little home in Lauderdale Manors is paid for and life is good, slow and easy.

They pull into the parking lot of the high school and they embrace, kissing each other on the cheek, Angelo pinches Jimmy's also. "Don't spend all your money at once," Angelo admonishes falsely, he cares not a bit, money is to spend or why have it? And his young son has the exact same sentiments in that regard.

Angelo drove Jimmy because its the first day, after this Jimmy will find his own way, as always. He may even ride the bus like the other West-side students, maybe-.

Ft. Lauderdale High incorporates all of the affluent East-side communities, and some of the far less moneyed West-side locales also. Jimmy has always moved easily and comfortably with both East-side upper crust kids, and his own middle class peers of the West-side.

However, he is now a ninth grade freshmen, the bottom rung of the high schools ladder so to speak. Social class will be more pro-nounced with the student body on the cusp of being young adults, the divide between the haves and have not's more evident in just physical appearances, the clothing, the vehicles or lack there of.

Jimmy has encountered the aloof snobbery in the lower grades too, and he has a vague sense of it all now, but not with a perfect clarity either.

He hears someone calling him, its his sister Christy. "Hey Jimmy, over here," she says waving to him. She hugs him and they also kiss cheeks. They're Italians, Italians kiss. Christy's best friend, Margo, is with her. They drove to school together in Margo's Corvair Monza and she now says, "Hello James, you look very nice. Should I warn all the freshmen girls about you?" She's teasing, she and his sister think Jimmy is very handsome. If only he were a little older, Margo muses.

From behind he hears, "Hello, Jimmy!" He turns and its Jill

Mayor! Wow! "Uh-, hi Jill. This is my sister Christy and her friend is Margo," he says.

By pure luck and not knowing what to say upon turning around and seeing Jill, the most beautiful girl on Earth, he looked mature and poised in making the introductions. Thank you God, he thinks.

Christy, the all knowing sister, can see he's awed by the girl so she valiantly comes to his rescue saying, "Have you known my brother long, Jill?" She replies, "Well, yes- I think, long enough that he should have already asked me out," and she laughs that musical laugh with her dazzling smile. Jimmy is smitten with her. Christy laughs with her and pokes Jimmy saying, "Well?" "Oh, yea! Yes, when? No, no I mean- wow," he's stammering and the girls laugh again.

The bell rings at that moment and Jill hands him her books saying, "Here, you can start by walking me to class, carry these for me?" She stands on tip toes and kisses him lightly on the cheek.

Jimmy is walking on air, he wants to shout to the heavens, he- grabs a hold of himself. "Nice to meet you Christy, Margo," Jill says waving as she leads Jimmy towards her home room class. At the door she takes her books and once again kisses him lightly, this time on the lips. "See you at lunch?", she asks. "Yes! Yes, fine, lunch," he answers. "I'll meet you on the patio, don't be late," she tells him.

Jimmy walks down the hall in a daze, he can't believe it! He shouts, "Yes!", he's got his hands up over his head like he just won the heavyweight Championship of the World. If he knows nothing else he knows he loves high school. He's had a crush on her since elementary school, fifth grade. She kissed me twice!, he thinks. He's afraid he'll wake up and it'll have been a dream. Just then, the second bell rings, he's late. His first day of high school and he's late.

Jill and her best friend, Nicole, are hugging and jumping up and down squealing with delight and emitting gales of girlish laughter. "I can't believe you did it, Jill! I saw everything! I'm so proud of you," Nicole says and they begin another round of hugging and laughing until the teacher, Miss Chance, clears her throat quite loudly and glares at the two of them. They both sit down quietly and Nicole whispers, "You have to tell me, everything!"

Before the end of September Jill and Jimmy are steadies. She wears his sterling silver I.D. bracelet proudly and they sit together every morning on the patio awaiting the start of classes and again at the lunch period. Jimmy was a guest at the Mayor home the previous evening for dinner.

Hugh Mayor, Jill's father, had unexpectedly popped up at the school, surprising his youngest daughter. Her family had noticed the bracelet and her moon-eyed look the last few weeks, so Hugh thought perhaps its time they meet the young man.

When the bell ending classes for the day rang, he sat leaning against his car watching the student's streaming out to the buses, or cars for the older ones. Jill came out holding a young man's hand chatting animatedly and didn't notice her father.

But, Nicole did- she was with them, so she said quite loudly, "Hi, Mr. Mayor, what are you doing here?" He was leaning casually against the car, like it was the most natural thing in the world- his being here at the school, in the middle of the business day-?

She poked Jill and she snapped out of her reverie with the young man and happily skipped to her father. She gave him a big hug and said, "Hi, Daddy! There's someone I'd like you to meet." She hurried back to Jimmy and took his hand and led him back to Hugh. "Daddy, this is Jimmy Carosa, and Jimmy this is my father," she said.

Hugh looked directly at the young man and the boy returned his gaze quite confidently. It impressed the politician that Hugh most certainly is, so he offered his hand and they shook, quite firmly, also good Hugh noted. He liked Jimmy's poise already and was glad Jill had seemed to choose her first boyfriend wisely.

"Well ladies, no need for the bus today. Jimmy are you waiting for someone or do you ride the bus? I'd be happy to give you a lift if you'd like?", Hugh addressed them. Jimmy usually took his time getting home, as long as he was there by 6:00 p.m. for supper.

"No sir, I-," Jimmy began but Jill interrupted, asking, "Daddy, can we-, would it be alright if Jimmy joined us for dinner?" She said this so hopefully that Hugh chuckled good naturedly and said, "Why honey of course! James will you do us the honor of joining us this evening?"

Jill's insistent stare saying he'd better accept, so Jimmy teasingly throws up his hands in a gesture of surrender towards Jill, and then smile's and says, "Yes sir, and thank you sir!" Of course he would have accepted anyway but it was nice to know Jill wanted him to meet her family.

She had taken his hand just now and squeezed it, looking very pleased with herself. "Well then, gentlemen, ladies, shall we?",

Hugh said and opened the car door for Jill and Nicole.

When they arrived at the Mayor estate, a walled river front villa of truly palatial splendor, Jimmy is awed by the mere sight of it. He can't help himself, as the car passes through the electric gate in the walls opening he says, "Wow!" The three look at him questioningly. To Hugh and Jill its just home, Nicole lives a mile or so North on the same river, in a home just as magnificent. Wow, indeed.

Jimmy had to stop himself from gawking as they entered a huge marble floored foyer. An older black lady, the maid, met them at the door and said, "Good afternoon Mista Hugh, you early, and mah, mah, look at mah two princesses." Both Jill and Nicole hugged the old woman, she's like a second mother to the girls. They call her, "Auntie Jewel." She's been a part of their lives since they were first graders.

It was then that Jewel noticed the young man in the foyer's alcove. She looked first at Hugh and then Jill before Jill realized they hadn't introduced him.

"Oh Jewel, Jimmy, excuse me! That's so impolite," Jill gushed with embarrassment and then introduced them with far to much formality to atone for her gaffe. "Please to meet you Mista Jimmy," Jewel said and thinks, the boy very handsome- so, this is Missy Jill's boy?

"Hugh? Jill- is that you, darling?" Its Jill's mother, Cynthia. As she steps around the corner she smile's brightly and kisses Hugh saying, "You're home early, what a pleasant surprise- and you've brought a guest I see." She says the last looking at Jill. Here's the young man Jill is so enamored of, she muses.

"I'm Cynthia, Jill and Lisa's mother," she says, extending her hand. Hugh has his arm around her waist as he says, "Yes, my dear, we've invited him to dine with us this evening," quickly adding, "If that's ok?" "Yes, of course, we're glad to have you Jimmy," Cynthia says.

She is dressed in a faded pair of jeans and a blue chambray work shirt rolled up at the sleeves. Like Jill, she has long ash blond hair and the clearest blue eyes. It's easy to see where Jill's beauty comes from, for Cynthia, with the barest trace of lip gloss and so simply dressed, is a stunning beauty.

"Do you kid's want a snack? Something to drink? Nicole, are you staying for dinner or-?" Cynthia takes charge acting the hostess and asking questions to each.

Nicole informs her, no, she won't be staying as Hugh says, "Well, my dear, I'll certainly take you up on the drink."

Jill and Jimmy decline anything so Hugh and Cynthia retire to the family room and the bar for Hugh's nightly scotch.

Later, after the dinner is finished, the girl's are talking over the days events with their parents.

Lisa has joined them for dinner, she is Jill's 15 year old sister. She's in the same grade as Christy, the eleventh, but Jimmy is quite sure that's the only thing Lisa and Christy have in common, Lisa is such a snob.

As soon as they were seated for supper, Lisa said, "I see you've met Jill's amour, James Carosa," to her parents and Jill had blushed as they all laughed. Cynthia asks if the girls had decided what this years Junior League project is and Lisa had responded avidly, "Mother, its good. Miss Jensen is compiling a list of all the area boy's in Vietnam, we'll draw their names out of a hat and they'll be our pen pal!" "Really dear? That sounds very noble," Cynthia says, sounding anything but, in her tone. Noble?

Cynthia thinks, who are these boy's? What kind of families or background do they come from?

"I'm worried, I mean, what do I write about?", Jill asks. Indeed, it's a very poignant question.

What does her 13 year old daughter write to some poor young man in some far away place fighting in a war? Cynthia hasn't an answer. What she does say is, "I certainly feel blessed that we don't have sons, who would be called upon to go off and fight in a war in some God forsaken little country I've never even heard of." She's looking directly at Hugh as she's saying this.

He had wanted a son badly. He loves his daughters but every man wants a son, too. Cynthia hopes the recent events, with the war in Vietnam escalating, may be of some solace in their not having any sons. Had Lisa been a male and her being 15 years old, the draft would be looming ahead for all of them.

"Well, with that damned cowboy in the White House its liable to drag on for quite some time," Hugh says, and then adds, "We shouldn't even be there at all, but that's the Democrats- that's what they do, start wars."

"Oh Daddy, do you think it'll be over before Greg turns 18?,"

Lisa asks. She's referring to her present boyfriend, who will be her ex-boyfriend far before they get anywhere near 16, never mind 18, Jimmy thinks maliciously.

"Well honey, let's hope so. Greg has a bright future ahead with his father, and they're allowing boy's to defer military service to attend college. I'm sure by then it'll be over," Hugh reassures. He can see real concern on all three Mayor ladies faces. He thinks: maybe it will be... Damn wars, there are far to many of them and this one in particular is unnecessary meddling by the Democrats.

"My brother, Joseph, is at West Point," Jimmy finally chimes in. He had sat quietly listening to the families discussion. All conversation ceased, instantly, like a plug being pulled on a record player.

Hugh finally gathered his wits back and asked, "Really Jimmy?", impressed. Perhaps the Corosa family has political clout? Something? An appointment to West Point has to be a political nomination from a Senator, Governor or Congressman. You cannot gain entry by merit alone, being a top scholar is insufficient.

"I'm sure your family is very proud, who nominated him?", Hugh asked, trying to sound casual.

Jimmy smiled and said, "Senator Connie Mack, Mr. Mayor. My brother was an honor roll, Dean's list student and he scored a perfect 1500 on the SAT. Mayor Lindsey personally proposed to the Senator for my father." Well indeed! Who is this boy? Hugh thinks, he'll have to find out. Jimmy and the entire Carosa family have just grown immeasurably in Hugh's eye's.

Jimmy is bursting with pride. He is very proud of his older brother, even though his life's goal at this tender age is to beat Joseph in a boxing match. They, the whole family, are very proud of Joseph, no one more than their mother, Nettie.

Joseph had aspired to West Point since he was an altar boy at Mt. Carmel Catholic School in the Bronx. He is brilliant, and no-where can that brilliance shine more than at the finest military academy in the world.

GeJo loves Angelo as a son. To him, little Joseph is like his own grandson, (at the time Joseph was little, 9 years old), and he's worthy of Mayor Lindsey's recommendation. The kid is a true genius and its a bonus award for Angelo's life time of service to the old Mafioso. And, Joseph is of his own people, he's Napolitano. He's in-. Mayor Lindsey endorsed Joseph when he was in the ninth grade, in 1960, to Senator Robert Kennedy of New York. Since Joseph will finish high school in Florida, the recommendation has to come from the Florida Senator. Senator Mack was only to happy to oblige the soon to be President's brother. One hand washes the other.

Lisa says, "Come on Jill, just because your beau is here you can still help me clear the table." Jill smile's at Jimmy and excuses herself to help Lisa.

"Jimmy, let me grab a quick shower and I'll run you home," Hugh tells him.

When Hugh's car pulls out through the gate, Jill and her mother watched them go. Cynthia runs her fingers through Jill's hair and caresses her face with the back of her hand saying, "So, you want to tell me about it?" "Oh, what mother?", Jill asks shyly. Cynthia laugh's and says, "Well, Sweetheart, you look absolutely charmed." Jill doesn't respond so her mother pulls her in for a hug, and Jill hugs her back firmly. Looking up she asks, "Do you think he like's me, mother? I mean, as much as I like him?"

Oh, young love! Cynthia muses and says, "Well honey, it looked like your young man was charmed himself, even your dear old Dad noticed, and for him to notice anything its pretty obvious, hmmm?"

Jill smilé's happily and hugs Cynthia again. "I hope Daddy liked him. Do you think he did?", she asks. "He seemed very impressed with him. Jimmy is very much the gentlemen," Cynthia reassures.

They were in the kitchen and had about finished up when Lisa entered and asked, "Can I help, Mom?" Cynthia replied, "No Lisa, we're about done."

"You like Jimmy Carosa a lot, don't you?", Lisa states, it's not a question. Jill blushes again but Lisa hugs her little sister and says, "You don't have to be shy, its just us girls."

Jill says, "oh, Lisa, he's so cute and, and-," she now looks at Cynthia before continuing, "the way he kissed me!"

"Oh, well now! That is serious," Cynthia mildly admonishes as she exchanges knowing glances with her older daughter. Perhaps it's time to have that talk with Jill? Already?!

Her baby Jill, it seems just yesterday she was a proud little first grader in pig-tails and jumper, and now? Now she's on the threshold of becoming a young woman. She'll be 14 in November. Where have the years gone?

"Jill honey, your still a little young to be kissing boys,"
Cynthia warns. "Oh, mother, I'm not a little girl and Jimmy is so...,"
she replies wistfully, "special."

"Well, just the same- proper young ladies must be careful.
Kissing and holding hands can-, um, lead to-," Cynthia is stammering nervously as Lisa bursts out laughing and says, "Oh, mother,
really! Little Jimmy Carosa isn't going to try to feel up your precious little baby, Jill."

"Lisa, please! I don't want to hear you speak so crudely,"
Cynthia scolds.

"I'm sorry, mother," Lisa replies primly, but she's winked
at Jill as she says this, and to Jill, Lisa is the best big sister
in the world. Jill hugs Lisa tightly in gratitude for defending her
and Jimmy.

Mr. Mayor and Jimmy chatted amiably and easily on the drive
to the sturdy little home in the West-side neighborhood of Lauderdale
Manors- that is smaller than the garage at the Mayor estate.

They talked baseball, the two pennant's and the World
Series just weeks away now. Hugh did manage to surreptitiously
query young Jimmy as to his father's line of work, and Jimmy being
an old pro at this line of deception, dutifully answers, "My father
is a bookkeeper for Holiday Inn," and there is truth in that reply.

Angelo does log hours at such a position as a night auditor,
his legit job, 5 nights a week from 10:00 p.m. - 6:00 a.m. His real
job, the book, is from 8:00 a.m. - 2:00 p.m., 7 days a week, 365 days
a year.

Mr. Mayor appears to accept Jimmy's answer as he doesn't probe any further. However, he does think to himself, how did his son get an appointment to the United States Military Academy at West Point? It is the singularly most difficult institution of higher learning to gain entry to on Earth, period.

Perhaps the father is a Medal of Honor recipient? How does a bookkeeper know the Mayor of New York city? Well enough that the Mayor endorses his son to a U.S. Senator, for his nomination? None of it makes sense, he intends to look into it but not out of ill suspicion, no. Maybe the politically connected father would be a valuable asset in Hugh's own future ambitions. He's not going to be in the legislature too much longer, ahead is the U.S. House of Representatives and possibly the Senate. All the wheels are greased.

As they pull into the driveway of the small home, Mr. Mayor and Jimmy again shake hands and Hugh says, "We'd be delighted to have you over for dinner again, anytime, you're most welcome." A politician always keeps all doors open, it's the first thing you learn in the profession.

"Thank you sir, and thank Mrs. Mayor for having me," Jimmy replies. He shuts the car door and walks up the stone path into his home.

Hugh ponders the utter paradox of the boy's humble lineage and apparent meager financial circumstances, the small house on the West-side, to the nearly impossible to obtain appointment to West Point.

Let it go, he tells himself, whatever the situation the

young man's brother, Joseph?, would soon be leading men into battle.

Hugh's own life is becoming more complicated daily. The girls, his daughters are fast becoming young ladies. Even little Jill, the boy he had just dropped off her first real boyfriend.

He smile's and thinks, you did well honey, the boy seems honest and straight forward. Maybe his father, Andrew? Albert?, no, its more Italian sounding, Aldo? Whatever- maybe he's a war hero? And his son's? Hero's beget hero's.

With that he thinks again about the American boys who are right now this moment dying in the jungles of South East Asia. He turns his car towards the country club, he needs a drink.

CHAPTER TWO

May 1966

"Yellow tigers, crouched in jungles, in her dark eyes."

White Room/ Cream

Nicole's mother, Victoria, is a dark smoldering beauty and its evident Nicole will turn out to be her equal, perhaps even surpassing her mother's fine, exquisite perfection.

Victoria, Dr. Henried Wright Smarts' beautiful wife, is only 34 years old, but this morning she feels 24, and almost looks it as well. She is wearing tight white shorts and a pale blue silk tube top with a man's white dress shirt over it, tied at the waist and the sleeves rolled up. Her long, luxurious raven hair is tied back in a loose pony tail.

She has recently taken a lover and just the thought of his hard, smooth body pressing against hers increases her anticipation.

"Nicole, darling, are you ready? I told Cynthia we'd be there for Jill at 8:00 a.m. sharp," she informs her daughter.

"Yes, mother," Nicole replies entering the mirrored foyer where Victoria is seeing how she looks from behind in the tight shorts.

Aranxa, the Cuban emigre housekeeper in charge of all the other domestics, which include a chef and his assistant, a gardener, and an all around maintenance handy man, is attending to Victoria for any last minute instructions or details.

"Aranxa, if the Dr. calls or arrives home before we're back, you can expect us by mid-afternoon I should think, tell him we'll dine at 6:00 p.m., unless he'd prefer to dine without us," Victoria instructs. "Yes, Mrs. Smart, will that be all?", the maid asks. Victoria looks around and decides, yes, she's in too much of a hurry for anything further.

She is taking the girl's, Nicole and Jill, to Southern's Bridal for gowns for the father-daughter ball at the club, the girl's first. Once their fitted and accessorized- which Victoria knows will proceed inexorably slow, she's allotted 3 hours for it, she hopes there will be sufficient time to inadvertently run into Hugh at the Club.

He is scheduled to be there for a working lunch drawing up a new amended charter, redefining the necessary requirements for membership appointment. Specifically, an exclusionary rule to facilitate rejection of less qualified candidates.

Victoria has, of course, planned the entire chance meeting, down to the very last detail in fact. She is very aware that all she needs is 5 minutes to have him totally enrapt with her. To cover her attendance at the Club her ruse is to sit and chat with Nicole's new steady boyfriend, Barnaby Casworth Jr., "Caz".

He and Jill's boyfriend have a lunch date with the two young ladies, and by her having just spent the entire morning getting the girls fitted for gowns, decided for an impromptu meeting with the young man.

Nicole and Jill didn't take quite 3 hours but it was close. They arrived at the Club shortly after 11:00 a.m.. The valets greeted all three ladies cordially, addressing each by name, (membership definitely has privileges here).

"Good morning Mrs. Smart, Miss Smart, Miss Mayor," the young man greeted, nodding to each.

"Good morning, boys, and thank you," Victoria dripped sweetly, adding just a slight extra sway to her hips as she walked to where the doorman waited, knowing that when she glanced back over her shoulder the poor boy would be staring, which of course he was. The doorman bowed deeply as if she were a queen and the girls princesses.

As they were being escorted to a table, an attendant in full foot-man regalia of the previous century, informed the ladies that they were the guests of Mr. Casworth, and would they please follow him. Jill and Nicole giggled, but one icy glare from Victoria immediately silenced both.

When they reached the table, Caz and Jimmy rose to greet them. Two more attendants, dressed exactly as the first, appeared out of nowhere to seat the ladies. Both boy's remained standing until the ladies sat. Victoria quickly appraised both saying, "Hello, Barnaby, oops- Caz." Here she acted flustered before coquettishly touching his hand and continuing, "How are your parents?" Before Caz could reply she abruptly turned to Nicole and queried, "Nicole, have you forgotten your manners, darling? Who is your new friend?"

"Oh, excuse me mother. This is James Carosa, a classmate of Jill and I. You didn't give me a chance to-," Nicole is answering, but with one glare from her mother she immediately becomes silent.

Victoria asks, "Do I know your parents, James?" Jimmy smiles and says, "No ma'am, I don't think so." He's still smiling, just the thought of Angelo and Nettie meeting this fraud- Ha! Not only hasn't she, he's absolutely certain she never will either, it's pretty funny. As he looks at the two girl's they begin to giggle also, but once again Victoria silences them both with one stern look, as she asks, "Do you ladies have something to share? Hmmm? I'm sure we'd all like to hear it." "Nothing mother, excuse me," Nicole says quietly and Jill echoes the same apology also.

Victoria now begins her query anew but the waiter approaches for their beverage orders. They all order iced-tea except for Victoria and Jimmy, who get coffee.

Victoria's ire is piqued by this young, arrogant boy and she will not tolerate any insolence, or even the mere hint of it.

Jill, sensing further confrontation, tries valiantly to deflect Victoria's wrath away from Jimmy. She squeezes his hand under the table and says, "James is taking the advanced curriculum and get's straight A's- he may seek an appointment where his brother is. He's helped Nicole and I quite a lot and-."

Victoria interrupts again and asks, "Where is it your- um, brother?, where does he attend-?"

But Jimmy, as politely as he can, interrupts her and says, "West Point," and smile's confidently.

They both hold the stare for just a brief moment before Victoria says, "Oh! Well- hmmm, that's quite a challenge, James." She is now talking very sweetly, her whole demeanor has changed.

The beverages arrive and they order lunch. It had been a draw, the verbal duel between Victoria and the young Jimmy. Neither had lost but- Victoria reassesses her youthful challenger. The boy is a mystery indeed, an unknown. Perhaps Hugh will know more? After all, Jill is his daughter, and the boy is her steady...

After lunch the youngsters excuse themselves and go for a stroll. Victoria had agreed only to have a reason to delay her departure. Where is Hugh?, she thinks.

She needn't worry. At noon sharp he strides in shaking hands, slapping backs, a natural politician. He is very good looking, 6 foot tall, slim, fit and tanned with just the slightest trace of graying beginning to appear at the temples of his blond hair. Her breath quickens at the sight of him.

As he turns and sees her, he has a brief urge to flee, before regaining himself and walking over to her confidently. She stands on her tip toes and kisses him lightly on the cheek cooing, "Oh, Hugh! What a pleasant surprise." She's taken his hands and is still holding them.

"Well Victoria, yes it is," he says. "I'm here with the girls and their boys," she tells him, trying to act the role of proper mom.

They are standing very close, her hand caressing his lapel, her lips glistening, her scent intoxicating him. He feels her heat.

"Daddy?" Its Jill. They didn't notice her approach with Nicole and the boy's. Victoria and Hugh look- caught?, something, even the adolescent teens sense it.

"Oh, Honey! Hello, how is my sweetheart?", Hugh says as he hugs his daughter. Jill love's her Daddy sooo much, she attributes the momentary delay to his extremely busy persona that's in effect 24 hours of every day. He is constantly and continually campaigning, working a room, any room, smiling, giving compliments here, a small amusing barb there, always remembering the tiniest detail to remark upon later, whether a week or a month past.

Many supporters, political and otherwise, are grateful for that personal touch that his recollections provide.

Hugh smile's at the two boy's and says, "Hello, Caz. How's your father? Tell him to call me, the fish miss him," he jokes, and then, "Hello, Jimmy, you've been absent from our dinner table lately. My little girl didn't scare you off, did she?" He make's a comical gruff face at Jill as he says this and she giggles.

"Nicole? Why so quiet?", he asks, as he walks over to her. "Hi, Mr. Mayor," she says shyly.

"Ah-," he replies knowingly, it's the young Barnaby she is shy about.

"Daddy?", it's Jill, "Can we stay?, if we can ride with you?", she asks hopefully. "Why certainly, sweetheart, give your Dad 30 minutes, ok?", he answers. Jill smile's brilliantly up at him.

"What brings you here?", Victoria now asks.

"Oh, just a minor detail with the Club's charter. I'll only be a few minutes," Hugh replies. He's looking for a server to take his lunch order.

"Jill, honey, if you'd like, take a walk through the gardens. I'll have you paged when I wrap up here," Hugh tells her, and the four young teens go out into the lush gardens, after making very proper and formal farewells to Mrs. Smart, of course.

Outside, Caz audibly exhales and whispers to Jill and Jimmy, "Man, am I glad your Dad's giving us a ride, Mrs. Smart make's me jumpy," and they all laugh, but are nodding yes in agreement.

"Hugh, can we arrange an appointment for tomorrow? I'm starting early with the pledges for the new pediatric wing, get ahead start. Henry is so worried we'll fall short," Victoria pouts sexily. Henry is Victoria's husband and Nicole's father, the renowned master neuro-surgeon.

She is once again standing very close to him, her finger's tracing up and down his neck-tie, her dark eye's under incredibly long lashes burning into him.

Victoria is very aware of the effect she is having on him, and quite pleased with herself. "What about lunch? Say, 12:30 p.m. at Stan's?", she asks.

He cannot say no, he hasn't the willpower to. He says, "yes, that'll be fine." She again stands on tip toe and brushes his lips very lightly with hers. It's like an electric shock to him.

"Bye, Hugh- see you tomorrow," she breathes.

After a brief instant, he is once again the confident politico as he enters the conference room where the Country Club board members await.

As they strolled through the garden hand in hand, Jimmy bends low and kisses Jill by the ear. "Stop it, Jimmy, that tickles," she laughs. "Um- Today, with Mrs. Smart," he begins-

"It's ok, Jimmy, she was being a real toad," Jill interrupts. Jill is a good girl, she doesn't curse, ever, a toad being her worst slur.

"Well, its not just that Jill, you told her I was taking the advanced curriculum? Straight A's?" He's smiling at her, he's squeezing both her hands in his, they're facing each other. Jill never lies, girl scouts honor, etc... But today she had lied, for him.

Jill blushes deeply, "I, uh- I- well," she's stammering, very self-consciously. Jimmy hugs her and gives her 5,6,7 quick little pecks all over her face.

"Oh, Jimmy, you see! Now I've been bad for you," she wails,

but its only half serious and she pokes him. They both laugh and kiss again, the kiss is magical.

"Miss Mayor, Miss Mayor." It's another footman, at least that's how he too is attired, paging them, it's time to go.

At home that evening, Jill is relating the day to her mother. "The gowns are so beautiful," she tells her. She tells of the lunch, her Dad's unexpected appearance there.

Later, while Cynthia is preparing for bed, she thinks its odd that Hugh didn't mention Victoria. Well, he's so busy, she attributes the lapse to. She makes a mental note to call Victoria, perhaps tennis and lunch at the Club next week.

"Hugh, darling, I'm going to bed. Do you-," Cynthia is saying, but Hugh has risen and before Cynthia can finish he's picked her up and kicked the bedroom door shut as he theatrically says, "Shush wench, tonight I shall have you."

Cynthia's giggles sound just like 14 year old Jill's, the same. They have a very good night indeed, with Hugh especially amourous. She is watching him sleep, he's so handsome she thinks. I am blessed with Hugh and my girls, and those are her last thoughts before sleep.

Hugh's last thought had been of Victoria, it was her, not his loving wife Cynthia- no, it was Victoria.

CHAPTER THREE

September 1966/ December 1966

"Street fighting man."

Title song/ Rolling Stones

September 1966

Barnaby Casworth Jr., "Caz", the object of young Nicole Smart's affection, is the son of Barnaby Casworth Sr., President and CEO of Florida First. A consolidation of banking, real estate holdings and land development companies, it is a huge financial conglomerate. Barnaby Sr. began in 1947 by acquiring a banking charter with one branch, the main one, in Ft. Lauderdale.

His grandfather, Alexander Casworth, had been an investor in Henry Flaglers railroad- "the railroad that leads to nowhere," or so it seemed at the time of its construction.

Many of Alexander's peer's thought him foolish. "Why, the railroad goes to an endless swamp, uninhabitable by civilized whites," they had cautioned. At the time they were indeed correct, it was mostly Seminole indian country, with a few settled "Forts" in the lower peninsula the only white settlements.

"Well, I'm a fool then," Alexander had replied. But he was no fool, nor was Henry Flagler. Both men gained enormous reward for their stubborn determination to forge ahead with their plans.

Alexander Casworth staked and settled claim to 100's of thousands of acres of swampland, beginning at the Atlantic shore and continuing westward some two dozen miles from the Fort of Capt. Lauderdale. He extended the North and South boundaries of his claim another dozen miles in each direction. A huge tract of land, swamp once, today that land area is Broward County, some of the priciest real estate in not just Florida, but the entire country.

Barnaby worked tirelessly, 18 hours a day, 7 days a week for months straight without respite. He hired land developers for limited cash contracts who agreed to accept a portion of the payment with land.

With the post World War II housing boom expected to need literally millions of homes, as well as the advent of Air Conditioning becoming a practical appliance, the potential was limitless. Florida First was well on its way.

And now, with the great Northern migration to the sunshine state, particularly South Florida, Barnaby has amassed a burgeoning empire of truly colossal proportions, it will become a multi-billion dollar enterprise within the next decade.

"How's school going, Caz? Everything all right with your teacher's? Your classes?", Barnaby asks his oldest son at the breakfast table.

"Yeah, Dad, everything's cool," Caz replies.

"How about you, Richard? You like your new teacher at East Side? What's her name again?", Barnaby asks his younger son.

"Oh, yes Daddy, she's real nice, and pretty too!", Richard gushes excitedly, and when they all laugh at his pronouncement of that fact, he turns beet red. Barnaby reaches over and tousles his young sons hair.

Mrs. Casworth, formerly Catherine Grace, a one time Miss Florida and a runner-up to Miss America in the 1949 pageant as well, looks at her family, Barnaby and her two boys, affectionately. She is very proud to be his wife and the boy's mother.

Barnaby is a very good father to the boys and an excellent husband to her, she could not ask for more than she has. She love's Barnaby as much as she did when they first met and began dating- could it actually be 16 years ago?, she thinks.

He has never denied her or the boys anything, only the best is what he demands for the three of them. His tireless work in getting Florida First off the planning books, and into the actual realm of developing the huge tracts of land into real estate properties, is a great achievement.

She now says, "I met Miss Butler, darling, and she is quite attractive, as our little Romeo here has informed us," and here she reaches over and brushes Richard's hair back off his forehead with her fingers, before adding, "She seems very patient and capable also," she smile's at him.

Of course, Barnaby thinks it would've been Catherine's #1 priority to meet her young son's teacher.

"Well that's fine, my dear," he says, and turning to his young son he continues, "When I was your age, our old school marm was so mean and ugly, why- she had to sneak up on a glass of water!", which his youngest son finds hilarious and they all join in his laughter.

It is a close and loving family. Barnaby too is proud of his family. Catherine is as lovely now today as when they had married, and both sons share their mother's good looks.

Barnaby himself is not unpleasant in appearance. Although of only moderate height he is quite stout and muscular, ruggedly handsome, where as Catherine is very beautiful, tall and statuesque.

Barnaby's inquiry to his oldest son Caz about school isn't idle talk, however. Caz has had difficulty in learning as a small boy, he had to repeat his fourth year. He was considered unmanageable and disassociative, possibly learning disabled.

He was removed from public school and enrolled at the Adelphi private Academy where he remained for three years before returning to public school to begin the seventh grade, a year older than his classmates.

That seemed behind them now and that's good. Barnaby has high hopes and expectations for his oldest boy and namesake.

He now asks Caz, "You boy's go for new school clothes yet?" They normally go after the new school year begins to have a chance to observe the latest fashions.

Caz looks at his mother and she says, "I've made an appointment for tomorrow but I can change-"

Barnaby interrupts saying, "No need to bother, Catherine, Caz is old enough to buy his own clothes and I'm sure he won't object to helping his brother, will you Caz?"

"No! Uh, no sir, no problem, Dad," Caz answers, thinking-all right! He hated going for clothes with his mother, it makes him feel like a little kid.

Catherine looks a little worried and she starts to give voice to her concern, but catches the quick shake no of her husbands head and so she stays silent.

Barnaby reaches into his pocket and pulls out an enormous wad of bills, all 100's, and hands Caz ten of them saying, "This should cover it but if not, lay away anything you want and we'll have them deliver it, ok?"

Caz hugs his father tightly, not for the money, the money means nothing. He's hugging him because somehow his Dad had known how he felt about shopping for clothes with his Mom. Barnaby is acknowledging Caz becoming a man.

Caz now says, "Thanks Dad, I'll help Richard, no problem," feeling very responsible in guiding and assisting his younger brother's selections.

Which is exactly the lesson Barnaby wished to impart on him, personal responsibility and being responsible for others under your leadership. Someday Florida First will belong to Caz, and Barnaby can't start grooming his son for it soon enough, so when the day arrive's he'll be ready.

However, the constant flow of money to the boy's, especially Caz, will actually hinder his appreciation of it, and more importantly, where it comes from. He'll enter adulthood with the ill conceived notion that money is just there, never comprehending where it mysteriously derives from.

He will never master economic principles or corporate revenues relation to net profits and actual earnings. Nevertheless, Florida First, by birthright, is destined to become his, whether he is prepared or not.

It is indeed a vast fortune he will control, and Barnaby will continue to impart any and all knowledge he can, regardless.

December 1966

Christmas time in South Florida is definitely unique. Not only is there no snow, but the average December temperature is 68-71 degrees, and today is no exception.

Jimmy is pretty wound up as he walk's into the school, his brother, Joseph, will be home for four days over the Christmas week-end. Joseph has been at the Academy continually since September 1964, when he entered the storied grounds as a young plebe at 17 years of age. He is working straight through, no summer recess leave, so he can receive his full commission as a junior grade lieutenant in September 1967.

The rigors of the United States Military Academy are world renowned. It doesn't turn out soldiers, it make's the leaders, the generals, even some Presidents.

The most able men on Earth emerge from West Point, there are no equals to it anywhere in the world. And Joseph Carosa has all the necessary, inherent abilities and characteristics to equal those distinguished cadets who proceeded him. Most certainly!

The escalating war in Vietnam, and increasing tensions world wide because of it, have enabled the Commandant of the Point to select and promote exceptionally gifted and intelligent cadets, of impeccable record, (no demerits, even one disqualifies the candidate from consideration), to accelerated commissions. By taking no summer leave the four years can be fulfilled in three, 36 consecutive months.

Accounting that completing the task in four years is rigorous, doing it in three years is far more daunting. Most cadets cannot do it, very few can, Joseph Carosa is one.

The Commandant is allowing the cadet: four days leave/ family visit, before returning to finish in September 1967. He will then go to his "corp schooling" before returning to graduate with his class in June 1968, just for the tradition, he'll be commissioned a junior grade lieutenant in September 1967.

It will be the only four day leave in a 36 month continuous consecutive attendance, a truly remarkable record.

The Commandant is allowing it because Joseph is an exceptional cadet. He will be first in his class, of that the old General is certain.

As Jimmy enters the patio he looks to where Jill, in all her loveliness, is sitting with Nicole. He attempts to surprise her but she looks up at the last moment and see's him. She smile's her dazzling smile and his heart races. I have to be the luckiest guy in the world, he thinks.

He bends down and kisses her as she makes room for him to sit. "Good morning, Jimmy," she says, and he replies, "Uh, uh, one more kiss and then it will be." She laugh's but grants his wish. "Good morning, Nicole," he says, and she nod's and says, "Hi, Jimmy."

Nicole is looking towards the entrance where Caz should be any minute now, and sure enough, just by Nicole's entire demeanor changing- Jimmy turns and there's Caz. Nicole is smiling broadly.

Jill and Jimmy exchange a glance, they both know just how she feels. Caz is with Rex Randall, a guy he rides into school with on occasion.

They walk up and Caz and Nicole, who he calls, Nicky, kiss. He's the only one she'll let get by with it. Her mother has never allowed anyone to, as Victoria put it, bastardize her name. To Nicole, it is very sweet.

They all exchange greetings and Rex Randall starts cracking jokes, very stupid ones as far as Jimmy is concerned. Most are racial slights or Jewish barbs, but to be polite the girl's laugh. However, enough is enough.

Jimmy is about to tell Rex to get lost when Rex says, "Hey, Carosa, what's an Italian helicopter sound like ?"

Jimmy doesn't respond, but Caz see's his face tighten and knows his buddy, Jimmy, is about to lose his temper, in a very bad way, especially for Rex.

Caz attempts, to late regretably, to shut Rex up before Rex says, "Guinea, guinea, guinea, wop, wop-," are his last words. Oooof! Oh! Oh! Oww! Uhnn-

"Stop it! Stop it! Please, stop!" It's a girls voice, but Jimmy is not stopping, he's tearing Rex to pieces. All the larger boy can do is try to cover up, but that doesn't work either and down goes Rex, out cold.

Jimmy is breathing deeply but that's about all. He says, "Don't ever insult me!", to the unconscious boy laying prone on the school patio and then he look's around.

There's a wide berth around him and the knocked out, Rex. Two teachers and a school janitor come running over. Shit! Jimmy thinks. Shit! Shit! Shit!

He walk's over to Jill and Nicole and their holding onto
one another crying. Jill almost shies away from his touch but stops
herself on time and let's go of Nicole and hugs him. She's shaking.
Shit, he thinks again.

"Jill, Jill come on. Come on, it's ok," he says.

"Oh, Jimmy," she moans and presses her face against his chest
before looking up at him. Jimmy wipes her eye's with his white hanker-
chief, that men carry for just this purpose he supposes, and kisses
her cheek.

She look's around him, the two teacher's and the janitor
have managed to get Rex sitting up. Jimmy turns and look's too as
Caz walk's up and slaps him on the back saying, "He deserved it. I
knew what was coming and tried to shut him up, but- I was too late."
That he was. Rex still can't stand up on his own, he's wobbling and
sits back down.

"Young man," it's Mr. Garrard, the American History teacher,
"Will you come with me, please?", he asks.

"Where? Why?", Jimmy answers. He wants to tell him a lot
more than that too but Jill says, "Jimmy, please."

Coach Kirk is there now too and he says, "You're just going
to the Dean's office James, please." Coach Kirk look's back at Rex
who's still sitting on the pavement. He turns back to Jimmy and
gives him a quick little grin and raises his eyebrows. Kirk thinks,
Rex is about 5'11" and a 180-185 lbs. He knows from gym class the
Carosa kid can't top 140 lbs. soaking wet, he's a skinny 5'9".

"Your friend's can come, we just need to know what happened,"

Coach Kirk tells Jimmy.

"All right, Coach," Jimmy answers.

Jill tells Nicole, "Come on, we're going with you." The janitor steps way back as Jimmy walk's by.

It was the talk of the whole school, all the boy's re-hashing the fist to cuffs, quite a few impressed with Jimmy's showing. The girl's, now that the actual violence was over, were tittering and squealing, you could hear the occasional, "Eww, gross!", from some as you passed by, but it was over.

As they waited in the Dean's office, Rex was taken, quite shakily, to the school infirmary.

Christy came rushing in, she'd just arrived. Margo was runn-ing late this morning. "Jimmy, what happened?! They're all out there saying you beat up some other kid? Who? Are you ok?" She's asking half a dozen questions all at once. He's standing looking at her, she has a hold of his arm's and is looking up at his face. She grabs it and turns it first one way and then the other, looking for marks, nothing.

Jimmy lift's his fists and she sees the knuckles on both hands cut, bleeding and starting to swell. Jimmy says, "It was Rex Randall and I'm fine, Christy. He insulted me, all of us." By us, he means Italians.

Caz jumps up and give's Christy a re-enactment, shadow box-ing, complete with sound effects, "Pow! Pow! Pow, smack, smack, boom! Down goes Rex!" He laugh's and slaps Jimmy on the back again, which causes Jimmy to smile.

Christy smile's also, looking from Jimmy to Caz and says, "Good, he'll know better next time. Spoiled ass rich kid's," and immediately regrets saying the last. She looks at Jill, Caz and Nicole and says, "Not you guy's. You all know I love you three to death," and she does and they know it.

"Don't worry, Christy. What are they going to do to Jimmy?", Jill asks. She's starting to panic again.

"They're not going to do anything, Jill, not while I'm here. You want me to call Dad, Jimmy?", Christy asks.

"No, no, no Chris. Don't bother the old man," he tells her. He's begun calling his Dad old man, but it's out of respect. For some crazy reason it flashes through Jill's mind, Mr. Carosa, Jimmy's father, would take care of it, she is certain. She almost says, Jimmy call him.

Caz takes up his shadow boxing routine again and Jill's had it with his childish antics. She almost shouts, "Will you stop with that stupid boxing, Caz! Maybe they should throw you out of school." Everyone, the entire office, becomes deathly quiet. Jill's never yelled at anyone, it isn't lady like, according to the always proper and correct Cynthia. Always talk civilly to everyone, never lose your temper she had instructed both Jill and Lisa.

They were all staring at her, in shock, with the eerie silence in the office lengthening. "Oh, gosh, I'm so sorry. I'm just so, so...," Jill says, as she begins to cry again.

Christy and Nicole quickly comfort her and Jimmy kneels down in front and takes her hands. He's very touched, her concern

for him is causing all this. "Jill, come on, don't- I'm going to
be ok. Please, Jill, don't cry," he soothes and she hugs him.

"Will you give me your handkerchief, please?" She snuffles
and says to Caz, "I'm sorry, please forgive me, Caz."

Finally, the girl's Dean comes out and asks the girl's to
come with her. "Give the boy's and Mr. Shultz a chance to talk,"
she says.

Jimmy is asked, not ordered, but it is requested that he
start the holiday early, "Like today, James," Shultz suggests.
"Give a chance for the dust to settle, so to speak," the Dean advises.
It's just one week, many student's are not in attendance for travel
to family anyway. Christmas is a week away, next Monday, what the
hell. "Sure Shultz, no problem," Jimmy tells him.

"Thank you, James, and Merry Christmas," Shultz answers.

The Randall boy is beaten up pretty bad but nothing broken
or anything permanent, according to the school nurse. Shultz also
suggested that Rex Randall begin his Christmas early, today, and
Rex was happy to oblige. The whole school is laughing at him getting
knocked out by Jimmy for his off color, rude jokes.

Caz shake's his hand for the hundredth time this day and
says, "Hey, I'm going to start early too, fuck it Jimmy," and throws
a few shadow jabs again and laugh's hysterically. They both get a few
extra days off together, that doesn't sound to harsh to either of
them.

They don't get a chance to see Jill or Nicole, they were
sent on to class. But Christy is waiting when they emerge from

Shultz's office. She's his sister and she's not leaving until she see's him.

She confront's both Shultz and Jimmy asking, "You're sure? He's not making you leave? Swear it to me, Jimmy! You're not suspended?" She's glaring at Shultz as she's pressing Jimmy.

"Christy! Geez- take it easy. I'm not suspended and he's not making me leave, ok?", Jimmy says calmly and slowly. His little sister is hot, she's older but she's 5' flat and under a 100 lbs. He laugh's and says, "Come on, before you beat up somebody too. Let's get out of here."

Outside they hug and she tells him, "Ok, will you go straight home? And don't get in anymore trouble." Once again the older, wiser sister giving instructions she knows he won't listen to or obey- but, she has to at least try anyway, it's an ingrained habit from all the years she helped raise him.

Jimmy laugh's and he's nodding yes to her and says, "Tell Jill I'll see her after school." They hug again and go separate ways.

Jill has calmed down by the time school lets out for the day. Enough to actually be very angry, now that she is over the initial scare and knows that nothing bad has happened to him.

School is finally out and Jimmy is waiting by their bus, she is furious. "How could you do this, Jimmy? The whole school is talking about it," she asks. He didn't expect her fury and tries to dismiss it with just a shrug of his shoulders, but she will not have any of that, no sir!

"You listen to me, Jimmy Carosa, promise me, promise me right now, that this will never happen again, ever!", she demands. "Ok, ok- I promise," he says very sincerely.

She look's into his eye's and they are so sparkling green, and all the fight goes right out of her. She's been stressed all day- whew! She says quite calmly now that she's vented, "Ok, I forgive you, but just this one time and I mean it. You'd better-"

Jimmy kisses her on the lips, silencing her in mid-sentence and says, "You look beautiful when your mad, maybe I should do this more often." He's teasing her but Jill doesn't think it's funny, not at all.

He did tell her she is beautiful though- and he's so handsome she can't stay mad at him.

"Oooh, Jimmy," she says, and shakes her fist at him but they both laugh and now she kisses him. All is right again.

The entire bus applauds, Caz and Nicole included. It is only then that they realize their first fight had been a very public affair indeed.

Caz insists Jimmy take the cab, and $20.00 cab money. "How will you get home?" he asks. "I'll call you in the morning, Champ," he says and laugh's again.

"Come over to my house, the old man will cover you with the Dean's office," Jimmy tells him, and then adds, "Three days at my house, my Ma will stuff you like a pig."

They both got a jump on the Christmas holiday, great!

"Oh, yea! Now I got to eat all those delicious Italian

dishes, just to make your mom happy of course- man, that's a pretty stiff penalty," Caz calls back, laughing. Nettie is always telling him to monga! monga! (eat! eat!).

The two cab's drive away going in opposite directions, one East for Caz and the other West for Jimmy, but both towards home nonetheless.

dishes, just to make your mom happy of course- man, that's a pretty stiff penalty," Caz calls back, laughing. Nettie is always telling him to monga! monga! (eat! eat!).

The two cab's drive away going in opposite directions, one East for Caz and the other West for Jimmy, but both towards home nonetheless.

CHAPTER FOUR

Christmas 1966

"Homeward Bound."

Title Song/ Simon and Garfunkel

Twenty minutes later, after giving the cabbie $10.00 for
a $3.00 fare, Jimmy's home. To the many thank you's of the cab
driver he calls back, "You're welcome, have a good night."

He walks into a very familiar scene, the smell of the frying
breaded veal cutlets making his mouth water from the aroma.

As he enters the kitchen, his mother Nettie, who has a
spatula in one hand and the other is ensconced in an oven mitt, tries
to hug him using just her forearms. She holds her face up for his
kiss on her cheek.

"Hi, Mom," he says. He love's his mother, she is an angel
to him, truly.

"Where do you go everyday? Such a busy young man," she admonishes mildly. Looking into Jimmy's face she sees her own, almost
like a mirror, except of course his face is her's 30 years ago.

Antoinette, "Nettie", is full blooded Italian, just as Angelo
is. Her father, Vito, is from Naples, Napolitano. Her mother, Rosa,
is from Sicily, Siciliano. Since her father is Napolitano then
that is what Nettie is too, Napolitano.

In Italian families it is the father's bloodline that decides
what particular heritage the children will be. It is definitely a
patriarchal society.

As long as the mother is Italian, whether Napolitano,
Siciliano or Calabrese, her husbands bloodline will determine what
their offspring will be. If she wed's a Siciliano, then the children
are Siciliano, and so forth.

Angelo is Napolitano. Both of his parent's came from Naples, but had his mother come from somewhere else in Italy, his father being Napolitano would've determined Angelo's being Napolitano also.

Only the father's bloodline counts- the mother must be Italian though for the children to be full blooded, and her ancestral lineage must be pure Italian as well. Any mix discounts a pure heritage.

The napolitano and Siciliano factions have alternately controlled the Mafia, both here and in Italy. All the gangland war's dating back to the St. Valentine's day massacre in Chicago in 1929 is for that control.

The Napolitano's kill the bosses and they take control. A few years later the Sciliano's kill them, now they take control. Back and forth.

Charles "lucky" Luciano had managed to settle the dispute with no one side getting more than the other, by creating the Commission, a national governing body with representatives from every crime family- who made all the top executive decisions, if you will. With his deportation in 1946, the war's recommenced.

Nowhere is a man's home his castle more than an Italian one, and this holds true here in the Carosa home as well. Angelo has the final say on all family matters. Whatever he decide's, that's it, there is no more discussion.

The Carosa home runs in the same tradition of Italian homes from previous centuries, literally. All the domestic chores inside the home are done by the women, the cooking, dishwashing, laundry, etc... Joseph and Jimmy have never done any chores inside the home, nor were they expected to, by Nettie or their sister Christy either.

Nettie and her sister, Asunta, (Susan), had always done the housework growing up, why would it be any different now? Italian girl's growing up are proud to learn the domestic arts from their mothers. It is a family tradition and heritage being passed from one generation to the next. How would they learn without practice? Nettie learned from Rosa and now Christy will learn from her.

Angelo is a strict critic of Italian fare, either heaping praise or criticism, freely. He compares Nettie's cooking to his oldest sister, Nina's, the best. Angelo's mother, Mary, and sister Inez, died in the turberculosis epidemic of 1918, in the squalid ghetto that was then the lower East-Side of Manhattan. He was 5 years old when they both passed within two weeks of each other.

Nina, the oldest sibling, raised the remaining Carosa children and looked after her papa Joseph, never marrying. Her younger brother's and sister's needed her, especially the baby of the family, Angelo, so that became her life. Now, when Angelo proudly declares Nettie's cooking the equal of his cherished sister Nina's, there is no higher compliment he could make.

Nettie now tells Jimmy to, "Go get your father up, the foods on the table," which it isn't, not yet, but it will be the moment Angelo takes his seat at the head of the table.

This is Angelo's bedtime, everyday from 2:00 p.m. to 6:30 p.m. He work's for Holiday Inn 5 nights a week from 10:00 p.m. to 6:00 a.m. Then, beginning at 8:00 a.m., he'll take bet's over the phone until the second race of the day, which comprises the second half of the daily double, is completed, usually 2:00 p.m., depending upon which horse track is holding it's seasonal meeting.

The daily double is a very popular wager for both the casual wagerer and the compulsive die-hard gambler. The bettor must simply pick the winners of the first and second races of the day.

Angelo will get hardly a break continually from 8:00 a.m. until at least the first race is completed. His day will finally end with the second races. His hours are 10:00 p.m. to 2:00 p.m., 16 hours. No matter that the illegal gambling trade, (the book), is a high salaried job, it still take's putting in the hours just as if he were standing on an assembly line, or chasing down sales leads, its a job. The primary source of income for the Carosa household is derived from "the book". The Holiday Inn job is, in practice, his second job.

If not for the income from the book, they might not be eating expensive veal cutlets, or living in this house. Angelo's full time effort is the reason they are, and they're all very aware of it. The lesson's of New York are well placed in their collective memories.

The shower is running, the toilet's been flushed a half dozen times and finally Angelo emerges, a cloud of steam pouring out behind him.

Nettie and Christy now begin bringing in platters of food piled high with every Italian dish imaginable, pasta ala oyla, the veal cutlets, asparagus, artichoke hearts, tomato salads, olives, and a huge loaf of fresh baked bread. It's a feast.

Angelo sits down and Nettie and Christy both kiss him on the cheek. He pats his daughters face and says, "Hello, doll," and to Nettie he says, "Oh Nettie, sweet, it smells delicious, come on sit, lets eat." He knows she won't sit, not yet.

"I have to get the wine," she says and hurries back to the kitchen again, the first of many trips she'll make throughout the meal. She's always done it and no one knows why except her of course. Everything must be perfect, not good- no, perfect, for her to be satisfied.

As Angelo digs in and the meal progresses, any issue that needs to be addressed, any problem, or approval their mother told them to ask their father for, any money needed, etc... now is the time to do it. There is only one issue tonight, Joseph is coming home for Christmas.

Christy nor Jimmy have even thought of mentioning today's fiasco at the school- Jimmy will tell Angelo out of hearing from their mother, and Christy knows that. She also knows her father will pinch Jimmy's cheek's and say, "Good! Fachime! He's bigger than you too? -yea?, good!-fuckin' American bastards, they hate us," and gives Jimmy another pat on his face.

Angelo is proud of his tough little son. Nettie had regaled him while he was away with stories about his youngest child, perhaps 4 years old then, how he had beat up "poobie", fat Bernard from around the corner's nickname, or almost biting off Richie Fusco's ear from next door.

All the mobster's on the corner had begun betting on little Jimmy every time he got into a fight, they loved the ear biting.

Nettie and Christy have cleared the table. Nettie will be gone a few minutes making the espresso so Jimmy has time to tell Angelo all about his day at school. Angelo does exactly as Christy had done in the Dean's office. He takes Jimmy's face and turns it one way first, and then the other, nothing-

Nettie hears Angelo and Jimmy laughing and carrying on at the dinner table and she smiles. Angelo love's his youngest child, they're always having private father-son chats, Jimmy bringing happiness and laughter to his father.

"Don't say nothing to your mother, Jimmy," Angelo cautions, but of course he needn't worry, it's an unspoken rule that Nettie is kept in the dark, about everything.

"Bring Caz here, you hear me? I don't want you two running around all day," Angelo instructs.

"Ok, Dad, you'll have to call-," Jimmy began, but Angelo finishes for him saying, "I'll call that Jew bastard, don't worry. It's a good thing he didn't try to fuck you around! I'd a told him the kid was twice my son's size! How the fuck you throwing my son out?!", he exaggerates and smile's and they both hug.

"Here, take this, make it last you the week, Jimmy," Angelo says and hands him a $100.00 bill.

Nettie comes in with the strong black espresso and some canolis, a delicious Italian pastry. She smiles at the both of them and actually sits down, the back and forth routine is out of her system now. Her life's mission, at least for this day, being complete.

Jimmy pours all three of them a cup in the small, fine China espresso coffee cups, each cup and matching saucer is hand painted with a blue floral design.

Nettie is so excited, Joseph is coming home! He is her favorite. She love's them all of course, surely, but Joseph is the apple of her eye.

Angelo takes her hand now and he says, "JoJo is coming home," he's smiling. They are both bursting with pride. Joseph is the shinning knight, the Carosa who will become somebody.

Angelo still calls his oldest child JoJo, like he did when Joseph was a toddler. Their pride is not a false one. Joseph has an exceptional, truly remarkable, gifted intelligence and capacity for learning.

When he was in the ninth grade he wrote a science paper on D.N.A's relation to cancer, a theory he had. The entire faculty department was stunned by it- how does a ninth grade freshmen write a graduate level thesis? They were confounded by his utter brilliance and by the time he graduated he was teaching his teacher's. He had also mastered both the German and Russian languages, and of course he was already fluent in Italian.

Jimmy finished his coffee. He kissed both his Mom and Dad and went off to shower and then bed. His hands were aching and swollen, both knuckles on each hand cut quite deeply.

He wonders what his brother JoJo will be like. He finds it amusing that his Dad still calls his brother, JoJo, and laugh's to himself. Jimmy is no longer the little boy that Joseph had left in

1964, over two years ago. He can't wait to see him, only four more days, Friday!

The two brother's were very close and always had been, from the time Jimmy could remember. He felt sure that wouldn't have changed, no matter what else may have. The two brother's closeness was the same that they both had with their father, all three of them, it would never change.

Angelo and Jimmy are waiting at gate #11, terminal A, for Eastern Airline flight #77 in bound from JFK in New York City to Ft. Lauderdale International. The plane bearing Angelo's oldest child, Joseph, has just touched down and is taxiing to the gate at 5:23 p.m. It will be the first meeting of father with both son's in over two years and they are all very excited.

As they wheel the departure stairs up to the gleaming silver plane, the exit door just rear of the cockpit opens, and, "There he is, Dad!", Jimmy shouts, pointing.

Angelo wears glasses to correct his lack of farsightedness so he's having trouble locating him, and asks, "Where? Where is he, Jimmy?" He's scanning the disembarking passengers, squinting.

"Oh yeah! There he is! Hey, fachime! Over here! JoJo!", Angelo's shouting, and then the three are embracing.

Angelo is hugging Joseph so tightly he about lifts him off the tarmac. "Oh boy my son! My son!", he's saying. "Look at you, Joseph, your a man- my boy is a man," he says almost with disbelief as he holds him back at arms length to look at him.

"Come on JoJo, Jimmy, let's go, your mother is dying to see you! She's been cooking since last night. Christy can't wait to see you either," Angelo tells them both and grabs a suitcase, but Jimmy takes it from him and says, "I got it, Dad, come on," and they walk through the airport.

Angelo is staring at Joseph as they make their way through the crowded concourse and out into the parking lot. He says, "You look good, babe." He's smiling and nodding yes as he says this. It feels like he's solid brick to Angelo, and he seems taller too.

"How's everything down here? Still the same? Nothing come up?," Joseph's asking his father. He's inquiring about the book operation, Angelo can hear the concern in his voice.

"Nah, nah, nothing. Everything is good JoJo, it's quiet down here, not like New York," Angelo tells him, easing his mind.

"And what about you, Gatz?", Joseph asks Jimmy. "Gatz" is a nickname Joseph has used for Jimmy for as long as Jimmy can remember. In a loose translation to English, it means: runt.

"You staying out of trouble? You're not screwing around with nothing, are you?", Joseph continues his query. He's asking if Jimmy is experimenting with any drugs. They've become prevalent lately.

"No! Hell no. What are you crazy?", Jimmy laugh's in response and then adds, "I got the best looking girl in school," he brags.

"Oh, yeah?", Joseph asks, he's smiling. Jimmy is a charmer with the girls, always has been, and that's a fact.

Joseph looks at his Dad for conformation. He knows its unnecessary but it'll give Angelo a chance to boast about his youngest

son. Angelo does have a good eye for the ladies, that's where
Jimmy got it.

Angelo smile's proudly and raises his eyebrows, nodding yes
as he says, "She's a doll, JoJo, and her family is loaded," and
they all laugh.

In the car they catch up with each other. It's been two
years and three months but it seems like its been ten. Angelo and
his two son's are very close. Joseph nor Jimmy ever lied to Angelo,
maybe to everybody else in Jimmy's case, not necessarily Joseph's,
but not to him, never! They don't need to lie to him and Angelo
will always be straight and on the up and up with them. They can
discuss anything openly and truthfully.

No matter the gravity or seriousness, Angelo wants his son's
to come to him. He's told both of them their whole lives, "I don't
care what it is, you come and tell me and we'll both figure out
what to do or where to go, you hear me?" He meant it and both boy's
have done exactly as he told them to.

Another lesson, "I don't care if they catch you red-handed,
you don't admit to nothing. You talk to me first," he had instructed.
All the Carosa children were wise from the start anyway. When asked,
"What's your Dad do for work?", the standard response was, "He
works for Holiday Inn," or whatever legit job he held at the time.

That is a big reason Angelo even holds down a real job, for
just that purpose, it give's all of them a valid response to any
outside probe. The book earns him a week's pay in one day, sometimes
even better depending on the season. Football, basketball and
baseball joins with the horse tracks action.

"Dad, in Mom's last letter she said GeJo's gone, huh?",
Joseph asks.

"Yea, well, JoJo, he was old and he had a good life. If I
can go like him I'll be happy," Angelo answers.

"Yea well, not too soon, Pop. Make it to his age first, ok?",
Joseph tells him, and then adds, "He kept his word to you, Dad, on
everything. I wouldn't be at the Point and no safe life down here
away from New York for you guys," he looks back at Jimmy as he says
the last. Boy, the kid grew up, he thinks. And, of course, the
little Gatz would have the prettiest girl in the school. The girls
always loved little Jimmy. He remembers him as a toddler and the
girls holding him down and kissing him. His bawling away adding to
the girls zeal to continue. He laugh's at the memory.

"Jimmy, what are you going to do if you don't marry this-
uh, what's her name?", Joseph asks.

"Jill, Jill Mayor," Jimmy answers, "And if I don't marry
her, I'll work for Dad," he adds in all seriousness.

"What?!", his father and brother say at the same time.

"Why not? I could do it," Jimmy tells them both.

"Yea well, forget about it, you don't need this shit.
Your young, your a smart kid, you can make a life for yourself,"
Angelo is shaking his head no as he is saying this, for emphasis.

"You could join the Army, or the Air Force," Joseph cuts
in. "Your smart, Gatz, you could go to O.C.S, become an officer,"
Joseph is telling him, (O.C.S is Officer Candidate School).

"I'm not talking about being a grunt, so don't give me
that look," Joseph says.

But Angelo is giving him the same look also, so Joseph says, "I'm not talking about being a grunt, Pop," he says this defensively. They both have the same expression, Jimmy and his father.

"Listen, JoJo, your brother's not you, he'd end up beating up one of the officers and get thrown out- after he got out of jail," Angelo says and smile's at his two son's. And of course he's right, as always.

"Tell him about the punk you knocked out, Jimmy," Angelo says proudly.

"Oh yeah? No shit, Gatz? Out?!", Joseph asks. And now Jimmy regales his older brother with the same story he had tickled Angelo with four days ago.

At home, Nettie comes running out of the kitchen, "Oh, my son! My son! Look at you!", she cries, and she literally is crying as well. She hugs him and hugs him.

Joseph laugh's and says, "Ma, Ma," and tilts her face up so he can kiss her cheeks, twice. She is wiping her eye's with the back of her hand as Angelo walks over and starts blotting her tears with his handkerchief and put's his arm around her. Nettie is still hugging her son as if to make sure he's really here, she can't believe it.

"Mom?", its Christy. She's in a bathrobe with a towel around her head, she's just getting out of the shower.

"Oh my God! Joey! Joey, look at you!" She rushes into his arms. Nettie's let go of him long enough so that he can hug his

little sister but she's still standing close and looking at him.
She thinks, my son is so handsome.

"Look at you!", Christy squeals again. "All my friends are
going to die when they see you! Joey, thank God your home, come on,"
she tells him and he takes both her hand and his mother's and they
all go sit at the dining room table. Nettie is on one side and
Christy on the other as Nettie runs her hand over his close cropped
hair. He has beautiful thick hair normally and she misses it.

They all start asking questions at once, rapid fire like
a machine gun. It's so familiar he knows he's indeed home. He laugh's
and tries to answer as best as he can, first one, and then that one,
and this one. He's so glad he made it home, it'll be his last
Christmas here at the Carosa home for quite some time. He ponders
how to tell them what's ahead.

No sense spoiling the mood, he's got four days, let them
be good ones, happy ones. He'll tell his father and Jimmy and then
the three of them can figure out what to do with his mother and
little sister.

Angelo finally interrupts the questions saying, "Ok, come
on, he just got here, let him take his coat off. JoJo, you want
a beer? A glass of wine?"

"Beer, Dad, beer's good," Joseph answers.

"Wait till you see what I made you baby, everything you like,
your favorites," Nettie tells him. Of course she has, she's been
cooking since last night so it's perfect.

"Sit. Sit right here, I'll be right back," she says, and
then, "Christy, go put some clothes on and then come and help me

in the kitchen," she says as she makes the first of what's surely to be dozens of trips to and from the kitchen this night. Her darling son is home, it has to be extra perfect for him. As a blur, the day's literally fly by. It'll be time to go back soon, too soon.

Saturday night he went with Christy and little midget Margo, as he used to call her anyway, to a party.

When he first saw Christy in her bathrobe and toweled head, she appeared unchanged from when he'd left. But seeing her later, and now again tonight, he can't believe how much she has changed, Margo too.

Christy is a senior in high school, and at 17, the bratty little 14 year old sophomore he left behind is now a porcelain skinned doll. And Margo is no longer a midget, either. She's a petite auburn haired siren. Boy!, they certainly have changed, he thinks.

Margo too had made a big fuss over him and he was a little embarrassed. He's the shy brother, definitely not like Jimmy is with the girl's.

At the party, as Christy had foretold, all the girl's are flirting with him. They too remember the boy he was vs. the man standing here now.

The girl's are wearing very short skirts, mini-skirts they're called, the latest fashion. Christy's in one but she didn't leave the house like that. No, she had a much more modest length skirt on over it. Her father, Angelo, would've never let her out of the house like that, Joseph thinks to himself and smiles.

Some of the boy's are asking about Vietnam. Is he going? Is it real bad? Many of these boys will be issued draft cards and draft lottery numbers as soon as they turn 18. Some here tonight already have their draft cards and are only awaiting the lottery number drawing in January.

So, the questions their asking are not out of idle curiousity, they're worried he can tell. I'll be leading boy's not much older than these. They'll be expertly trained and prepared but not a whole lot older than these boy's, nope.

"No, fella's, its not that bad, yet," he tells them now, adding the "yet" after the briefest of pauses. It's going to get a lot worse, too," he's saying, and again here he pauses, looking at the young men staring at him, ashen faced. Then he smile's broadly and says, "For them, because we're going to kick their ass!" The boy's actually cheer and begin slapping him on the back, smiling.

Christmas eve the family stays together at home for the traditional seafood feast. Seafood is the chosen food for Italians on this night. They open their presents and drink annisette laced egg-nog.

Christy has one small box, its gift wrapped of course, and as she's opening it she's asking, "What is it, Dad?" It, is a set of keys? Keys! Ford keys! "Oh, Wow! Wow! Daddy, you didn't? You did! Oh my God, you did! Oh Daddy, Mom!", she's stammering.

Angelo and Nettie are on the couch. Nettie has her arms around Angelo and his is draped over her shoulders. They're both smiling at their little girl, she'll always be their little girl to them.

She runs over and hugs both of them as Angelo says, "Ay-you going to see it?, or-." But he need say no more, Christy is out the door and there it is, Joseph leaning non-chalantly against it.

It's a brand new 1967 Mustang, red, with black bucket seats, wood grain interior, accessories, and a 289 V-8. Christy is literally shaking.

"Come on, Christy, take me for a spin," Joseph says. They hop in and Christy tears out of the driveway. The car is fast. As she guns the engine they barely hear Nettie, she's yelling something to them. She's saying, "Your shoes!" Nettie is holding Christy's shoes, to her chagrin Christy goes barefoot most of the time. Nettie can't understand it, these kid's down here, Florida, don't own shoes? They never wear shoes, she's shaking her head as she goes back inside.

Much later, as Nettie has gone to bed, Christy is still on the phone to all her friends telling them about the car.

Joseph, Angelo and Jimmy are sitting at the dining room table. All serious discussions occur there and tonight's subject is definitely serious.

Joseph tells his father what's ahead for him once he returns to the Point. "I finish in September, they give me my commission, and my term there is complete. I'll return to graduate with my class in June 1968," he tells them.

The three are drinking beer, Jimmy's old enough, he might not see his brother for a long time after tonight.

Joseph continues, "I finish at the Point in September. Then

I go to Ft. Benning for jump school for three months. After that I go to Ft. Walton Beach for Ranger training, six months. Then it's back to the Point for graduation, and then assignment.

He made it sound easy, simple, it is neither. Jump school is for airborne para-troop training, and Ranger training is one of the two most intense, grueling courses the United States military has, (the other is the Navy Seal program).

Angelo says, "JoJo, I'm not stupid JoJo. All this training, what the fuck they going to have you do, JoJo?" When Angelo is nervous he repeats himself, and he's far from calm right now. Will he see his son again?, he's wondering-

"Pop, the more training I get here, the better I'll be prepared, ready, there," Joseph replies.

"And where the fuck is "there", JoJo? Vietnam, right?", Angelo states, he doesn't need an answer.

When they had spoken about West Point, Joseph was still a kid, and there wasn't any war. Even in 1960 when GeJo pulled the strings with Mayor Lindsey- but now...

"I'm going to be leading boys, Dad. I-," Joseph was saying, but Angelo cuts in saying, "Your just a kid yourself, JoJo." He pats his son's face, he's very proud of him.

"Your mother and I will come to New York for your graduation," he tells him.

"Whoa! What about all the old problems? And GeJo gone too-," Joseph asks.

"Ain't no problem I can't come and see my son graduate,"

Angelo replies. He said son with so much pride it almost chokes
Joseph up.

Angelo hugs his son tightly, "Don't say nothing to your
mother. You either, Jimmy," he warns his boy's, unnecessarily- they
both know.

"Let's go get some sleep," the old man says, and tonight,
for the first time, Angelo actually feels old.

CHAPTER FIVE

September1967/ April 1968

"So glad we got the real thing."

The Real Thing/ Tammy Terrel & Marvin Gaye

Although Jimmy's sister, Christy, and Jill's sister, Lisa, attended the same school and were in the same grade together, they had never been friends. On occasion, if they saw one another in between classes, they may stop and chat, the conversation usually about their younger siblings, both singly and as a couple.

Christy and her best friend, Margo, had associated with a different crowd. The supposed "bad boy's" who smoked, cursed and maybe even drank a beer or two on Saturday night. The main divide between Christy and her set, and Lisa and her's, is family income.

The boy's in Lisa's crowd also smoked, cursed and drank. And, more than likely, with far more frequency than their less moneyed peers.

Christy's group hung out in public parks close to home, while Lisa's usually had a vacant villa without parental supervision to retire to.

The latter group indulged in much riskier behavior behind the walled and gated manor than the public park crowd ever thought about.

But good or bad is ones perception, it matters little in real life.

So, in September Christy is beginning her third month of employment as a waitress at Patricia Murphy's, an upscale restaurant located at the Bahia Mar Yacht basin. Her friend, Margo, is also employed here. The tips are very good and both girl's are glad to have their jobs.

Lisa Mayor is a freshmen at the University of Florida in

Gainesville, as are many of her friends. She is likewise happy with what she is doing.

Jimmy and Jill are still a couple. They're Junior's in high school now and there is already talk of future matrimony of the two. In high school two years is eternity.

Joseph is completing his last weeks at the Point. He'll make his first jump from a tower erected for just that purpose, at the jump school in Ft. Benning in less than 30 days. Ten days after that it's live practice out of air transports.

Christy and Margo are getting an apartment together. They both anticipate that by no later than Thanksgiving they'll have saved and put away everything their now amassing to furnish and accessorize their new abode.

All are young and eager for the future, and what's ahead is greatly anticipated, by most anyway.

Many of Christy and Margo's high school friends, the boy's- are awaiting their draft lottery numbers. They're 18, or will be before the year is out, and the lottery is held in January 1968. There will be no college deferments for them, no.

Christy's boyfriend from high school is contemplating joining the Air Force or the Navy. At least he wouldn't be in those same jungles he see's every week night on network news. Or, jumping out of helicopters, or worse, being carted back to those helicopters shot or blown to pieces. Vietnam, live in your home every night, courtesy of ABC, NBC or CBS.

The young men of Christy and Margo's crowd are nervous.

They'll go if called, no cowards or draft dodger's here, not amongst
this group. Not yet, there will be some few thousand in later days,
but not yet. Going to Canada takes money, not many West-side boy's
will be found in Toronto, or Quebec, or Vancouver.

The class of 1967 is still patriotic, the huge pot of dis-
content is just now being placed on the stove to boil. Most of the
young men are readying themselves, steeling themselves if you will,
to watch the big barrel roll and the initial number to come out
of it, designating all young men born on this specific date, 18 years
ago, with their Selective Service System number. It literally can
mean life or death.

It is with mixed sentiment that the young await the holidays,
Christmas and the New Year. Some with dread, others avidly- The
Draft Lottery looms for some, not all-.

April 1968

Lisa Mayor is not a frivolous or foolish young lady. As
1967 became 1968 she is very aware of the war. Everyone is, especially
the young, for it is their blood, or their peer's blood that is
being shed in South East Asia.

However, it hasn't touched her personally yet. No one she
knows, no one she attended high school with, no boys from the river-
fronted community she grew up in, have been effected at all.

The boy's she date's at the University of Florida are
safely ensconced there, college deferment intact. Their biggest worry
is flunking out and becoming draft eligible. Scholarly or not,

they know the consequence of failing grades. They must pass and so they do. Safe for another semester.

During the annual Spring break, Florida becomes "the spot" for college student's East of the Mississippi River. They flock to its beaches by the hundreds of thousands.

Lisa has experienced the crux of it her entire life in Ft. Lauderdale. And so it is that she agrees to go to Daytona with her two sorority sisters, Beth and Joanne. At least it will be different, she thinks.

After two days she realizes that its no different at all. It's a bunch of loud, rude, boisterous, very intoxicated boy's, as well as girl's, acting like fools.

She is considering returning to the University of Florida Campus. At least she can study there, she's definitely not enjoying-this? Beer and liquor controlled riot, she thinks.

As she's strolling down the shore contemplating her choices of stay or go, she runs right into a young man who, prior to her collision with him, was taking a photo of four young ladies, all in mid pose.

"Oh, excuse me," Lisa says. She nudged him just enough to spoil the shot. He turns around and- wow!, she thinks, before feeling even more embarrassed because he is so good looking.

He smile's at her, bows theatrically and says, "Lt. Gordon Rollins, at your service," and snaps her a quick salute. She's standing there and he just keeps looking at her, expectantly.

She finally snaps and says, "Oh! Excuse me- again - I'm

Lisa Mayor. I don't know what's come over me." And now she really
is embarrassed-

By now, the four girl's are very annoyed with Lisa for
interrupting their handsome young man and the taller blond girl
asks, "Hey, are you going to take the picture, or?"

"Excuse me one moment, Lisa?", he asks. He executes a neat
about face, walks to the girl and says, "Or!", and hands her the
camera.

Lisa is laughing. He holds out his arm to her and she takes
it. "Will you have lunch with me? I'm an officer in the Navy, your
perfectly safe," he assures her, smiling.

"All right- yes, thank you," Lisa replies. She can't believe
she just accepted a lunch date with a stranger, what is wrong with
her today? She's picked up a sailor on the beach! If her prim and
proper mother only knew. The thought is so amusing she laugh's out
loud-

"I'm sorry, Gordon, I'm in a very strange mood today," she
says and actually shakes her head. He finds this very amusing and
now he laugh's too, saying, "I've been known to have that effect on
women, I must warn you." He says this very seriously but his eye's
are dancing as he looks at her and they both laugh. She again thinks,
Wow!, and chastises herself, "Stop it, Lisa!" She is behaving far
out of character, she's never been forward with boy's before.

Through lunch, Gordon told her all about himself. He's on
day three of a ten day leave from the Jacksonville Naval Air Station
where his ship, the carrier U.S.S Enterprise, is preparing to set
sail 7 nights from tonight for the South China Sea. His parent's

live just South down the beach in Cocoa, where his father, Colonel
John Rollins, is with NASA. This is where he grew up, Cocoa Beach
is home. He's 24 and a naval aviator of F-4 Phantom fighter craft.
These are his last days stateside until after the Enterprise returns
late next year.

To Lisa, he is the most handsome man she has ever been with.
Tall, dark haired, although it is clipped very short, polite and att-
entive, he is unlike anyone else she has dated in the past. He is
a man, the other's were boys.

They talked and laughed the hours away, literally. The
beach crowd had actually thinned to the point of being deserted.

"Oh my! What time is it?", Lisa asks, "I'm supposed to
have dinner with my sorority sisters," she adds. Punctual, concise
Lisa is late - there's a first time for everything.

"It's 6:20 p.m.," he tells her.

"Oh, no! I'm late-" She is truly stunned, what's happened
to her? "I have to go - Gordon, I-" She is getting her things together, but she doesn't want to just leave. He's sailing in 7 days,
she may never see him again, she-.

"Lisa, come to Cocoa Beach with me, get away from - this,"
Gordon is asking as he indicates the crazy college frat house
mentality here in Daytona.

She stops and looks at him and thinks, "Yes, all right. I
have to get my thing's from the Howard Johnson's," she says, "Room
523. Do you have a car, or-".

"I'll get my gear and pick you up. I'll ring you from the
lobby," he tells her. Twenty minutes later they're driving South

on Highway A1A to Cocoa Beach.

They spend the next 6 days on the quiet white sands of Cocoa, swimming, surfing - well, he tried teaching her. But their nights!

After an early supper, they'd return to the Cocoa Hilton and make love all night. They watched many a sunrise on the beach wrapped together in a blanket, a thermos of coffee and a feeling of bliss. They both knew what happened but were afraid to say.

On the last morning, Gordon was to report by 1800 hours, 6:00 p.m., He said, "Lisa, come with me. We'll drive up and you can see me off dockside, its Navy tradition."

"Isn't that only for family? I don't want to intrude," she asks, but Gordon is shaking his head, no, and he says, "No, I want you to come. I want you to meet my mother."

"All right, yes, I'll go with you," she answers. It's music to his ears.

He kisses her deeply and they both nod, yes, its there all right- whatever "it" is, they've got it.

They stopped at the Cape so Gordon could see his father, and then they headed North.

"Gordon, are you going to be safe? I mean are you- uh, I'm afraid, what if-?", Lisa is saying but he silences her with a kiss.

"I'll be fine. If your here waiting for me nothing will stop me from coming back to you, ok?", he asks.

"I'll be here. You promise me you'll come back and I'll be here waiting," she assures him.

"I'll be back," he soothes and they kiss. "I can't wait for

my mom to meet you, Lisa, she's going to be thrilled," he tells her now. He love's her and he's going to marry her, as soon as he gets back, he thinks.

Meeting his mother, and seeing him off dockside- maybe he'll propose, she muses.

At 1745 hours/ 5:45 p.m., Lieutenant Gordon Rollinsreports to base.

His mother had flown, compliments of the Navy, from the Cape with other Navy and Marine family members.

She is waiting for him in the officer's club. And, as Gordon predicted, she was thrilled to see her handsome son with a most beautiful girl.

Mrs. Rollins, who instructed Lisa to call her, Barbara, has been a military wife for almost 30 years. She now asks, "Gordon dear, how did you find such a lovely young lady to come all this way with you, only to watch you sail off into the night?"

She's teasing them both of course. She had watched his father Jack depart for war.

"Well, we ran into each other on the beach, and...," Gordon says mischievously as Lisa playfully slaps at him.

"Actually, Mom, I'm going to ask her to marry me when I get back," he announces to the shock and surprise of both ladies.

Lisa is blushing and when Barbara see's this she says, "Why Gordon! Your suppose to be a gentlemen, and I believe Lisa is just now hearing this for the first time. Shame on you," she scolds but not seriously.

"Lisa, darling, don't mind my son's bad manners, I believe love has addled his senses," she says.

"I'm uh, oh, Mrs. Rollins, Barbara, Gordon, I'd be honored, yes!", Lisa says, she had been tongue tied by his surprise.

Gordon kisses her, Barbara hugs her and says, "Welcome aboard, is the way we say it in the Navy Lisa dear. Now Gordon, will you please get me a drink? I'm a little too old for such surprises."

At midnight, Barbara and Lisa stood together watching the great ship put to sea. Both had taken an immediate liking and affection for each other. Barbara thought Gordon lucky. She could see the love shine from Lisa's beautiful eyes.

They heard the National Anthem and then the Navy's own Anchors Away. The entire 5,000 sailors, marines, aviators and technicians top side as 8 huge ocean going tug's pulled her out to sea. They both had tears in their eye's as did many of the women and some few men as well. Their boy's were sailing off into harms way.

When the hulking vessel was but a dark spot on the sea, Barbara hugged Lisa and said, "Lisa, come home with me for a few days, I want you to meet Jack, Gordon's father."

"Well, are you sure, Mrs. Rollins?" Lisa asks.

"Mrs. Rollins isn't sure, but Barbara is positive. Now come along, dear," she replies warmly.

On the drive back, they were in Gordon's rental. Barbara regaled Lisa with Gordon's entire life story and her own courtship and marriage to his father.

Jack was taken with Lisa as well, she is a lovely girl, he thinks. He, too, fills her in with stories about how the young boy Gordon was, from his first catch of a blue Marlin right off Cocoa Beach to his most recent achievments of graduating in the top 5% of his class at the U.S. Naval Academy in Annapolis, MD., his rapid advancement through combat air maneuvers and carrier air craft training that resulted in his present stationing on the U.S.S Enterprise. He is very proud of his son.

Jack had flown missions off the "Lady Sara", the U.S.S. Saratoga in World War II in the Pacific campaign, with the first Marine Air Wing. This was in support of the invasion of Guadalcanal to seize what became Henderson Field, for use by the heavy bombers of the Army Air Corp.

He had flown dozens of missions in each invasion up the Soloman Islands, Tarawa, Tulagi, up to Borneo and finally to the Japanese home islands of Chi-Chi Jima, Iwo Jima and Okinawa.

He's confident, he tells the ladies, that Gordon would prove himself valiantly and return home safely.

What he didn't tell them is war is a very unpredictable affair, the unexpected happening often, you needed luck on your side too.

When Barbara and Lisa tell him they would be praying for him, Jack knew he would also.

CHAPTER SIX

December 1968

"Lonely days, lonely nights,

where would I be without my woman."

Title Song/ The Bee Gee's

Dr. Henried Wright Smart ia a scion of the wealthy social class. He is a brilliant neuro-surgeon who received his medical doctor degree from Duke University, and then his doctorate of neural sciences at John Hopkins in Baltimore, MD.

He is one of the top five neuro-surgeons in the country, and East of the Mississippi River by South of the Mason Dixon line he has no peer, he is the best.

Dr. Smarts practice consists of five neuro-specilists. The Chief neurologist, Dr. Warren, is the elder doctor of the group. It is his diagnosis the four surgeons discuss when a patient becomes the groups responsibility.

Further, Dr. Warren assigns patient's on a case by case basis to the appropriate associate surgeon. The most difficult and delicate procedures are assigned to Dr. Smart.

The four surgeon's of the Ft. Lauderdale Neurological Group are responsible for the entire county of Broward. All emergency room head trauma injuries are responded to, and treated by, one of the four surgeon's on a seven day rotating schedule on emergency room stand-by.

This week is Dr. Smarts seven days of Emergency Room stand-by so it is quite late when he finally returns to his river front home where he resides with his wife, Victoria, and his daughter, Nicole.

As he passes the door to the master bedroom, he looks in on his sleeping wife. He almost considers waking her, as he had once done so often during his first year residency at John Hopkins. Those day's truly seem an eternity ago, as if they only existed in his imagination, as he stands here in the doorway this evening.

He closes the door without entering. He goes to the bar and pours himself a Scotch, two fingers, and quickly tosses it down.

As he sits there in the quiet mansion, he reflects again on how quickly the years seem to have passed.

Nicole is a young woman, she'll be off to college in the fall. It seems she was just a little seven year old, dressed as the Virgin Mary in her elementary school play. What is it now, ten years ago?

He feels like a stranger in his own home, he hardly knows the two women who are his wife and daughter, his family.

He and his beautiful wife no longer make love spontaneously, it's been years since they have. Victoria allows him the pleasure once a week, on Sunday. She hasn't the desire and has made it perfectly clear that she is unavailable at all other times. Henry has rationalized it as her being a woman with a low sex drive who doesn't want or need the physical act of sex.

After Nicole was born, he had wanted more children but Victoria had flatly refused. She had borne him a daughter, and as far as she was concerned, she had fulfilled her wifely duty. She had abhorred her pregnancy and was cross the entire nine months of it. Never would her body be thick with child again. She had no intentions of giving anymore of herself than she already had. Not to her husband Henry.

But to Hugh, oh yes, completely, hungrily. Victoria and Hugh have been lover's for two and a half years now and they both still can't get enough of each other. She remembers yesterday, and how he had looked at her. He was so inflamed with desire that had it not been high afternoon, but the dark of night, she was sure he would have taken her right there in the car. She enjoys having such an over powering effect on Hugh. That he is the husband of her best friend, Cynthia, doesn't quell her enthusiasm, quite the opposite, it actually adds to her pleasure. Poor Cynthia, her pale blond beauty is no match for Victoria's feminine intoxicating allure to the helpless Hugh, completely in her spell.

But, Victoria has played this game far too long already. She has tired of it and intends to demand an end to it soon. Hugh is her's. With Nicole going off to college in the fall, as well as Hugh's daughter, Jill, also going to the University of Florida at Gainesville, there will no longer be any obstacles,nothing more that Hugh can object to. The time is quite near, she has no doubt of who he will come to when she puts her foot down and he is forced to choose.

The law firm of Mayor, Jetts, Steadman and Kuhl is a powerful and influential entity in it's own right.

The represented clientel of the firm control vast fortunes in Florida, the United States and globally.

Hugh's position as a State Senator in the Florida legislature is to ensure unimpeded prosperity and continuity for his client's within the state. But, the time has arrived for Hugh Mayor to perform on a much larger stage, the United States Senate.

He has incorporated a campaign committee and the financing

of such through the law offices. He plans to run for the national seat in the elections of 1970, and has been assured by the power brokers, the mover's and shaker's in both the state and national party's hierarchy, that the seat is his.

They are very aware of Hugh's unwavering pro business advocacy as a state Senator. They are assured by him personally that he will utilize his U.S. Senate seat in almost the same capacity. The election is a mere formality, he will be the next Republican Senator from Florida. How could he not be?

His background, his upbringing, education, along with his record on public service, are impeccable. He has the presence and exude's the confidence of every natural politician.

His tall, trim frame and thick hair with just the slightest touch of graying at the temples, along with his deep baritone and self effacing qualities, literally shout, Senator. His beautiful blond wife and his two pretty blond daughter's complete the package that the public will see, There is no way he will lose.

But, Hugh has one very dark secret that no one knows of, no one can even guess at except, of course, Victoria.

He doesn't know how he ever let it begin, how he could have been so foolish. And, the worst of it is that it yet continues. He's told himself time and again that it has to end, he must put a stop to it. But, then she is there and he is helpless in his desire, he must take her.

He hasn't the answer of what to do about Victoria. For such a powerful man, he is powerless with her.

At the Mayor home, Jill and Nicole are wrapping Christmas gifts. Lisa is expected later tonight from the University of Florida at Gainesville.

Cynthia thinks this is the last year like this. Next year it will be Lisa and Jill coming home for the holiday's, and with that thought comes a slight melancholy. Her girl's are young women and the world awaits them.

Jimmy is expected at any minute. It's the night before Christmas eve and Jill won't see him again until after its conclusion. He has a motorcycle that his father, Angelo, bought him and Cynthia has forbidden Jill to ride on it. Jimmy must park the bike there at the Mayor home and then he and Jill can go in her car. They know that if the bike is parked there Jill won't be on it. Of course, she has ridden with Jimmy, many times on a Saturday afternoon or a weekday lunch period you could find the two motoring around together. She loves it, and Jimmy drives very safely when she's with him.

Jill love's Jimmy very much and Jimmy love's her. What are they going to do in September when Jill goes away to the University of Florida?

Jill toyed with the idea of changing to the University of Miami but Jimmy insisted that she go to Gainesville.

"Are you trying to get rid of me, Jimmy Carosa?", she asked teasingly.

He replied with mild sarcasm, "Yes! I want to date all my other high school girlfriend's, don't you remember them all?"

Jill was frowning at him as he said, "There was Jill, and

then angry Jill, and then uh, bossy Jill." Jill had started to
giggle. "And, Oh yeah, my favorite! You!!"

He chased her as she sprinted away saying, "Catch me if you
can!" She was laughing happily.

He caught her easily and they rolled to the ground with
her on top.

"Are you at least going to miss me," she asked.

"Every hour of every day," he answered, and she leaned in
and kissed him.

Cynthia had observed the two of them and even caught a bit
of their conversation. They had been steadies since the first day
of high school. The expectations of youth, she mused. Jimmy was
a part of their home, she and Hugh liked and approved of him.
Would the reality of living apart, living separate live's in the
real world make an exception for Jill and Jimmy? Cynthia regretfully
didn't think so.

"Mom? Jill? You guy's here?", Lisa calls from the foyer.

"Oh, hello, Jewel. I didn't see you," she continued.

As the old woman attempts to take her bags, Lisa says,
"No, no, Jewel, I've got them, its ok."

"But Miss Lisa you'll work me out of a job if'n I don't
take them," Jewel chides but Lisa hugs her and says, "Shoo, or
I'll fire you for insubordination."

Cynthia rounds the corner and, "Hi! Your early," she hugs
her oldest daughter.

Jewel has attempted to take the bags again but they both
shoo her away, smiling, as Cynthia says, "You have coffee to make,

Jewel, and thank you."

Jewel smile's broadly in return and says, "I hope Mista Hugh don't fire me for alls the work I don't do no more."

Mother and daughter laugh, Jewel is part of the family and they all know it.

"Who's motorcycle, Mom?", Lisa asks. Then she hears Jill and Jimmy in the other room carrying on and her and her mother exchange smiles as Cynthia shakes her head and raises her eyebrows.

"Well, if it isn't James Carosa," Lisa says, adding a false disapproval in her tone as she enters. Then turning to Jill she adds, "I see you haven't tired of him yet, hmm? They say love is blind, so...," but she is smiling broadly as she is saying this and has her arms open as Jill hugs her, and Jimmy leans in for a quick peck on her cheek.

Jimmy has grown up, Lisa sees. He was always a cute little devil but now, wow! If only he were a little older, she muses. Those eyes! She can't pinpoint it but it's not the color or the shape, it's the emotion that pours out of them. 17 year old boys aren't suppose to have eye's like that.

Seeing the way Jill and Jimmy look at each other, Lisa can see their love and thinks, just as her mother had earlier, will they stay intact once Jill's at the University of Florida? Looking at them now she can almost believe, yes. After all, she is a world away from Gordon but as close as the night he sailed away.

She write's him everyday, twice a day sometimes. The interminable wait for his letter's would go on seemingly without

end, until she'd get 8,9,10 letter's all at once. She'd read them
front to back, most recent to oldest, and then back to front, again.
Mail from the South China Sea was uncertain, slow and spotty, but
to her it was received with such great elation and relief that she'd
call Barbara in Cocoa and they'd talk for two hours.

It had been eight months now, seven more till the Enterprise
departed her station and returned to port. Lisa was literally counting the days.

At the Carosa home it was a subdued Christmas, Joseph was
in the minds of all of them, of course. Angelo and Nettie had indeed
attended his graduation in June, bursting with pride and overcome
by emotion in parting the next day.

Nettie believed that he was going as an advisor, trainer to
a base in Japan, and he did, for 30 days. Angelo knew that after his
son left Japan he was going into the jungle somewhere in South East
Asia, to a classified military posting to prevent any possible
trace back tying him to official orders of the High Command, should
he be captured or, killed.

If Angelo were ever afraid before you'd never have known
it by looking at him. But the day he and Nettie boarded the Silver
Meteor in Penn Station, where Joseph stood on the platform watching
the train pull out, if you looked very closely you'd see what no
one before had, Angelo was afraid. He kept looking back at his son
till the tracks curved out of sight.

Joseph called once from Japan, and he had written five letters,
one per month. Angelo knew no news was good news. They'd only hear,

God forbid, if something happened. Joseph told his father that if he failed to report back to base within 3 days of his ETA, the Department of the Army would assume he'd run afoul and was M.I.A, K.I.A, or a P.O.W., only then would they be notified.

They hadn't, of course, so, Angelo smiled at his wife, at Jimmy, and at Christy, and they all had a toast, to Joseph-salud, to Dominick-salud, to the New Year- salud.

Christy's boyfriend was home on leave before shipping out January 2, 1969, an Army draftee.

PART II

UGLY MEN

CHAPTER SEVEN

December 1968

"Better run through the jungle."

Title Song/ Creedence Clearwater Revival

Gordon is flying at 5,000 feet, a circuitous path around the battle fleet, while the A-6 bombers for this morning mission are being launched from his mother ship, the U.S.S Enterprise, and her sister ship, the U.S.S Kitty Hawk.

From fighter group Alpha, which Gordon is a part of, there are six F-4 Phantom fighters to escort an even dozen A-6 bombers from bomber group, Zebra. The bombers are a second Marine Air Wing detachment, deployed, South East Asia operations, South China Sea, Naval Task force.

The Alpha group fighter's are escorting the twelve bombers to their target destination in Vietnam. While the bomber's proceed directly to their targets, the fighter's will engage and neutralize all resistance, from aerial challenge, ground anti-aircraft fire, and surface to air missles.

The much slower A-6 bomber's are easy prey for MIG-19 fighter's deployed by the North Vietnamese, piloted by Soviets.

The MIG-19 is the primary reason for the F-4's presence. It is the most superior fighter craft in the world. Flown by a skilled combat aviator, it has no equal. The scrambled MIG's are quickly diverted by the lead F-4'S and now it is the ground defenses that open up, throwing walls of flak into the flight paths of the attackers.

They can only hope the initial barrages are insufficient to disable the lead crafts. Once the anti-aircraft batteries fire, they are exposed and ensuing fighter's quickly destroy them.

It is the surface to air missiles, made in China, that

the U.S. attack squadron is most concerned with. Any direct contact and the aircraft is surely lost. But more importantly, if the pilot is unable to, "make the soup", get his craft back over the open sea where Naval recovery and rescue can be made, he must eject into the jungle.

If the damage is so severe that he must immediately abandon his aircraft, he most surely will be parachuting down into hostile enemy territory. Friendly rescue and recovery is doubtful.

Captain John Avery, "Hunt", Lieutenant Gordon Rollins, "Surfer", his wing man, are flying tree top level raining fire below from their wing mounted .50 caliber machine guns.

Once the incoming fighter threat, bogey's on the aircrafts radar, have been diverted by two of the F-4's of the fighter group, the remaining 4 craft's are ripping the jungle below, literally shredding it to mulch.

Any hostiles present who manage to survive the onslaught will still not have managed to get aloft any surface to air missiles or much anti-aircraft flak.

The A-6 bomber's are in close formation, tight behind the fighters. The fighters own radar targeting is scanning the area 360 degrees, finding and storing coordinates, so they can be destroyed by their wing mounted missiles. The kill rate of course, is not 100%, the North Vietnamese Army air defense batteries will send some ordinance aloft no matter what the fighters lay down.

Gordon has flown several missions where the air was thick with pier piling size projectiles all around, right, left, front and back. He was surprised that none made contact.

Gordon has been on station now for seven months, since May. He has flown dozens of sorties into North Vietnamese airspace, as well as over the central highlands and the Mekong Valley in the South. He has one confirmed kill, a MIG-19 that he shot down in air to air combat.

He has killed many of the enemy on the ground and feels no remorse. It's his duty, his mission. They have begun using a new weapons system called, Napalm, a jellied petroleum accelerant, extremely combustible with super hot temperatures over 1,000 degrees, they are burning all of Vietnam to ashes.

After this sortie, Alpha group has fulfilled its part in the mission. He's in a return holding pattern waiting for the last A-6 to rendezvous. He and Jeremy, "Germ", Fulmer, from Alabama, are flying wide arc's off the coast.

"Germ to Surfer Alpha," comes over his radio and he clicks his mike to acknowledge.

"Hunt 1 has ordered me to proceed South to rendezvous station 0101, request escort per Hunt 1 discretion," Germ radio's.

Lieutenant Fulmer, "Germ", is asking Gordon, "Surfer", to proceed South with him as his wing man.

"Roger, Germ, I'm on your wing," Gordon radios back.

"Hunt 1 all Alpha squad, Zebra intact, going dust," Captain Avery announces over the radio. Going dust means going home, back to the carrier.

"Hunt 1, Germ, your - ah, wing?", Avery asks.

"Hunt 1 Surfer Alpha is my wing," Germ radio's back.

"Copy, Hunt 1 out," the Captain signs off.

Germ and Surfer, Jeremy and Gordon, are flying a slow cruising speed of 400 miles per hour when they make contact with Air Operations radar control. They roger the identification and cross over land and begin to descend to 2,000 feet, then 1,000 feet. They are in supposed friendly territory. They are flying very loose, its a joy ride until they reach rendezvous 0101.

Gordon is checking all his instruments, armaments, gauges, and air-speed indicator when Germ arcs off into a slow Westerly decent. He doesn't give it much thought, they are still in visual contact. He see's Germ's wing cannons firing bursts. What's this?

He bank's hard right and brings up his speed to close on Germ. The only reason his cannon would be firing is enemy engagement.

Gordon radio's, "Germ, Surfer Alpha, What's your sighting?"

He hears a malicious snicker before Germ says, "Oh, nothing ole Surfer boy, just a little target practice. Country boy needs to knock the rust off, that's all."

Gordon is looking down and sees nothing.

"Germ, what are you saying? Talk straight," Gordon radio's.

"Well, I took care of a few gook's fore they get their pajama's on tonight, just a little prevent ole-," Germ is saying.

By now, Gordon realizes what's happened and he says, "Goddamit, Germ! Goddamit! Tell me your joking?! Are you crazy?! You son of a bitch! You-," Gordon is yelling into his mike.

"Hey! Mister! Can it!", Germ snarls, but Gordon is red hot.

"Are you fuckin' crazy? What about your numbers? What about-",

Gordon is still yelling.

"Ain't nobody left around to tell nobody nothin'," Germ replies, adding, "Everyone I get now is one less pajama wearing mother fucker they got to get later anyway."

"Germ, two things. As soon as we're on the deck I'm kicking the living shit out of you, and number two, I'm reporting you to Hunt 1." Gordon almost screams this over the radio.

"Surfer, you can't do the first, and you ain't going to do the second, either, Germ out," Germ barks over the radio.

They make the 0101 rendezvous without another word and then escort the big, slow medivac prop plane from Danang to Tan Son Nhut airport. It's just a precaution, MIG's have snuck over the Cambodian border for quick strikes.

The U.S. aviators cannot understand why they are not allowed to make strikes over the border. There are North Vietnamese Army supply lines and aircraft using Cambodian territory and airspace for strikes into South Vietnam, and then quickly making haste back to Cambodia and virtual sanctuary. The war is there, the North Vietnamese are there, why aren't the American's?

"Enterprise control, two incoming Alpha group, clear for catch?", Germ radio's the ship. Germ is the senior airman, he make's all radio contact and mission commands.

The ship radio's back, "Alpha, Roger, catch one loop one, copy?."

"Copy. Surfer, you copy?", Germ says.

"Copy, Germ," Gordon replies.

Seven minutes after initial radio contact with the ship,

both aircraft are on the deck. Germ's is already on the elevator being lowered into the bowel of the massive ship.

Germ is jawing with a couple signal men on the flight deck. When Gordon approaches, he grabs Germ's shoulder, wrenching him around and- boom!

"Come on, Surfer, Come on boy," someone is slapping him lightly on the face. He's propped up to a sitting position, he's fuzzy, confused. Why's he sitting here? What happened?

Someone is pinching his face, shaking his head.

"Come on, boy," he hears Germ drawl.

Ah- now he remembers.

He shake's his head and removes Germ's grip from his face, pulling his hand away. Germ is smiling at him.

"Why you-," Gordon begins but Germ grabs him under his arms and hoists him up on his feet like he was no more than a sack of potato's. Gordon almost crashes dizzily back on his ass and actually has to lean on Germ.

Germ smile's at him with a slow chuckle before saying, "I tole you you can't do the first and you ain't gonna do the second, neither."

Goddamn hillbilly hits like a mule kicks, Gordon thinks.

The two airmen are still standing there, stunned speechless.

"You two are dismissed," orders Gordon, and the two sailor's say, "Aye- Aye, sir." They snap a quick salute and go.

"Why ain't, er- why aren't I going to report you, Germ?", Gordon asks.

"Well, we's on the same side for one, and between you, me and this here empty deck, Hunt 1 is where I picked up that little ole trick," he answers.

Germ is smiling as Gordon stares open mouthed at Germ's definitely unexpected response.

Hunt 1, he thinks, holy fuckin' shit!

Germ gives that low rumbling chuckle and says, "Come on, let me buy you a drink."

He throws his arm around Gordon's shoulder and helps the still dazed Gordon down to the officer's lounge.

-Along the Vietnamese/ Cambodian Border-

Lieutenant Joseph Carosa, two sergeants, two Hmong scouts and twenty five enlisted men are breaking camp, its 0300 hours. The Ranger platoon is hunting inside Cambodia, where they have been causing massive disruption and distruction far beyond their meager number.

They've destroyed tons of ammo, medical supplies and all types of ordnance, from heavy Russian artillery to grenade launchers from North Korea. They've also been doing demolitions to infrastructure, railroad tracks, switching stations, bridges and river barges.

This is the eighth patrol this Ranger patrol has been out on and they are seasoned far beyond a mere five months operating as a unit. They wear no insignia denoting rank, no emblem identifying any military branch, nothing. There is no single outwardly observable demarcation distinguishing one soldier from another, except So and

Chi, the two Hmong scouts with the platoon, being oriental.

The platoon has over a 1,000 confirmed kills of the North Vietnamese Army. That figure doesn't count the dozens of Russian advisors and technicians, nor Viet Cong in South Vietnam.

They have not lost a Ranger yet, and G.I. Joe, Lt. Joseph Carosa's bush name, has no intentions on that happening on this patrol either.

The unit's patrol duration is 14 days. They take only weapons and ammunition. No food stores or non-lethal equipment. They live on whatever they can gather during the expedition. While laying in ambush that could be grubs, monkey meat, snake and bugs. After the raid, they will gorge themselves on captured food stores taken from the enemy. They take no prisoners, just the food rations.

After making a deep infiltration into Cambodia to start this patrol, they had stalked and ambushed a North Vietnamese army reinforced, mechanized company of almost 200 troops. All their support equipment, except for the valuable food stores, was destroyed by sheer cunning and military prowess. It is text book Ranger tactics.

They had lain in wait through the night and before the North Vietnamese Army could muster for the days march, they had attacked.

"Mac, take Ruckus, Cotton, Jake and Hammer," G.I. Joe says.

"Chi you got a good look?", G.I. asks his scout.

"Yea, I got it G.I.," the small, slight Hmong trooper replies.

"Ok, wire that mother fucker flat," G.I. tells his demo Sgt. Mac. By "flat", he means no delay fuses, blow it on contact, as soon as their clear. The target is a levee.

"I'll be a 1,000 yards on the East. Weegie, take your squad West," he tells his other sergeant.

"Nobody gets out. When them slant's break we'll enfilade, and Mac, any that get by you got em, right?", Joseph says, looking to make sure everybody's got it. They all nod assent. Chi and So take no offense at the slur, "slants". They are Ranger's, the enemy are slants.

When the levee blows, a huge torrent of water swamps the sleeping North Vietnamese Army camp. Many drown in their sleeping bags and tents. Those who managed to get out are now trying desperately to find footing or a hand hold, something to avoid being pulled into the sudden deluge.

The two squad's open up chopping the North Vietnamese Army to pieces. They have no avenue of escape from the water except directly into the machine guns of the Rangers.

When the panicked and confused enemy finally realize what's happening, they begin shouting, "No shoot! No shoot! Surrender! Surrender!" When they tried raising their hands, Weegie's greaser, (a Thompson sub-machine gun), hammers into them.

Mac's squad and Joseph's clean up any that slipped away. They stripped all the food, shot any slant that showed a maybe, (maybe he's not dead), and tracked East towards the frontier and into Vietnam. Primary mission of this patrol complete, one left.

The North Vietnamese Army and American command both know there are enemy operations by each in Cambodia, clear violations of international law- Cambodia is a neutral. Neither can accuse the other, it is the silent front.

The second task is to seek and destroy a Viet Cong enclave that is hidden among a group of small villages close to the border. The platoon lay in re-con for two night's observing with infra-red night vision binoculars and scopes.

Joseph is moving between the observation points asking, "Chi, what do you think? It looks like Khe don, a lot of traffic for a small village."

Chi smiles and says, "I take one from village, G.I., he tell us!"

Joseph playfully knocks off his bush hat and says, "That's your answer to everything, we don't have the time."

He goes post to post, nobody is certain.

When he gets to, So, who he considers his best scout, his gut instincts uncannily on the money, he asks, "So, what do you think, what's your gut say?"

So, a man of few words, says, "Khe Don or Ta Rheto."

"Which? Which, So?", Joseph presses.

So shrug's his shoulders and begins looking through his scope again.

Fuck! Joseph doesn't want to kill the wrong village. Fuck! Fuck! Fuck!, Joseph thinks.

He takes a dime out of his pocket, his good luck charm, and says, "Call it, So."

So smiles and says, "Tails."

Heads Ta Rheto, Tails Khe Don. Joseph flips the coin. Its-, Tails it is, Khe Don.

Joseph nods, he tells his two sergeants, "Mac, Weegie Khe Don." He points at Mac and says, "Go around East, lay off 100-150 yards, hold," he stresses the hold by staring at Mac till Mac nods, yes.

"Weegie, you go in on top. I'll go in on the bottom, crash your side at," he looks at his watch, its 0216 hours, "Its 0216 now, at 0226 sharp."

Weegie looks to make sure his watch is with Joseph's.

"I'll need two with greaser's on the West, they'll be thick, you'll hear 'em before you see 'em, don't leave any," he says.

Ruckus and Cotton both step forward and ask, "Where to, G.I.?"

"Lay in about halfway back this way," Joseph answers and hands Cotton his greaser as Weegie hands Ruckus his.

"Ok, 8 minutes to party, let's go!", he orders and the squad's all peel off to point.

At 0224 hours, Joseph, Chi, and So enter (crash) the village and begin yelling in Vietnamese, "The Americans! Many Americans are coming! They're coming! Run! West! Go West! Hurry! Americans, many Americans! Coming from the East!"

The dirt street is instantly packed, crowded and swarming with villager's who are screaming and confused. It is mostly old women and small children. The bulk of the village has indeed fled West, almost to a man.

Not one man has stopped to help. They are hastily retreating from the village.

He grabs a young girl who is screaming and slaps her quite sharply. She shuts up and he tells her in perfect English, "Take them and go East! Move! Move! Go!", he's shouting. The young girl grabs a young boy and an old woman and starts running East. They all follow her.

It is 0226 hours exactly and Weegie's squad has crashed the village, firing bursts into all the huts on their side as Joseph and his two scout's begin spraying a deadly swath of lead on theirs. As if in concert, they hear the chug, chug, chug of the two greasers join in the symphony of slaughter.

In 4 minutes, the Ranger's have killed the entire village except the women and children who fled East. It wasn't perfect but it was the best he could do, at least he saved some. He is aware of other platoon's who spared none.

He and Weegie meet in the middle of the now deserted village, corpses laying about in the dirt street.

"Let's go see Mac, So, Chi, take a look around?", he tells them, and they head East towards Mac.

Mac has the villager's in a loose circle and Joseph is surprised to see two young men with them. Where'd they come from, he thinks. He and Mac find an old lady and a young girl to question. He tells Weegie to go bring the two men over.

The old woman explains that about a month ago, the Cong came to the village. They killed all the men who would not fight for them and then they began raping the young girls. The mother's of the young girl's tried to trade themselves, to use them and spare the daughter's, but they also were killed.

The old woman is weeping at the horrific memory, so is the young girl.

In Vietnamese, he asks the girl, "Child, these two men? Tell me-."

She is shaking and mumbling, but then he hears her saying, "He killed my mamaison, he killed my ma-." She is crying to hard to say more but she had indicated the taller man.

Joseph walks over to where Weegie has the two men and pulls his .45 out of his holster and puts it to the man's temple. He hesitates for just a second before pulling the trigger. The report sounds deafening, the huddled women begin to shriek and weep out of fear.

The other man has fallen to his knee's but Weegie pulls him up by his hair.

Joseph says to the women and children in Vietnamese, "Anyone have anything to say? Why I shouldn't kill him?"

Before Joseph can raise his gun, Weegie has buried his bayonet to the hilt in the man's chest.

Joseph continues on in their native tongue, "Go East. I'll get you food and water. Your safe, go."

He then says in English, "Mac, burn it. Burn the mother fucker."

The platoon heads East with the small group of villager's following, trying to stay close. Some of them are touching the young soldier's, smiling.

Joseph look's at his men, they are all seasoned battle-hardened men. No matter their youth, they are the best the United States Army has.

With this patrol completed, they'll get ten day's leave instead of the usual five. Joseph has no plans but to eat and sleep for all of it. And that's what he's going to do.

He's undressing in his barrack's when a knock comes at the door. His two sergeant's, Weegie and Mac, enter.

"Hey, G.I., thought we'd have a drink," Weegie says.

"Well-," Joseph begins, but Mac says, "Just one, sir. A toast, for good hunting and no casualties, again."

Joseph smiles.

"All Right, take a seat," Joseph says, nodding at the two men.

"Hey, G, what do you say? Me, Ruk and Mac here are going down to sin-city. If the booze or whore's don't kill us, well, we'll let the gook's give it another go," Weegie says, smiling, and asks, "You want to come?"

"Ah, well,-," Joseph begins but Mac jumps in to stem his commanders refusal, "Hey, Lieutenant, you lead us through the jungle and we all got back in one piece. Now let us return the favor, Saigon ain't that," Mac's saying, as he now thumbs towards the surrounding jungle, "but it's close," he grins.

Weegie is smiling too, and Joseph surprises himself by saying, "Ok! ok. Why not, sure."

"All right! I told you he'd go. West Point or not, I says G's one of us," Weegie crows and he's slapping Mac on the back as he says this.

Joseph laugh's, "I guess that's a compliment, Weegie?", he

asks, and they all roar as Weegie replies, "Damn right it is, sir," and now he snaps a neat salute as well.

As they're leaving Weegie says, "Oh, Merry Christmas, sir."

Merry Christmas? Holy shit! He's been in the bush so long he's forgotten all about it.

Joseph asks, "Hey, Weegie, is it Christmas here, or-?"

"There, sir. We had our's yesterday. Didn't it feel Christmassy to you out there?", Weegie replies smiling.

Yesterday they had been burning Khe Don.

"Ok, thanks, see you in the morning," Joseph says.

He walk's over to the communications hut and tells the corporal the number state-side.

The corporal says, "May as well take a seat sir, it'll be a while making the connection."

So, he sits and waits. His parents have been waiting months for this call, since last July, right before he shipped out from Japan.

It's only about twenty to thirty minutes, he thinks, but not a moment too soon either.

CHAPTER EIGHT

December 1968/ January 1969

New York - Miami

"I always thought that I'd see you again."

Fire and Rain/ James Taylor

White Plains, New York, December 1968

On a quiet residential street in the North end of the Bronx, the Italian neighborhood of, Carmine Stracci, represents the fortunate. The people who live here have, through hard work, or other means, moved out of the South Bronx. Away from the over-crowded projects inhabited by black's and Puerto Rican's, many on Home Relief, (Welfare), and the old decrepit tenement's that still house many of their Italian compatriots. They have achieved middle class and have optimistic hope of attaining more.

In the kitchen, Carmine is having espresso with a splash of anisette liquor in it. With him are two Mafioso lieutenant's, Ralph "Chink" Chinesse and Alfonso "Porky" Pignacio.

Carmine is a Capo, a boss, an overseer, for Philip "Philly Black" Catalanotto, who has taken control of all of GeJo's operations in New York and Miami since the old man's death, of natural causes, a truly rare event in this business, two years ago.

Philly Black is the final authority concerning any and all of the business he inherited from GoJo.

That is the reason that the three men are having coffee tonight. Carmine feels a change is needed. It's time for new manage-ment, so to speak, and he knows just the right man for the job. Himself. Chink and Porky also think its time for a promotion, and Carmine is now telling them exactly how to go about getting it.

"Tomorrow night, I'm going to the Bella Napoli at about 9:00 p.m.," he says.

The Bella Napoli is a restaurant in the old neighborhood.

"Philly wants to see me. You think he gives a fuck I don't like that Napolitan sanguinach?, or that the fuckin' scungilla is almost raw?!", he bellows.

"No, he don't! Every fuckin' time it's, Carmine see me at Bella Napoli, we'll eat. For that alone I want that fucker hit!", Carmine is roaring as he slams his ham sized fist down on the table.

"One more time tomorrow I gotta eat that shit," he says, and then looking at Porky he continues, "When he sends Ray to get the car, you take care of him. Bring the car around front like your Ray to pick him up, you-," he points to Chink, "Your on the floor in the back. When Porky tells you, go, you come up and give him the bye-bye, head shots, remember! The fucker might have a vest on," Carmine instructs.

He's smiling now, just giving the order's has soothed some of his anger.

"Ok, Boss, we got it, you want us to-," Porky is saying but is cut off.

"You stay away from everybody for a couple of days. Then, after I talk to Jimmy, ("Jimmy Blue Eyes", Abaticcio), in Miami, I'll call Madea and she'll tell you where to see me, you understand?", Carmine instructs.

He looks hard at both men.

Chink says, "Sure, sure, Carmine, ok," and Carmine glares at Porky until he too says, "Ah- sure, Boss, sure, gotcha!"

"Ok, good. Now get the fuck outta here, I'll talk to you next week," Carmine growls.

"Ah- one last thing, Boss, you gonna stay, ah- inside?, or what?", Porky asks, continuing with, "I don't want no, ah- you know."

"I'm gonna be inside. I'm gonna eat some al dente linguini with scungilla while the Napolitan fuck is dying in the fuckin' street," Carmine says, and he's once again smiling. It's as good as done.

Angelo and Nettie were so glad they had the chance to speak with Joseph. Once it got late on Christmas Day, they were both resigned to thinking he wouldn't call. Maybe he was too far from any place with a phone? When the call did come late, very late Christmas night, it was an answered prayer.

They had talked for over an hour, one parent on each extension talking a mile a minute, Joseph laughing, at the utter familiarity of how fast his Mom and Dad talked, both to him and each other. It was a three way conversation but the two elder Carosa's had surely far outtalked their son. Joseph didn't care. They sounded good, safe and happy and that's all that mattered to him.

He told them, "God bless you both, I love you," and was gone.

That had been four day's ago, everything was back to normal now. Angelo had work to go to, both at the Holiday Inn and in the back room with the phone.

Angelo felt at ease, things were okay with his three kid's. He knew Joseph had played down his own danger, but talking to him he sounded good.

Joseph had said, "Usually, I'm guarding some ammo dump, Pop, nothing to it."

Angelo knew his son didn't get all that training for that, but... Nettie had insisted he call, "At least once a month, we're dying over here, your father and me, for five months!", she admonished. He promised he would.

Two days left in the year, tonight and tomorrow. Angelo had to go see the Boss tonight. Coco was old but when he told you to come, you came, and you got there early. Everyone had expected him to step down, "retire", but his mind was as sharp as it had always been, so why should he? He had killed for the family, many times over. He was made Boss of Miami because he was smart, yes, but also more important, because he was ruthless. He would go when he, and only he, decided it was time.

Angelo was to meet Mr. Eddie Coco and his right hand man, Jimmy "Blue Eyes" Abaticcio, at The Place for Steak on Seventy-ninth street in Miami. He was told 8:00 p.m., He's there at 7:30 p.m.

When Mr. Eddie arrived, he was accompanied by only his button man (body guard).

"Ay Angelo, hows my paison? You okay? You need anything?", Coco asked.

Angelo hugged him and kissed his cheek.

"I'm doing good, Mr. Eddie. My wife, Nettie, says hello and she'll make the Ravioli anytime you say. Anytime your welcome," Angelo says.

"I know, I been busy, I ain't had time to do nothing. You

know when GoJo, God rest his soul, went, all the mongemedes was circling, waiting to see me go down, Angelo. I been in this business 50 years!", the old Mafioso is telling Angelo.

"Fifty years! You think I got here because I'm stunad??", he says.

"I still got the biggest book outside of New York, Angelo. When it's time for me to go, nobody gonna have to tell me, I'll know," Coco said.

Angelo wondered, where is Jimmy Blue Eyes?

"Mr. Eddie, there's no problems anywhere? I, uh- with my book?", Angelo asks.

"Forget about it! What are you, you imbabid?", Coco says, patting Angelo's cheek.

"No! No, I was just, you know, wondering," Angelo replies. Where is Jimmy, he thinks again.

The waitress brought the espresso first. Maybe later he'll get a steak, burnt and extra well done. For now, just the coffee.

Coco talk's, he's in the mood. He regales Angelo with stories about the old days, "way back", he says.

He asks about his son, the one at West Point, "Gonna be a fuckin' general," he jokes, "Maybe even the President, make all this shit we do legal, put us outta a job." He's rolling right along. You don't interrupt him when he's going like this, you listen. You smile at the appropriate time, you laugh or frown according to his particular view on something.

Angelo is nodding along with him as he says, "The kid's

these days are shit, they got no respect," Coco says.

He's still going when Angelo look's up. Someone has approached the table... and, BOOM!!

He's been punched hard in the side of his head and he's falling over. He feels something wet and warm on his face, and then, nothing.

It's Friday, Jimmy's getting ready to jump on his bike and go to school. Tonight is New Year's Eve. He and Jill are going to a ball at the outdoor pavilion of the Ft. Lauderdale Yacht Club. He's rented a tuxedo and Caz has hired a limo. They'll pick up the girl's in it at Jill's and then go to the club. It's all haute couture snobbery but Jimmy love's every bit of it.

He whisks Jill into his arms when he arrives at school and dances her in a circle, in what he hopes are waltz steps.

Jill laughs happily and kisses him in what Jimmy calls her dear prudence school kiss. It's a quick, prim little peck. He tries to get a real kiss but she dances away from him and says, "That's all you get, you'll have to wait for tonight, and don't give me that look either, James Carosa." She is feigning annoyance in saying the last.

"If you haven't the patience to wait for me for," she look's at her watch, "13 hours, how will you manage once I'm all the way up in Gainesville? And you'll only be able to see me, maybe, on weekends?", she says, and stretches out the maybe.

For just the briefest instant he looks so sad that she

immediately regrets saying it.

"Maybe I'll come to Gainesville, maybe-," he answers,
dragging out his own maybe, as he tries to tease her right back.

"Now, can I have a kiss? Just one?, to take me through the
next 12 hours and 59 minutes?", he asks.

Jill kisses him hard and says, "If you can't wait don't
worry, you can have all you want," she is whispering.

He looks and she has tears in her eye's? What's this?
"Jill, uh- what's," he starts to ask but she laugh's and says,
"Nothing, kiss me!", and he does.

How will she be away from him? For weeks?, she thinks. How?

In the first hour of home room class, Mr. Proctor tells
Jimmy the Dean's office has called for him. As he's making his way
there, he's wondering what it could be?

Mr. Shultz is standing waiting for him, looking nervous.

"Come with me, please, " Shultz says.

In the office, he tells Jimmy to take a seat.

"There's been a family emergency, they've asked that you
call immediately."

He take's the phone and turns it towards Jimmy and says,
"Dial 9 for an outside line. Would you like some privacy? I can
step out."

"No, that's okay," Jimmy says. Joseph had just called a
few days ago, it couldn't be him. Family Emergency?

His Mom answers on the first ring. Why is she answering
the phone?, he thinks. Post time for Hialeah is hours away yet.

Something is definitely wrong and he knows with a sinking dread it's his Dad- busted? Something.

"Mom, why are you answering the ph-? Where's Dad?", he asks.

She's crying, "Come home, Jimmy, please! Right now, come home!"

"I'll be there in 10 minutes! Hold on Ma, I'm on the way," he says, and slams the phone down and is out the door before anyone can say a single word.

He runs every stoplight and stop sign on the way home, slowing just to check on-coming traffic. Fuck the cop's or a ticket, he can only think of getting home.

The old man's car isn't there. He didn't come home from work this a.m.? He remembers it's Friday. His Dad is off Friday's and Saturday's so he doesn't go to the Holiday Inn Thursday's at 10:00 p.m., which means he should've been home this morning when he left for school, but he wasn't. Fuck! Fuck! Where was he all night? He didn't come home at all? Nothing make's sense.

"Ma? Ma! Where are you?", he's yelling.

The house is empty, no, he hears her crying in the bedroom.

"Mom, Mom, come on, come on," he's saying, trying to get her to look at him.

"Mom, where is he? In jail? Which jail? Come on, Mom, talk to me," he urges her gently.

She's crying worse than he's ever seen, she mumbles, "Dead. He's dead, Jimmy."

She collapses into him, she's shaking. She's under 5' and less than 100 lbs, she feels like she'll break if he doesn't hold on to her. He realizes that there are tears on his own face, his tears. Dad? Dad, my God, what happened? Why? How?

They both sat there crying for a few minutes on the same bed his Dad had just been yesterday.

"Come on, Mom, we can't just sit here like this. Let's go have a glass of wine in the kitchen, come on," he says.

Nettie walk's like a zombie with him and then collapses into her chair at the dining room table. Just looking at Angelo's empty chair she begins crying again.

"Here, drink some of this," Jimmy says, and hands her a water glass filled with Chianti.

"Did you call, Christy? Does she know?", he asks.

"No. Nobody Jimmy, I called you," she sobs.

He's patting her, trying to soothe her. Should they call Joseph? For what? Best not to tell him anything, he's in a war.

"What happened, Ma? Car wreck? What? What happened?", he probes.

"He was shot, Jimmy, him and Mr. Eddie. The police don't know why," she tells him. She look's crushed, will she ever be able to get over this?, he wonders. Would he? My God, Dad, what happened?

He had to take care of his Mom. There was no time for him to grieve, not now, later, but not now, he's got things to do. He called Mrs. Mayor and explained as best he could before breaking down on the phone. She told him she would pray for him and his family, and she'd tell Jill his message.

"It's a bad time to call. I'll call as soon as, well, as

soon as he felt able," is what he said.

In the ensuing week, after having to console and prop up Christy and his Mom, he made all the funeral arrangements and not-ified the Army so that once Joseph re-emerged, from wherever, he'd call.

Jill had to be almost physically restrained from going to him. How could she not? But her mother and Lisa convinced her to wait, give him some time. She made up her mind, if Jimmy needed her, she would postpone college for a year. He was more important than school, he was more important than anything. It could all wait, her resolve was absolute.

But, not as absolute as Hugh Mayors. It was front-page headlines in the following days newspapers, not for Angelo, he was a side note. He had merely been sitting there with the infamous and notorious, Eddie Coco, mafia chieftain of Miami since the 1940's, rumored to have killed over a dozen men on his way up the ranks.

Hugh was incensed, how could he have been so stupid? A man of such meager financial means, living in a small three bedroom house on the West side, working for Holiday Inn, and his son get's an appointment to West Point?

Mayor Linsey should've been all he needed, everyone knew that he was the mob's mayor, and one politician to another and, hell, Connie Mack wouldn't blink an eye.

Jill would not see the Carosa boy again. There would be no argument and no discussion. She was a member of the social registry and the daughter of a soon to be U.S. Senator. She would not, could not, consort with offspring of a common hoodlum. He would not allow it, period.

There was much ado made out of the gangland style slayings in the Miami steak house. Papers flew off the racks. Another execution style hit had occured in New York, one Philip "Philly Black" Catalanatto.

The FBI was saying the two were connected. An in-house shake up of the hierarchy was taking place according to organized crime specialists with the bureau.

For two weeks the media saturated print, radio and television news programs with the unfolding and never ending story.

At the Carosa home, Nettie was disconsolate and listless. She sat drinking coffee in her housecoat and slippers, not cooking once, not even frying an egg. All the joy's she had gotten from her life's calling, being a wife and mother, were gone.

It was all Jimmy could do to get her to eat a piece of Provolone cheese, some bread, a few olives, anything.

Angelo had money put away for the present and immediate future. They'd be okay. The house was paid for. There would just be the property taxes and of course the utilities and living expenses. They were solvent for now. His father's friends had all offered money, but he refused. They didn't need it.

Jimmy didn't return to school, he was finished with school.

Caz called to console his friend, he felt terrible for him. He knew how close Jimmy was with his Dad.

"You need anything, you call me, Jimmy, I mean it. Whenever

your ready, I'm here for you, Champ, anything, you got it, ok?",
Caz told him.

Angelo liked Caz and Caz had respected old Angelo.

Jill called and cried through the entire call. "I'll
postpone college for a year and stay here with you if you want. I
love you," she told him.

He never heard from her again. He didn't have to, her
father, Hugh, called and told him all he'd ever need to know.
Hugh expressed his empathy and concern. Perhaps it'd be better he
suggested, if Jimmy didn't contact Jill again. She'd get over
it and so would he.

Jimmy was filled with grief and sorrow for his father
and worried about his poor, broken hearted, mother. There wasn't
any more room for additional sadness, he was full.

He had room for anger though, and that's what he felt for
Hugh and all the rich, disconnected shadow people for whom the
appearance of propriety is far more important than actually having
it.

Morality is inversely proportional to financial and
material wealth. The less you have of the latter, the more you
possess of the former-.

CHAPTER NINE

June 1969

"Angel came down from heaven yesterday."

Fly on my sweet Angel/ Jimi Hendrix

The war in Vietnam continues, there is mass unrest on college campuses throughout the country. The growing death toll, the continued escalation of U.S. troops, that now number 500,000, and the failure of the new administration of the Nixon White House to advance peace talks, yet again, is the fuel that fires the peace movement.

Jimmy is working two jobs. He works construction during the day and washes pots at a seafood restaurant at night and on the weekends. The only thing he has time for is sleep.

He's cajoled, badgered, begged, and wept from sheer exhaustion in his efforts to get his mother up off the couch, out of her housecoat and slippers and back to the living. It hasn't been easy but she is almost whole again.

Christy is also spending most of her free time with Nettie. Brother and sister make it their duty for one of them to always be there with her.

Joseph had called within days after Jimmy had contacted the Army. He had just returned from an unrestricted leave, hence the Army was not able to locate him until he reported back to base.

He was devastated, he had just spoken with his father on Christmas night. To have this news awaiting him at his return was a nightmare. The safe life in Florida? All a lie.

Joseph wept. He couldn't help it. He offered to come home, he could get leave. Jimmy told him no, despite Christy and his mother's objections. Angelo had already been laid to rest the previous afternoon. It would only be worse when he had to go back. If they didn't forge ahead now, starting today, they'd never break free of the sorrow and malaise that firmly held all of them in its deadly grip.

It had worked. Not a day went by that one or the other wouldn't cry, the hurt and the loss were so deep, but together they slowly, gradually moved forward.

Joseph sent his Army pay to Nettie. It wasn't much, even for an officer in combat, but it helped.

Christy floated the idea of moving back, but again, Jimmy overruled her. If they didn't force their little mother to get up, stand up to this tragedy, she herself may give up and die. Once again he was right.

Nettie fussed over him to the point of smothering. He let her, he was all she had now. She made him such abundant lunches to take to work that he could have fed half the laborer crew on the construction site. He let her, it gave her a much needed purpose. The same thing with supper at night. She had started her back and forth routine to the kitchen again, and to Jimmy, that was the last missing piece of his fragile mother's former self. She made it.

Jill never called. Hugh had foretold Jill that he wouldn't call her.

He had rode his motorcycle to the school on a rain out day from the construction job. He sat there, waiting for the lunch bell, in the rain, like a fool, before kicking the bike to life and riding away. What was the use?, he thought. She would've called him long before this. How could he have been that wrong?

That mistaken?, with the girl he swore he knew so very, very well. He would never understand it, how could Jill have just up and turned away? He'd have moved heaven and Earth for her, she never called.

Hugh had tried to console her. It was his opinion that the Jimmy she knew, that they all knew, was a carefully crafted, assumed persona. I mean didn't the boy know his father's occupation? He concealed that truth quite expertly, didn't he? Maybe there a lot of truths the young Carosa kept hidden.

Jill listened to her father. She didn't believe it, not any of it. Hugh told her if you don't call him he won't call you. I'll bet you he doesn't. He sounded very sure of himself.

One week became two, two became four, and then... He never called.

He dropped out of her life like he was never there, without so much as a good bye, nothing. That last morning she had seen him on the school patio, when he had danced her around, when she had teased him about being far away, was that really sadness she had glimpsed? Could it have been something else? Is it possible he knew then, that morning, that they'd never see each other again?

She lost weight, too much. She was skin and bones according to her mother and Lisa. Her grades plummeted but she did well enough on th S.A.T. that she'd graduate and go to the University of Florida in the fall. She couldn't wait for September, maybe a new location, a new start up there in Gainesville would help her forget, maybe.

Lisa is counting the weeks. The U.S.S Enterprise is scheduled

to port in Jacksonville on August 5, 1969. By her count that was
two weeks late. The Navy has it's own way of counting, she thinks,
April 1968 to July 1969 is 15 months, but the Navy counted from
the time that the vessel entered the operations theatre, sailing time
to station is not counted, it's 15 months on station. Still, it's
close, so very close now...

South Vietnamese/ North Vietnamese Frontier

Joseph and his platoon are 4 days into a 30 mile deep
foray inside enemy territory. It's slow going because they cannot
alert the North Vietnamese Army of their surveillance.

They are collecting intelligence on a heavy concentration of
the enemy, believed to be at least a division in strength, that
has moved to the near frontier of South Vietnam. Can this be another
Tet?

The American command isn't waiting to find out. As soon
as the Ranger troop reports back with all the pertinent data, they'll
decide whether to preemptively strike using Naval bombers.

The Ranger's are to collect intelligence - the supply line?,
how much equipment?, artillery?, armor?, food and medical stores?,
for how many troops?, for what duration?. They entrust the Ranger
commander to give accurate estimates.

The platoon is a couple of 1,000 yards behind the North
Vietnamese Army rear echelon troops of supply, communications and
medivac units.

"So, my count is 20,000, what'd you come up with?", Joseph asks his scout.

"Yah, G.I., my too, I think is good. I no see reinforcement battalions, only one division," So replies.

Let's see, he's got 30 trooper's with him. Hell, 30 against 20,000 that's not to bad. He has to stifle a nervous chuckle.

He falls back over the rise where the platoon has formed up. Weegie and his squad reconned East and Joseph took the West. Neither has seen any trace of reinforcement battalions in those sectors. Mac, Chi and Ruckus went North, perhaps 15 miles. They could move quicker with just the three of them, to make sure this division doesn't have delayed reinforcement troops or material in route from the North. They are looking specifically for trains on side tracks, possibly loaded for quick movement South. As soon as he returns they'll have all the data the general's need. It's sunset, 1900 hours.

U.S.S. Enterprise/ South China Sea 2400 Hours

Gordon is on deck awaiting the loader. As an airman wheels it over, Gordon is bumped from behind, it's Germ.

"Hey, good lookin', we gonna kill a whole bunch of gook's tonight? Hunt 1 said division strength," Germ says and rubs his hands together in anticipation.

"I heard the briefing, Germ, why at this hour?", Gordon asks. He'd been asleep an hour ago.

"Heh, heh, heh," Germ snickers exaggeratedly, and says, "Need your beauty sleep, son?"

"No, I was dreaming about my girl. She was saying- hell, I don't know, you know how dreams are," Gordon replies.

"Well, we'll be back fore sunrise and you can go right back to sleep and ask her. It'll be good practice for married life," Germ says, and then howls with laughter. His laughter is infectious and Gordon laugh's too.

Since the day they had scuffled, they had become good friends. Gordon was taken in by the group as an accepted member. The mantra being,this is war, we kill the enemy, whenever and however we can, there are no terms.

This war is different from other wars, it's not an army vs. army. It's us against them, the entire country, it's open warfare. The same man working in the rice paddy today, will be your killer later that night.

Gordon's initiation had been that first recon with Germ. His indoctrination began that very night in the officer's lounge, and tonight it's in his blood.

There are six air groups. Each group has 6 F-4 Phantom fighters and 12 A-6 bombers. The target coordinates are inside North Vietnam, 15 miles from the frontier with South Vietnam.

The lead group crosses over land and immediately the fighters begin raining bullet's into the jungle beneath. The group's are tight, 300 yards separating them. It's a continuous, nearly uninterr- upted, barrage. It is 10 miles to target, mere minutes, as the group's

arc off to their specific target areas. Alpha group is first,
they are the initial spear-head.

Joseph and his Ranger's have made almost 5 miles tracking
South-Southwest through the jungle when they hear the roar of the
jet's cannon's. It's deafening, even at this distance. The bomber's
are plastering the interior while the fighter's are chopping up
the exposed flanks.

The North Vietnamese Army are throwing up everything they've
got. It can't all miss, and it doesn't. An A-6 blows up in a giant
fireball, both crewmen killed instantly. Another has taken heavy
flak and it's control is severely damaged. The pilot maydays as he
tries to manoeuvre South and East, trying to "make the soup".

The F-4's are firing their wing mounted missiles at the
North Vietnamese Army surface to air missile launching hubs. The
U.S. missiles are radar sighted. Heat seeker's are ineffective
against ground based weapons, there's no heat. The pilot in the
aircraft must maintain position until his missile arrives on target
using his weapons radar. It's only seconds but those seconds can
seem like an eternity. Gordon is locked on, 1second, 2seconds,
3 seconds, - a hit!!

He throttles back to full power and pulls into an almost
vertical climb straight up. Before his aircraft can respond the
plane is, buffeted? And then there is a tremendous explosion and
impact. The wind buffet was the airstream wake of the missile that
missed, the collision is the one that didn't. His F-4 loses all
manoeuvrebility, every bell and alarm is activated. He tries to

steer but his leg's won't press the rudder pedals. He tilts the wings South and East and his plane actually slides into that heading.

He's losing altitude fast! He's a low-level attack fighter, 1,500 - 2,000 feet, he can't go below 500 feet or his ejection will be fatal anyway. He has to act now or...

He pulls the lever and the ejection caps blow the seat straight up almost 500 feet before the parachute release pops. As he slowly descends into the darkness, he hears, "Surfer! Surfer!!"

Germ has maydayed Surfer. Gordon didn't and Germ thinks maybe his buddy is unconscious, unable to mayday or pull the ejection lever. Germ is peering through the sky and, there it is! He's ejected! Thank God, Germ thinks, and then he starts yelling into his radio, "Surfer! Surfer! You read me boy, it's Germ! Surfer!"

"I read you, Germ. I can't feel my legs, how am I going to fly? Mother fucker! Mother fucker!", Gordon is shouting.

"Listen to me boy, you'll be back jet-jockeying in no time, but first we gotta get you outta there. You got your .45, your survival kit?", Germ asks.

"Yeah, big fuckin' deal. I can't feel nothing from my ass down, how am I gonna-," Gordon trails off.

"Turn on your locator beacon, I'll fly loops over you till we get rescue here, stay with me! Surfer?! Surfer!", Germ's yelling. Nothing.

When Gordon awakens, he's sure that he's in hell. The cords of his parachute are snarled in the jungle canopy's roof. When he finally finds his knife in his belt, he cut's himself down and lands on two broken legs and who knows what else. His ass, balls and everything below his stomach feels broken. He thinks, I'll never see Lisa again, and then he passes out.

When he comes to its full daylight. He can see shafts of sunlight peeking through the canopy. He suddenly realizes that he's not alone, someone is slapping him, "G.I.!, G.I., you wake now!", says the filthy Vietnamese soldier as he grins, showing black teeth. "You lieutenant! Good, good, I get promotion for you," he says.

Gordon is thirsty, thirstier than he's ever been. He creaks, "Water? Can I have some water?"

The soldier's all laugh. Black teeth opens his trouser's and pisses all over Gordon's face as they all howl with laughter.

"Yankee, you wish you die before we get you to camp," Black teeth says, and spits in Gordon's face. He says something in Vietnamese and two soldier's come over with a small, wooden square. They roll Gordon onto it, his broken legs, hip, pelvis and lumbar vertebrae scream!

It's his screams he realizes, and when he next awakens he is strapped to the tiny board and the two soldier's are dragging him through the jungle. His broken leg's bouncing and jarring every foot of the way. He screams until he is unconscious again.

When he next rises out of the murk that has become his mind, the troop has stopped and made camp. Blach teeth comes over, bends down and gives him a cupful of water.

"G.I., you no lieutenant. I kill you right here, you lucky, I make sure you live one more day, then we get to camp, no die G.I.!, one more day," he warns.

Gordon wishes he were dead, the filthy gook had been right. He tries to feel for his knife, maybe they missed it? At least he could try to stab the son of a bitch! He feels his belt, but that's it, nothing, he's naked from the waist down.

Listen up, So, Chi you guy's go ahead about 200 yards North of the camp. It's 2200 hours," Joseph is saying and the two Hmong scout's set their watches. "How long to go?", he asks them.

So and Chi look at each other and Chi says, "2210, we be 200 yards North of them."

"Okay, at 2220 you encroach to shouting distance, 50 yards?, but do not engage. I.D. yourself as Fifth battalion, North Vietnamese Army," Joseph orders. He continues, "When they give you the okay to approach, light that mother_fucker up like Broadway."

He wants the scout's to rouse the camp and then fire white phosphorous flares into the jungle canopy, turning the dark jungle into blinding daylight.

"Weegie, you take the West and I'll come in behind them from here. Chi and So, once you light it up get flat, we'll be shooting waist high right at you. It's 2203, lets go!", Joseph orders.

The Ranger's have tracked the North Vietnamese Army platoon all day, with Gordon's screams it wasn't difficult. That's how they first located the platoon, by Gordon's horrible screaming when they had strapped him to the small, wooden board. How far had his scream traveled? A mile?, Two?, a long way through the jungle.

The Ranger troop arrived within minutes to the spot where Gordon had been strapped to the board, but they were gone of course. They could have easily taken the platoon in daylight, an easy task for the Ranger's, but not if they intended to rescue the pilot alive. To much could happen, at night the ambush would be a lock, like ducks in a barrel, blind slants, and, the pilot would be flat on the ground.

At 2221 hours, Chi walks up to where a skirmish line would be. They have no sentry, their complacent, they are in their own country. He feels immediate contempt for them. These are not soldiers, they are like children playing soldiers.

He calls out in Vietnamese, a perfect Hanoi inflection, "Soldiers! Comrades! Don't shoot! I am N.V.A Fifth battalion, don't shoot!"

The camp instantly swarms to life, every man has his rifle at the ready. Black teeth utters what will be his last words, saying, "Show yourself, you may approach."

At that moment, the jungle comes to instant full daylight, like a noonday sun in the desert. The N.V.A. are blinded, literally. Gordon is flat on his back and he also can't see anything. It's like a 1,000 flash bulbs popped in his face.

But he can still hear, and what he hears are the deep chug, chug, chug of the two greaser's and the heavy staccato of the M-16's on full auto. There is screaming, screaming and cursing, in Vietnamese. His last thought is, angels, it must be, it's the angels who've come to save him.

The Ranger's swarm the now deathly quiet camp. They've ripped off their black goggle's, and as the men make sure everyone is dead, Joseph grabs a mosquito net that one gook died in. He, Ruckus, Sluggo and Jake all give a hand in getting Gordon into the netting.

"Who are you guys?", Gordon croaks.

Joseph says, "Get him some water."

So comes over and hands Joseph a morphine surette, he has four more.

Joseph looks questioningly at So. So points to the dead N.V.A. medic. Joseph pushes the needle into Gordon's exposed ass cheek as Sluggo is pouring water into his mouth.

"All right, lets go, one man on each corner," Joseph orders.

"This may hurt but we have to lift you, ready?", Sluggo warns Gordon.

Before he can reply, he's lifted off the ground and the Ranger troop is jogging double-time, South, into the jungle. Its 2229 hours.

They track South and West, putting some jungle between them and the destroyed platoon, and then West to the river. If they can get to the river he'll break radio silence and request a Navy swift boat for the pilot. He's in bad shape, he's black and blue from his navel to his toes.

They tracked for five hours. It's almost 0330 hours when they reach the Mekong River. They are still in North Vietnam, maybe as much as 6 or 7 miles up river.

"Weegie, come here," Joseph says.

"Yea G, what's up," he answers.

Joseph has a dime again, "Call it," he tells Weegie.

If Weegie is right he'll break radio and call for a tub, if not, they'll make camp in the jungle and wait for nightfall, 16-17 hours away. He doesn't think the pilot will make it that long.

But a rescue by swift boat is risky, its two hours to dawn, he's putting everyone in danger.

Oh well, Weegie calls, "Heads." And its- heads! Good! The pilot might make it now.

He radio's, "This is Ranger G.I. Joe, I'm req'ing a tub, Mekong, approximately 6 miles up from home, copy?"

U.S. Marine rescue in Khe San picks up the transmission, "Marine one copy, Ranger bird won't work?", the radio man asks.

"Negative, got a winger badly broken," Joseph replies.

"Roger, got two tubs in route," the marine informs him, "Marine one out."

Sixteen minutes later they hear the tub's way down stream, it sounds like a freight train. The Skipper of the lead boat spots Jake. They pull him aboard and Jake directs them 100 yards up stream to where the platoon is waiting.

Every gun on both tubs is manned and the fuckin' river is lit up like a Christmas tree! How can the slants not see this? In their own country?, Joseph thinks.

They hand the netting with Gordon in it to Jake, the Skipper and his ensign and they lift him aboard. Then they all board and the two boats roar away, hitting 40 M.P.H., going South.

When they reach South Vietnamese territory, the tubs Skipper with Gordon radio's for medical dispatch to meet them at

DaNang. He'll go from there to the field hospital.

As they off load Gordon at DaNang to the medics, he'll be stabilized there and then flown to Japan as he is seriously injured, he's trying to ask the Ranger something.

"What's your name?", he finally croaks. He has screamed his voice away in the jungle.

Joseph leans close and says, "G.I. Joe, fly boy, good luck to you," and then he snaps Gordon a salute.

Gordon is crying. He had walked, no, he'd been dragged through the valley of death, and an Angel had saved him.

An Angel named, G.I. Joe?

He actually smiles and dozes off into a morphine induced slumber.

CHAPTER TEN

December 1969

"The fool on the hill, see's the sun going down."

The Fool on the Hill/ The Beatles

Lisa and Jill are driving home for the holidays, the University of Florida is recessed until the New Year. Lisa plans on stopping at Barbara and Jack's home on the way back up. They're spending the Christmas holidays with Gordon at Bethesda Naval Hospital in, Maryland.

Lisa had spent the Thanksgiving holiday with him and all three of them had been there awaiting his arrival from Japan, via San Francisco, at the esteemed medical facility last July.

He arrived in a full body cast, from mid torso down, but he was home and alive. It was a miracle to all concerned. Gordon had attempted to tell them the entire amazing story of his daring rescue when he had phoned from Japan, but his voice wouldn't cooperate. It had not fully recovered from his screams in the jungle.

Jill was quiet. Lisa kept initiating small talk but Jill would merely nod yes or no. It has been almost one year since she's seen or spoken to, Jimmy.

Caz is at the University of Florida also and Jill would occasionally run into him, both exchanging casual greetings before parting. After seeing him around the campus, at the coffee shop or on a rare occasion when she did go to a party, she finally asked him, "Caz, do you ever hear from Jimmy?", hoping beyond hope that maybe he did.

But Caz had responded, "Not since right after, uh, his Dad-."

She could see he was uncomfortable talking about it so she let it go and said, "It's okay, Caz. I guess I'll see you," and she began to walk away.

"Hey! Hey, Jill!", Caz called to her, "Lisa asked me about him too, she was angry I think, I don't know. Anyway, it was real bad, Jill, I stopped by after school like two weeks after his Dad, and His Mom, man! She looked devastated, terrible. Nothing like the happy lady she used to be, always trying to get me to eat, monga! monga!, she'd say." Caz said this and had to look away.

"It's okay, Caz, you tried. Maybe I should've too," Jill said. She kissed him lightly on the cheek and walked away.

The girl's arrived home and auntie Jewel greeted them warmly saying, "Mah, mah, ya all looks so grown up and purty, what happened to my little un's?" The girl's both kissed the old woman. She held Lisa's eyes for just an instant before absently trying to lift one of the suitcases.

Lisa thinks, what is that?, before she says, "Stop it, Jewel, no suitcases for you," and she playfully slaps Jewel's hands away from the handle.

"Befo ya all go's back to school, yo Daddy gon fire me. Nobody let me do nuthin' aroun here no mo," Jewel gently chided.

"Nobody's going to do anything, Jewel, we'll fire Daddy first," Jill said and actually laughed.

Well! Lisa thinks, perhaps all is not lost? When Jill had teased Jewel again, Jewel had cut her eye's towards Lisa. What in the world? I'll talk with her later, she thinks, I want to call, Gordon.

Jill and Jewel are going down the hall, Jill has both
suitcases but as a compromise Jewel is carrying the one overnight
bag. Jill is actually giggling at something the old woman is saying.
Thank you, God, for Auntie Jewel, Lisa muses gratefully.

"Ah, the prodigal son returns," Barnaby Casworth greets
his son upon his arrival home. They hug and the father asks his son,
"You learning anything up there? Aside from chasing skirts, I mean."
He's smiling.

Barnaby is sorely disappointed in his oldest son for not
qualifying for a better college. However, Caz can learn more at
his father's side than any education available at the higher
learning institutions.

"It's slow, Dad, economic's is, uh, boring. How did you
ever master it?", Caz asks.

"Son, no one masters it completely. Things occur that no
one has ever faced before, at least not in their own lifetimes,
and then we all look like jackasses," his father replies.

"I never knew there were so many different factors involved-
cash flow, interest rates, consumer spending, whew! I may never
get it right," Caz says quite truthfully.

He is stumped by all of it, not just economics.

To Caz, college is another four years of high school. The
only thing he's paying attention to is keeping all of his different
girlfriend's apart, separated. His life today is no different than
it's ever been. It's just as care-free as it was last year and
the year before that.

"You'll get it, son. It'll take you some time but you'll get it," his father says with much more confidence then he feels.

The great land boom is upon South Florida, Florida First has doubled and redoubled it's networth. The land out in the Western edge of the county is being developed rapidly. Canals are being dredged to drain it, sewer and water pipes are being installed, and electric power lines are traversing West on massive high tension towers to electrify the budding cities that are rising up out of the swamp. The cities of Plantation, Sunrise, Tamarac and Coral springs are all projected to have populations exceeding 150,000, overtaking Ft. Lauderdale by doing so.

Florida First is involved in every phase of this development. It owns the land and is financing all dredge operations, a huge undertaking that many less ambitious men had shied away from, but not Barnaby.

The contractor's installing the utilities the future cities must have, are financed by Florida First to have the working capital needed now. Florida First will reap tremendous profit from municipal bonds the cities will issue upon incorporation, it will literally own a percentage of them.

Caz has only a vague notion of the financial behemoth that Florida First is. As far as he's concerned that's plenty enough. It is years before the mantel will pass from his father to him.

Right now his date with, Sharon, the best looking cheer-leader at the University of Florida, and whose also from Ft. Lauderdale, is the only thing on his mind, so he asks his Dad, "Can you give me a few dollars? I've got a date and-." As Barnaby peels off some hundred's, he tells Caz not to drink and drive, and Caz, grabbing the cash, says, "I won't, Dad. Thanks! See you later," and he's gone.

Barnaby shakes his head. Well, he's still young, he'll settle down, it's still his first year, he thinks. And, there is his younger son, Richard. He's straight A's and honor roll, maybe he'll got to Wharton. He smiles thinking about him and feels better already.

The Mayor's have a quiet dinner. Lisa went out to do some last minute Christmas shopping so it's just Jill and her parents. Her mother seemed oddly distracted, and her normally boisterous father was quite subdued. Something isn't right, Jill can feel it.

As Jill and her mother clear the table and easily fall back into their old routine, Jill suddenly asks, "Mother, what's wrong with you and Daddy?"

"Wrong? What could be wrong, dear?", her mother replies.

"Mother, I'm not blind, nor am I a little girl anymore. There's something wrong and I want to know what it is," Jill says, and looks at her mother before continuing, "Are you or Daddy ill? Is something wrong with either of you? Please tell me, I want to know!"

She is sounding alarmed so Cynthia stops loading the dish-washer and comes over and takes Jill's hands and leads her to the breakfast counter where they sit.

"Jill, honey, your father and I, we-, we may be getting a

divorce," Cynthia says. Divorce? Jill is stunned, divorce?

"Mother, I- uh, divorce? Why? Why? What's happened? Is it you?", Jill asks this last accusingly and immediately regrets it as she see's her sweet mother's face fall.

"Oh, mother, I'm so sorry, forgive me," she says and then thinks, if its not her mother its...

"Mother, its Daddy?", she asks, incredulous.

Her mother is just nodding, yes. Her head is down and she's begun to weep. Dear God, what's happened? Her father? The loving, dedicated family man, the only person she's ever felt completely safe and protected by, being held in his big bear hug as a scared young girl growing up. What could've happened? Why would he destroy it? All of it? Is it because she went away to college, she wonders.

"Mother, I can come back home, I'll go to the University of Miami or Nova, we can be a family again, if that's it-", Jill is saying.

"Oh, dear sweet Jill, baby its not that, its not you," Cynthia says and here she hug's her, "It's another woman," she says. She says it so matter of factly that Jill is even more stunned by this than the news of the divorce had on her.

"Who is it, mother? Do you know?", she asks.

Jill finds the whole thing unbelievable, her Daddy with another woman? Who?

"I'm not sure, honey, but does it even matter? He's still- um, beholden to this person. He thinks I can't tell, that I don't

notice, but after 20 years of marriage I know his every thought,"
her mother says.

"Lisa? Lisa doesn't know?", Jill asks.

"No, we were going to tell you both together, but-,"
Cynthia drops her head and sighs.

"Go to bed, baby, we'll talk in the morning, okay?", her
mother soothes, back to being calm and proper again.

"I love you, Mother," Jill says. She hugs Cynthia and now
it is she who starts to cry. From this moment on she would no longer
be a girl, an innocent or naive. Her world had just come crashing
down on her as she sat in the kitchen with her dear, sweet mother.

Jill stayed awake. After she showered and put on an old
sleeping T-shirt she drank some coffee, which even Jewel looked
askance at but didn't say anything. Coffee at this hour, she
thought.

When Lisa finally got in it was past 10:00 p.m. She had
taken advantage of some of the bigger stores staying open late
and not being so crowded.

Jill had collapsed into her arms and weepily related the
entire episode with their mother in the kitchen earlier that
evening. Lisa listened patiently letting Jill cry it out of her
system, patting her, kissing the top of her head, soothing.

Finally, Jill got up off the bed and went to their bathroom and started blowing her nose. Now that she had stopped feeling
sorrow, she immediately began feeling angry.

Lisa said, "It's Victoria Smart, Jill," very calmly, like

she was talking about some trivial everyday occurrence instead of their father's betrayal.

"Mrs. Smart? Nicole's mother?!", Jill asked in horror, would it never end?! She almost covered her ears to block further indignities from reaching her.

"I know it is. She couldn't keep her hands off of him at your graduation party last year," Lisa said.

"I, I didn't notice, Lisa. I remember Daddy looked very uncomfortable, but-," Jill said.

"Let's got talk to mother," Lisa says. She starts to head for the door but Jill stops her saying, "Right now? Its late, do you think mother knows?"

"Of course she knows. The question is, what does she want to do? Can she forgive, Daddy?", Lisa says hotly.

"Mother said that, Daddy's still, well, that it's not over, Lisa!", Jill says, and her voice is panicky again.

Not over? Not over? Lisa's hand is covering her mouth, an automatic gesture of shock. This isn't a one time lapse of marital fidelity? It's a continuing affair? Lisa collapses, sitting down on the bed, all her fervor and zeal gone. She's running her fingers back through her hair, another automatic gesture, this one despair.

"We'll wait. After Daddy's gone to work, I have to find out from mother what is going on," Lisa says.

The sister's hug and Jill looks like she wants to cry again so Lisa says, "Don't Jill, don't baby, we'll figure something out," she soothes. But she's not so sure there is anything to figure out.

Cynthia is sitting out by the pool staring out at the passing skier's and boat's on the river. The occasional gale of laughter echoing in off the water seeming to mock the dark mood of the Mayor home.

As Lisa approaches, her mother, trying to sound bright and cheerful says, "Oh! Good morning, Lisa," but one look at her daughters face and she knows Jill has told her.

Lisa quickly crosses to her and they hug, remaining that way for a moment. Lisa giving her love and support through the embrace. Finally, Cynthia is able to speak, saying simply, "You know?"

"Yes, Mother, I know," Lisa says, having to restrain herself from blurting out her accusation of Victoria. She needs to let her mother bear that bit of news if she decides to share it with them.

Lisa has never seen her usually exuberant mother look so deflated, it's heartbreaking.

"Mother, how could Daddy do this? To you? To us? How could he?", Lisa says, and now she has started crying. She had promised herself that she wouldn't, not in front of her dear, sweet mother.

Now Cynthia embraces Lisa and Jill walks up and embraces them both. The mother and two daughter's, who all look very much alike, sit there crying.

When Lisa's tears are out, and she can't contain her anger, she says, bitterly, "It's that bitch, Victoria!"

"Lisa! Please! Honey, don't use that language, no matter what you may think of Mrs. Smart," Cynthia admonishes.

She is still using the proper form of address for that adulteress whore, Lisa thinks. And, even facing such betrayal, by both her husband of 20 years and her best friend, she has the presence of mind to confront Lisa's vulgarity.

"Oh, mother, you are always so gracious," Lisa says, and hugs her again,

Cynthia is a lady. She was raised as one, and she passed through all the societal rites into adulthood as one. A lady must never lose her composure, never, or use vulgar or profane language. Even in confronting a crass, insulting more pedestrian person she must always remain composed and civil.

Cynthia Mayor is the epitome of graciousness, even now, alone here with only her daughter's present and confronting such utter betrayal.

It makes Lisa even more furious at her philandering father. How could he choose that slut, Victoria, over his own beautiful, devoted wife? Over all three of them? He hadn't only betrayed Cynthia, but Jill and Lisa as well. And Nicole? Nicole and Jill are like sister's, what will this do to their friendship?

Lisa shakes her head as if that will clear all these terrible thought's out of her mind. How can she face her father? Look into his eyes? Eye's that all her life had shown only love and devotion. And trust, trust?!

He had betrayed their trust, would any of them ever trust him again? No! Lisa had already decided that that trust had been shattered into a million pieces and could never be put back together again.

Though Jill is 18 years old and a young woman, she cannot confront her father with his treachery. But Lisa can, easily, and she intends to do just that, force him to explain himself eye to eye.

Hugh Mayor has just entered the foyer when Lisa confronts him.

"Father," she says.

"Lisa, honey! How's my-", he begins but stops. He had tried to enfold her in his arms but she had stepped back. His face clouds with guilt and shame.

"Lisa, please, let me explain," he says.

"That's what I'm waiting for, Daddy. How could you do this to mother? To all of us?", Lisa is almost shouting at him.

"Lisa, Lisa please, let's sit down, come-", he asks quietly, adding, "Will you fix your old Dad a drink? Two fingers scotch-."

"I know your drink, Daddy, I used to make it when I was 10 years old, remember?" She hurls these words at him. She wants to cause him to hurt, to suffer, like he's done to them.

She brings him his scotch. She love's her father, he's always been there for her and all of them, but now?

He's sitting in the same chair he's always sat in, when he was the one who'd listen when she revealed her mistakes, her failings. Now, for the first time ever, it was the other way around and she feels unsure. How she wished it was the same as it had always been, that he could hug her and tell her, as he had so often in the past, that everything would be all right, her old Dad would take care of it. Not this time she knows.

"Lisa, this has been the hardest thing I've ever had to face in my entire life. I've misled you and Jill's and your mother's trust, I have no excuse and I won't attempt to offer one. What I've done is inexcusably," he tells her solemnly.

"Who is it, Daddy? Who?", Lisa demands, her words harsh. She wants him to personalize this shadow that's destroyed their lives.

He hesitates just a breath and then says, "Victoria, Mrs. Smart." He has to turn away from her hateful glare.

Lisa can't help it, she is livid. "You betrayed, mother? All of us? For her? For that, bitch? How could you? How could you, Daddy?!", Lisa is screaming at him.

Before he can say more than, "Lisa," she has bolted from the room.

Over the next week, both girl's begged off all engagements. Nicole had called several times but Jill wouldn't even come to the phone and refused to see her.

They had so much to talk about with their first months away at college. What could be happening?, she wondered.

On the night before Nicole's early morning red-eye flight back to Philadelphia and Bryn Mawr, Victoria's alma mater, she made up her mind, she was going to Jill's and would not leave without seeing her.

Lisa answered the door and was surprised to see Nicole standing there.

"Hi, Lisa. Can I come in?", she asked.

"Yes, of course,please. Jill's not feeling well, I don't know if she'll want to see you," she tells her.

The normally welcoming, boisterous atmosphere that is the Mayor home isn't here, its gone. There is a pall over the house, its eerie.

This house has been a second home to Nicole. A good deal of her life growing up has been spent right here. What's happened? Is Mr. or Mrs. Mayor ill?

When she had questioned her mother, Victoria, about just that, she had snapped, "Cynthia and I are no longer on good terms, she may have turned Jill's allegiance to her, I think its obvious."

Nicole had replied, "But mother, Jill and I are best friends, we've grown up together and Mrs. Mayor is like a mother to me."

Victoria had cruelly parroted back, "She's like a mother to me! I am your mother, Nicole,have you forgotten that in such a short time away?"

Now she is standing here in the family room, so familiar but...

"Sit down. Do you want something? Tea or?", Lisa asks.

"No, no. Just please tell Jill I only need five minutes," Nicole implores.

A few minutes later Jill appears and Nicole is stunned, the despair written so plainly across her face.

"Oh, my God! Jill! What has happened?", Nicole gasps. She

is sure it is nothing so trivial as a disagreement between their mother's, her friend is devastated. Nicole has crossed the room and she now attempts to hug Jill, but Jill shrinks back away from her embrace and crosses her arms. Nicole feels as though she has been physically slapped, she is hurt deeply by Jill's reaction.

Jill says, "Nicole, I don't want to talk to you, it has nothing to do with you. What's happening right now is personal and I don't want to discuss it. I, uh- I think it would be best if you leave."

Nicole has had enough and now screams at her, "I will not leave, Jill!", her eyes are filling with tears, "How can you dismiss me like I'm a casual aquaintance?! We're like sisters! Damn you! Whatever has happened, please Jill, let me help!" but Nicole is crying to hard to continue.

Now Jill crosses to her friend and they embrace tightly, both girl's are crying. After a few minutes, Jill can finally speak and says, "I'm so sorry for avoiding you, this has been the worst week of my life. Mother and Daddy may get a divorce. I didn't, I couldn't face anyone, Nicole, I-", Jill sighs.

"Oh, Jill, I'm so sorry," Nicole says, she too is disbelieving, the Mayor's divorcing?

Both girl's are still wiping their eye's. Their noses are running as Lisa steps over and hands both a kleenex, she's using one herself. Nicole is like another younger sister to her.

Jill and Nicole chat for two hours, catching up with each other. At the door they hugged each other, neither wanting to let go.

-

"I'll call you tomorrow, in Gainesville?", Nicole asks.

Jill nods, yes.

"I love you, Jill. I'm so sorry, maybe things will work out?", Nicole says hopefully.

But Jill is shaking her head, no, and says, "I don't know if that's possible, but we can hope, right?" She's trying to sound optimistic, it doesn't work.

Nicole hugs her again and says, "Please, take care of yourself, Jill. Promise me."

"I will, I promise," Jill answers. She watches Nicole pull through the gate, and keeps on looking until the gate closes and locks behind her, before closing the front door.

Both girl's kiss their mother good-bye the next morning, but neither arose to say good-bye to their father.

He had stopped at their doors hoping for some consoling words, but the words did not come.

"I love you, Lisa. Please try not to hate me,"and at Jill's he knocked, "Jill honey, I'm leaving for work. Sweetheart, are you awake?" There was no response. "I love you baby, please try to forgive me," he finished, but again there was no response.

He left his home with the heaviest of hearts, feeling like a complete abject fool.

Lisa and Jill both cried after he left, feeling ashamed. The hurt and the wounds were deep, to fresh still. They loved him but could not forgive him. He had destroyed their family.

Cynthia determined to put on a strong front for the girls. She insisted she was fine, she'd be okay. They had each other, they all embraced, not wanting to be the first to cry. The three ladies willed the tears in their eye's not to fall.

-

CHAPTER ELEVEN

May 1970

"Can you tell me, Please don't tell me."

Questions 67 & 68/ Chicago

Jimmy looked at the clock, it read 9:55 p.m. Finally, his long day is over. He stacked the fry pans back by the grills, took off the rubber apron and pulled off the pot washing gloves he's had on for 6 hours.

He goes into the employee rest room to wash his hands and he hears an argument in the manager's office. The wall separating the office and the rest room is only one sheet of dry wall. He is sure the manager can hear every fart, and he smiles to himself.

As he steps out of the rest room, the manager is rubbing his face and has ahold of Melissa, a recently hired waitress, by her arm.

"You bastard, I told you to keep your hands off of me," she yells at him.

They both now notice Jimmy and the girl looks embarrassed.

"Why don't you just let her go, Menard," Jimmy tells the manager. He still has a hold of Melissa's arm.

Instead of releasing his grip he squeezes harder, and says, "Ay, dishwasher, why don't you mind your own business."

Jimmy can see he's hurting her.

"I told you to let go of her," Jimmy says quietly. As he's saying this he's taken a hold of the girl's free arm, by the elbow, and gently but firmly is backing her up a step.

The manager actually tilts his head back, peering at Jimmy between slitted eye's. The look he's trying to effect is supposed to be menacing.

Jimmy cuts right into him, back to back left upper cut, right round house combos, and the fat manager is out before he hits the greasy kitchen floor. He's knocked over a wheeled rack of stainless steel bowls on the way down. It makes a tremendous noise that causes other employee's to come and see what's going on. They stare at Menard and then at Jimmy. The vegetable prep man, Cuban Charlie, starts clapping and everyone joins in. A few of the workers are clapping Jimmy on the back and offering handshakes and compliments.

Jimmy nods and then turns away to leave. Oh well, so much for this job, he thinks.

As he walks out the rear employee exit, he hears, "Hey! Hey, James!" Its Melissa. "Aren't you at least going to give me a chance to thank you?", she asks and then smiles.

"Well, I figured I better go before Menard calls the cops, you okay?", Jimmy asks.

"Yes! Thank you, I'm fine. Say, would you-, do you want to go for coffee? I only live a few blocks ," she asks.

Jimmy looks at her and nods, yes, and then says, "Okay, sure. I'll follow you on my bike?"

"Yes, give me two minutes, I want to grab my purse," she answers.

He follows her to a small house minutes from the restaurant. He;s surprised upon entering to see her mother and what appear to be three younger sisters watching T.V.

"Hi, Mom!", she says, and then kisses her and the two older girls before picking up the baby and rubbing noses with her, to the little toddler's delight.

"Mama, this is James Carosa, and this is my sister kate,

and Debbie, and the little one here is, Tina," she says indicating the little girl.

Tina is looking up at Jimmy and holding her hands out to be picked up, she's a little doll. He bends and swoops her up. Turning slowly he holds her up high toward the ceiling. The little girl, perhaps three years old, is laughing and squealing in delight.

He lowers her down to one arm and brushes her cheek with the back of his hand, saying, "Hi, Tina. I'm Jimmy."

"Jimmy, are you going to marry Mellie?" The little girl asks this so seriously they all laugh. Jimmy just says, "Wow!"

The little girl persists, "Are you going to be my Daddy?"

He laughs and says, "She's persistent, isn't she?"

Melissa is enjoying how easily Tina and Jimmy converse. Tina is very comfortable with him, she wanted to be picked up by him immediately.

"Ok, you, time for beddie bye. Say good night, sweetie," says Melissa, as she takes the toddler from Jimmy, "I'll be right back. Katie will you please get him something to drink?", she calls out to her sister as she goes into a bedroom with Tina.

She's back in 15 minutes. She's showered and has on a pair of short shorts and a small tiny t-shirt. She's combing her long dark hair that's still wet and Jimmy thinks, Wow! Fuck! She's beautiful! And she is. She's 18 with long dark chestnut hair and light gray eyes. She has no make-up on and doesn't need it.

He's never really looked at her, since the, a- split with Jill and all that had happened, he hasn't had the time nor inclination to take up with anyone. Seeing the waitresses at work, he didn't really look. He was coming from his day job at the construction site where he had busted his butt in the hot sun all day, by the time that he arrived to wash pots, he was running on automatic pilot.

For the first time since Jill, and those terrible days that followed, he's actually looking. He thinks, I must be stupid, blind, or both, and actually shakes his head as if to wake up.

Melissa notices and smiles at him, and says, "Penny for your thoughts?"

He smiles back, "I was thinking I must be blind or need

glasses," he says this so truthfully that Melissa laughs.

"Well, you would look quite handsome in glasses too," she teases and says, "James that was very nice of you tonight. I feel bad because for helping me you've probably lost your job."

"It's all right, I work days for Whiteside Construction. I'll find another pot washing job, hell, I've got experience now," he says.

She smiles and leans over and kisses him on the lips. She lingers just a moment and he can smell her sweet skin. She pulls back away from him and says, "Will you have dinner with me tomorrow night? I'm off, unless I'm fired too?", and they both laugh.

"Okay, I'd love to," Jimmy answers. Why not? He's been pining away for Jill for a year and a half, fuck it.

"Pick me up at 7:00 p.m., okay?", she tells him at the door.

"All right, I'll see you at 7:00p.m.," he says.

"Yes!", she thinks as she closes the door. She's very attracted to him and has been way before the events of tonight. He's so handsome and those eye's! But he never made any gestures towards her or the other waitresses. He seemed so very serious for an 18 year old guy. She had heard the restaurant job was a second job and wondered what he would need two jobs for? She is determined to find out who he is, no one at the restaurant knows anything.

The next night as he's dressing after a shower, he tells Nettie, "I met someone, Ma, she may be your future daughter-in-law," he joked.

"Oh, Jimmy! I'd be so happy. Your so young with no happiness, I worry," she tells him.

"Don't worry Ma, I'm okay," he says and hugs his little mom.

At 5 minutes to 7:00 p.m. he's there and Melissa opened the door and, Wow! Wow! Fuck!, he thinks, she's beautiful, where the hell has my head been the last year and a half?!

"Well, do you want to stand there, or would you prefer to come in?", she asks.

"Oh yea, yes, thank you," he says and steps in.

Her sister's are giggling and little Tina recognizes him immediately, saying, "Jimmy, pick me up! Like yesterday!

He scoops her up and really spins her, she's laughing and squealing. He finally slows and holds her against his chest, saying, "How's my, Tina tot?"

"I'm fine. Are you going to marry Mellie?", the little imp asked again!

"Well baby, Mellie might not want to marry me," he answers, figuring that will be the end of it.

But the small child says, "Mellie told Katie she would!", and Melissa blushes. She comes and takes Tina from him and with mock indignation says, "Naughty girl, we girls aren't supposed to share our secrets."

Jimmy did notice the quick glance the two sisters, Melissa and Katie, shared when Tina announced that.

In the car he asks, "Have you eaten? Want to go for a steak? I know the best place-"

Melissa silences him with a kiss, fully on the lips, in mid-sentence. "I'm not hungry," she says.

"Uh, you want to go for a drink?", he asks. He's confused and doesn't know what else to say.

"No, I don't want a drink either. Let's go someplace we can be alone, I don't bite," she says and smiles. She doesn't have to tell him twice, he's already making a U-turn to go down U.S. 1 to the motel strip.

Melissa had playfully mentioned to Katie that she would marry him, but the little toddler had heard and told Jimmy in her very serious for a three year old tone.

As soon as he closed the door she dropped her skirt and stepped out of it. She came over and kissed him and started un-buttoning his shirt. Jimmy lifted her onto the bed and they stayed there all night, talking, making love, talking some more, both shedding tears when relating the extreme sorrows both had endured.

They were 18 yaers old, both had far more life experience than their tender ages.

Melissa's questions were determined. She wanted to know who this young man with the beautiful green eye's was.

When Jimmy got to the rough part about his Dad, not the 5 years in New York, the real bad part, he couldn't. Melissa took his chin and made him look at her, saying, "Tell me."

When he tried to look away she held his face firmly. She tilted her head so that his eyes had to meet hers, and repeated, "Tell me, Jimmy."

And so, he did, everything, how close his family is, his brother, who she see's he's very proud of, his mother who he loves and takes care of, and his sister being like a second mother in raising him. He told her about the 5 years in New York supposedly buying Angelo and the whole family a new life out of New York and down here, his brother's appointment part of the reward. They made love again and then Melissa told her story, as best she could.

She was the oldest daughter born to John and Marilyn Kamp in Queens, New York. The family had moved to Florida when she was a girl. Her father was a golf course grounds keeper. Their move to Florida was on the basis of there being a lot more golf courses in Florida than in New York.

A few years back he got sick and they all thought it was his ulcers again. But after a week straight her mother insisted he go see a doctor.

The doctor admitted him to the hospital for tests. The

results were that John Kamp had cancer throughout his internal
organs. He was given 6 months to live, 3 months later they buried
him.

He left behind his wife and daughters. Melissa, being the
oldest, did her best to be brave and console her mother and younger
sisters. She had to grow up quick. Her mother had to work and
therefore she was left to care for her sisters. She learned to
cook, sew and was a fierce disciplinarian regarding her charges.
She made sure they did their school work and minded their manners.
She had done an admirable job, the girl's got straight A's in
school.

She couldn't tell him this: Melissa had dated a boy named,
Jay Forrester, for almost 3 years. They had planned on always being together. But Jay was the son of a wealthy family, and as
time elapsed it became evident that Melissa was not to be a part
of young Jay's future.

When she happily told him that she was pregnant, what
could've been the happiest moment of her young life, became her
saddest. He wanted nothing to do with her or any child. She was
crushed. When she confided in Marilyn that she was with child,
Marilyn threw a fit. How could you? How can we afford an infant?
They were struggling so already.

She made it hard on her daughter those first few weeks.
But then Marilyn felt guilty and ashamed. She scolded herself for
being so selfish and inconsiderate. Little Melissa had taken
charge of the household chores when John had passed and it was
often she, Marilyn, who sought the consoling arms of her oldest

child. She would stand by her now.

Melissa had never given it another thought but to have the baby. She has never regretted it. Tina was a bundle of joy from her very first moment, she was seldom cross or ill-tempered. The three girl's had all taken to the baby as if they were all her mother. They all took turns changing diapers, and when Tina began bottle feeding, they split that up too. Tina would be three in a few weeks, she needed a father and that thought brought her back to the present.

She looked over at him and he smiled. They were holding hands and he gave her's a reaffirming squeeze. Oh, Jimmy, dear sweet sexy Jimmy with the sparkling green eyes!

She hadn't known him for more than 24 hours, but the passion of this night and how they had talked and talked, laying here together now it feels so perfect and so right, this the boy she's waited for.

She would have to tell him about baby Tina, but how? What would he say? What would he do? Would she lose him?

They awoke in the morning wrapped together. Jimmy gave her a quick little kiss and drew back looking at her. She felt under the covers and, oops! She kissed him back and they made love again. They showered and dressed.

In the car, Melissa asked, "Are you coming over tonight?"

"I've got to stop home and change for work. Come with me, you can meet my mom," he tells her, and squeezes her hand.

"Am I going to meet my future mother-in-law at this hour? Won't she think I'm bad keeping her boy out all night?", she asked.

He smiles at her and says, "She's probably expecting us.
I told her before I left last night I'd met someone and- don't
worry, she's going to love you, I do and so will she."

"Whoa, mister! Will you repeat that please?", she says.

"What? That my Mom will love you?", he answers, knowing
that's not what she wants to hear.

She pokes him with feigned annoyance and says, "Not that
and you know it, the other thing."

He laughs and then says, very seriously, "I love you, I do!"
He waits for a reaction, nothing? One second, two seconds and then
her eyes flew open and she threw her arms around him.

"Oh, Jimmy! Do you mean it?", she asks.

"Of course I mean it, what about you?", he asks.

"About me? Oh!", she says, and starts giggling like a
young girl before saying, "Yes! Yes! I love you too, Jimmy. Lastnight-
I've never felt like this." And now she actually has tears in her
eyes.

"Mel? What's wrong? Are you okay?", he asks.

"Oh, you silly boy, I'm way more than okay, this is the
most wonderful day," she tells him.

She has tears running down her face so she stops hugging
him long enough to get a kleenex out of her purse.

They drove on holding hands, every now and then one or the
other giving a reaffirming squeeze. She should be so happy but she's
wrestling with her dilemma, she has to tell him about Tina.

"Mel? You all right? You're awful quiet over there," he
says.

"No, I'm fine Jimmy, what could be wrong? I've just spent the most beautiful night of my life and you tell me you love me in the morning. It's like a fairy tale," she says.

They finally arrive at the Carosa home, its just getting light out.

"Are you sure its okay? We won't be waking her up?", she asks.

Jimmy silences her with a kiss, "Come on, she'll be up. She'll be so happy to see you, even if she were in a dead sleep it wouldn't matter," he says.

Jimmy leads her up the walk and into the house.

Nettie is awake. She hugs her son before stepping back and smiling at Melissa.

"He told me last night that he might be bringing me a daughter-in-law, and your so cute," Nettie says and hugs her. She continues, "I hope its you? Jimmy, is this her?", she's teasing.

"No, Ma, that's her sister," Jimmy shoots right back at her and Nettie acts like she's going to swat him.

Melissa notices how easy they get along and she can see Nettie adores him.

Nettie takes Melissa's hand and leads her to the dining room table. "Jimmy, will you get us some coffee? I want to sit and talk with my soon to be daughter-in-law," Nettie says.

"Okay, Ma." He can tell she likes Melissa already.

They were talking away when he brought the coffee in.

"She told me you beat up that fat bastard at work for

bothering her, good! Fuck him and that job," Nettie says, and she means it to.

"He's a good boy, Mellie, I would've never made it without Jimmy," she says, and pats the chair to her other side for Jimmy to sit.

"Does she know about your father?", Nettie asks.

Jimmy and Mellie exchange trusted, knowing glances before Jimmy says, "Yea, she knows, everything."

"Well, he was a good man, Mellie. He did everything for his family, for us," Nettie says, her eye's filling with tears.

"We're getting married, Ma," he says.

"What? When?!", Nettie asks, and looks at Mellie who looks just as surprised as her. Mellie decides right then to tell him about Tina.

"Jimmy, we need to talk. I have something to tell you-," she begins.

He cuts her off saying, "We have to tell Tina tot."

Melissa looks confused and says, "Tina?"

"Yeah, Tina. She asked if I'm going to be her Daddy-," Jimmy says evenly.

"Jimmy, you don't-", Melissa is saying, but then she understands, perfectly, he knows!! Nettie is looking from one to the other, she is confused for certain.

Melissa is so overcome with emotion that she bursts into tears and lowers her head into her hands.

"What did you say to her?", Nettie asks sharply, and she

takes Melissa in her arms, "What's wrong? Poor baby, Nettie soothes. Melissa looks up, she's smiling through the tears. Jimmy comes around and kneels in front of her, taking her hands.

He says, "Her little daughter, Ma, she's a doll. I'm going to be her Daddy." He smiles and Melissa is laughing now and wiping her eyes with the kleenex Nettie took out of her housecoat pocket.

She feels silly and wants to explain why she didn't tell him last night. "I swear I wanted to tell you, I almost got the courage to but- I was afraid, I-", she's telling him.

"Don't worry, it's okay. How could I not know? After last night?", Jimmy tells her.

"Well, forgive me for thinking that your just a shallow love machine," she says, and playfully pokes him. By the look they exchange, even dear old sweet Nettie notices and says, "Gosh, don't anyone light a match, they'll hear the explosion 10 blocks away!" They all laugh.

"Listen, I got to get moving, I'm going to be late already. Ma, can you take Mel home?", he asks.

He used the car last night. His bike is outside but he'll be late if he takes her home. He's already lost one job, he can't lose this one too.

"Don't worry, I'll take her home. Please drive careful, better late than never," Nettie says worriedly. She knows he'll ride recklessly if he's late.

"Don't worry, Ma. I love you and I love you too," he tells both of them. He gives each a kiss and he's gone.

"We'll tell Tina tonight, together," he hollers back.

Jimmy called Melissa and said he was coming straight from work. As soon as he walk's in, Marilyn, Melissa's mother, embraces him warmly. She's so happy that she has tears in her eyes. She trusts Jimmy. He is in no regard a boy and she hasn't seen Melissa look this happy in years, if ever.

Little Tina is clamoring for attention. Jimmy lifts her up, way up and twirls her around as she howls, laughing.

This time when the little girl asks, "Are you going to be my Daddy?", they all laugh, she is so persistent, but he says, "Yes baby, is that okay?"

Tina asks, "Does Mellie know?", and they all laugh again.

As he and Melissa kiss, little Tina tot is trying to wriggle her face in, she wants kisses too.

They both kiss one cheek each, together.

CHAPTER TWELVE

September 1970

"Down by the river, I shot my baby- dead."

Down By The River/ Neil Young

"Hugh Mayor For The United States Senate", read the
boxes of bumper stickers, windshield flyers, and pamphlets extoll-
ing his many qualifications, background, family and education.

The most recent polls show him with a slim majority over
his democratic opponent in the general election less than two
months away.

He is roaming the large expanse of lobby at the Governors
Club Hotel in downtown Ft. Lauderdale. He is greeting donors,
backers, associates, old political allies, and some few former
opponents as well from past legislative battles who are now behind
him in his bid to be the first Republican Senator from Florida
since reconstruction 100 years past.

"Hello, Judge, who is the lovely lady with you this
evening?", Hugh inquires, as the lady in question giggle's like
a teenager.

"Oh Hugh, you old rascal, you know darn well who I am,"
says Teresa Cabot, still acting the coquette.

Her and the Judge have contributed an even million dollars
to Hugh's campaign war chest along with immeasurable votes garnered
by the Judge's endorsements.

The Judge is no longer a judge and never actually had
such an official designation. The name derived from his absolute
control of the vast regions of Southwest rural Florida the past
50 years. It was virtually his own private fiefdom. He and the
lady Cabot owned half the citrus growing regions in the state.
All disputes were taken to the Judge to be settled, his decision
usually being the final word.

Hugh Mayor move's quite easily through the crowd. He's shaking hands, slapping backs, a wry comment here, a poignant question there. A true plitician, he forgets nothing, the most trivial minutiae as regards certain backer's he can recall instantly, reassuring such men, and women, that they are indeed on a personal level with the soon to be Senator.

It is past 10:00 p.m. and though he appears to be spry and alert, he is coming to the end of a very long day, one that Victoria had made seemingly endless.

He had met her at their love nest, a very private water front condominium he had purchased for just that purpose.

They had made love hotly, no tenderness, both physically consuming the other. Victoria liked to be taken roughly, often teasing him to a blinding lust just to push him to such extremes.

He would tear her tight sheer mini-dress off in his rush to take her, just as he had done today. He had not lost his raging desire for her, it was as overpowering as it had always been.

After they had slaked their burning passions, he told her, "I have a $1,000 a plate dinner tonight at 7:00 p.m. I'm taking Cynthia, I have to-."

Victoria did not give him a chance to finish, she asked, "Your what?!"

"Victoria, please, its only-," he began again and once more she interrupted saying, "No! No more, Victoria please! That's it, Hugh, and I'm serious. I'm not going to put up with this any- longer, the girl's have been away at college a year already!",

Victoria fumed.

"Victoria, please, just listen to me," Hugh tried but she would not.

"You listen Hugh, you tell that pale little wife of yours exactly what your doing, now, this instant, and I'll inform poor dear Henry as well, but no more delays and I mean it!", Victoria insisted with finality.

She stood up away from his attempt to hug her, and wrenched free, grabbing her panties and shoes. The dress is torn, she remembers, so she throws it in his face and grabs a shift out of the closet. Slamming the door to the bathroom as she enters it, he hears the shower running. He leans back into the pillows and contemplates the situation.

Victoria is being unreasonable, only two more months, less actually and the election will be over. He'll be free to divorce Cynthia and they can live here until Dr. Smart vacates the house on North River Drive.

She must wait, it's his entire political future at stake. He's worked his whole life to arrive at this juncture and he will not throw it away now that he is so very close. Not for her, not for anyone or anything. He'll do what he must to win in November.

When Victoria emerges from the bathroom, she has on her panties and heels and she's stepping into the demur cotton shift she'll wear home.

Hugh says, "Victoria, listen to me, please, you've waited this long, its only two more months. Less after tonight, I'm almost there," he beseeches her.

"No Hugh! No! That's it. Today is Tuesday, Friday night you either tell Henry and Cynthia, or- I will." She says the last very evenly.

"Victoria!"

"No Hugh! No." She is at the door and she stops and turns and says, "Friday," slamming the door on her way out.

Someone is saying something, and that brings Hugh back to the present.

"Oh, excuse me, Mr. Rooney, I must have fallen asleep on my feet," Hugh laughs heartily.

"That's quite all right, Hugh, got to get it when and where you can. I know the rigors of the campaign very intimately. I used to catch a nap here and there just like that myself," says Mr. Jonah Del Rooney. He is a Republican party insider. No one can win a Republican chair without his being on board, it's that simple.

"Everything going okay? No last minute surprises? No snafu's I need to know about?", Rooney asks very casually, like it doesn't have any import to him one way or another.

"Oh no, Mr. Rooney, not a thing," Hugh replies confidently, feeling anything but confident. The spat with Victoria and her threats loom large. He has to neutralize her ultimatum somehow, but how?

"You have a lovely wife, Hugh, and you daughter, Lisa, is an asset beyond calculation," Rooney informs.

Cynthia and Lisa have spoken on Hugh's behalf at various functions around the state. Lisa's position as a senior at the University of Florida and her being very active in the anti-war movement there is fueling the youth vote for him.

"Well thank you, that's very nice of you to say so," Hugh replies.

Cynthia finally sees him and comes over saying, "There you are! Hugh, I have a busy day-"

"Say no more my dear, we're off," Hugh gratefully interrupts.

They bid Mr. Rooney good night. Hugh makes one last circuit around the lobby clasping hands. At the exit, the crowd applaudes as he bows graciously and Cynthia waves proudly, and then they depart, the ideal couple.

Hugh comments about Rooney's observations and general feeling of tonight's dinner. Cynthia listens politely, they haven't slept together as husband and wife in quite some time. It is an uneasy truce at their home.

They both understand the importance of their appearing to be in perfect marital and family harmony and unity, how crucial it is to Hugh's Senate bid, and so it continues.

Jewel unexpectedly greets them at the door, "Evenin' Miz Cynthia, Mista Hugh."

Cynthia mildly scolds her, "Why Jewel, you needn't have waited for us. It's late, you should've been asleep hours ago."

Jewel says, "That's ok, Miz Cynthia. My ol bones a little achy sometimes and I can'ts sleep."

"Well, you go on now. We're home safe, okay? And thank you,

Jewel," Cynthia tells her.

Jewel walks slowly down the hall towards her rooms. She knows there's trouble tween the Miz and Mista. She hopes they comes to an understandin'. Peoples be foolish, she cant knows why.

Hugh and Cynthia sleep in separate bedrooms. Cynthia is in their old master bedroom while Hugh is in a guest room further along the hall.

She is so tired, is this what her life's become? An actress? Acting the happy wife and mother? And Lisa, she's agreed to play a role also but not for her father though. She is adamantly anti-war as is Hugh and that is her only reason.

What is mine?, Cynthia thinks. Do I still love him? Undoubtedly yes, but can I forgive him? She doesn't know. She feels so empty, so alone, She begins to cry and it is hours later when she falls asleep.

Hugh is wide awake, Victoria's words echoing over and over. He must find a way to stop her, but how? Tomorrow, tomorrow he will plead with her, beg her. She must listen to him, she must.

Hugh places a call to the Smart residence the following day under the guise of some legal, contractual issue he must discuss with the Smarts.

The Hispanic housekeeper who answers the phone says, "I very sorry, Dr. Smart is at the hospital. It is his week on Emergency Room standby so I not to sure when he expected. Will you like Mrs. Smart?", she asks.

"Yes, that will be fine," Hugh says.

"This is Mrs. Smart, how may I help you?", Victoria answers into the phone.

"Victoria, it's me, please- I need to see you, we need to talk, you must listen," Hugh begs.

"I believe we've already discussed this matter as much as I'd care to. My position has not changed and it will not change, so- I'll see you, um- Friday?", she answers coldly and hangs up.

Hugh is in a panic! He tells his secretary and legal assistant to cancel the rest of the days appointments, he's not feeling well. He needs time to think, alone, he must stop her!

He goes to the Country Club and sits there quietly drinking. He must figure out some way to avert this impending disaster.

If she tells her husband, if Cynthia knows that Hugh's philandering is not past but that it is an ongoing affair, what will she do? His campaign, the millions of dollars already invested by the powerful, his backers and supporters, all will abandon him.

His political life would be extinguished now and forever. No one would ever get behind him in any bid, even his seat in the legislature would be forfeit.

He has worked his entire life to arrive here where he now stands. Every casual aquaintence he's made, every contact, every move he's ever made pre-calculated to further his goal. He cannot let this happen, he will not let it happen!

Hours later when he leaves the Country Club he's fairly intoxicated, but the employee's would never dare address such an issue with a member, it's yes sir, no sir and good evening sir, and that's it. They need their jobs.

When he arrives home its near dusk. Jewel greets him but he brushes right by her. She smells the liquor and just rolls her eyes thinking, that man hate hisself, he lose his family and now he losen his mind.

Cynthia hears him enter but he doesn't acknowledge her at all. He looks- odd?, she thinks.

Fifteen minutes later they hear the 24' Kingfisher start up and then it roars away from the dock into the twilight.

Victoria has just stepped out of her bath and Aranxa has laid out her robe. She now asks, "Mrs. Smart, you need something more from me tonight? or-."

Victoria thinks for just a moment but decides, no, she has no further need for Aranxa tonight, and says, "No, Aranxa, that will be all. Dr. Smart should be home shortly and we'll dine together when he arrives."

The chef and his assistant have the meal ready. Whenever Victoria wishes to begin, she'll ring the kitchen, Aranxa is done for the night.

Hugh has slowed the boat to an idle cruise. He's taking long swallows from the bottle of Scotch, Dewars White Label, that he's brought from his bar at home, his brand.

He looks about, it's a clear, beautiful starry night, but no moon. He gulps another swallow and pushes the throttle forward to full, going North. He's decided what to do, and if he doesn't hurry and do it now, right this instant, he may never be able to.

The estate's along the river are set back from it in huge park-like grounds. There are walls surrounding the entire property. From the dock, as you move inward, you would pass perhaps a guest cottage, a large pool and sauna area, and gardens before approaching the main residence.

Most of the estate's have a multi-car garage over which there are small apartments for the servant staff, as there is here also.

The Mayor home is on the river to the South, a short distance of perhaps one mile from where Hugh is now.

He is tying the Kingfisher to the dock at the rear of the Blackwell estate at 2450 N. River Drive. He has not come to see old Ned Blackwell, nor his boozy wife, Elinor, known as "Tippy" for the obvious reason. They won't be in tonight, or the next, or the one after that. They are at their Northern abode in Suffolk County in Long Island, New York. They won't be here until Thanksgiving.

Hugh has come to see their neighbor at 2440 N. River Drive. He quickly but quietly covers the 100 or so yards from the Blackwell dock to the property line, where he must breach a small protrusion of hurricane fencing that hangs outward from the seawall, separating 2450 from 2440.

He does quite easily and he is now in the rear of the house

at 2440 N. River Drive. It is dark, but the main house is at least visible beyond the small guest cottage and the pool/ sauna area. It is all unlit except for the light coming from the windows at the back of the main house. Hugh now crosses the large expanse of lawn and closes to the rear of the residence.

There is literally a wall of glass sliding doors spanning the width of the house. Most are curtained but he can see several that have the light on within.

He see's a shadow pass across one on the far left, closest to the garage on the North side of the property. All the garage apartment lights are off except the one that looks directly into the backyard, where he is now standing.

He again notices the shadow pass behind the curtains of the same door. He knocks very lightly on the glass, nothing. He raps a little harder and the curtain is immediately pulled back. It's Victoria, and she has a small, black automatic pistol in her hand.

She is livid! She unlocks the glass door and he staggers in. "You scared me half to death! What are you doing here, Hugh?!", she seethes.

"Here, have a drink with your old boy," Hugh slurs, and holds up the bottle of Dewars.

"I will not have a drink, and if you don't leave I'll call the police," she tells him, but it sounds ridiculous even to her.

"And what will you tell them, Victoria? That the soon to be Senator I'm blackmailing is here?", Hugh snarls.

Victoria is frightened, she has never seen him like this. "Hugh, darling, why don't you just calm down. Here, take a seat," she says, and pats a loveseat by the bed.

"You bitch!", Hugh growls, and lunges at her. She attempts to bring up the small gun that's still in her right hand but he has grabbed her arm and is bending it back, almost breaking it.

When she rakes at him with her free left hand, she misses his face but sinks her nails deep into his neck and chest and scratches him all the way down.

He backhands her and the hand she's been holding the gun in loses it's grip. She tries desperately to hold on to it, but it slips from her hand as she reels from the savage blow.

Hugh picks up the small gun and---.

Henry is finally done, he can go home now and at least get a shower and eat dinner. If another head trauma case is brought in, at least he'll be refreshed.

He pulls into the gated wall entrance and drives the car to the garage but does not pull it in. He leaves the car on the driveway in case he has an Emergency Room call to attend.

As he steps out and closes the car door, he hears a sharp pop, not from the door mechanism, from inside?

He hurries to the door and upon entering nothing seems amiss. As he walks back to the rear of the house he calls, "Victoria? Are you here?"

He opens the door to the master bedroom and, Oh my God! "Victoria! Victoria!", he begins yelling. She is lying in a pool blood! He removes his suit jacket and has propped her head up on it. The curtains are blowing in on the sliding glass doors- he hears what sounds like a boats engine being started.

His gun is lying beside his wife. He grabs the gun and sprints out towards the sound of the engine. Just as he gets to the seawall, he see's a boat about a 100 yards North along the Blackwell dock, pulling away. Henry shoots once, twice, but the vessel keeps going.

He runs back to the house and grabs the phone and dials "0" for the operator. He's kneeling by his wife and when the operator comes on he screams directions into the phone.

"I'm Dr. Smart, 2440 N. River Drive, I have a gunshot wound! I need an ambulance, hurry!"

Being the address is where it is, the ambulance and police are there in seven minutes flat. They ring the door bell and then enter the residence.

"Back here! Hurry! Hurry!", Henry is yelling.

The two cop's and the ambulance crew proceed into the bedroom. Henry has Victoria in his arms, blood is boiling out of a horrific wound in her chest.

"I am a doctor! I need a thoracic air compress and oxygen, hurry!", he yells at the medic's and they rush out to get them.

A uniform cop and a detective, who is off duty but heard the call come in over the radio on his way home, have responded to Henry's urgent call.

Detective Todd asks, "Dr. Smart, who did this?"

"I don't know, I just got in. It's my on call night, I-,"

Henry is saying, and then, "Victoria! Victoria! Who did this?", he asks.

Victoria opens her eyes and looks right at him. It is her last lucid moment before death.

She says, "Henry, Henry, why? -uh, why did?, you?, Why did you?", and then she's gone.

PART III

MONSTERS

CHAPTER THIRTEEN

September 1970

"Killer on the Road."

Riders On The Storm/ The Doors

James Carosa had taken Melissa Kamp as his lawfully wedded wife exactly 3 months ago, the first Sunday in June, and that is what they are celebrating tonight.

Since they are extremely limited in spending money, it doesn't hurt that tonight's fete is on the house, by Louie, an old friend of Angelo's. He is the proud proprietor of an Italian bistro on the Hollywood Circle.

Louie's call of a few days previous seemed like divine providence, right on time to toast 3 months of marital bliss.

Jimmy is once again working two jobs and Melissa is back waitressing. They decided to live with Nettie at the Carosa home for a variety of reasons, the main one being that Nettie could not be left alone, not this soon, her son Jimmy is her life.

And, Nettie has no income, even had she become accustomed to the not so distant tragedy. She still has the rainy day money that Angelo had put aside, but better to leave it intact for even worse times should they arise.

Jimmy, Melissa and little Tina are seated in the back of the small restaurant. A small bottle of real imported Chianti is brought to the table along with a tiny bottle of grape juice for the baby.

"Everything is on the house, enjoy," said the young waitress. They toast all around, Tina too, for the 3 idyllic months and the many, many more still to come. Jimmy and Melissa kissed, and of course Tina tot wants her share of kisses too and they happily oblige.

Melissa has a big surprise for Jimmy and she is bursting with anticipation, but she has decided to wait until after the meal is done. He's told her quite frequently that Tina is his little girl too, without reservation, and Melissa knows it. But, he has mentioned, in his unassuming way, that he would like to add to their little family. Maybe a little brother? Later, perhaps a little girl too?

Melissa had laughed, "Of course, all you want, it's not you that will get fat and ugly," she had teased.

He had wryly replied, "It'll be more of you to love," and laughed as she poked him.

But tonight... After they had finished and were awaiting the espresso, Melissa said, "I have something to tell you, Jimmy." She sounded so serious at first that he was alarmed. He looked and saw the amusement in her eyes and she had begun to smile.

He kissed her and brushed her cheek with the back of his fingers and said, "Ok, tell me sweetie. You look like the cat that ate the canary."

"I stopped by my doctor's office on the way home and...," she drew out the last just long enough to see his eyes widen, before finishing, "I'm pregnant, Jimmy!"

"Your kidding? Your not kidding?! Your serious? Really?! Oh fuck, Mellie!" He almost shouted the last and she laughingly covered his mouth saying, "Shhh! Everyone is staring silly boy," and then she kissed him.

"Oh Mellie! Wow! Wow! I'm going to be- a Dad! Again! I hope he? or she? whichever, looks just like you and Tina," he said, and then laughed and kissed her.

"Ay Jimmy! How ya doin? Who's the pretty goil witch ya? Ya didn't marry this bum, did ya?", Louie asks the last to Melissa, he's joking with them as he shakes Jimmy's hand and pinched first Melissa's cheek and then little Tina's.

"Ya look good, Jimmy, and you got a nice little family. Stay outta dis shit. I'm very sorry about your fadda," Louie says.

"Thanks, Louie. Thanks. It was real tough there for awhile, I was worried my Ma wouldn't-, you know, it was bad for her," Jimmy tells him.

"Well, come on in da back. I gotta couple bottles of good wine, you take dem to ya mudda, tell her me and Irene send our best. She need anytin you tell me, I'll make sure she get it, Jimmy," Louie says as he squeezes Jimmy's shoulder.

"C'mon, get the vino," he says, and Jimmy says, "Sweet, I'll be right back."

"I'm going to take Tina to the potty, take your time, Jimmy," Mellie says and blows him a kiss.

Jimmy follows Louie as he waddles behind the counter of the small deli and through a curtain into the back of the establishment.

He brings out a small bottle of Amaretto and pours two fingers into each glass. "Sit, Jimmy. Lets have a small shot, to ya fadda," he says, and Jimmy sits at the small table.

"You know dat fuck Jimmy Blue Eyes set up da hole ting, dat's why he wadn't there," Louie says.

Jimmy is getting mad, again, for the 10,000 th time. Fuckin' old wop ass bullshit got his Dad killed.

"Who did the- uh, who shot them, Louie?", Jimmy asks, "For what? Why?!"

Louie says, "Well, when Philly Black was taken out in New York, Coco had to go here, no two ways about it. Your fadda just happened to be there. Dat shouldn't a mattered, a real pro wouldn't a hit Angelo, it was only Coco. I seen hits, Jimmy, nobody but da target get it, it was a sloppy job," Louie finishes.

A sloppy job, a sloppy fuckin' job, a mistake, and his Dad gets killed.

"Who, Louie? Who did this?", Jimmy asks.

"Well, you know Jimmy, just business, changing of the guard shit, its-," Louie is saying.

"I'm not talking about that, Louie. Who did the job? The sloppy job? You said it yourself, who?", Jimmy demands.

Louie looks Jimmy in the eye and he knows the kid's got that coming. "Two Ton Tony, Tony Gallante, working for Blue Eyes outta New York, Carmine Stracci's people," Louie tells him.

"Where is this-", Jimmy asks but Louie stops him cold saying, "Forget about it! Forget it! You got a wife and kid, live your life, kid. Leave all this shit, this garbage behind, forget about it, Jimmy! Please!", Louie tells him and stares until Jimmy looks away.

"Here, salud, to ya fadda," Louie says and they touch glasses and Jimmy says, "Salud."

"C'mon, let's go back to your little goil, take the wine,"

Louie says, and they hug as Louie pats his face.

Jewel hears Hugh entering the back patio door that leads
to the dock and goes to see if he wants anything. He was quite
drunk when he left earlier.

She meets him coming down the hall, he's staggering.

"Mista Hugh, you alright? Want me to fetch the Missus?",
Jewel asks and turns on the hall light.

She gasps, "Mista Hugh! You hurt! You bleedin!", she says.

"Shut that fuckin light off!", Hugh roars and shoves past
her into his bedroom, slamming and locking the door.

Cynthia has heard the commotion and comes out of the
master bedroom and into the hallway. "Jewel, what is going on?
Where is Hugh? I heard-," she says, as Jewel points silently to
his closed and locked door.

Cynthia tries the door and then knocks.

Jewel says, "Mista Hugh hurt Missus. He bleedin' on his
shirt and he, uh- he been drinkin."

Cynthia knocks louder and says, "Hugh! Hugh! Open the door!
Are you hurt? Please Hugh, open the door, I want to see if your all
right."

"Go away!", Hugh hollers, and then he passes out.

Cynthia continues banging on the door but there is no
response. Should she call the police? No, she doesn't want to
draw any negative publicity. "Jewel, could you tell? Is he hurt
badly?", she asks.

"I not to sure, but he need sleep Missus, he drunk,"
Jewel answers.

"All right, Jewel, and thank you. I'll see you in the morning," Cynthia says.

She listens at Hugh's door but hears nothing. She goes
back into her bedroom but is unable to sleep. It will be hours
before she dozes off.

The police are all over the Smart residence. Detective Todd
has called for Homicide detectives and Crime Lab technicians. They
have finally removed Victoria's body to the morgue for an autopsy.
The lab people have photographed the entire bedroom, the scene of
the murder, dusted for fingerprints, inventoried and catalogued
every item within the bedroom.

Dr. Smart is sitting with two Homicide detectives, a
Lieutenant Arena and a Detective Price. The lab people have informed
the two detectives that the doctor has gun powder residue on his
hands.

Henry is drinking a tumbler of Scotch as the two policemen
ask him questions. He has told them the story twice from beginning
to end, he will not tell it again.

They have sent uniforms out to question the servant staff.
If any have information they are to be brought back here to the
residence. So far, nothing. None of the domestics have seen or
heard anything, no boats in the rear of the property, no shots,
no strange intruder lurking outside the master bedrooms sliding
glass doors, zero.

Only the Doctor apparently has seen this mystery boat, or the report of the two shots he claims to have fired at it.

Detective Todd, and the responding uniform officer, Snow, have told the Homicide detectives Victoria's last dying words. Detective Arena is weighing this heavily, he is in charge of the investigation. The Doctor is a scion of the societal elite, a respected and renowned physician. He has to be very careful.

"Dr. Smart, tell me once more of your first inclination that something was wrong," Lt. Arena asks.

"I've told you! Twice. I will not tell you again Lieutenant. While you sit there wasting time with me, the man who murdered my wife is out there!", Henry shouts at him.

"Take it easy, Doctor. Take it easy," Detective Price soothes, "We're trying to help," he adds lamely.

"You should be out combing the river, going dock to dock, finding the craft the murderer made his escape in," Henry says forcefully. He is out of patience with these two bumbling fools! Why are they sitting here with him?

"Doctor, I'm going to ask you to accompany Detective Price and I downtown, just need to go over some things," Lt. Arena says.

"What?! I will not accompany you anywhere! This is preposterous! I'm calling my attorney right now!", Henry shouts at both of them.

"That's your privilege and your legal right, Dr. Smart, call him," Lt. Arena says smugly. This rich doctor doesn't scare him.

Robby Keebler is drinking shots and beer chasers, "Boilermakers", they're called. He's drank at least a half dozen of them and he's pretty darn drunk to say so himself.

He gets a double shot of whiskey and one beer chaser, for the road. He tosses off the whiskey, takes a big swallow of beer, and stagger's out the rear door of Freddie's Anchor Bar on State Road 84 and U.S. Highway 1.

It takes him several minutes to find the ignition of his pick-up truck with the key. His truck is elevated, up on stacks, for off-road treks. He finally finds the ignition and inserts the key.

Jimmy and Melissa are thanking Louie for having them as guests.

"You two, and the little one of course, anytime you's want, ya come here, ya welcome here, ya hear me? Don't be strangers," Louie tells them. He hug's Jimmy and pats his face, saying, "Ya got a life, kid, don't fuck it up," and shakes his finger at him.

"I won't, Louie, thanks," Jimmy answers. He knows exactly what Louie means, but Melissa just thinks its an admonition to live right and enjoy the life they have together.

He contemplates the irony of his father's murder coming at the hands of an incompetent hit man. The incompetence, or sloppy job in street parlance, wasn't the hit being botched where the intended target survived, no, it was the untargeted Angelo being killed too.

The Mafia doesn't approve of any innocents being harmed.

It's a surgical strike, not a hatchet job.

Two Ton Tony has gotten a pass this time only because Angelo was not a true innocent, he was connected. But since Angelo's killing wasn't approved, Tony had still fucked up. He would not be trusted with future hits of this variety.

True pro's could hit a target right beside the Pope himself, and not a drop of the victim's blood would stain the Pontiff.

Nobody looks and nobody pays attention. Nobody cares, as long as the killing is contained and their only doing it to each other. If just one citizen is killed or harmed in any way, then everything changes.

They are in Mellie's 1967 light blue Ford Falcon, it has a bench seat in the front. Usually Tina would sit between her mother and Jimmy, but often, as now, she is sitting between Mellie's legs and leaning back against her mother comfortably. The little girl is tired and she is napping peacefully.

Jimmy and Mellie are holding hands, their young life together just beginning. Even Nettie is rejuvenated, she has a family to fuss over again.

It is a Wednesday night, just after 9:00 p.m., the traffic is relatively light. The young newlyweds are driving along doing the posted speed limit of 40 m.p.h. They are just South of the New River Tunnel on U.S. Highway 1, going Northbound.

As the Northbound traffic merges from three lanes to two lanes, the tunnels width, a pick-up truck going much to fast realizes it too must merge. However, instead of slowing or stopping, the driver attempts to merge directly into the already merged traffic's two lanes, there is no space for the extra vehicle.

The errant pick-up must do something, it is rapidly approaching a concrete abutment where the tunnel right of way begins. The pick-up swerves directly into the near side lane where a red Corvette and a blue Ford Falcon are already occupying that lane.

The pick-up hits the concrete abutment with the right front side of the trucks passenger side, and being the truck is jacked up on stacks, elevated, it becomes airborne before coming down on its driver's side, right on top of the small Ford. Both vehicle's are sliding down into the tunnel's entrance, the Falcon with the pick-up on top of it as all the other Northbound traffic slams into both vehicle's.

The two Northbound lanes into the tunnel become a dozen car pile-up. As vehicles behind come upon the unexpected log-jam, and are unable to stop, they too crash into the pile of mangled cars.

It will take hours to unsnarl the destroyed vehicles. It will also hinder rescue and medical help to the injured in several of the cars.

At close to midnight, the Fire Rescue Department crew has finally managed to cut the three occupants of the Ford Falcon out of the wreckage of the two vehicle's. Only one is alive and is sped by ambulance to Broward General Medical Center.

The phone is ringing at the Smart residence. The two

detectives, Henry, and his attorney, Joe Baron, are awaiting a Circuit Court Judges decision on whether to issue search warrants for the residence and Dr. Smart's medical offices. But, more significantly- whether Henry can be barred from both until the searches are complete. The Judge was not happy about the late night call.

Joe Baron answers the call, saying, "Dr. Smart's residence. Joe Baron speaking, how may I-?"

He is interrupted by an Emergency Room doctor summoning the good Dr. Smart for an inbound head trauma.

"Henry, its the hospital," Baron tells his friend and hands him the phone.

"Yes?", Henry says into the phone.

The Emergency Room attending physician says, "Auto accident head trauma, bone fragments possibly imbedded in brain, on life support."

Henry listen's to Dr. Keilor's diagnosis and then says, "I'm on the way!", and slams down the phone.

"I have to go to the Broward County Emergency Room," he's telling Joe Baron but Lt. Arena starts to protest saying, "Hold on here Dr.-", but Henry brushes right past. He's not holding on at all, and says, "Out of my way, you fool." He's already out the door and heading to his car, left outside the garage hours earlier for just this reason.

The attorney, Baron, looks at the detective with a withering glance, as Henry pulls his car out through the gate and speeds to the Emergency Room.

The patient is a young male, 5'9", 140 lbs., perhaps
18 years of age. The right rear quadrant of his cranium has been
fractured and there are bone fragments touching the brain.

His brain has already begun to swell and Dr. Smart is
examining the x-rays. He has no time to lose, he must relieve the
pressure that the swelling brain is causing. That is what he must
race against now, without delay, before possible permanent damage
occurs.

Dr. Smart begins barking orders, "Janet, operating room #2,
need Neural Anesthesiologist. Call Cameron, tell him to get here
for assisting neural extraction. Call Warren, he should supervise,
lets go." The Emergency Room staff disperse, gathering the necessary
implements.

In 44 minutes, James Carosa is in operating room #2.
Dr. Roman Cameron is the assisting physician, Dr. Edwin Warren
is the supervising physician, and Dr. Henried Smart is the primary
attending physician. The Anesthesiologist is Dr. Paul Blumen. He
is the best for such an extremely delicate procedure as this. He
will be responsible for keeping the patient aerated and his heart
functioning for the duration of the procedure.

For 6½ hours Dr. Smart slowly and meticulously extracts
tiny slivers of cranial bone fragments. Some of the fragments are
literally as tiny and of the same weight as a flake of dandruff.

He has removed a small section of the cranium in close
proximity of the actual wound to alleviate pressure from the
swelling brain. It is exacting, demanding work but Dr. Smart is

a master. Any error in his judgement and the patient could lose vast portions of brain function. One small probe a 1/100th of an inch and he could lose the patient entirely.

Finally, Henry looks at Cameron, and then Warren. They both nod, he's done it, perfectly. They only have to replace the small section that was removed, excised temporarily, to relieve the pressue that was on the patient's brain.

For this relatively routine procedure, Dr. Cameron will be the primary, with Dr. Warren as the assisting and Henry will be supervising. Which in this instance, will be mere spectating.

He is exhausted, mentally and physically. And now that he is no longer holding another life in his hands, emotionally also.

For now, the still raw, fresh loss of his wife, Victoria, all comes rushing back to him. He collapses into a chair and begins to weep. It is all too much for him to absorb without respite. It is many minutes before he regains his composure.

He walks to the scrub room and washes his hands and is splashing cold water onto his face. It is time to go home.

It is full daylight, almost 8:00 a.m., when Henry walks out of the hospital to his car.

His lawyer, Joe Baron, is waiting for him. "Henry, I spoke with Chief Judge Morris. Your uh, -you're to surrender to the Broward County Jail by 5:00 p.m. today. I know, I know," Baron says, holding up his hands as he see's Henry's astonishment.

It turns to disgust and exasperation as Henry says, "Joe,

you've known me, what?, 15 years now- do you think I killed Victoria? No, no, do you think me capable of doing so? That's what I'm asking."

"Of course I don't, Henry, it's preposterous! But this Lieutenant Arena, you've made an enemy there, Henry, a dangerous one. He's the lead detective on the case, we have to be careful," the lawyer answers.

"Just great, a total ass in charge of finding the man, the animal, that killed my Victoria. Let's charge the husband! Why not? Save a lot of police work, sure," Henry says sarcastically as he shakes his head, he has no more words.

"I've got a bail hearing set for 1:00 p.m. in chambers," Baron is saying, 'When you report to the Booking Desk your bail will be set. I'm asking for a PR, personal recognizance release, but we'd better have a bonding agency just in case.

Henry just nods absently. Victoria is dead! She was so beautiful and relatively young at 38. He hasn't even called, Nicole, at Bryn Mawr, how will he tell her this tragic news?

"Do what's necessary, Joe. I'm leaving this all to you. I have to call my daughter," Henry tells him.

Baron shakes his head, yes, and says, "Meet me at the Booking Desk at say, 4:45 p.m., get you out of there by 5:30, ok?"

"All right, Joe, thank you my friend. I'll see you then," Henry answers him, and then gets in his car and heads home.

Melissa Carosa and Tina Kamp were pronounced dead at the

scene. Robbie Keebler was unhurt except for minor cuts and bruises. He was booked into the county jail on charges of D.W.I, causing an accident that resulted in death or grevious bodily harm, driving with a suspended license and having no insurance. There were several injured in the pile-up but Melissa and Tina were the only fatalities.

From Mel's drivers license and the car's registration in the glove box, the police were able to obtain her home address as the Kamp residence.

A uniform was dispatched to bear the grim news and upon hearing it, her mother, Marilyn fainted dead away. Medical attention was required to revive her.

Hugh Mayor awoke hung over and sticky from his own blood that had congealed to the sheets and mattress. He was confused and foggy but then he remembered the events of the previous evening. He rushed into the bathroom and puked. Finally climbing into the shower he felt terrified, what had he done?

He went out to find Cynthia seated at the breakfast table. She took one look at him and he crumbled in front of her on his knees, sobbing uncontrollably he buried his face in her lap. She was frightened, what had happened to him?, she thought.

When he finally was able to speak, he begged Cynthia to forgive him. He loved her, he could not go on without her.

She stroked his head in her lap and talked very softly trying to soothe him. "It's okay, Hugh, everything will be all

right honey. We'll be okay, shhh-," she babied him. He looked
up into her face and she kissed him on his forehead and stroked
his hair.

"I'm taking leave from the office. We'll go away for a
week, two weeks. I won't return until after the election. We'll
get away, Cynthia, just the two of us, can we?", Hugh pleaded.

"Of course, darling, anything you'd like," Cynthia
reassured. He hugged her close, holding onto her for dear life
as she murmured comforting words in his ear.

Maybe the bad times were behind them. They could start
anew. She hoped so, she had prayed for this, to have Hugh back,
her husband once again, and the girl's their father too, a family.

James Carosa remained unconscious for 5 days. When he
finally awakened, Nettie and Marilyn were ushered into the I.C.U.
room where he was on continuous observation.

He wasn't sure where he was or why he was here. He didn't
recognize Marilyn, and what was his mother doing here?

Marilyn started to cry as she told him about Melissa and
Tina, and that's when he remembered,everything.

Melissa's last dying breath telling him that she loved him,
the enormous weight on his chest he couldn't lift off of them.

He struggled to get out of the bed and alarms began sounding with hurried beeps and whistles, as the I.C.U. nurses came on
th run. Nurse Cannon, the I.C.U. supervisor, immediately administered
a large dose of pento-barbital through his I.V. tube.

Within minutes, Jimmy is once again unconscious, in a dreamless sleep.

CHAPTER FOURTEEN

December 1970/ August 1971

"But I know that he won't stay, without Melissa."

Melissa/ The Alman Brothers

Dr. Warren is making his rounds at Broward General Medical Center, it's 6:30 a.m. The patient in room 732 is being discharged today, his recovery complete.

A tiny plug of synthetic fiber has been surgically implanted in his cranium, where it had shattered into the 41 fragments that Dr. Smart had removed over 3 months previous. Even on close inspection you'd be unable to detect any physical scarring. The patient is as good as new neurologically and physiologically. The deep scars are within, emotionally and mentally, and Dr. Warrens expertise has no answers for those afflictions.

"Good morning, James. You'll be discharged this afternoon, anything you need to discuss? Anything bothering you? Balance? Spatial perception?" Dr. Warren greets his patient's with questions, it's a long standing habit.

"No sir, Dr. Warren, I feel fine. I'm ready to go, I got a lot to do, the world awaits," Jimmy answers with false enthusiasm.

Dr. Warren is concerned that the young man has refused any grief counseling and has not once spoken of the accident or the ensuing devastation of losing his wife and daughter.

Dr. Warren cannot force him to disclose his thoughts, that is the young mans decision, but still the Doctor is concerned.

"I'll need to see you in our medical offices in, say, two weeks. I'll make the appointment. It will be in with your discharge papers. Do you want me to prescribe something for sleep? or do you-," Dr. Warren is asking but Jimmy interrupts, saying, "No, I'm okay Dr. Warren. I don't need anything."

"Well then, James, I'll see you in two weeks. If you need

to be seen before then, call and Shiela will get you right in, okay?", Dr. Warren says, and he holds out his hand and they shake firmly, "Good luck to you," the doctor closes.

"Thank you, Doctor, for everything, and please tell Dr. Smart I said thanks, too. I owe him, Dr. Warren," Jimmy tells him.

"I will, James," and Dr. Warren is gone.

Dr. Smart had only done the first initial follow up examination on Jimmy. Mainly looking at x-rays and his E.E.G. graphs, asking very few questions of the patient himself.

Henry is a surgeon, he is more comfortable with hard scientific data and the exacting pressures of the operating room than bedside conversation with patients.

"Everything okay, Mr. Carosa? You feeling well?", Henry had asked only to be polite. The x-rays and E.E.G. had shown that indeed the patient had come through just fine.

"Yes sir. I uh, I'd like to thank you. The nurses have told me how bad it was and that, uh, your the best," Jimmy answers.

Henry nods and smiles saying, "It helped me a great deal that you are a young and healthy patient who could endure such an invasive procedure."

"Dr. Warren will be seeing you hereafter, Mr. Carosa. He's our Chief Neurologist. If you need anything, or should some imbalance or visual difficulty arise, be sure and let him know. Good luck to you," Henry said in farewell.

Henry had literally surrounded himself with his work. There was no need to retire to his residence on the river. The large villa now an empty shell of a home, he has contacted a realtor to put the estate up for sale.

Nicole had come home for Victoria's funeral, staying only three days before hurriedly departing back to Philadelphia and Bryn Mawr. Henry is alone.

Christy had moved back to the Carosa home. Nettie needed her and she needed Nettie.

Her friend and former roommate had moved back with her mother. Her boyfriend, John Zimmer, had been killed a month after arriving in Vietnam. He was a helicopter door gunner. The life expectancy of door gunner's in Vietnam is 30 minutes. John Zimmer made it a whole 30 days.

Christy felt terrible for, Margo. All the fun and gaiety had drained right out of her friend. Christy had even begun to feel guilty that her boyfriend, Dominick, has survived.

The nurses frequently gossiped about their superiors to one another, and occasionally, to the more familiar patients.

There was an abundance of criticism for many, but never one word about Dr. Smart. Nurse Cannon, call me Karen she had instructed Jimmy, related the entire sordid story about Dr. Smart's present troubles.

It was often the focal point of many an argument between

nurses and police who were frequently at the hospital on business.

Jimmy was going home to his mother and sister. The medical bill's were over $100,000 but that was the least of his problems now, he had Nettie and Christy to think about.

No time for moping he had told them both. He would not tolerate their tears or sorrow for him. It would be much easier he knew if they believed he was okay, although he was anything but okay. No sense in showing it, he would only weaken their resolve.

Christy and his mother silently thanked God, he did seem all right, and they soon resumed a regular day to day rhythm with Jimmy in control.

He went to see Marilyn, and of course she cried. He made it over often after that, for coffee, to reassure her and the girl's that he'd always be there. They had only themselves and Jimmy, the huge void without Melissa and Tina gaping openly.

He went to Louie's. Louie actually wept as he hugged him. Louie had went to see him in the hospital, right after. He looked like he'd be better off dead, his hurt from losing the baby and his wife crushing him.

He was surprised to see Jimmy looking this good now. It was too much, first his father and then the accident, he's a kid for Christs sake.

"C'mon, lets have a glass of wine. Ay Ralphie, I'll be in da back if ya need me, I'm gonna talk to Jimmy," Louie said as he led Jimmy to the little table in the back room where they had sat five lifetime's ago, it seemed.

"How ya doin? I got a few dollars for ya, a tousand, here, take it," Louie says as he holds out the money.

"I don't need to take your money, Louie, you don't have it like that," Jimmy is saying, but Louie will not hear it.

"Ay, ya take dis! Ya wanna insult me? Say I can't give ya a few dollars," Louie orders.

So Jimmy takes it, they'll need it he knows.

"Thanks, Louie, thanks, but I didn't come here for money," Jimmy tells him.

Louie looks at him and says, "I know dat, but ya goin to need it. Now, tell me what ya really want."

Jimmy meets the old guy's stare with his own, he knows Louie knows what's on his mind. "I want to take care of my own, that's all, Louie," Jimmy answers.

"Ya mudda and ya sista need ya. Ya don't want to do nuttin stupid, I was a pro kid so listen to me," Louie is saying. He grabs Jimmy's hand on the table and Jimmy looks at him.

"Ya wanna take care of dis fuck? I'll help ya, but ya gotta do it clean and get away, ya hear me?", Louie asks.

Jimmy nods his head, yes. He's surprised, he had expected an argument out of the old gangster. But the old gangster knows, Jimmy needs redemption, he may not be able to live without it.

"Louie, I'm going to need-, hell, I'm going to need everything," Jimmy says.

"Don't worry, I'm gonna show ya everytin, and I got what ya need too. Ya sure ya wanna do dis?", he asks, but he's laughing and patting Jimmy's face as he says it.

"C'mon, c'mon up stairs wit me," Louie tells him and they climb the old back stairs up to the storage area.

Hours later when Jimmy leaves he's got the iron, a .22 caliber with a small wire muffler that screws on.

"When ya done, ya come back here. I don't care what time it is, ya hear me?", Louie says.

Jimmy's nodding, yes, and he says, "All right, I'll see you, the end of the week. Thanks, Louie."

They hug and Louie holds Jimmy for a long second before letting him go. He pats Jimmy's face and says, "Be neat."

He watches until the motorcycle is out of sight.

On New Year's Eve at Sneaky Pete's, a Hallandale night club across the street from Gulfstream Park, the horse track, the clientele this evening is mostly people of the same persuasion and occupation.

Many of the Mafioso are accompanied by their wives, some are with their girlfriends, and some, who really like living dangerously, have both. Of course the wive's don't know that but the girlfriend's are very aware.

There are many associates of member's here also. A lot of the big boy's will make an appearance here tonight, it is "the party" for all of South Florida's underworld.

The wive's are afforded great respect by all in attendance,

while the girlfriend's get very little, if any. They are relegated to a side room of sorts, where they will commiserate with each other, the misfortune of being only the girlfriend vs. the wife.

The wive's are chatting happily, some hurling insults at their Mafioso husbands bad eating or bathroom habits, which of course only they can get away with.

But, everyone is having a good time, the booze is flowing and it's nearing midnight.

Outside, the young valet parkers are jumping. They've had to park close to 200 cars, that wouldn't fit in the night clubs rear parking area, across the street at Gulfstream.

They will make over $1,000 each, almost every car is a $20.00 tip, if not a $50.00 or a $100.00 Every mobster will throw them such a lavish stipend. Money is nothing to such men, it's like monopoly money, they have no regard in spending it.

The big boss has made his appearance, like a King annointing his loyal subjects by his presence. As soon as the New Year arrives he will make his exit. He's tired of hob-knobbing and just wants to go home to Susan and sleep.

He has come alone, except of course his button man, Two Ton Tony is with him. At midnight, the balloons descend, hundreds of them, the mobster's and their ladies popping them with their cigarettes, laughing, hugging, kissing and toasting. Many are drunk.

But not Jimmy Blue Eyes, he's had only coffee, espresso, with a little anisette in it. He tells Tony to go get the car, he'll meet him out front in 5 minutes. Tony lumbers off to do his bosses bidding.

Louie has described Blue Eyes to Jimmy and he can definitely see how the name was ascribed to the man, the cold blue eyes his most prominent feature, dead flat icy pools.

Jimmy has a bus pan and he begins to clear the table the instant the fat button man lifts himself away from the table. He has a card, its a greeting card that says, "Wishing you well this New Year." Jimmy casually takes it out of the bus pan and hands it to Blue Eyes, who looks at it and see's its for Two Ton Tony. He looks up confused but its too late. Jimmy has taken the small .22 with silencer out of the bus pan and puts three bullets into Blue Eyes, two in the chest, right into the heart, and one into his temple. It didn't take five seconds total from the moment he handed him the card to now. He has the gun gripped in his hand inside the bus pan and he's walking away.

"Hey! Hey, you! ", Jimmy hears someone calling him but he doesn't turn.

"Hey, boy, you heard me," its some boozy old lady and she's gotten ahold of his sleeve. "We want more champagne, over there," she says, and points to a table and begins to giggle, "Hey, your cute, why don't ya come over and have a drink with us," she slurs.

"I'll grab the champagne and be right back, two minutes, ma'am," he tells her.

"You hurry now, I'll be waiting," she orders and staggers off towards the table she had pointed to.

Jimmy turns into the kitchen. He's jammed the pistol into

his waist and now he drops the bus pan on a rack full of them, peels off the red vest he's had on, grabs his coat and helmet, and goes out the back kitchen door to his bike.

No one has taken any notice, the place is a madhouse and its packed full in there. He kicks the bike to life and pulls out, slowly, down the rear alley out to Hallandale Blvd. and then North on U.S. Highway 1, to Louie's on the Hollywood Circle.

Jimmy Blue Eyes is dead. His button man, Two Ton Tony Gallante is finished, he can't shine shoes for the mob after this. The greeting card found in Blue Eyes hands for Tony, apparently left by the gunman, an insurmountable personal insult.

Happy New Year, Dad, I still miss you, Jimmy thinks.

August 1971

Jimmy is back at Whiteside Construction, he's directing crane's on a 30 story condominium named, The Points of America.

The construction manager knows about the accident and Jimmy has worked for Whiteside for over two years now, excluding his three month hospital stay. He's earned a step up, the crane director makes $11.00 an hour and he doesn't have to bust his ass lugging materials all day.

Tomorrow, Jimmy has to be in court, Robbie Keebler's sentencing is docketed. Marilyn has asked him to come with her and he can't tell her no. It's not his first trip there with her, it hurts every time. He cares little what they do to the drunk driver, it won't bring Mellie or Tina back.

He meets Marilyn in the courthouse lobby at 9:00 a.m. She hugs him. Tears have leaked out of her eye's and she's dabbing at them with a kleenex. Seeing her still hurting makes him mad all over again, his own crushing sorrow reopened.

"Come on, Mari, you want to have coffee upstairs? We have an hour," Jimmy says. He takes her elbow, just as he had taken Mellie's that night he socked up Menard he remembers. Being with Mari it all comes flooding back, every time.

They ride the elevator up to four where the lunch counter is, just like the last time, when Keebler had entered his guilty plea.

He grabs them two coffee's and they sit by the glass window looking down onthe river. Marilyn tells him about Kate and Debbie, how big their getting, that they still get straight A"s in memory of-, she stops and looks down. When she looks back up she turns her face away once again looking out the window, and Jimmy sees the tears pooling in her eyes.

Poor sweet Marilyn, Melissa was her little trooper when John died. Her hurt is too deep, it may never go away.

"Mari, come on," he says taking her hands, "You have Kate and Debbie and they need you, and I need you. You have to go on for all of us. We're going to make it, okay?"

She smiles through her tears and leans over and hugs him, saying, "I knew the very first night I saw you, Jimmy, that Mellie had found her prince, we all love you," and they hug again.

At 10:00 a.m. Robbie Keebler is brought into the courtroom.

He see's Marilyn and quickly looks away. At least the son of a
bitch feels guilty, Jimmy thinks, he can't face us.

The Judge rattles off a litany of legalese that he must
say to the Defendant before he sentences him. Finally the Judge
hands down Keebler's punishment. He will serve one year in the
county jail, with credit for the time he's already served since
his arrest last september, 11 months, and he is further ordered
to complete 5 years of probation. During that time he is not to
possess or consume any alcoholic beverages. He will attend counseling sessions as ordered or directed by his probation supervisor,
he will not operate a motor vehicle except for the purposes of
going to and coming from his lawful place of employment, he will
pay all costs of the court and his supervision during his probation-
ary period. The Court is adjourned.

And that is the price of two lives lost forever.

Jimmy walks Marilyn down the hall towards the elevators.
She is quiet, the relief she had hoped for didn't come. He has his
arm around her shoulders, she feels so small and frail, he aches
for her.

They have come up on a large crowd blocking the hallway,
completely, wall to wall. There are camera men and reporter's
cueing up. They look as if they're awaiting some Hollywood movie
star or someone famous.

At that moment a tall gray haired man, impeccably dressed
and carrying a large briefcase, emerges from the courtroom and into
the hallway. Flash bulb's immediately begin lighting and the crowd

of reporter's all start shouting questions to him at the same
time.

The tall man has his hands up as if to attempt to slow
the torrent of questions he's being peppered with. The young man
with him, also nattily dressed, is fielding some of the query's.

Jimmy is shielding Marilyn from the press of the jostling
crowd and he manages to get Marilyn and himself through the throng.

He hears the gray haired man vowing to appeal.

Several of the reporter's are shouting questions, "How did
the jury come to this verdict?" "What was the Doctors reaction to
the guilty verdict?"

Jimmy hears the shouted questions but he isn't paying
attention, he's only thinking about Marilyn.

In the lobby, he promises to stop by in a few days. The
girl's want to see him, she says. He hugs Marilyn and they part.
He watches the petite woman walk away being swallowed up by the
bustling crowd, all rushing to keep their date with justice.

Justice is only a word, there is no justice for the just
or the unjust.

The crowd of reporter's are trailing after the tall gray
haired man they've followed down into the lobby and are still
hammering away with questions.

Jimmy stops a cameraman and asks him, "What's the commotion
about?"

The cameraman hollers back over his shoulder, "The jury
came back with a guilty verdict of murder against the Doctor."

The doctor? Jimmy see's an elderly bailiff standing by the elevator so he walks over and asks him, "Excuse me, sir, do you know the name of the doctor they're talking about?", he nods in the direction of the mob of reporter's who have followed the tall man out onto the sidewalk in front of the courthouse.

"Yep, they're talking about the rich society man, a Dr. Smart is the name," the bailiff tells him.

Dr. Smart? His first thought is, he's not guilty! Every nurse in that hospital had swore by it.

"What's the tall gray haired man's name? He's the Doctor's lawyer?", Jimmy asks.

"That he is young man and his name is, Joe Baron. The Lord of the Court he's called. He's the best attorney in Broward County," the bailiff replies before stepping onto the elevator that's just arrived.

Robbie Keebler is exiting the elevator, he has all his belongings in a large manilla envelope, and someone, a friend? Maybe his brother, they look similar, has come to pick him up.

Jimmy is about to walk away but he hears the guy Keebler's with say, "Got you a cold one in the truck little brother, a whole case. I know you dreamin about one," and he laugh's and claps Keebler on the back.

"Goddamn right, Jesse! Fuckin' county jail, a year feels like five," Keebler says back to the guy with him.

The one year sentence is served, fulfilled, by the 11 months Keebler has served in waiting for sentencing.

Jimmy is in a black -coal black- mood. He's had to see the

unending hurt in Marilyn's eyes, not just today but everyday
he goes to see her. It rips open his own terrible sorrow like a
scabbed wound. But he must go to her anyway, she needs him.

He gets on his motorcycle, its parked right in front in
an area specifically designated for that. He watches Keebler and
the other guy cross the street and get into a black pick-up truck.
It's on stacks, elevated, just like the truck that...

He follows it South on U.S. Highway 1. Beer cans are being
tossed into the bed of the truck, two, then four, then six as the
truck winds its way through lunch hour traffic.

When the truck reaches State Road 84's intersection with
U.S. Highway 1, the truck hops a curb right past a corner and
turns into a parking lot there.

Jimmy rides past looking at the businesses. There's a tire
store with several cars awaiting service out front, a travel agency,
and, Freddie's Anchor Bar, a tiny hole in the wall establishment.
It's location just outside the Ft. Lauderdale city limits, at
the entrance to Port Everglades, enabled the owner to procure a
full liquor license cheaply.

Jimmy parks the bike and goes in. The two occupants from
the truck are shooting pool and neither notices him, Jimmy walks
right by Keebler and looks him dead in the eyes-, nothing, Keebler
doesn't recognize him. He had always seen Marilyn in the courtroom,
but he never took notice of Jimmy.

The small bar is near empty, its early in the day. Jimmy
orders a beer and picks up a newspaper that's lying there on the

counter and begins leafing through it, feigning search of the classified Help Wanted ads.

He and the bartender have exchanged opinions on the war, the job market, women, everything.

It's been close to two hours and Jimmy still has the same untouched beer in front of him. The barkeep thinks it odd, but hell the place is empty, its not like the guy is keeping a spending customer from sitting.

The two brothers, Jimmy has ascertained that much, are no longer playing pool, their to busy drinking. Both are pretty drunk, getting loud and slightly obnoxious.

The bartender has finally had enough and tells them that's it, no more booze, they've had enough and he'd like them to leave.

The man with Keebler walks up close to the old barkeep and says, "Fuck you, old timer! I'll kick your ass and take all of it. What are you gonna do?"

Robbie is telling his brother to forget it, let's go, but Jesse doesn't forget it, he spits at the bartender, swaying drunkenly.

He looks at Jimmy and says, "What the fuck you lookin at, punk? You want to try me?"

Jimmy is off the bar stool in a flash! He hits Jesse four times before Jesse can even begin to scream. He's flattened his nose and broken his jaw. It looks as if he has a small baseball squirreled away in his cheek.

Robbie tries to hit Jimmy with a pool cue stick. As soon as Robbie made his swing, Jimmy side stepped it easily, and he's on Robbie like a rabid dog. He beat him for five minutes straight, not letting him collapse on the floor, he backed him against the wall and laid it on viciously.

Jesse was to fearful to try to stop it, he couldn't even yell because of his jaw. It was finally the old barkeep who snapped Jimmy out of his black rage and got him to stop the brutal beating.

"I gotta call the cops! You may want to leave," the barkeep says, he too is afraid of Jimmy. No way that guy is re- covering from that savage attack, he thinks. The guy is beaten horribly, its the worst the old guy has seen, and he's seen a lot of them in his time tending bar.

"I'm not going anywhere, call them," Jimmy tells the bartender, and he walks over towards Jesse. But Jesse doesn't want no part of it and runs out the back door exit, leaving his brother right there.

CHAPTER FIFTEEN

December 1971 - July 1972

"There must be some kind of way out of here,

said the Joker to the Thief."

All Along The Watchtower/ Jimi Hendrix

The blue state prison bus slowly rocked its way across the old wooden bridge leading to the Florida State Prison, "The Rock", the familiar moniker to both prisoner and guard alike.

The prison houses over 3,000 convicts, 2,500 on the line, (Prison parlance for General Population), and 500 plus in the infamous East Unit. Of the 500, there are a 135 condemned who await a seat in "Old Sparky", Florida's electric chair. The remainder are left to rot, some in perpetuity, designated as unmanageable by the Administration.

There are 12 other prison's throughout the state, all housing dangerous and violent criminals. Raiford, "The Rock", is the end of that line, and is usually reserved for prisoner's who've run afoul of the Administration in other prisons.

Convict's who are frequent disciplinary problems, or exhibit unruly and disruptive behavior, have an unusually high number of assaults on other inmates, or any type of threat to staff, are sent to Raiford.

Once here, if the unacceptable behavior continues, you assault guards or murder your fellow convicts, you earn your own private cage in the East Unit.

Threat of placement there does not deter the overwhelming atmosphere of violence at The Rock, the convict's on the line don't have the luxury of options. The only way a prisoner can walk the line is he must have the respect of the other convicts, and the only thing respected is the immediate and instantaneous homicidal retaliation to any challenge. Any challenge, no matter how small or trivial.

A mere verbal slight, reaching over you or behind you, any approach without first procuring consent, or cutting ahead of you in line, any line. Prison is lines, for everything, food, showers, laundry, and the prison store, where the inmate's can buy cigarettes and miscellaneous. Everything is a line.

Any disrespect on any level, whether real, perceived or imagined, must be addressed, right then on the spot. You cannot retreat or back down, ever, not one inch. It is truly a jungle where only the very strongest survive. You must be a lion, anything else is failure, and failure here is death, or a fate even worse.

The Rock is a brutal, violent prison. Once here, you alone are responsible for your own safety, none will be provided.

Any guard will tell you, "If you are afraid of being fucked, better sleep with your thumb up your ass," and then he'll walk away laughing.

There are three youthful offender prisons in Florida for persons under 25 years of age. One in Gadsen County, one in Desoto County, and one in Sumter County. The first two have young offender's who in all likelihood will be released back to society.

The last, Sumter, houses young murderers whose offense has aggravating circumstances, such as rape, or extremely callous and heinous characteristics as part of the act of murder. Most of these young offenders will not be released back into society, ever. Their crimes so brutal they are not entitled to a second chance, once was enough.

No one should mistakenly interpret the "youthful offender"

designation as the mere missteps of youth inherent to all as part of the maturation process. These offender's are vicious killers without remorse.

They are spared a seat in "Old Sparky" only because of their age, it being deemed cruel to execute minor aged persons. It is a poor excuse, most do not merit that consideration, ask their victim's.

The blue bus is pulling up to the West gate of The Rock. It is Friday morning. Every Friday morning this same bus arrives bearing new prisoners, fresh meat for the meat grinder that this particular institution is.

Dr. Henried Wright Smart is prisoner #021120, a lifer, never mind that it is his first offense of any kind. In his first experience on this side of the criminal justice machinery, a system he supported and believed in as a necessary function of a civilized society, he has short cut the normal journey to The Rock.

He is part of the lucky, or unlucky, who didn't get an assignment to one of the other 9 adult facilities first, and then "earned" their way here by bad conduct or escape threat.

Henry has refused to admit his guilt, a sign of defiance to the corrections intake screeners. Thus Henry was assigned here at his initial classification a few weeks before, during the the reception medical center intake procedure.

He is 49 years old, he has a life sentence for murder, why send him South to a less severe or violent facility than the end stage Rock?

He's just more scum to classification officer Whitehead,
who's family has worked and virtually ran the North Florida corrections facilities for generations.

To keep a racial balance they need white convict's at
Raiford. They can't have too many of one race. Even though its
65% black, out of the remaining 35%, a quarter of them are Hispanic.

Generations long nepotism is still alive and functioning
perfectly in the Florida Department of Corrections.

The esteemed classification officer, Whitehead, has
determined that Raiford, The Rock, is the proper facility to
house inmate Smart for the rest of his natural life. Or, until he
is killed by one of his fellow convicts, or kills one in his own
defense. Then he'll get his own personal cage in the East Unit,
unless of course he gets to "ride the lightening", a seat in
"Old Sparky".

Ha, ha, ha, yep, classification officer Whitehead finds
it pretty dern funny. High falutin big shot society Doctor gonna
be eatin slop with the nigra's, probably one of them big bucks
may take a shine to the old doctor, take him for a wife! Ha, ha, ha-
another hard days work done and society is still safe, thanks to
classification officer Whitehead.

There are a 1,000 convict's on the yard watching the bus
disgorge the 28 new prisoners, 19 blacks, 7 whites and 2 Cubans,
all "new cocks", the familiar moniker all new men are known as.

The 1,000 convict's start hooting and hollering at the
"new cocks", "Hey, purty young thang, you gonna be mine tonight,"
or, "Jes cause you old don't mean a nigga won't fuck you," and more.

The verbal barrage has a purpose, to see which of the new men looks frightened.

The 28 men pick up their meager belongings and the gate to the yard, with the milling throng, pops open as they are lead out into it by one disinterested guard.

The "new cocks" walk through the crowd to their cell block assignments. The scared men are being jostled, threatened, propositioned and maybe even molested in route.

Some have had their personal property ripped out of their hands, and watched helplessly as it is handed back, hand over hand, into the crowd until it disappears.

There are actually fights breaking out amongst the convict's to settle the issue of who will have the first turn at some particular young, soft looking prisoner. It's serious, its not idle posturing at all, they're establishing position.

And, its not all one sided either. There is the rare instance when perhaps an article is snatched from one of the new cock's, only this particular individual may not be someone you'd want to anger, not at all. Though the prisoner in question may not have uttered one word, he is afforded room, a personal space not to be violated. With one look he has conveyed lethal, mortal danger. Any article taken from such a man is given back immediately with profuse apologies. And that may end it, but maybe not.

Killer's come in all shapes and sizes, same with cowards. Big tattooed barrel chested toughs will be getting sodomized that night, while some skinny, baby faced youngster is killing any challenger one cell away.

Nothing is as it seems. Its an upside down, topsy turvy world.

Of the 28 men who arrived that morning on the bus that delivered Henry, only 11 are still on the line after 30 days. Four are transvestite homosexuals and seven are equals, peers. Only two of the seven are white and only one is Cuban. The winnowing process is by fire, no faint of heart need apply.

Henry is one of the two whites who awakens with the cell doors popping open on D floor, in January 1972. He is in a six-man cell, two other whites and three Cuban's are his cellmates.

It is breakfast in 10 minutes. Oatmeal, powdered milk, watery coffee and an orange. One positive about doing time in Florida is that you get a lot of oranges, every day.

Henry isn't going to breakfast. He can't eat the slop for one, and for two, he's had some of his teeth knocked out. Quite a few at that.

He put up a good fight for a slightly built 160 lbs., 6', 49 year old man. He fought a big, muscular black named, Junior.

Henry had just purchased two donuts and a coffee at the prisoner's store. As he was stirring the sugar into his coffee, the donuts were sitting on the small counter. Junior had walked up and grabbed the donuts, stuffing one into his mouth. Henry just looked at him, but Junior said, "Fuck you, cracker, I'll take your ass bitch," and made a move like he was going to backhand the old doctor.

Well, the coffee from the prison store is strong, not like

the chow hall stuff, and- its very hot. Henry dashed the scalding coffee into Junior's face and began hammering away at the big buck, ineffectively though.

As soon as Junior could open his eyes, he smashed a ham sized fist into Henry's mouth and teeth went flying. A few more of the powerful blows and Henry was a bloody mess. Two of Junior's homey's stopped him, Henry had had enough.

The one other white prisoner who arrived with Henry, that was still on the yard, Scotty Fair, picked up his old cellmate and half carried and half walked him back to the cell saying, "Well, you shore showed that sumbitch," and laughed that slow, sardonic laugh that he had.

Scotty liked the old guy, even old Doc's insisting he was innocent didn't bother him. Scotty would yes him to death, "Yea Doc, we all is, hell, I ain't shot that deputy. It was a sumbitch looked just like me," he'd say and issue that mirthful laugh.

Since that morning, Doc sits with Scotty in the chow hall. Doc had to take that first step himself, but now, anybody fuck's with Doc and Scotty will beat them half to death.

Scotty Fair is one of the toughest white men in The Rock. He's got a one punch knock out with either hand. He's laid out a pile already, whites, blacks and Cubans, armed with knives or not. One crazy Cuban named, Wahillo, had a knife in each hand, it didn't matter.

The boxing team is trying to get Scotty to fight for The Rock when The Rock fights teams from the other prisons. Sometimes even pro's from the outside come in and there's some very competitive bout's staged. Scotty's thought about it, he might, but he don't cotton to no blacks and a team with blacks and him on it don't seem like a good idea.

Scotty is an armed robber. He shot a Clewiston Sheriff's deputy while making his getaway from a pawn shop stick-up.

Henry is a murderer. Guilty or not, it doesn't matter, that's what he is in this community.

There are no white rapists on The Rock, any that are are punks and used for deviate sex by the killers who like that perverse shit.

Scotty ain't with it, but he jokes old Doc to death about Doc needing to get one, a punk, for his self. Ha, ha, since he's got life may as well get one, marry one, buy a two man cell on J floor and live happily ever after. Ha, ha, ha.

Henry has been here almost six weeks. He hasn't received any mail except from his attorney, Joe Baron. He's written to Nicole but so far nothing. He can't understand it.

The estate sold for six million. Baron has placed that money, with all the rest of Henry's assets, stocks, bonds, personal savings accounts, into a dividend paying retirement account, with Shearson- Lehman Brothers that is 100% safe. Henry has directed Baron to have the dividend payments deposited directly into Nicole's personal cash account.

Baron has filed the direct appeal to the Fourth District Court of Appeals in West Palm Beach and has petitioned for a supercede's bond to be set pending the appeal. Still, Henry waits.

"Hey, Doc, c'mon, me and you," it's Scotty and he's shadow boxing, acting like he expects Doc to get up and spar with him.

Doc laugh's, and to Scotty's surprise, he jumps off of his bunk and clumsily throws a few uncoordinated blows, saying, "Why, if I were a little younger, I'd show you a thing or two. I used to be quite the pugilist in my college days."

Scotty looks confused, "A what? What the hell is a pug-pugh? That some fancy doctor shit?", he asks, and throws a few very soft body taps at Henry, which he easily deflects and actually starts bobbing and weaving like he really knows what he's doing. It looks comical and Scotty starts laughing.

"Doc, you gotta set your feet right to start with, here," he shows Doc how to stand, left foot out front, right about a step and a half back, then says, "You got your left hand and shoulder out front but your leaning back on the right foot. Now, don't that feel better? You use your left to feel out your opponent, but your coiled and ready to go," Scotty says, and then shows, Doc. Doc is always amazed that such a big brawler like Scotty can move so cat quick.

"Listen, it all looks and sounds great, but I want to know how to do that knock-out trick with either hand, can you show me that?", Doc asks, smiling.

"I could show you," Scotty says all serious, "But then I'd have to kill you," and laughs that slow laugh as he throws a couple more soft, slow powder puffs that Doc easily deflects.

Well, Doc thinks, I have one friend in the world at least, it could be worse.

June/ July 1972

Lisa and Gordon have been married two years today. It's June 2nd, their anniversary. Gordon is as handsome as he was the first time she literally ran into him on the beach in Daytona, over four years ago.

It took a full year and numerous surgeries before Gordon was made whole again. If it weren't for the world class doctors and facilities of the Bethesda Naval Hospital, he may not have recovered so spectacularly, a slight limp the only hint of his ever being injured.

With the exception of his fused lumbar vertebra, all his broken bones have fully healed either by self regeneration or bone graft.

His aviating days are over, they came to an abrupt end the night a Chinese made surface to air missile, fired by the N.V.A as his squadron attacked their division, collided into his aircraft.

They had thrown up everything they had in defense of the massed ground troops but it had not been enough, the division was destroyed by the Naval air attack.

Germ came to see him in Japan before he shipped state-side. The hardened veteran wept in relief. He was sure that he was either dead or worse, captured. It was widely believed that Naval aviators were treated especially cruel, physically tortured by their captors.

The story of his rescue by Army Rangers inside North Vietnam was nothing short of a miracle. With Gordon's injuries he may have perished in route to an N.V.A prison camp or shortly after arrival.

They hugged and then Germ saluted him, saying, "I'll see you state-side." Fourteen days after Germ said those words, his F-4 Phantom fighter was shot down over North Vietnam. He is listed as M.I.A, still.

Gordon and Lisa are both attending the University of Florida Law School. He is one semester away from recieving his degree and then the bar exam, Lisa has two years to go.

They have a small apartment in Gainesville but they spend every hour they can over in Cocoa Beach, recreating those heavenly but oh so brief days before he sailed away. Without God's divine intervention, in of all things a soldier called G.I. Joe, he may never have returned, Lisa is certain.

With Germ's fate as an exclamation point to just that, he cannot argue with her. They live every day like it is a gift, which it most certainly is, not to be squandered or taken for granted.

"Do you love me more now than you did before? Or are you just making sure everything is still working?", Lisa asks teasingly. They have been in bed all morning, both savoring one another. Lisa is a stunning beauty, the 18 year old girl is now a 22 year old woman. Gordon can look at her endlessly without tiring of the effect she has in him.

"Well, I don't know, Miss, would you say everything is ship-shape with your old sailor?", Gordon teases right back. Lisa laughs and impishly takes her hand and waffles it, indicating a so-so approval before leaping from their bed before he can grab her.

She loves teasing him. Even though Gordon is an ardent, excellent lover, it doesn't hurt to keep him sharp, she muses. He is now chasing her around the bed with her laughing wickedly as he says, "You are so bad! I'm going to spank you, young lady."

"Oh! That sounds like fun! Maybe I'll even let you catch me," she says, and actually almost lets him grab her before sprinting away again.

By now Gordon is in avid pursuit and he easily catches her. As she squeals in mock terror, they both collapse to the floor, slightly winded by the chase.

The doorbell rings. Gordon puts on a pair of shorts and goes to see who has come, while Lisa herself dons shorts and a t-shirt. She thinks, who came without calling?

She goes out into the living room and sees, Jill.

"Hi, sweetheart! What brings you to our little den of iniquity?", she asks, as she hugs her younger sister.

"Hi, Lisa. Hello, Gordon," Jill says, and then continues, "I'm going home this afternoon and I thought I'd stop by now. Are you going over to Cocoa later?", she asks.

"Well, yes, we're going over tonight and we'll be staying with Gordon's parents for the week," Lisa says.

She knows Jill has something on her mind and she wonders what it is. She looks at Gordon and he understands her look, she wants to speak with Jill alone.

"I'm going to the store, you all need anything?", Gordon asks by way of taking his leave.

"No, I'm fine, thank you," Jill says, as Lisa shakes her head, no.

When Gordon leaves, Lisa takes Jill's hands and sits her down on the couch. "Do you want to talk? What's going on, Jill? Something is weighing on your mind so lets have it," Lisa insists.

"It's Nicole, Lisa. I'm going to see her tonight. I don't know what to say to her, her father is, uh-, she hasn't written to him and she doesn't intend to go see him, ever," Jill tells Lisa. Hmmm, that is a sticky subject, Lisa thinks.

"Well, you can't push her in any direction, Jill, that's her decision to make. Just stand by her with whatever she decides," Lisa advises.

There's more, Lisa can tell. "Um, what else? There's something else, you can't fool me, Jill," Lisa says.

"It's Jimmy Carosa, Lisa. It was in the newspaper down there." By down there, she means home, Ft. Lauderdale.

Jimmy Carosa? The newspaper?

"What was in the newspaper, Jill?", Lisa asks, she's confused.

"He was convicted of attempted murder. He beat some poor guy half to death at a bar," Jill says, and sighs knowingly. She still remembers the vicious attack on Rex Russel at school that day, over 5 years ago.

"Jill, Jill honey, there is nothing you can do about that. He wasn't who you thought he was, what we all thought he was. Daddy was right, he had sides of himself that he concealed very well, and no one knew anything about that Jimmy," Lisa imparts wisely to her younger sister.

Jill looks ashen, pale. How could she have been so wrong about him? These doubts still plague her so assuredly that she has not, to this day, had anything more than a casual relationship with anyone.

Lisa is very aware of Jill's fragile psyche in that regard and she has an intense dislike of James Carosa for being the cause of it. Damn, him! Maybe he'll go to jail for a long time, where he belongs, Lisa thinks.

"I'm going to go see him, Lisa. I have to," Jill tells her.

"What?! You will do no such thing, Jill! No way! Why? Why would you want to go see that, that-," Lisa is sputtering, she is incensed.

"I have to know, that's why!", Jill replies testily. She will not be told what she will or won't do, she is no longer a child.

"Know what? That he made a fool of you? Of our whole family? We accepted him as one of us, but he was never one of us and never can be, grow up!", Lisa is nearly shouting.

These harsh truths effect Jill almost as a physical assault, as if she had been slapped. She begins to cry. Lisa feels terrible, she immediately tries to hug Jill, saying, "I'm sorry. I'm so sorry, please forgive me, Jill. He hurt you and for that I hate him." Jill has shied away from Lisa and that makes her feel worse still.

"Jill, honey, please don't," Lisa says very softly. Jill

relents, falling into Lisa's arms she begins sobbing harder and Lisa rocks her little sister speaking softly, soothingly. She hates Jimmy all over again, even worse, for hurting Jill. She hopes he goes to jail forever!

Not quite. The jury found James Carosa guilty of attempted murder for Robbie's brutal beating, and aggravated assault for the broken jaw inflicted on, Jesse. He was sentenced to 10 years and 5 years, respectively. The sentences were to run concurrently which means his total obligation is 10 years.

Robbie Keebler has suffered brain damage, he's a mumbling, slobbering idiot now. Jimmy feels no remorse whatsoever. It is partly that lack of remorse that he exhibited to the jury, when he took the stand in his own defense, that netted him the dual convictions.

The jury had considered Robbie's conduct in consuming alcohol in violation of his probation, but his mild aggression towards the barkeep and James at the pub did not justify such a vicious response.

The jury did not hear of the D.W.I accident that resulted in Melissa and Tina's deaths, in relation to these present proceedings.

Jimmy Carosa is prisoner #028989. He is 20 years old, a first time youthful offender.

However, they need white prisoner's at Sumter, and the wise sage intake screeners decide, why not? A young tough like this inmate will be good for some lively action at the boiling cauldron of hate that Sumter is, and so, he is classified and designated to that facility. He is one of 115 white prisoners at the 1,000 bed prison. If Raiford is a meat grinder, this is an abattoir.

CHAPTER SIXTEEN

October 1972 - December 1973

"There are many here among us

who feel that life is but a joke."

All Along The Watchtower/ Jimi Hendrix

The prison van has 9 occupants ranging in age from 16 to 22 years old. Only two have release dates in this, the 20th century. James Carosa is one of the two.

The small van is taking its human cargo to Sumter Correctional Institution, a horrific, mismanaged, out of control killing ground. It's that simple.

You won't read that in its policy statement. There you'll read an authorization to provide a separate, specific, age-orientated confinement facility to house persons under 25 years of age, who have committed serious crimes and have lengthy terms of imprisonment to serve.

It is determined that such offenders are more amenable to rehabilitation and it would be detrimental to house these youth's with older incorrigible criminals.

In some far fetched theory, these poor, misguided, abused youngsters who have been mistreated for most of their short lives, may respond to positive corrective measures such as counseling, psychological re-orientation and drug abuse classes.

In practice, in reality, that can all be thrown right out the window. Of the 1,000 prisoner's here, 866 have killed another human being, either premeditatedly with malice aforethought, or during the commission of another crime where the murder was the end result. Of the 866, over 600 have a sexual offense as the primary motive of the criminal episode.

Many of the victim's were small children, such as 3 year old, William Dooley, and 6 year old Rory Pike, sodomized

and strangled by a 15 year old- youth? Other's were the elderly-
Ester James, 86 years old, Thea Boone, 79 years old, and her 82
year old sister, Maude Black, were raped, beaten and left to burn
alive in the fire at their home that the - youthful?? 19 year old
assailant hoped would conceal his crimes.

The list of atrocities goes on and on, ad nauseam.

The 1,000 prisoner's are 80% black, 12% white and 8% Cuban.
Of the 115 white prisoner's, 60 are housed in a protective custody
unit and 30 of the remaining 55 are forced homosexuals. The 25
that are left are totally, without question stubborn survivors.
They live in a terrifying, bizarre, nightmare come to life, where
each and every morning is a challenge to live and survive that
one seemingly endless day, only to have to face the same the next
morning, and the next, and the next...

Today will be different, today 3 will be dead by noon,
but not from the 25, no- From the 722 who reside there in open
population, there are 78 black prisoner's in the protective custody
unit also.

Jimmy arrived yesterday and today he has killed Alfonso
Jordan and Mikel Suggs. He walked right up and stabbed Alfonso in
the neck and chest and then chased Mikel 50 feet before plunging
the fatal blows into his abdomen.

The boy who arrived with him yesterday, 18 year old Nelson
Brock, a 120 lbs. on a 5'10" frame making him look like a scare-
crow, has killed Ulysees Norton.

These two and one other, Danny Skidmore are awaiting a
transfer van to Raiford's East Unit. Skidmore supplied the knives

and helped with the stabbings. He hit Sammy Tremont 4 times in
the neck and chest with his knife. Sammy is clinging to life at
a nearby local hospital, (He doesn't make it. He dies at 3:05 p.m.
that afternoon).

Skidmore is serving 12 years for burglary, Jimmy has the
10 years for the attempted murder and aggravated battery, and Nelson
has 16 years for cat burglary. Cat burglary is distinguished by
the fact that the break in occur's while the occupants who reside
there are home. Nelson was thieving while the occupants were
sleeping. Its a dangerous and serious crime, vs. burglary of
empty homes or businesses, hence the 16 years.

They are here because this fine correctional institution
hasn't enough white prisoners, that is the only reason. The geniuses
at the reception center picked these three unfortunate's to be
sent here to address that need. Never mind that the only criteria
they qualify in is age. Skidmore arrived last week and he was
beaten senseless and awoke in the hospital. He demanded to be put
back in population, he would not serve his time in the protective
custody unit. Last night the three young men, by absolute necessity,
hatched today's plan.

When Nelson was approached by a group of thugs and told
to choose a man, (for deviate sex), he chose none. He was beaten
up, in turn, by the group, and they promised to be back today so
he could choose. The same happened with Jimmy, although Jimmy put
up a much better account of himself and the in turn plan had to be
abandoned, and he was attacked and beaten by the whole group at once.

Today, just before any choosing or talking, or anything,

Jimmy, Nelson and Skidmore attacked and killed four of the group, tsk, tsk, tsk.

Upon arrival at Raiford's East Unit, the three were thrown into bare concrete cells with no mattresses, sheets or blankets. They also had no clothing except the one pair of boxer shorts they had worn on the drive up from Sumter.

There they were kept, in near total deprivation of everything, except food and water, for 95 days.

The authorities in Sumter County declined to file criminal charges, none of the deceased had family interested in pressing the State Attorney's office to prosecute.

Some people, if you can even classify them as such, are so vile and so evil, even a mother feels nothing but revulsion. Apparently the four deceased were such. Not one had a single human being who would speak out for their silenced voice.

When God asked Lot to produce just one man, who was not corrupt, to save Sodom and Gommorah, he could not. There is the precedent.

On the 96th day, Jimmy, Nelson and Skidmore were released to the main line, general population, where it would recommence one final and last time.

After parking their state-issued clothing and bedding in their cells on G floor, the three head out to the yard.

Before they can exit the cell block, two stout looking toughs nod to the three youngsters, and the older one asks, "You all them boys from Sumter they had over in the unit?"

Jimmy looks at Skid and Nelson and nod's, yes, saying, "Yea, why?"

The two older con's smile and the one who asked the first question, says, "Take it easy, partner- we's on the same side. I'm Chuck, and this here's my brother, Calvin."

He offers his hand and Jimmy shakes first, and then they all do, introducing themselves.

Chuck says, "Here, you boys going to need these-" He's got two steel knives that look like bayonets, and a pair of brass knuckles.

Jimmy hesitates but Chuck laughs and says, "You ain't going to owe nothin- you got that comin, take em."

"Okay- thanks," Jimmy says. Nelson and Skid take the knives and Jimmy takes the knucks and puts them on his hands, he's ready.

They know there's unfinished business to attend to, and no time like the present. They felt the stares and tension directed at the three of them. There wasn't no way around it but to face it head on and finish it.

In mere minutes, a stout muscle bound black, who had the moniker of Popsicle, approached Jimmy with two of his homey's, Ice Water and Showdown.

"You the cracker kilt my little cousin, Ulysees?", Popsicle seethed.

"No, it was him," Jimmy said pointing at Nelson. This caught Popsicle off guard, and that was just too bad for him because Jimmy tore his ass up, he was knocking pieces , literally, off his face with the brass knuckles, steel knuckles actually, and he's shredding Popsicle with them.

Showdown and Ice Water wanted to jump in but Nelson and Skid were armed and ready, and they knew it. Any move by either of them and its dying time, for a certainty they wouldn't all be walking away.

There were a couple of hundred convicts circled around cheering on both. There wasn't any favoritism, black or white, the best man wins, simple. And, anything goes, pipes, knives, knucks. No such thing as dirty fighting in prison, as long as its heads up, one on one.

Showdown kept asking Popsicle, "You done? You wanna stop?" Finally, Popsicle had enough.

"All right, that's it! That's it!", Showdown hollered, and Jimmy quit.

Ice and Showdown grabbed Popsicle and steered him away. There was some grumbling but nobody was going to take up the fight, for Popsicle or no one. A man is his own man, period.

"Excuse me, young man, are you-?", Henry says, but he can't recall the name. "Fractured cranium, I removed 41 bone fragments from you cerebellum," Henry finishes.

Holy shit! "Dr. Smart! Son of a bitch! Dr. Smart! I heard about you and I couldn't believe it, your not guilty! Why are you still here?", Jimmy is saying, with torrents of emotion spilling out of him, pent up anger, fear and hate. Every emotion inside of a human being is flooding out all at once.

Doc is staring at him, one tear is slowly leaking out of his left eye and he hurriedly wipes it away.

"What is your name, son? er- uh, excuse me-," Dr. Smart asks. He hadn't meant to call him, "son". In this looney bin it could be taken as an insult.

"Jimmy, James Carosa, Dr. Smart. How are you, sir?" Jimmy asks. He still can't believe it, why is he here?, Jimmy wonders.

Henry was overcome emotionally by Jimmy's statement, "You're not guilty, why are you here?", indeed.

"James, this is Scotty Fair, a good man and my friend," Henry introduces them.

"Hello, Scotty," Jimmy says and sticks out his hand and they shake, the big guy saying, "Well, you shore did show that sum bitch, little fellar. Damn right you did," Scotty is smiling and issuing that slow laugh.

"This is Skid, and this is Nelson, all 100 lbs. of him pure, mean killer," Jimmy says and laughs.

They shake all around and Henry asks, "Where is your cell assignment? What floor?"

"We're on G floor, all of us," Jimmy tells him.

"Well, Scotty, lets see the officer and get these boys, uh- men, moved, now if we can?" Henry asks the big man.

"Shore, Doc. Ask them if they prefer a yard view or the flat top back dock view?", Scotty answers, but he's smiling and laughing that slow laugh.

These three are mere boys, the youngest convicts here most likely. But that doesn't mean much, all three will kill if anybody, anyone, even thinks about getting out of line. They've already done so, it was all over the yard at The Rock an hour after they got out of the van from Sumter.

The bad part, the down side to this, is that the three young men would never again be the young, care-free youths that had come in the front door of the Florida Department of Corrections. They were forever changed, and not for the better. They could live in this jungle, this parallel upside down nightmare world, yes, but can they now return to and live in the real world?

Maybe, they were young and you could hope, but it is highly unlikely. They are different animals today than they had been just a few short months ago.

The human psyche is a fragile entity. It can bend without breaking, it can be knocked full of holes and heal, the holes almost fully restored, almost. The bend will never return exactly to the way it was before being bent, close, but not exact.

A person cannot face death, nor a horrific, degrading near death, and completely recover. No one can. The emotions asscoiated with, or unleashed by, such experiences, cannot simply be put back whence they came, all neat and tidy as if they had never been loosed. When someone has crossed over the invisible line to madness, no matter how brief, can they ever return back to the safe side of that invisible line?, without the memory haunting them forever? The only answer is, maybe, its possible, but the finished product may not be what was hoped for.

Henry still uses the proper form of address in talking to

or describing one to another of the various prison officials.
It is the officer vs. the hack in this instance, and the officer,
Mr. Griffiths, has no problem moving the three men over to D floor
from G. There's always room for white convicts in The Rock, its
better than a two to one ratio.

Henry can't get enough of the young James. It takes him
back to his former self, former life, the master surgeon doing
the most intricate and delicate procedures.

"Dr. Smart, have you seen your, uh, family? Didn't you
have a daughter? Nicole, right?", Jimmy asks. Why would he not
have familial support? He's innocent!

"Well, no James, I haven't, not even a letter. I don't
understand it, Nicole knows I loved her mother, Victoria, and
that I-," Here Henry sighs deeply, the sound is so full of despair
that Jimmy actually flinches.

"How could I have harmed the woman I loved?, adored. Since
the first time I looked upon her, I was smitten, bewitched by her
loveliness," he says. Henry is looking off wistfully, into an
image only he can see.

Every gossipy nurse at Broward General Medical Center
had been positive beyond any doubt, Dr. Smart was innocent. But
if so, how could he be in here?

"Dr. Smart, what's that lawyer's name? Is he doing
anything about you, uh-, you being here?", Jimmy asks.

"Baron, James, Joe Baron, the Lord of the Court, the best
attorney in Broward County," Henry answers with a sardonic laugh.
"He's filed an appeal and petitioned for a bail pending a ruling,
but so far, nothing. The bails been denied several times already

due to the probability of my appeal being denied," Henry says, and again emits that bitter laugh.

"Do you know, Dr. Smart, that every nurse at the hospital said you were innocent, every single one, and believe me you'll never see a group of gossips as bad as they are," Jimmy tells him. He's trying valiantly to infuse some hope in the old doctor.

"Well, James, I could've used a few of them on my jury," Henry says with good humor.

Jimmy nods, yes. He can see that this place, a tough, brutal prison, has eroded much of the Doctor's faith and belief in justice, in goods triumph over evil.

The good Doctor hasn't quit by no means, but his confidence in the system, the American judicial system of truth, fairness and ones day in court, the proper functioning of such that he believed in his entire life, is gone. He is innocent, yet he is here, how can it not be broken?

Henry has a bridge, false teeth, now. Custom made by a prisoner who works in the dental lab. They fit and work quite adequately. He is still adjusting to eating with them but at least he can eat.

And tonight, to celebrate the young trios arrival, that's what they do. Henry is buying a steak and french fry dinner for all. It's $3.00 each at the outdoor patio restaurant that also serves bacon and eggs, chicken wings and hamburgers. Just like the streets, almost.

It's January 1973, the war in Vietnam is concluding. The peace accords have been reviewed and signed by all parties. Its over, its finally over! There are 2,000 M.I.A's, but that number won't grow. Amen.

Just before Christmas, as another year is coming to a close, Jimmy is summoned to visitation. Nettie and Christy made the trek last summer and although Jimmy was glad to see them, his little Mom looked so old and frail, he made them promise not to do it again, and he meant it.

"We'll write, Ma. I don't like you two on the road by your-selves. I'm okay here, you don't have to worry, all right?", Jimmy had instructed.

Who could this be?, he wondered. He was always worrying it'd be the cops for something in his past, you never knew.

He goes through the strip search and emerges into the visiting room looking to see who... its Joseph!

"My God, Joe! Holy shit!", Jimmy says. The two brothers hug and remain that way for long minutes, both wiping their eyes furiously trying not to spill the tears that are there.

Jimmy finally says, "Come on, lets sit down. How's Ma and Christy?"

"They're fine, Gatz. You should let Ma come, she wants to see you, even here. She doesn't care, you're her baby," Joseph says, and then pinches Jimmy's cheek like his Dad used to.

"I write her, Joe. Ma writes me every week. I don't have much to say, you know? Being here, I let her down, Christy too, they needed me," Jimmy says.

"Forget it, Gatz, you did what you had to. According to Ma, you probably saved, Marilyn?, Marilyn's life. Ma said Mellie was an angel, and the baby a little doll, so-, I'm sorry, Jimmy, I can't even imagine the, uh-," Joseph says shaking his head.

"Yea well, even though I know everyday that that punk is shitting his pants and someones got to wipe his ass for him, it don't change-," Jimmy is saying, but stops. He's shaking his head as if to shake all those thoughts out. The anger is right back, all over again, like its been three days instead of three years.

Joseph can see it plain as day, he knows its far from over for Jimmy, he's not okay.

Just to change the subject, because he's already looked into the, -uh, trouble at Sumter, he's still curious so he asks, "What happened at the other place, Jimmy?"

"Nothing! Not a fuckin thing, Joe! So don't ask," Jimmy bites back.

Whoa!! Joseph thinks, Jimmy's still pissed about it, wow!

"Hey! Don't get mad at me, Jimmy! I'm on your side, remember? Shit!", Joseph comes right back.

"You killed two guys, I mean-, that ain't nothing, you son of a bitch," Joseph says, with a touch of amusement in his voice.

When Jimmy looks at Joseph he's smiling, smiling proudly to boot! Jimmy smiles now too. It's Joe, he has to remind himself, they're as close as two brothers can be.

Jimmy says, "Yea, Joe, fuck them two animals! Fuck their

mama's for having some garbage like that!"

Joseph laughs, proudly again. His younger brother did a good deed, a positive, he won't even attempt to diminish that truth.

"Listen, the world is full of bad people, Jimmy. The cops get some, but not all of them, so- you just gave them a little help," Joseph says, and shrugs his shoulders.

Jimmy laughs. Of course he understands, its Joe for Christs sake, he has to keep reminding himself.

It's been seven years since they last saw each other, Dad was still- with them, and Jimmy was in high school.

They talked for another two hours, about everything, Joseph casually mentioning that he'd went by and saw, Louie. Joseph looked at Jimmy just an extra second before moving the conversation along again, after patting his cheek like Dad would, Jimmy thought.

Joseph is stationed at Ft. Benning. He's a Captain, a Ranger Company Commander in the 101st Airborne Division. He'll train an officers qualifications test once a year at the Ft. Walton Beach facility. He could've gotten Jimmy out right now if not for the incident at Sumter. That made pulling any strings impossible.

Keebler got what he had coming and so did the two prisoners, as far as Joseph is concerned. Jimmy's four word summation of, "Fuck them two animals," was dead on the money, Joseph couldn't agree more.

As they're saying good bye, Jimmy asks Joseph to take care of Marilyn if he can, you know, throw her a few bucks. "She'll try to refuse so make her take it, Joe," Jimmy tells him. Jimmy knows that his Mom and sister are okay now that Joseph is back living here in the U.S., they'll be just fine. Just before Joseph steps up to the massive barred door, Jimmy tells him about Dr. Smart. At first, Joseph is looking skeptical, but as Jimmy continues on he begins to see the possibility of what Jimmy is saying.

"I want to help him, and I may need you to help me help him, okay?", Jimmy asks.

Joseph nods his head, yes, and says, "Let me know what I can do."

He watches Jimmy walk back into the prisoners search room and thinks, he'd have made an excellent Ranger. Coming from Joseph, its the highest compliment Jimmy could get.

The United State Supreme Court had abolished the several state's Death Penalty laws earlier in the year, the convicts on Death Row were released to the main line. Most anyway. Some had done things so heinous and vile that they'd have been killed on the yard in minutes. So they chose to remain on lock down in the East Unit for protective custody.

A man can be a vicious killer, even a cold calculating murderer for financial gain, death is just another way of doing business. Harsh, but there it is.

However, no sexual deviates, no predators of women, or children, or the elderly and helpless, no rapists. If they hit the line at Raiford, they're killed a lot faster than the death processes effected by the state. The state takes years, 10 possibly 15 or more, to finally execute the condemned. The convicts take minutes, maybe an hour, no more.

Dr. Smart's appeal has been denied at the Fourth District Court of Appeals. It is now being appealed to the Florida Supreme Court. It's been over three years since the initial filing at the Fourth District Court of Appeals. It will be at least that same duration before the high court hears his case, so, Henry waits.

No one writes to him, no one has visited, he has ceased to exist. Only his lawyer, Joe Baron, stays in contact. Henry's continued imprisonment is very hard on the esteemed attorney. He is working tirelessly with no respite but without success as yet.

Nicole has made an appointment to see Baron, not to inquire about her father's well-being or the status of his appeal, no. She needs money. The money she receives from the dividend payments are sufficient, however, she believes that she should be the owner of the trust, not her father.

Her father is a murderer. He killed her dear mother, why should he be the owner of the trusts assets that was jointly held by both parents?

She intends to sue, unless of course her father will agree to forfeit all the monies and holdings in the trust. In exchange, she'll allow him to keep possession of the $600,000 in his personal savings account, but that is all.

Joe Baron politely asked her to exit his offices, he will not even consult his friend Henry before refusing to even entertain such a preposterous tender.

The following afternoon, Joe Baron and Henried Wright Smart were served with notification of intent to seek compensatory renumeration in the amount of 10 million dollars, for one Nicole Smart.

Henry had finally heard from his daughter, not as he had hoped or dreamt of, but nonetheless in quite commanding fashion, to say the least.

Here's some salt for your wounds Henry, Happy New Year.

CHAPTER SEVENTEEN

September 1974

"The things that pass for knowledge

I can't understand."

Reeling In The Years/ Steely Dan

Gordon has been employed as a special investigator for the U.S. Attorney's office, in Miami, for close to two years. In that short span of time he has become the resident expert on organized crime as it exists within the Southeast United States.

He is a respected and thorough fact finder who very seldom misses even the most minute, trivial detail, the loose thread so to speak, that will unwind an entire intricate and complex criminal enterprise.

Gordon is credited with bringing down Anthony "Tony Pro" Provenzano, and his multi-million dollar racketeering and extortion ring, that operated with impunity in Florida since the 1950's. At one time it was believed that Tony Pro's outfit was skimming $10,000 a day from various nightclub owners and their service providers throughout South Florida for protection.

The expensive protection they were purchasing was from the provider himself. Pay or disappear, for good, and the club would be torched for the good publicity it would garner.

However, just as with sharks teeth, when one is broken off or lost, there is another one right behind it to fill the newly vacated gap. In the organized crime business, it is the same.

Less than a year after the downfall of Tony Pro's outfit, a new outfit has stepped in, The Black Tuna Gang. They are an especially vicious group of killers. Ricky Cravero, Ronnie Chandler, Johnny "Side Burns" Cerella and the Sessa brothers are demanding and receiving even more than Tony Pro's old outfit. They have killed an estimated dozen in the last several months. By the end of their reign of terror, the gang will be attributed with hundreds of murders.

It is this group of cold blooded killers that Gordon is trying to find the weak link to. Whether that is an insider willing to inform on the gang, or some loose end, a loose thread somewhere, a minor oversight, some small detail, anything, that will begin the slow painstaking pursuit that will result in the demise of the Black Tuna Gang.

"Gordon, its your wife, Lisa, on line two," says Brenda, his legal assistant and secretary.

"Hello, Sweetheart, to what do I owe this pleasant surprise?", he says into the phone. Lisa never calls him at work unless its absolutely necessary.

"Are you sitting down? Are you ready?", Lisa asks.

For a brief second Gordon is alarmed, but the tone of her voice sounds anything but dire or grim.

"Uh, yes I am. I just happen to be at my desk and I'm actually quite busy, Lisa, this better be good or," he is saying, but Lisa cuts him off with, "I'm pregnant!" Whoa!

"What!? Will you say that again, did I just hear you say you're pregnant?", Gordon says. He's gotten up from his desk and walked around and shut the door to his small glass enclosed office.

"Yes! Ooooh, yes! We're expecting! Finally Gordon, you're going to be a father and I'm going to be a mommy!" Lisa is ecstatic! She is gushing with joy and delight. Finally, he thinks.

"Lisa, I'm just so, -so, wow!", Gordon says. He is speechless.

They've been trying for four years. They had all the tests.

Gordon was quite potent and Lisa very fertile, there were no physical obstacles. They certainly made love frequently enough, and they both still desired each other as much as they had as newlyweds. It was a mystery why Lisa hadn't become pregnant, but that's behind them now.

They're going to be parents to a little baby- "Do you know if its a?, uh-," Gordon asks.

Lisa laughs before saying, "No, silly, I don't, but Gordon! We're going to have a baby!" She squeals delightedly.

"Well, this calls for a celebration! I'm taking you to dinner tonight and I won't take no for an answer," he tells her. Lisa has been very tight, penny pinching. They've bought a lot right on A1A just North of Sunrise Blvd., and Lisa has been saving all their money to build their dream home. Now, with the baby a reality, its time to start the actual building of the house.

"All right, just this once I'll let you win, but no more extravagances after this," she warns.

"Aye, Aye Captain," Gordon teases her, "I'll see you tonight," he says.

Lisa is a prosecuting attorney with the Broward County State's Attorney's Office. She's tried two cases already, both successfully. One was presided over by the Chief Circuit Court Judge, Leroy Mims, who is very strict and demanding on both attorney's in his courtroom, prosecution and defense.

Lisa promises to be a formidable opponent. She already displays the tenacity and assertiveness to exact candid disclosure from witnesses on either direct or cross examination.

She's won both of her two jury trials and has bargained very toughly on negotiated plea agreements. She definitely bears watching in the ensuing tears.

Jill is back home at the Mayor residence. She could easily live elsewhere but with her father away in Washington D.C. most of the time, and Cynthia alone, Jill has opted to live here. Its better to be here with her mother than living alone by herself.

The aged maid, Jewel, is still in residence although she no longer has near the duties she had in years past. The three ladies are very much atuned to one another, the familiarity bourne of years in the same domicile.

Jill is working on her Masters Degree in Psychology at Nova University. She is presently employed at the Coral Ridge Psychiatric Hospital where the rich and their offspring often seek sanctuary. Either personally for some perceived oddity or, more often, as a means of subverting some run-in with the local authorities, a drug possession or driving under the influence charge.

Jill knows that the majority of the patients she sees are of the latter variety and are affecting a sham, a ruse, to avoid real penalties that could be imposed in a court of law.

The Coral Ridge Psychiatric Hospital will provide their patient/ client with a legitimate, medically diagnosed mitigating circumstance to offer the courts that the court cannot ignore or disregard. In street verbiage, a guaranteed out from any real punitive sanctions. There is often monetary renumeration to the effected parties but no criminal convictions, no record of any kind in fact. Guaranteed, a very tidy arrangement indeed, but only for the few, the hospital is very, very expensive.

Jill actually does treat some mentally disturbed patients, they are a definite minority but some do exist. She is presently counseling a young adolescent girl who has what her parents have called unusual aggressiveness and masculine interests. Hmm?

She is a tomboy, that's it. She likes boys, although she feels pretty sure she could beat up half the ones she knows, and she's better at some sports than many. She is only 15 and she hasn't had any sexual activity or experiences yet, which is in her favor of course. She thinks the whole damsel in distress posture girls are forced to affect is ridiculous and she will not conform, period.

Jill likes her. She is a free spirit, a free thinker, and someday she'll make some boy a fantastic mate.

Her parents want her to make her debut in October, next month. They insist she must metamorphose into a sophisticated, poised and proper young lady by then. Or else!

Jill thinks its preposterous, but she must come up with some way to help the girl. The problem is the girl's mother, not the girl. And, Jill's had prior experience with this particular type of mother - daughter assertion for dominance and control, Victoria and Nicole.

Their archetypal battle of wills had been a main force in Nicole's adolescent years, and Victoria had won in that instance. Nicole had finally broke free when Victoria was-.

Jill shakes her head to clear out that thought. When Victoria was what?, she thinks. Murdered? Yes, certainly, she didn't shoot herself. Victoria would not have committed suicide, she loved herself too much, Jill thinks, and then immediately chastises herself for having malicious thoughts about a deceased person.

Nicole has never written to her father, and she certainly has never considered going to the prison to visit him. Jill actually feels bad for Dr. Smart, he was always so kind and considerate towards everyone.

What an odd pairing that had been, she thinks now. Victoria 10 years younger, and often cruel and unforgiving, Never a kind word for anyone, including Nicole, who as a youngster was in constant fear of her mother. Victoria always demanding and finding fault capriciously, selfish and egotistic, she seemed to actually take pleasure in humiliating the less fortunate.

Jill shivered. What is that?, she thinks, again reproaching herself for thinking ill of the dead. She makes a mental note to call Nicole. Maybe the two of them can have lunch at the club this weekend. Its been quite awhile since the two childhood friends had seen each other, over two months Jill realizes. They were so close growing up, closer than sisters, and now months would pass without even a phone call between the two.

Hugh Mayor, the United States Senator from Florida, is at the HayeAddams Hotel in Washington D.C. this evening. He is being entertained by a group of businessmen who are interested in the possible opening of off shore oil drilling sites in the Gulf of Mexico, off the Florida coast.

Should that bill, now being debated upon on the Senate floor, make it to a vote, the group is seeking a pledge from the distinguished Senator that he will indeed vote in favor of it.

The mineral rights awarded, should the bill pass, will make the members of the group wealthy beyond imagination. The oil embargo is not yet a year past. The country's had a good preview of what a lengthier embargo could entail, the economic havoc that would be wrought by just such an event.

Hugh has tacitly been made aware that the groups indebtedness to him would know no bounds, literally. The esteemed Senator is nodding at just the right moment, uttering the necessary, "I see's" and "of course's". He is a master politician.

He is anxiously awaiting 10:00 p.m., but he wills himself not to look at his wrist watch. Instead, he smiles and pretends to be attentively listening.

Hugh has discovered that his position as a U.S. Senator has made him truly one of the most powerful men in the world. And not just here in the United States, he is feted by Japanese conglomerates and their trade delegates seeking favored nation status. There are Arabian princes and Sultanates wanting U.S. military protection, and of course the home grown variety of business tycoons like these gentlemen here this evening.

The power is intoxicating, and not just to him. The Washington ladies are all a flutter, as moths to a flame, over the tall handsome Senator, and Hugh is quite accommodating as well.

"Never refuse a lady, its ungentlemanly," he'll say, "but always, always be discreet." The guffaws he inspires from the buyers of influence with that statement are hearty and plentiful. It makes Hugh seem so much more accessible, like one of the boys, by bandying about such colloquialisms. But Hugh takes his own seemingly off the cuff remark deadly serious, while the others think its just amusingly risque.

The long dinner and ensuing drinking are finally winding down. Hugh shakes hands firmly all around promising his support, they need not worry.

It's just past 10:00 p.m. Hugh takes the elevator to four and quickly exits through the fire door, into the stairwell. He takes the steps two at a time to the sixth floor, where he emerges. After quickly scanning the hallway in both directions, he makes his way to #621. He inserts his key and enters.

Denise Eliot is waiting for him in a filmy, sheer, white shift. Sans panties of course. She is a tall lovely seductress, with magnificent exquisite breasts and long perfectly shaped legs. She is Victoria not quite 10 years ago, and the same age that she had been when Hugh and her had first begun.

He crosses the room and takes her in his arms as they kiss hungrily. She begins to unbelt his trousers as she breathes, "Hurry! Hurry please, darling!"

Hugh is inflamed and rips the thin cotton shift off. Yes! She loves seeing him like this, helpless in his desire, his lust for her.

It is several hours later and Hugh is preparing to leave, to return to his fourth floor suite before the hotel comes to life. They have been enjoying their nights together since congress re-convened in the early Spring, its now the beginning of Fall.

Hugh has bought her a brownstone townhouse in Georgetown, but they cannot meet there, not yet. Perhaps after his re-election, still two years away. She is satisfied with being his mistress, she cares little about the formalities of marriage.

It is well known in Washington that it is the mistress who wields the real power and influence over the elected represent-ative of the people. The wife is merely a prop to be brought out in election years to convey his commitment to the American ideals of family, God and country. After that, she is safely tucked away again. Hugh's wife is very good in her role and Denise has no desire or interest in unseating her, no, Cynthia's position is quite safe.

Barnaby Casworth Jr., Caz, and his father, the senior, are standing on the construction site in downtown Ft. Lauderdale where the 22 story Florida First office tower is now being erected. It now rises 16 stories into the clear blue late September sky. The completion date will be on time, scheduled for December 20th.

The expansion of housing developments now reach far out into the Western edges of the county. The building boom is in full stride, there is no such thing as being unemployed, not for anyone

willing to work. There is hundreds of millions of dollars in
the construction industry and the entire state is in full throttle.

Caz has been out of college for over a year, and Barnaby Sr.
has kept his son continually by his side since then. Perhaps Barnaby
Sr. is hoping that his young son and namesake will, by some magical
form of osmosis, become the astute business tycoon he himself is.
If only Caz stays close enough it may rub off on him? Possibly.

Barnaby Sr. is sorley disappointed in the boy, he seems
to have gleaned nothing from his four years at the University of
Florida. He's given Caz the very important sounding title of Vice
President of Marketing, that in actuality has no function whatsoever,
none. Florida First is an investment banking and real estate development conglomerate. They don't market anything, they finance and
build cities, period.

Caz earns a tidy six figure income, an office and a secretary,
that Barnaby is sure Caz is involved with, to some degree, beyond
Florida First business. He performs no duties in furthering the
goals of the corporation. Its not that Caz shirks any legitimate
tasks, it is more Barnaby's lack of trust in his son's sorely
lacking abilities.

As father and son stand at ground level admiring the soon
to open Florida First Corporation Headquarters office tower, Caz
seems to be avidly absorbing his father's continual, uninterrupted
soliloquy regarding Florida First's sprawling, colossal mission
for the remainder of the century.

Barnaby has divided it into nice, even compact 10 year plans.

The present phase, Broward West, began in 1970. The second phase
will encompass the extreme Southwest and Northwest, Broward County,
and partially Southern Palm Beach County. The last phase will be
all of Western Palm Beach County into Martin County.

The undertaking ahead is huge, gargantuan, the population
of the three South Florida counties will soar to 8 million inhabitants by centuries end. They have not a moment to spare, truly, this
present phase just the tip of the development ice-berg.

Caz is smiling and nodding, letting his father know that he
is enrapt by all the astounding plans for the upcoming 25 plus
years ahead.

In truth, Caz can't even give a presentation of this very
spot, this building, where he and his father are right now standing.
He is truly lost, the degree from the University of Florida more
a token of appreciation to Barnaby Sr. and his very generous
largesse to the school, than to Caz's proficiency in business.

Caz has his lunch date with Nicole on his mind. His wife
is often in his thoughts, but not today. He'll think about Trish,
nee Patricia Vance, when he see's her at home tonight.

What a cold fish that one is. His father persuaded him
that it would be beneficial to his, Caz's future, to have the next
Governor of Florida as his father-in-law. Yea, but his Dad didn't
have to sleep with her every night.

"So, what do you think, Caz? Are we going to make it? or-,"
Barnaby is asking.

"Oh, uh-, well-, Yes! Yes, I believe we will, Dad," Caz answers.

Barnaby grabs his son's shoulder in a reaffirming grip and nods saying, "Good, son, very good, I think so too."

"I've got to run, Dad, I, uh-, I told Rene I'd be back to, uh-," Caz is saying, but his father spares him anymore discomfort by saying, "I'll see you tonight, son, your mother expects you at 7:00 p.m." Barnaby knows Rene, Caz's secretary, has nothing to schedule him for, or her, unless its both? He begins to chuckle.

Caz is still standing there looking confused. He now asks, "Dad, why is Mom expecting me?"

Barnaby shakes his head, "Not you, son. You and your wife, have you forgotten? Today is the 23rd, and the 23rd is-?", he draws out the question giving Caz time to answer, but finally gives up and says, "Its your anniversary, Caz. One whole year of marital bliss to the lovely and very politically connected, Trish. See you at 7:00 p.m.," and he walks away.

There are times Barnaby actually wonders where Caz came from. He looks like Catherine certainly, but he has not one ounce of Barnaby's razor sharp intelligence.

Oh well, at least Richard is on his way, he's begun his second year at the Wharton School of Business at the University of Pennsylvania. He is sharp as a tack. He is a genius numbers cruncher with the ability to store huge amounts of data from several sources, and recall any single one, verbatim, on demand. Barnaby smiles and thinks, there is a God.

Fuck! Fuck! Fuck! Caz cannot believe tonight of all nights is his anniversary. Fuck! He can forget the late afternoon post lunch tryst with Nicole, won't happen. Why did he ever cocede to marrying that block of ice that is now like an anchor around his neck? Well, okay, he had to do as his Dad asked. He couldn't not do it, but still.

"Caz, since you'll be, -uh, away from the office this afternoon, can I have the rest of the day off?", Rene asks, giving him her brightest smile. She calls him Caz, not Mr. Casworth. I mean its hard to enforce protocol when you're whatever.

"Yes, fine Rene. Don't you think your skirt is, well-," Caz smiles roguishly.

"Too short? I'm sorry, I thought you-," she is replying but Caz interrupts, saying, "No! Its too long actually, remember? Finger tips, Rene, finger tips."

She smiles sexily and says, "Oh! Okay, I won't forget," and blows him a kiss. He wants her finger tips, with her arms resting at her sides, to touch the hem of her skirt. Hell, with legs like that, you got em flaunt em.

He rubs his hands together in anticipation of lunch and Nicole. Then once again remembers the cursed anniversary dinner, to celebrate one year of misery, married to Miss missionary, for 5 minutes only.

He grabs his suit coat and hurries out of his office, maybe he'll get a quicky in the car-.

Nicole is waiting impatiently. He is always late, she thinks, except in bed, then he's early, just like most of the men in her life have been.

Nicole has by far surpassed her mother's beauty. At 22 she is an extremely lovely woman. A head turner, literally, conversation stopping in mid-sentence to behold such beauty.

As the minutes pass, slowly, Nicole is becoming angry, Caz is a whole 5 minutes late. As if by command he is there, acting very contrite like he is hours late instead of mere minutes.

He knows Nicole's extremely, uh-, testy side. Caz remembers her mother all to well, and Nicole is definitely her mother's daughter.

He decides to act nonchalant and composed, it may blunt her venom. "Hi, doll face, you look beautiful, as always," he says, and smiles his best heart melting lady killer smile while trying to steal a kiss.

"You're late! And don't give me that doll face drivel, Caz, I'm not 14 anymore, remember?", she says, frowning disapproval at him.

If she weren't so out and out drop dead gorgeous, he'd get right up and leave, but- she is. Just one look at her and its as if he were welded to his chair, he can't leave.

Okay, time to retreat he tells himself, and says, "I am sorry, Nicky. I was stuck, uh- busy all morning with my Dad, at the tower project, you know, facts, figures and drawings." He's trying to sound knowledgeable and involved, but Nicole knows Caz couldn't build a sand castle in the sand box in kindergarten, then or now.

Still, she relents and gives him a quick kiss and says,

"okay, I forgive you, just this once though," and she wags a
finger at him. Even her finger wagging is sexy and he tries to
at least get a real kiss, but she abruptly turns her face away.

"Will you stop, please? I have some things I need to discuss
with you," Nicole says this sincerely, like she needs some sage,
wise advice from him. He immediately responds just as she knew
he would, becoming all concern and seriousness.

"What, Sweetheart? Are you okay? Talk to me, Nicky," he
says, the epitome of maturity.

She almost laughs, Caz, the perpetual teenager, acting
sooo grown up. But, she does appreciate his trying so she leans
into him and allows him a kiss.

"Caz, I'm having problems with my father's old attorney.
He won't give me access to the trust funds dividend payments. Since
I've filed suit, not one penny, and-, and-,," she's saying haltingly,
looking up into his handsome face, trying to affect the damsel in
distress all men are suckers for.

And what she has told Caz is true. She had been getting
the quarterly dividend monies from the trusts assets, over $300,000
a year, before her blatant and callous money grab. Now, Baron has
the dividends reinvested, he sends Henry whatever he needs, which
isn't much, out of his office budget. The fund is locked up tight,
no one can access the account except Henry himself.

Caz immediately decides to be her champion. With her looking
at him like that, how could he not? Talk about a sucker for a pretty
face.

"I can help you, Nicky, how much do you need?", he asks softly.

"It's only a loan, Caz, I promise I'll pay it back. I'll even sign an- I.O.U.?, whatever its called," she says, feigning ignorance of money matters.

"Don't worry, Nicky, this isn't business, this is you and I. Please, let me help you, ok?", Caz says, touching under her chin to tilt her head up.

She has tears in her eyes as she says, "Oh Caz, darling, thank you!" And her smile melts his heart, among other things.

"How much, Nicky?", he asks.

"A million dollars," she says, and seeing his surprise quickly adds, "I can pay it back, Caz. My lawsuit is for ten million, and my attorney is positive the fund will be turned over to me."

Yikes!! Caz thinks, a cool million, oh well. "Can you wait until Monday?", he asks.

"Oh yes! Caz, thank you! Thank you sooo much. I knew I could come to you, that you'd help me," she coos, and lets him get a very deep sexually charged kiss.

"Can we leave? I'd like to be alone, if you don't mind?", she asks hesitantly, shyly.

He doesn't need to hear it twice. Though neither have ordered anything, there is no check, in his haste to leave he tosses a $100.00 on the table and they hurriedly depart.

CHAPTER EIGHTEEN

April 1975 - January 1976

"His hands are clean, and you're the best

thing that he's ever seen."

Lay Lady Lay/Bob Dylan

Major Joseph Carosa is watching the early morning news on a television at battalion headquarters with Lieutenant Colonel Akers and Colonel Ridgemont. The three combat veterans, the Colonel of both Korea and Vietnam, are watching helicopters from the two U.S. Navy carriers on station in the South China Sea, ferry foreign service office diplomats, and their families, from the rooftop of the U.S. Embassy in Saigon.

58,148 dead, over 2,000 still listed M.I.A, for this. South Vietnam has fallen to North Vietnamese forces in less than two years since American withdrawl.

The three soldiers are bitter, everyone of them have lost men they themselves led into battle.

Major Carosa, the executive officer of the 2nd Battalion, 97th Regiment, 101st Airborne division lost only two. Only two, he thinks with disgust, two brothers in arms, blood and spirit.

Weegie, Sergeant Leonard Reeb, was Killed In Action, (K.I.A), in May 1970 in Cambodia, just as that country was recognized as a very real combat theater by the world at large. It was in all the newspapers stateside.

Weegie had destroyed an entire advance attack company of a North Vietnamese Army battalion, unassisted, using dynamite. The explosives were wired for instantaneous detonation purposely, no time for delayed ignition, if he was to successfully annihilate all 150 troops of the enemy.

By doing so, by wiring the explosives as he had, he chose his duty first and his own life second. A true hero, he put the success of the mission above everything. He is awarded a Silver Star with oak leaf cluster for his extreme valor, posthumously of course.

And young Ruckus, Pfc. Brian Kubik, K.I.A in South Vietnam, while engaging heavy enemy fire and already severely wounded, he crawled over 100 yards through hostile enemy occupied terrain. And then he tossed two grenades onto the dug in Viet Cong, killing 14, and himself, in the explosion. He also is, posthumously, awarded a Silver Star.

Weegie 24, and Ruckus 20, Army Rangers to the last, sacrificing themselves doing their duty.

Colonel Ridgemont gets up and turns off the T.V. Both Joseph and the Lieutenant Colonel start to voice their opinions, but the Colonel puts up his hands, palms out in a stopping gesture, and they both stop in mid-sentence.

"I know exactly how you feel, both of you, so can it. I'm as pissed as anyone, politicians can't fight wars, that's why they have us, the military," he says, looking evenly at both men before continuing, "We lost a 100 boys from our battalion at Inchon in less than two hours, and another 100 before nightfall in the retreat." The retreat was down the Korean peninsula with 2 million Red Chinese in pursuit.

"At Ia Drang, in 65', 1,200 of the enemy engaged my lead company. Their Captain led them to far ahead against my explicit orders not to. Before we could reinforce them the entire company was lost. We annihilated the 1,200 the next day. I still hear only the voices of the boys in that lead company," the Colonel finished. He looked drained in the retelling of the defeat that was turned to victory.

The message he is conveying is that we only remember the lost.

The Colonel looks at Joseph and Akers and they both nod, saying, "Yes, sir." They can think of nothing else that needs to be said, he's said it all. Almost, but not quite.

The Colonel now says, "Carosa, you have command of Akers 2nd battalion until further notice."

When he sees the surprise and questioning look in both of their faces, he orders, "Akers, you are to report, by 1800 hours, day after tomorrow, to-," and here the old Colonel delays just a breath to add to Akers suspense, before adding, "The Army War College in Carlisle, Pennsylvania," He smiles broadly and sticks out his hand.

"Sir? Yes sir, Colonel!", Akers says, and snaps off a salute before pumping the Colonel's hand vigorously.

Akers will become a full,(bird), Colonel upon completion of the College of Command, it is fantastic news, to both. Major Carosa will assume command of the 2nd Battalion temporarily. It will become permanent as soon as the already submitted recommendation is recorded at Army Headquarters in Washington D.C., and he is promoted to the rank of Lieutenant Colonel.

The 97th Regiment, commanded by Colonel Ridgemont, incurred the highest combat casualties in the Vietnam war. Not because of unqualified or poor leadership, no, the regiment fought the highest number of engagements, twice the next nearest regiments.

It is an Airborne division, with multiple Ranger companies in its ranks, a war machine through and through.

"Push, come on, just a little more. That's it- push!", the ob-gyn nurse is coaxing Lisa, and, 'There! There you are!" She hands the small wrinkled baby to the doctor who deftly snips the umbilical cord and ties it off.

He places the baby on Lisa's gown covered torso and smiles at her, saying, "You are the mother of a perfect baby girl." The tiny baby is making little squeaks, but she isn't bawling or fussy as Lisa picks her up, awed! She is perfect!

The nurse says, 'C'mon Mom, I'll clean her up and she'll be back in a jiffy."

Lisa hesitates a brief instant but then hands her daughter to the nurse.

Gordon is waiting outside the delivery room when they wheel Lisa out. He bends down and kisses her sweat soaked brow. Lisa is beaming, "It's a beautiful, perfect baby girl," they both say the, girl, together. He was told by the attending Physician just moments after the delivery.

They are holding hands as the bed is being wheeled through the halls back to Lisa's room.

"I want to see her, Lease," Gordon is saying, but as they are arranging Lisa back into her own bed, the nurse enters with a tiny pink bundle and hands her to Lisa.

Now Gordon is awed! She looks like him, the nose anyway, and yes! She's smiling at me!, he thinks. They are both overjoyed and touching their precious little daughter. The baby does appear to be laughing, isn't it too soon?, they both think.

"She's beautiful, Lisa! My God, I love you!", he says, and then looking at the tiny baby, he also tells her, "I love you too my sweet baby girl." He holds out his finger to her and the baby actually grabs it!

To both their amazement, they are new, first time parents. There's a lot of amazing's ahead, every moment. Lisa squeals with delight and they both hug, very carefully, with the tiny baby in between them. Thank you, God, thank you, he thinks, without You I wouldn't have made it back for this. He kisses his wife and daughter.

Gordon hasn't been able to discover who the soldier is. G.I. Joe, that's all he knows. His vocation and profession is investigation, detection, yet he has been unable to put a name to him. Ranger operations were, and still are, very hush, hush - on a need to know basis, and he doesn't need to know, not officially at least.

He hopes the soldier didn't perish in the jungle, not that guy he assuredly thinks, no way. He vows to continue digging until he knows. The soldier and his comrade's saved Gordon's life. Lisa, his parents, and himself consider his rescue a miracle.

He surely would have perished, if not enroute to the P.O.W camp, then once there. Would he have been alive after three and a half years in captivity? Doubtful, and had he lived to be returned

with the P.O.W's who had survived, he certainly would've been a
cripple. His injuries were severe, his legs needed bone grafts
and his vertabrae was surgically fused.

No, he wouldn't be "standing" here right now. I'm going
to find you, soldier, I won't quit until I do, he thinks.

Jimmy is fighting in the middle weight class even though
he barely tips the scale at 141 lbs. He's 10 pounds below that class.
He's been on the boxing team over 2 years now and he's undefeated
as a middle weight.

Maybe they'll have to bump him up to cruiser weight, 159 lbs.,
he thinks and smiles. He's not cocky, he's good. Henry is lacing
up his sparring gloves, their going to have a three round warm-up
in preparation for this weekends bouts against the Sumter's team.

Should be some pretty good boxing in store. Its a big
event every year, and it won't be any different this year either.

Henry is the unofficial team doctor. He enjoys the comradery
and in turn he is well respected. His protestations of innocence
are no longer laughed off, by Scotty or anyone.

The story behind the old doctor has been in the newspapers
in Ft. Lauderdale and Miami. Many now believe that maybe the doctor
didn't do it after all. The convicts see many holes in his conviction
themselves.

A truly innocent man is a very rare extreme in such a place
as this. This is The Rock, a lot of the prisoner's here have made
many stops at lesser prisons before arriving here. A man may actually

be innocent somewhere else, not likely but possible.

But here? A lot of the convicts are here for committing crimes at the other prisons, that is why they are here. Nope, no innocents here, uh-uh. Well- except, maybe there is one, perhaps, the old Doctor.

Jimmy is the only fighter the Doctor attends to with the lacing and the taping, the other boxer's have their own managers. Henry enjoys managing Jimmy. He occasionally attempts to impart boxing tips to his young fighter and Jimmy actually pretends to take them into consideration.

They've become very close. If Jimmy's not working out, pushing a little iron, (not too much, it'll slow him down), or running/ training with Scotty, he and the old Doctor can be seen out walking the yard or having coffee at the patio restaurant.

Though Scotty isn't on the boxing team, he still pushes the iron and runs with Jimmy everyday. They are both naturals. It is their speed, the velocity of their punches particularly, that makes them both prolific boxers.

They've discussed Henry's case every possible way it can be looked at, front to back, and back to front again, for over 3 years now, and its still a blank.

Henry has told Jimmy that his beloved wife named him, Henry, as her killer, but he doesn't know why. The mystery assailant and his speed boat getaway is another blank. Jimmy knows he's innocent, without a doubt.

He still addresses Henry as Dr. Smart, not Doc or Henry,

Dr. Smart. This man picked 41 bone fragments out of his brain the night his wife was murdered. Jimmy is only aware of that particular coincidence due to Henry's retelling of the story, his story.

Henry, his attorney, with the police, were awaiting a Judges phone call deciding whether to issue or deny a search warrant for his residence. Instead, a call came from the on duty Emergency Room physician reporting a head trauma accident, that required Dr. Smarts attention. Henry, without a moments hesitation, sped to the hospital, leaving the police and his lawyer sitting there waiting for the Judges call.

How could a man, any man, kill his wife, and then mere hours later perform an extremely delicate and complicated surgical procedure? The clincher is, Henry loves Victoria, still, right now today.

Jimmy is stumped, why did she name Henry as her killer? He cannot find an answer to that question.

He hit the speed bag, it sounded like a machine gun. Then the heavy bag, its loud thud, thud, thud echoing across half the yard. He sparred three rounds of three minutes each to keep his body movements and footwork sharp. Its a tune up for Saturday.

It's near dark, late December. The daylight doesn't linger much past 5:00 p.m. Doc unties Jimmy's gloves and they walk back towards the cell blocks. The yard is closing with the onset of night.

Jimmy has a year and a half left before he'll max out the 10 year sentence. In Florida a prisoner serves about half of the court imposed sentence. He could do far less if he is granted parole but parole is pretty elusive. The prisoner must have clear conduct, an impossibility at the main facilities where violence is the norm. The incident at Sumter will bar any parole consideration, unless it is granted at, or very near the end of his term, in a bid to have him on supervised release once freed.

He earns work gain time of 20 days per month, and receives an additional 10 days per month statutory good conduct time. Every day served counts as two, 10 years expires in 5 years.

Had Louie not posted his $10,000 bail, he'd have received credit for all the jail time served prior to the imposition of sentence. In July of 1977, Jimmy will have fulfilled his obligation.

It's almost certain that he will be offered parole 6 months before then. It enables the state to monitor the former inmate in society, with the added threat of violating his parole and returning him to the inside for any minor infraction.

He can remain in prison until July 1977 and walk out free, no obligation. Or, he can leave in January 1977, possibly even an early release for the Christmas holiday in December 1976, but be obligated for all unserved portions of the imposed sentence, 5½ years, should he violate the terms of parole.

Much depends on the individual prisoner, many hardened convict's refuse parole and await expiration. Some married inmates, or the less experienced, take the first chance they can get to be free.

Henry has offered Jimmy any help he'll need to begin his life anew. But Jimmy can never return to the young man he was a lifetime of heartache ago. He won't take the Doctor's money, he doesn't need it or want it. Possibly some good old fashioned, hard, bust ass in the hot South Florida sun, work, will leech some of his anger and irreplaceable loss out of his heart and soul.

The day after Christmas the boxing tournament is a good one, a wild one. The first 3 bouts go the 10 round distance, with no K.O.'s.

Jimmy's doesn't. The bigger opponent hits him with a couple of good round house rights that get his attention. After the third round he's got the other fighters best moves countered easily. Thirty seconds into round four, the 154 lbs. man throws his left hook, right cross combination, only the left hook misses and the right cross never gets launched.

Jimmy easily pulls back out of the path of the slow hook and counters with a straight right, to set up a left upper-cut, right cross double combo, boom, boom, boom, boom, fast-, and, bye-bye, the guys out.

The referee jumps into the ring and steers jimmy away from the sprawled out man on the canvas. He goes over and counts, slowly, using his fingers theatrically, until he's used all ten of them. He now goes over and takes Jimmy's right hand and raises it, as the crowd of prisoners, black, white and Cuban roar their appreciation. It's a biased audience, they're Rock convicts, they pull for the home team.

Jimmy exits the ring and Henry is awaiting him, beaming like a proud father watching his son's first fight. They hug right there at ringside. They get down from the elevated ring and Henry begins unlacing Jimmy's gloves, saying, "You looked good out there tonight. You've actually gotten better, and there wasn't much to improve to start with."

"Thanks! I've been using some of your pointers, Dr. Smart," Jimmy grins at him. Henry ruffles the boys hair, he knows Jimmy is teasing him.

To celebrate the New Year, 1976, Doc has purchased some very potent home made wine, called "Buck", in prison parlance. It's made from the over abundance of oranges the prisoner's get so often, with a lot of sugar, and left to ferment, after adding just a teaspoon of yeast, for 5-6 days.

It's strong, real strong. One quart is plenty, you're quite intoxicated if you drink that much. If you drink two quarts, you've over done it, for sure. Nobody on The Rock can drink two quarts of good Buck without becoming sloppy, staggering drunk.

This is a very dangerous place, its very unwise to get in that condition here, a lot of bad things could happen.

Doc has bought two gallons, 8 quarts, for $15.00, enough for the whole crew and some left over. None of the five, Doc, Jimmy, Scotty, Skid or Nelson drink regularly, so this is a rare occasion for all.

It doesn't take 30 minutes and they're all getting pretty tanked, the stuff is strong. The shit talking starts up with who can tell the bigger lie with the straightest face.

Scotty gets to retelling the night he shot ol goober,

thinking he was shooting a coon, the four legged kind not the other, down in Clewiston. Goober is the local junk man in the sugar cane town, the citizens trash is his treasure.

Once Scotty finishes the updated version of his oft told tale, the youngster of the group, Nelson, has a new joke, another of his corny racial jokes, but they're not mean spirited so they tolerate his telling of them.

"What did Jesus tell the blacks?", he asks.

He's laughing and feeling pretty darn good from the Buck already. When nobody answers, Jimmy says, "What? What did he tell them, Nelson?"

Nelson is laughing like crazy, he says, "Don't do nothing until I get back."

They all laugh- it is pretty good and none have heard it before.

As the minutes become hours, first Scotty lumbers off to his rack, he's had enough. Then Skid and the youngster Nelson. It's only Doc and Jimmy.

There's still two quarts left, they have taken one apiece and are sipping it. This stuff is like whiskey, it even smells like it.

Jimmy tells Henry about his first love, Jill. Henry has heard it before but lets him tell it again, why not? Jimmy is lamenting about how everything sort of went belly up, all at the same time. His Dad's murder, Jill's change of heart concerning him, all the bad one after another, until Melissa. And then, well, Henry knows that story too.

Now Henry retells his story, how he fell in love with Victoria on sight, she a Bryn Mawr freshmen, he at Johns Hopkins in his final internship year. She was 18 years old and so beautiful that it hurt his eyes to look at her. He was a very old 28 and already mastering intricate procedures.

When she spoke to him he had trouble maintaining eye contact, her beauty blinding him, literally. When she laughed, flashing perfect white teeth in such an inviting smile, he was hooked. She made him dance with her, not the crazy dances of today, but the romantic classics of the 40's and 50's.

He fell in love, that night, a year later they were married, and two years later Nicole arrived, and, and...

Henry is weeping, the booze partly responsible. All inhibitions leave, not just some.

"The night she died, she was in my arms, James, the blood-," here Henry takes a minute to compose himself before continuing, "She said, why? Henry? I had asked her who did this, Victoria, and she said why Henry?" Henry is sobbing uncontrollably now.

Jimmy feels terrible, he can see the Doctor's torment, he says, "Come on, Dr. Smart, give me that quart, you've had enough." He's trying to soothe his friend.

Henry is not stopping, he's struggling to continue the tragic story, he has to get it out.

Henry says, "She said Henry, why? Why did you? Why did you? Why did you do this?" He's sobbing but he's got it out-.

Jimmy had tried to stop him before he continued. Jimmy is drunk, almost anyway, but did Dr. Smart just say what he thinks he did? Why did you? Why did you do this? Suddenly, Jimmy has a flash of the Country Club, years ago, Victoria and Hugh- Hugh? Hugh?! Hugh!! Fuck! Fuck! Fuck!---

"Dr. Smart! Dr. Smart! Stop it! Goddamit stop it!", Jimmy is shouting, and he's snatched the quart out of Henry's hand.

Henry is startled and he's suddenly not so drunk and weepy either. Jimmy's frightened him and the adrenaline from his fright has a sobering affect, short lasting, but its enough.

"Its Hugh! Its Hugh! H-U-G-H, its not you, its Hugh! Its H-U-G-H, you understand?!", Jimmy is shouting it, loud, "It's Hugh! Hugh mother fuckin Mayor, Dr. Smart, shit!!", Jimmy is yelling this at Henry, loud enough for the whole Rock to hear it.

Henry's adrenaline sobriety lasts long enough where he does, indeed, understand what young James is shouting at him. Jimmy is hugging him and jumping up and down with the both of them. Henry is stunned speechless, and he's stone cold sober also.

"Listen, its Hugh Mayor, Dr. Smart. The mystery speed boat getaway? Its Hugh-! You're out! You're out! If its the last thing I ever do," Jimmy is repeating himself, he's delirious.

After all this time they've finally figured out what Victoria was saying, not you- Henry, Hugh H-U-G-H! He can't believe it, his thoughts are a jumbled mess. They are both hugging and Jimmy is still jumping-.

They finally settle down and sit. Henry is wiping his eyes,

he's crying real tears now, not drunken ones.

    "How? How are we going to prove this?", Henry asks, and
then adds, "He's a Senator, its been over 5 years now, I-."

    "Forget about it, Dr. Smart, that bit-, uh-, Nicole,
is going to help, and so is Jill and her stuck up snob sister, all
of them. You're innocent! I'll get you out. My brother will help,
I promise, Dr. Smart, we won't stop until you're free! You have
my word!", Jimmy tells him, and they hug. The old Doctor is
trembling, the innocent, falsely imprisoned Doctor-

    Happy New Year, Henry. This time its for real.

PART IV

ON THE SIDE OF THE ANGELS

CHAPTER NINETEEN

December 1976

"I'm Free."

Title Song/ The Who

The Christmas Eve holiday celebration at the Mayor home is an especially joyous one this year.

The entire family is here this evening. Gordon and Lisa with the simply adorable 18 month old baby, Carla, Gordon's parents, Barbara and Jack, Jill and her somewhat occasional boy-friend, escort, lover?, Hamilton Geoffries, "Ham" to the group that is gathered here, and of course the Senator and his lovely wife, Cynthia, round out the celebrants.

They are drinking hot rum toddies even though its 71 degrees outside. You have to create your own holiday atmosphere residing in the tropical South Florida environs, and there's nothing like a good stiff holiday beverage to facilitate it.

Nicole is expected to join the group. She is alone, without benefit of any family except this one, which has been like a second family to her most of her life.

The holiday season heightens such an absence and the Mayor's know to avoid any reference to that fact. Poor Nicole, she is so alone.

When she arrives, Jill greets her warmly. They are still the best of friends and they embrace closely.

Nicole knows everyone in attendance tonight except Gordon's father, Jack. She met Barbara at the baby shower.

She missed Lisa's wedding. She hadn't returned from Bryn Mawr to Ft. Lauderdale for the summer recess until the week after.

Nicole is introduced to, Jack, and she makes her greetings all around before oohing and aahing over baby Carla. "Look at you! You're a big girl, now! Aren't you precious!", Nicole coos.

She makes eye contact with Jill after the rest of the party resumes their conversation. Jill grabs two Rums and she and Nicole head out to the rear veranda so they can talk privately.

"Jill, darling, its sooo good to see you. Its been ages, hmmm?", Nicole utters smoothly.

"Yes, Nicole, it has been awhile, what's going on? Are you okay? or-," Jill asks. She's mildly annoyed with her for not getting right to the point, making her have to pry.

"Its Caz, Jill. He wants to divorce Trish and- marry me," Nicole says, emphasizing disdain when she speaks Trish's name, before feigning indecision as to what she should do.

Nicole's ploy for sympathy and affirmation/ approval from her childhood friend doesn't work. It's so transparent Jill almost laughs and thinks, sorry Nicky, not here.

Nicole has had her hooks into Caz for three years now. He's given her close to 2 million dollars as well. The money was placed into an account at Florida First, created by a personal check from one Barnaby Casworth Jr. That check, and the ensuing one for another $999,000, are being held, they have not been processed into the financial accounting of the corporation.

It can't be covered up in perpetuity either. Eventually the two checks will have to make their way into the banking divisions assets and holdings or, liabilities and losses.

Caz has persuaded the comptroller to omit the entire account from his yearly report, by, well- out and out bribery, to the tune of $50,000 since the account was created, to Dennis Calhoun, his secretary Rene's sometime boyfriend. Dennis has been successful so far due to the incompetence of the Chief Financial Officer, Jordan Grace, Catherine's brother, Barnaby Sr.'s brother-in-law. Nothing like a little nepotism to erode and undermine the financial stability of a company.

"Maybe you should insist that he not contact you again, Nicky? I'm sure that if you threatened to reveal the affair to Patricia he would have no choice-," Jill opines, knowing that's the last thing her friend wants to hear.

Nicole scowls at Jill, "I thought you were my friend? Is that all you can come up with?", she asks irritably.

"Nicky listen, you don't love Caz. You can't marry him. I know that he's been, uh- helping you, but you'd be miserable if you let that decide you agreeing to marry him," Jill advises her friend.

She's taken Nicole's hands and they are seated on the cedar love seat by the river. The dock is now empty, her father not being here often anymore with his duties in Washington D.C., there is no need for a boat.

"Jill, what am I going to do? I thought by now the suit would've been settled, its not, and it could be years before it is, how will I live? I have no income except-, well, Caz has been helping me," Nicole says, exasperatedly and shakes her head.

"Do you think Caz will, um-, stop helping you if you don't marry him?", Jill asks. She feels bad, Nicole is her friend and she is concerned about her. But, she also knows Caz is crazy about

Nicole, would he actually let her fend for herself? She doesn't know, and now Jill shakes her head.

"I don't know what he'll do, Jill. He says he loves me and wants to marry me. He doesn't love Trish, I know that," Nicole says, again with contempt for Trish.

"Have you considered, I don't know, maybe if you withdraw the suit your father's estate would recommence the quarterly payment?", Jill asks.

"I will not withdraw the suit! That money is mine! Father murdered mother, why should he have anything? He's not entitled to a penny, Jill. I will not compromise with him or that old miser, Baron," Nicole says with finality.

"Hey, there you two are," its Ham, looking very preppy in gray flannel slacks and a white cashmere sweater. "I'm not interrupting am I?", he belatedly asks.

The two women exchange a glance but Jill says, "No, not at all, Ham. We were just coming in to refresh our drinks."

The three of them stroll back up to the house.

Hugh had also taken a private stroll, out to the small greenhouse and garden, until his composure could return. With the help of two long pulls off the bottle of Scotch, Dewars White Label, it was just now arriving. Seeing Nicole had unnerved him, it was like seeing Victoria enter the living room. They had the same hip swaying walk, and her laughing and cooing with the baby, Carla, it was eerily identical.

Hugh takes another long pull from the bottle in his hand.

Feeling much calmer now, he also returns to the gathered guests, the supremely confident politico once again.

At the senior Casworth residence it is a smaller though no less joyous gathering. They too are very much in the holiday spirit. Richard is home from Wharton where he will graduate with a dual bachelors degree from the prominent business college this June.

He majors in both economics and mathematics, the last culminating in actuarial cycles and projections. Once so degreed, he will attend Princeton for his ultimate goal of attaining a doctorate/ fellowship in Public Monetary Policy and global financial management.

Richard is a true natural master in the science of economics and Barnaby Sr. is bursting with pride, as well as relief. Florida First, with Richard at the helm, will become the worldwide leader in investment and development of the third world.

Caz is there on this holiday eve with his wife, Patricia Vance Casworth, daughter of Lawrence Vance, the Governor of Florida.

With Richard's stewardship and Caz's political insider access, the state of Florida will become the launching pad to the worlds vast undeveloped territories. Africa, Asia as well as Central and Latin America. Trillions in revenue, hundreds of billions in corporate income and profit.

Grace and Trish are chatting quietly about their respective families. The Governor and the States First Lady, Trish's mother,

Lynn, always an interesting topic. Governor Vance is quite the
maverick, not what the people of this great state expected.

Caz is sulking moodily, he's drinking bourbon, not the
spiced Rum egg-nog the others are sipping. He's tried to get a
reaction from the ice queen, Trish, by being rude, ill-mannered,
and out and out hostile in his attitude towards her.

She has cooly deflected all barbs and pseudo insults he's
flung at her. She will not make a scene or join in his juvenile
temper tantrums this evening. It is Christmas eve, and she is
with her in-laws whom she is very fond of, especially the gracious
Catherine.

They will attend the midnight mass at the Methodist Church
of Coral Ridge later. Patricia is religious, not fanatical no, but
she holds a deep belief in Christian principles and faith. She
does not believe in divorce or abortion.

And, she thinks perhaps after all this time, she may be
with child. She'll know for certain once she see's her physician
right after the New Year. She hopes to surprise Caz with the news.
Maybe that will have a settling effect, and dare she hope, a
maturing effect, on him?

Caz is thinking about the- needed expenditure? Business cost?
Hell, call it what it is, the bribe, the needed bribe money on his
mind. To cover 1974, and then 1975's financial statements cost him
$50,000. 1976's statement must be on Jordan's desk close of business
one week from today, December 31st, at 5:00 p.m. Calhoun is looking
for his- stipend, that's what the money grabbing fool had called it.
Stipend?!

Now that the amount to be hidden is $1,999,000 he's insisting on another $25,000. The amount isn't an even two million because Calhoun advised Caz to stay below that threshold. Any expenditure two million dollars or more must be signed off by the President, Caz's father, Barnaby Sr.

Caz had been hoping to cover the two checks with Nicole's lawsuit settlement money, but its been two years now and next week its financial statement year number three, and still no resolution in sight.

His father won't throw him in jail he's certain, but what will he do? He has a high salaried position with all the perks. Without his job he's-?? He even bought Nicole a 3 carat marquis diamond ring for a Christmas/ engagement present, $15,000. How will he pay for anything?

Caz takes a swallow from the empty glass and almost hurls it across the room in frustration before catching himself. He strides over to the bar and pours the glass half full of bourbon before knocking down most of it in one swallow, and then refilling it. He exits the residences rear door, get some air to clear his thoughts, he thinks.

He walks down to the river's seawall and sits in a wrought iron chair under a huge stand of oaks. It's quite dark and he begins to relax, something will come up and he feels better already. Its the bourbon of course, having it's mind-numbing effectiveness.

After a few moments, he hears, "Caz?" Its his wife, Trish.

"Yea? What do you want? Please don't tell me I'm drinking too much," he says. He can't see her its dark, but he recognizes her voice.

"I don't care how much you're drinking, that's up to you, isn't it always, Caz?", she says with mild sarcasm. She couldn't help it, he's been itching for a fight all day and she has resisted, so far, to oblige him.

He's such a "spoiled baby", is what comes to her mind. If he weren't so handsome? He is truly a "beautiful man", that thought also comes unbidden to her. He's not just handsome, he is beautiful.

That's why she is here, both right at this moment and as his wife. They share very little affection, their love making is?, emotionless, purely mechanical. Trish has looked within to see if its just her, but its not.

How can she respond? Or be expected to respond? to a man who acts like its a chore, an unpleasant one at that, to make love to her? She is very confused. He is her husband for better or worse, she has to try harder. She will not give up.

She walks over to him and brushes his hair up off his forehead with her fingers. He pulls back away from her touch. It hurts, she is only human and she does love him, even though he acts this way and doesn't reciprocate. He used to to but now, lately, nothing.

"I love you, Caz. I always have since I first saw you, since our first kiss. Whatever has happened, I hope you figure it out," she says, softly. She bends and kisses him very tenderly on the lips, before walking back up towards the house.

This time he does hurl the glass, as far as he can out into the river. He feels ashamed. He doesn't know exactly why but that's what he's feeling. He walks up the stoned path back into the mansion. "Merry Christmas, you dumb fuck," he says to himself, "Merry fuckin Christmas."

Its almost 7:00 p.m., where are they? They should have been here by now. Maybe they had trouble with the car? Nettie is working herself into a panic with these thoughts. She's not actually voicing them out of old Italian superstition, "If you say it, it'll happen."

"They" are Joseph and her baby, Jimmy, who she's only seen the one time her and Christy went to visit. He had insisted they not make the trip to see him again, it was too far and he didn't want them on the road alone.

Jimmy, after 4½ years, is free. He was given a Christmas parole, and in exchange, he now is indebted for the 5½ years he didn't serve, of the 10 year sentence. Henry had tried to convince him not to take it on his account, but Jimmy refused, there was much to do and he could not begin quick enough.

Had he waited seven more months he wouldn't have owed the state one more day. He forfeited all earned work gain time and statutory good conduct time by accepting parole.

The way Jimmy himself looked at it was, fuck the paper,(time owed for parole), he'd either make it the right way, lawfully, or he wouldn't. If he failed the legal way the time he owed for the paroled sentence would be the least of his problems.

He and Henry had hugged at the Lieutenant's office gate, both holding on for long minutes before letting go. Henry had one single solitary tear running out of his left eye, his crying eye

Jimmy had often teased, and Jimmy's eyes were brimming full themselves.

"I'll see you for Father's Day, Dr. Smart. My mom will cook you the best Italian food you'll ever eat. Six months, old man, hold on six months, okay?", Jimmy had promised.

Its the only reason he's now sitting in the car with his brother, Joseph, and Joseph knows it too. The brother's are very close, always have been and always will be. Joseph admires his younger brothers dogged determination, with everything. Once Jimmy sinks his teeth into something he's not letting go, forget about it.

And, Joseph knows the entire Dr. Henry Smart travesty, not some overly exaggerated obsessed version, there is no inter-changing multiple versions at all, no- just the one God awful truth version, the one that makes even combat hardened Joseph sick.

Its not Jimmy getting justice for Dr. Smart, or clearing his name, they both are. Joseph is in for the ride till the wheels fall off.

"Here we are, Gatz, long time since we were both here, huh?" he says to Jimmy as they pull into the driveway. Its been 10 years to the day that he, Jimmy and their father had sat together for the last time that night, so long ago, at the dining room table. It goes through both their minds at the same instant, and they look at each other but don't say it.

Nettie comes flying out the door as soon as Jimmy steps out of the car. She is crying, laughing, hugging him, holding him at arms length looking, hugging him again, pinching his cheeks and then kissing him where she just pinched.

Joseph and Jimmy are both laughing, Nettie hasn't looked this good, this utterly happy in- 10 years. Angelo can't be here this night but both her son's are and surely he must be looking down from Heaven and know it.

Christy is expected any minute. All three of her kid's are home! Thank you, God. Thank you, my kid's are all alive and healthy and home, she thinks. She kisses Jimmy's face 10 times and will not let him go. She has to at least be touching him, she's afraid that if she even blinks it'll all have been her imagination and he'll be gone.

"I made everything you like! Look how skinny you are! C'mon, you're going to eat everything. Thank God your home, Jimmy, please, I almost died here without you," she says this very fast, no interruptions, and Jimmy laughs and thinks, I'm home!

He hugs his little Mom, "Don't worry Ma, I ain't leaving again," he says, and then adds, "I want some black olives, a chunk of provolone and a glass of Chianti first." He's thought about them for 4½ years. Nettie pinches his cheeks again and kisses him five more times before she sits him down in Angelo's chair. Then she hurries off to get the wine, cheese and olives for her baby.

Christy has a surprise for her younger brother, well its from Joseph but he's insisted that she take half the credit and no arguing with him either. Dominick is helping her, but where are they, Joseph thinks.

Jimmy is feasting, literally, on every Napolitan seafood dish ever made, and all the delicious side dishes too. He's eating some of everything out of the dozen or more platters spread all over the huge dining room table, as Nettie stands watch.

"Monga baby! There's more, don't worry about saving
anything, monga!", she's telling him, eat! eat!

Christy arrived an hour ago without Dominick. He's supposed
to be right behind her-.

She too made a fuss over her baby brother, she's awed at
how stout and hard he is! When she hugged him it was like hugging
a bronze statue, wow!

"Are you going to stay home this time? Please, Jimmy, me
and Ma can't go through it again," she says, as tears well up in
her eyes. He knows it was bad for both of them but Christy more so.
She alone had to prop up their mother until Joseph made it home.
No more, Jimmy thinks, we've all had enough.

They have one thing to take care of, to finish, Dr. Smarts
freedom. And with Joseph and the lawyer, Baron, they won't stop,
won't quit, until he's out.

Baron knows the horrific truth. Henry told him on an
attorney visit, everything. But, he was bade not to take any action
until all the loose ends could be locked down tight. Hugh Mayor
is a Senator and Henry is a disposable convict. A lot could happen
if the hand is tipped and Hugh becomes aware.

Henry could be murdered, right there in Raiford- easily,
by the guards, by the convicts, by both in consort. It happens
all the time but the outside world doesn't hear about it. Just
another convict killed by his fellow prisoner, or- a suicide hanging,
that's not a suicide at all. These are not paranoid delusions but
cold hard truths. They must be very careful, for Henry's sake.

They are very close now, its only a matter of time, putting the pieces together, can't afford to hurry and make a fatal mistake, literally.

Not after all this. Henry has suffered terribly, irreparably, even once things are set right, (if they are set right), the damage is done.

Victoria is still dead, the humiliation of his imprisonment and the lost years can't be erased, and- he's still there.

Setting things right is the sought for, hoped and prayed for result they seek. Nothing is certain. They could all die broken hearted, there is no guarantee of success. Fear is far to inadequate a word for failure.

Its late, Jimmy and Joseph are finishing off a bottle of wine. They've managed to ease Nettie's mind so she can comfortably retire for the night. They're not going anywhere, they'd both be there in the morning, they promised her. Both son's gave her a long lasting hug and a kiss good night.

Nettie hasn't felt this happy, this relieved and at ease in- 10 years. God bless you, Angelo. God bless your soul. We're all back together, home, she thinks as she lays down.

Christy motions for Joseph to meet her in the kitchen, and when he joins her she says, "That fuckin Dominick is drunk! Marie won't let him drive the bike over, do you-."

"Forget it, Christy, have him ride it over in the morning. I'd hate for the dumb ass to kill himself trying to ride it over tonight, drunk," Joseph says, and then adds, "We'd never forgive ourselves and Marie would curse the whole Carosa family for generations," he smiles. Marie is Dominicks Italian mother. All Italian mothers have a wicked ability to curse other Italian families. The ma'loika, its called, and only the mother applying this centuries old curse can remove it.

Christy hugs Joseph and nods her agreement.

We're coming, Dr. Smart. Good will triumph over evil, not every time, but it damn sure better this time. Its Jimmy's last thought before he too dozes off to sleep.

CHAPTER TWENTY

Christmas 1976 - January 1977

"You can't always get what you want."

Title Song/ The Rolling Stones

Jimmy is running the motorcycle up to full speed on the South bound lanes of I-95, towards Miami Beach.

The 750 Honda is fast, with the Kerker header he's installed adding another 15 horsepower its even faster. At 6:00 a.m. with traffic still light he can turn it loose, the top end an easy 130 m.p.h.

He's going to work on the 40 story condominium Whiteside Construction is building on the Northern tip of the very pricey beach front locale.

Gus, the general manager of the project, who Jimmy had worked for previously, hired him back on the spot without hesitation. He's a hard worker who will do it all, from the dirty and dangerous stripping, (the disassembly of the concrete support structure once a floor is poured, set and cured), to the less physically taxing but far more important responsibility of directing the on-site cranes movements of hundreds of tons of construction materials.

He doesn't complain and he's on time and sober. That put him in the top 2% of the 100 man work force at this job site, right behind old Gus himself as far as he's concerned.

Whatever the incident up in Ft. Lauderdale all those years ago, it's not Gus's business. Knowing the kind of kid Jimmy is the guy probably had it coming. Jimmy's not a malcontent trouble maker. He does his job and keeps his mouth shut, and that's all the old construction manager can ask for.

The first place Jimmy rode his new motorcycle to was the Kamp residence, early on Christmas morning.

Marilyn and the girls were up but they didn't know who the guy on the motorcycle out front was. Kate is 21, and Debbie, the youngest sister, is now 17, she's in her last year of high school.

As he walks up the narrow walkway to the house he's taking off his helmet. Marilyn doesn't need to see his face, uh-uh, that walk is Jimmy!

"It's Jimmy! Oh my God, it's Jimmy!", she is nearly shouting it. She is out the door in her housecoat and almost bowls him over as he picks her up, hugging her tightly.

"Oh my God, Jimmy! Jimmy, Jimmy, you're here! You're really here, sweet Jesus thank you!", Marilyn is half sobbing these words.

They can finally let go of each other, the girls have tears in their eyes too and Jimmy hugs them both.

"What happened to the little girls that used to live here? What have you done with Katie and Debbie?", he asks in mock horror and the girls laugh.

Debbie looks like Melissa. She's almost the same age as when he had met her at the restaurant, light years and a lifetime ago.

"Come in, come in," Marilyn says. "Are you hungry? You want some breakfast? When did you get out?" She asks all three questions back to back to back, before he can even answer any of them, so he laughs and thinks that's the Mari he remembers.

"No, no, and yesterday," he answers, and she looks bewidered until she figures it out and playfully slaps at him.

"Coffee?", she asks, and he nods, yes.

"I'll get it, Mom," its Debbie, and she goes into the kitchen with Kate, giving them a few minutes to talk.

"Jimmy, I'm just so- whew! I can't believe you're really here," Marilyn says, and then, "Your brother, Joseph, sends me money every month. I felt bad accepting it but he insisted. Did he tell you he came to see us? Oh, I don't know, maybe three years ago?", she asks.

"I told him about you, Mari, that you're my other mom, and the girls are my little sisters," Jimmy says, smiling. She hugs him tightly again, how she had missed this boy she now remembers, all over again.

"Don't worry about the money either, he knows you need it," Jimmy tells her.

"You look good," she says, and runs her fingers back through his hair, "I'm so relieved, we heard you ran into a little, um-, trouble at the one place? So they sent you to an even worse place?", Marilyn asks, and actually shivers.

Jimmy smiles, "Lets see, my Mom must have mentioned that-, right?", he asks, and smiles again.

Only Nettie could have worded the events of Sumter, and then the East Unit and Raiford like that.

"She was worried sick, half to death, Jimmy. We all were," Marilyn says in Nettie's defense.

"I know, Mari, wish I could've done things different. I left you all alone out here because I couldn't control my temper. When I saw that son of a -," Jimmy is saying, but has to stop. He's angry, red-hot, all over again, still.

Marilyn jumps right in, she's shaking her head, no, before saying it aloud, "No! Don't! I'm glad you did, Jimmy, and I mean it. That stupid dumb expression he had every time he looked at me, he wasn't sorry, he felt no remorse for what he did- nothing." She too is angry, they both are. The anger nor the sorrow will ever go away.

"Well! Merry Christmas to you too," he says, and it breaks the tension, for now at least, and they both laugh.

"I'm so glad you're here, you're home. You have to come for dinner, promise me we're going to see you? All the time?", she's nodding her head, yes, as she's saying this, and Jimmy's smiling and nodding, yes, right along with her.

Kate and Debbie are peeking from the kitchen, they don't want to interrupt. Jimmy sees them and says quite loudly, "This has got to be a plot. You girls are dragging me long enough on the coffee where, hell, it'll be late enough that I may as well stay for dinner?"

The two sisters giggle, "All right, all right we're coming," Debbie says. She even sounds like Melissa, and just as he thinks that he sees Mari thinking the same exact thing. As she looks at him they both nod and smile in agreement.

He stayed with them all morning. They want to give him a Christmas present but they feel bad for not having one for him. But, his being there was a complete surprise, so- how would they have known to get one?

"Goils!", he pantomimes Archie Bunker, and they all playfully swat at him.

When he leaves he hugs Marilyn, and she has to force herself to let go. "Please be careful, I'll see you Saturday, okay?", she says.

He kisses Kate and Debbie on the cheek, and says, "I'll be here, Mari, I love you guy's."

Marilyn blows him a kiss as he kicks the bike to life and roars off. She looks up at the sky and makes the sign of the cross as she whispers, "Thank you, God."

Joseph and Jimmy went to see Baron before Joseph had to return to Ft. Benning. They know of Henry's innocence but that's not going to change his sitting behind bars. There are many others who need to be convinced, beyond all doubt, to effect his release. Where to start?

With Jimmy. He is going to see Nicole and be the bearer of the good news of Henry's innocence. He will not disclose any critical information in regards to the true assailant. She is going to have to trust him, take it on faith that its not her father.

Should he encounter adamant resistance from her, well, the next stop is Jill Mayor, and Lisa Mayor too, why not? Make it a family affair.

But, Nicole has first at bat. Jimmy contacted, Caz, his old pal. He didn't know where Nicole lived, nor did Henry or the lawyer, Baron, so that's where he started.

Caz was floored! "Holy shit! Jimmy?! Where are you, Champ?", he asked, from the phone in his corner office of the now open

Florida First office tower. It afforded him a panoramic vista East, towards the sparkling blue Atlantic ocean.

They haven't spoken since right after Angelo was-.

"I'm at home, Caz. I just, uh-, got out, ah- I'm wondering if you still see Nicole? Or, where is she living now? Is she here in Florida?", Jimmy asks.

Well! Caz expected Jimmy to ask about a lot of things, but Nicole?

"Listen, can you meet me for lunch? Oh no!, I can't today, shit. Uh, how about you have lunch with me on Saturday at the Club, about noon? I'll bring Nicole along," Caz says.

"All right, yea, great. I appreciate it. I'm not imposing am I?", Jimmy asked.

"No, not at all, it'll be just like old times. Have you- uh, called Jill? Want me to bring her? She's not married, you know," Caz asked, mischievously.

That would really be a blast from the past, the four of them at the Coral Ridge Country Club! Ha!

"No, I don't think you should its, ah-, its not strictly a social call, Caz," Jimmy tells him.

Not a social call? What is that suppose to mean? Caz is definitely intrigued. "Okay, that's your call Champ, I'll see you Saturday, noon, at the Club?", Caz finishes.

Jimmy says, "Fine, thanks, I appreciate your cooperation."

My cooperation?, Caz thinks as he places the phone back in its cradle. What would Jimmy want to see her about? Is Nicole in some sort of trouble? Drugs? No! No, that's not it, but what could it be? Caz is very anxious for Saturday, it ought to be a lot of fun either way. Jimmy's definitely not one of the rich dull bores he deals with daily. Its going to be pretty darn interesting that's for sure.

That lunch date is whats on Jimmy's mind this Friday morning as he is speeding down the interstate towards work. He would've liked to have seen Jill. She's not married? Hmm- But, it's business. If he encounters a brick wall in Nicole he doesn't want to burn his second option, maybe even his last option?, with Jill, at the same instance.

And, what would he say to her even had this been a social call? Hi, how come you never again contacted me? During the most difficult days of my life?

He stopped being a kid the day he was called home from the school to find his heart broken, devastated mother lying on the bed sobbing. To learn that the man he loved, respected, admired, imitated and aspired to be just like when he grew up, his Dad, his beloved father was- gone.

Thanks, Jill. Sorry my Dad wasn't a rich powerful man. Maybe if he had been you wouldn't have turned away from me? Our time together, what was that? Nothing?

He shakes his head to clear out the thoughts, what does he know? It seems the wealthy, to his limited understanding, though not exact of course and not blanketly applicable either, value appearance above all.

Love, loyalty, fidelity, honor, etc..., matter little if at all. They can be applied capriciously according to circumstance. As long as one can believably affect those qualities, whether truly possessing them or not, has no import.

To the masses who are without great financial means, the actual possession of these attributes seem of utmost importance, because it is all they have, their character.

Money is a definite asset in the concealment of ones personal flaws, it paves the road of life's journey so to speak. Character is built on the unpaved road, and great character is built on the unpaved road up a mountain.

At 4:00 p.m., quitting time, Jimmy takes the bike up Alton Road to the 163rd St. Causeway. I-95 will be wall to wall cars and he'd rather cruise up the beach road and avoid the traffic.

He waves to bikini clad girls making their way to their cars. The sun is descending and the day is winding down. It's January, and even with the temperature a mild 74°, the day light is still short.

Jimmy turns 25 next month. Jill is? She's 25 already. She'll be 26 in November, the 11th, Armistice Day, now called, Veterans Day. She's older than he is? Why isn't she married? Caz didn't say she was divorced, only, "she's not married, you know."

He shakes his helmeted head to hurl these useless thoughts out, no place for them. Those days, those youthful, so full of hope and expectation times of yesterday, are never to be recaptured.

We can't have yesterday, there's only now, today, and

perhaps a tomorrow that's yet to come. Yesterdays gone- That thought saddens him, more than he can understand.

He takes the Causeway West towards the interstate and home. The only hope of tomorrow for Jimmy is the actual next day meeting with Caz and Nicole. After that, it's up to fate.

At 7:00 a.m., early Saturday morning, he pops into Marilyn's and insists that she accompany him, on the motorcycle, to the beach, and he won't take no for an answer.

"No Jimmy! I won't get on that thing, and what will you do with an old gal like me? I look terrible in a swimsuit," she says, and wrinkles her nose at him.

"Uh-uh, bull, get your suit on Mari. We're getting some quality time together, remember? You're the one who insisted that I come over often, and here I am. Lets get moving," he orders playfully and smiles. It'll be good for her to get out of the house for a couple of hours.

She hurriedly brushes out her hair and dons a one-piece swimsuit and a pair of baggy cut-off shorts. She's 44! What is she doing getting on a motorcycle with a boy half her age? Well almost half, close enough-.

She's mildly embarrassed as they pull away from the small house with both daughters hooting and hollering at her.

He drives slowly and carefully with her on the back. The beach is still deserted when they arrive. It's a beautiful bright sunny morning, the air a little cool yet at this early hour, upper 60's, before the midday warm-up, which today is supposed to be 77°.

They laid out a huge blanket and used their shoes to hold down the corners.

"Mari, I want to put in a few miles," Jimmy is telling her, meaning he's going to run, "Can I leave you here alone? Or will I have to chase all your admirers away when I get back?", he teases her.

"Very funny, you bring me here and now you're running off and abandoning me?", she tosses right back at him.

He laughs and says, "I'll only be 20 minutes and we'll take a swim when I get back, but just in case-, there's a shark billy in the gym bag, feel free to conk any oglers."

She swats him playfully, and says, "Go, go- shoo-."

He gets 3 miles in 22 minutes. On the sandy shoreline, even with the sand partially packed, that's not to bad. Its not his Rock time, but...

When he gets back, Marilyn is wading in the water, just her ankles. He scoops her up and plunges wildly into the surf with her, her laughing screams carrying up and down the nearly empty beach.

"Ooh- I'm going to get you for this, Jimmy," Marilyn pants as she pushes her hair up off her face. They are chest deep and the water is unsurprisingly warm. The ocean this far down the Florida peninsula is usually warm and mild.

Jimmy laughs and dive's beneath the surface. She looks but he's gone! Suddenly, he comes up right underneath her! In one smooth, easy motion she is perched atop his shoulders and he is wading in towards the beach with her laughing and pulling his ears. He had startled her so by sneaking up like that.

"To bad there's no one around, we could've challenged them to a chicken fight," he says. By now, he's close enough to the shore that he can run up onto the beach and to their blanket, where Jimmy kneels down and lets her get off.

"Well! Let's see, its been, um, 15 years since I've done that, maybe longer. The last time- uh, John and I with the girls," Marilyn says, remembering.

Jimmy looks at her, she;s still pretty and she's not that old either. "Why don't you-," Jimmy begins, but then he falters, he doesn't know how to approach the subject tactfully.

Marilyn does though, and quite bluntly too, "What? Date someone?", she says, and smiles. She can see Jimmy is mildly abashed and she finds it amusing, but is also touched by his genuine concern for her.

"I'm too old," she says, and puts her hand up in a stop gesture before he can voice his protest.

"I don't want anyone, Jimmy, really. The girl's are grown, I'll have grandchildren, my family, I can be content with that," she finishes.

"Well, all right. But if you happen to change your mind I'll ride you off into the sunset on my bike, okay?", he teases.

She laughs happily at that and says, "I'm sure all my nosy neighbor's believe you've already done so." And they both get a good laugh at that, indeed!

She looks good, relaxed. He remembers the hollow shell she was right after-, those days at the courthouse together. She seems okay now, much better, thank God.

Jimmy tells her about his lunch date today, in just a couple hours now, and its purpose. He tells her about the old Doctor himself.

Marilyn is horrified, "Oh, Jimmy, it must be terrible, that poor man- , do you think you'll be able to help him?", she asks.

"We're going to give it everything we've got. Could use some help, Mari, it wouldn't hurt for a little divine intervention," he smiles at her. Mari's a pray-er, and Jimmy believes her prayers for him have worked in the past. He needs them again now he's certain.

"I'll pray for you and him. I always pray for you, you know that, but I'll pray that you are successful. That poor man, Jimmy," she says shaking her head.

She kisses his cheek when he drops her off and hugs him, making him promise to call and let her know how the lunch turned out.

The fight for Henry begins now. Today is round one, its a 15 round bout- its the first fight Jimmy has ever feared losing.

Caz and Nicole arrive fashionably late, 12:30 p.m. Jimmy was on the guest list at the door and was escorted into the main dining room. He was offered a lounge seating until Mr. Casworth arrived, but he's not drinking, he prefers coffee, so he's at the reserved table when they arrive.

Nicole is beautiful, far more lovely than Victoria. Since she is unaware of the purpose and intent of today's lunch, she is quite pleasant to Jimmy as well.

"James! You look fabulous! Doesn't he, darling?", Nicole says liltingly, and holds her cheek up for the perfunctory kiss. Jimmy has risen at their approach and he quickly performs the obligatory peck to Nicole and shakes Caz's hand.

Caz will have none of that casual formality, no sir, he hugs Jimmy in a bear hug and booms, "You look great, Champ! You're like a solid hunk of granite," and he slaps Jimmy on the back as they sit.

The waiter hurries over and Caz orders a double bourbon, and then looks at Jimmy almost as if to challenge him to order something milder.

"That'll be fine," Jimmy tells the man, and Nicole says to Caz, "I'll have a vodka gimlet, darling," and Caz gives her order to the waiter.

Very strict etiquette Jimmy observes, Nicole refusing to speak directly to the waiter, as if by her doing so would corrupt her impeccable social manners.

Its not going to be as easy as he'd hoped, perhaps he underestimated her? Maybe both of them? Caz is worth a lot of money, like the pissing contest just now with the drink order.

Here goes- "Nicole, I was with your father at Raiford," he begins and looks at both of them evenly.

Caz has the beginnings of a small, tight lipped smile forming and he's quickly glanced sideways at Nicole.

She herself is sitting back looking very pleased and relaxed, her lips are parted just a bit. The two appear to be expecting some sort of peace initiative or compromise, something. From Henry? Via Jimmy? Something isn't right, their not asking any questions and they both seem only to willing to let him have the floor.

"He's innocent, Nicole, he didn't kill your mother," Jimmy says to both of them, looking from her to Caz, and then back to her.

Nicole's reaction is like lightening, immediately sizzling! She sneers, "How dare you?! How dare you come here and insult me?!, insult my mother's memory with that ruse?!" She is livid.

But when Jimmy looks at Caz he's actually smiling.

Caz is thinking, I knew this was going to be a live one, Ha!, the fire-works are just getting started.

The waiter approaches with their drinks and as soon as he places Caz's in front of him, Caz gulps it in one swallow and says, "Keep it coming," to the astonished waiter. This is the Coral Ridge Country Club, not some honky tonk, people don't usually consume their beverages in such fashion. He's never seen it in his entire 15 year tenure as an employee here.

"It's not a ruse, Nicole. Your father doesn't care about the lawsuit, the money, he's innocent! He wants his life back, he wants your mother back, of course that's not possible, but he still loves her," Jimmy finishes, imploring her to listen.

"Have you come to try to bargain with me? Perhaps my father is seeking a compromise? I'll give him 1 million dollars James, that's my final offer. Take it or leave it," Nicole replies.

She hasn't heard one word of what he's said.

"Nicole, its not about money," he says very slowly, very
calmly trying to get her to listen.

The waiter is back with Caz's drink. Caz is sitting on the
edge of his seat looking from Nicole and then to Jimmy, and then
back again, like a verbal tennis match. As fast as the waiter sets
the drink down, Caz again tosses it right off and smiles broadly
at the truly bewildered waiter, and says, "Don't stop, Jeeves, keep
em coming."

The members of the club are the elite, the monied, the
powerful, they are never wrong, never! Give them what they want
and do it quickly and without question, so the waiter hurries off
to replenish Caz's drink.

"You say it's not my father? That he's innocent? If he's
innocent, James, then who is it? Do you know? Am I to blindly
accept this? Your gut instincts shall we say? Do you have anything
more than mere speculation?", Nicole probed.

"I can't say, you have to accept what I'm telling you in
god faith. He's your father, Nicole, he's innocent!", Jimmy answered,
but it sounds hollow even to him.

Nicole frowned, "Not hardly, James. Caz, I'm going to the
ladies room, I'll be ready to leave when I return," she informs both,
the conversation is over.

Caz is giving Jimmy that same look he did in high school.
Its a mixture of admiration and devilry. Caz has never provoked
any deep emotion in women. They think he's beautiful, yes, but his

persona, his character, is so shallow that there is no depth to be pondered or revealed. Its always been a mystery to him, he's much more comfortable on the surface, skin deep, literally.

Jimmy is just the opposite, he seemed to always effect women deep within, even as a teenager.

"Listen, Champ, if I can help you I will, you hear me?", Caz asks.

Jimmy's nodding, yes, "Thanks, I'll call you in a few days if something comes to mind, Caz," Jimmy says and they shake hands, standing.

"Call me either way," Caz tells his old friend.

Nicole is walking back confidently, she slows just a moment to beckon Caz to follow, which he very reluctantly does.

Won't be any hanky panky today, not with Nicole acting like this.

CHAPTER TWENTY ONE

February - March 1977

"He's your oldest and your best friend,

if you need him, he'll be there again."

Beautiful Loser/ Bob Seger

Jimmy had no other options immediately available but to contact Caz. He waited until he could speak with Baron and his brother, Joseph, first.

They both agreed that Jimmy had acted correctly in not revealing anything tangible to Nicole regarding Henry's guilt being challenged.

That fact must be kept strictly confidential until they, the three of them, could present substantive, concrete evidence to the contrary. Should it become known prematurely by the wrong person or persons, a cover-up could be effected, making the gathering of exculpatory evidence in Henry's favor much more difficult to obtain.

Should the discovering party or parties panic, which must be taken into full account, Henry may very possibly be in mortal danger.

Jimmy was advised to proceed thusly, try to enlist the assistance of his old high school chum, Caz. They would then attempt to persuade Nicole to relent her out and out betrayal of her father by her adversarial position that is stemming directly from her civil suit against Henry's estate.

Of course, Jimmy has already tried that without Caz being on board, with no success. Nothing to lose by one more try- but, he doesn't expect any different result. The next stop is? Jill? Lisa? both? Maybe, Caz first.

Its a rain soaked day along Florida's Gold Coast, comprised of the three southern most counties along the Atlantic coast, of Dade, Broward, and Palm Beach.

This is the last inclement weather the area will experience until the Summer rainy season in late June and July.

Whiteside's condominium project has closed for the day. At 9:00 a.m., any of the crew that showed is sent home with a half days pay.

Jimmy is running his bike up I-95 through whipping sheets of rain because of just that reason, the half day rain out pay. Anyone who's ever worked construction knows the established companies will pay the half days for rain-outs. He needed that money so why not show?

He takes the Broward Blvd. exit and goes East towards the ocean. He's not going to the beach, of course, its a miserable day, chilly and wet. Its the last of the cold weather this winter.

He rides his bike up under the buildings facade. Its quite deep and he is no longer being pelted by the rain. He parks and gets off, shaking out the rain from his soaking wet clothes. Seeing himself in the ground floor lobby windows, he looks half drowned.

He does have a towel though, its under the seat of his bike. After removing his helmet he dries off the best he can, shaking the water out of his ears and hair. The rain was undetered by the helmet as he drove up the interstate.

He enters the vast lobby of the Florida First tower. There are at least a dozen bank teller windows on each side of the huge L that takes up most of the lobby. The remainder is a carpeted area with several desks of various bank employees. They are speaking in hushed tones to patrons who are seeking home or auto loans, or possibly establishing savings or checking accounts.

Jimmy walks through the bank towards the elevators where the building directory is located. Barnaby Casworth is on the 22nd floor, suite 2200. Barnaby Casworth Jr. is also on the same floor, in suite 2250, along with eight other top executives. He presses the elevator button but the door is already sliding open, disgorging its occupants. He enters and presses #22.

When he exits the elevator, he follows an arrow pointing left that says suites 2250-2290. He stops at 2250. On the glass door stenciled in black lettering, it says, 'Vice President, Marketing, Barnaby Casworth Jr."

He enters but there's no one inside. The receptionists desk is unoccupied. He hears a woman's laughter, throaty and sounding very amused.

He calls out, "Excuse me, is someone here?" Of course he knows that, he can hear her laughter, but it was the only way to make them aware of his arrival.

From the hallway leading to the offices a tall, very pretty blond emerges. She is wearing a navy blue suit with an extremely short skirt.

She asks, 'Hello, how may I help you?" She is looking at him with amusement. Jimmy is certain its because his clothing is soaking wet and dripping onto the carpet in the waiting area.

"Uh, yes, thank you. I'm James Carosa, I would like to see Mr. Casworth,Jr.," he adds hastily.

"Caz? Yes, -one moment please. I'll tell him you're here Mr.- Carosa?", she asks, but she is already retreating down the hallway back to the office.

"Jimmy?! Hey, Champ! Come on back, geez you're soaked. Rene, bring us some- coffee?", he looks at Jimmy as he says the last.

Jimmy nods, yes, and says, "Yea, thanks, maybe I can dump some over my head and get the chill out." The air conditioning in the offices combined with his wet clothing has given him goose bumps.

In Caz's office, Caz throws him a towel from the bathroom located behind a louvered door, and says, "Here, dry yourself off and get out of that shirt. I've got extras in the closet over there," he nods towards another door.

Jimmy strips off the wet shirt and uses the thick fluffy towel to dry himself, much more thoroughly this time. He's taken a white Oxford dress shirt, size 16"x35", from the closet. Jimmy wears a 15"x34" so its a little big, but that's okay, its dry and it'll do.

Rene brings the coffee and departs, closing the office door.

"So, what brings you here? Looking like that?", Caz asks, smiling. He's noticed the helmet so he knows why he's soaking wet.

"I'm coming from work, we were rained out. I figured I may as well try and see you while I got a day off," Jimmy explains. He almost added, some of us have to actually work, perform a task or function vs. flirting with your secretary, but of course he doesn't.

Caz, as if reading his old pal's mind, laughs and says,

"That's Rene, my executive assistant. She's quite the multi-tasker, worth every penny. Now, what do you have for me? Let's have it, Champ, I can see the wheels grinding," Caz is tapping his forehead as he says this.

"Caz, listen to me. I know some things, some pretty bad things, about- some very dangerous people," Jimmy tells him. He hesitated just that instant to phrase it obliquely. Not powerful people, or monied people, or politically connected people, all of whom could be quite dangerous also.

Caz is looking intently at Jimmy. He remembers Angelo. The old gangster is how he still thinks of him. It was the way he talked, every gesture, every nuance. Jimmy has some of it too, but not even close to the old man, his father, Angelo.

When Jimmy's Dad talked, you listened. It was like getting lessons, free lessons, in life. He could spot a phony, a fake, a mile away. In mere minutes, Angelo would either be able to vouch for you, "He's a 100%", or caution against you, "He'll turn on you in a minute." Never mind that the old guy had known you a whole 5 minutes before rendering such judgements. The truly amazing thing? He was never wrong! Never!

He could do it with women, too. "You gonna have your hands full with this one," or, "She's good, you see your mother? same thing."

"What did your Dad ever tell you about me, Jimmy?", Caz asks now. The question coming out of left field like that catches Jimmy off guard.

"About you?", Jimmy says, he's stalling, feigning misunderstanding of the question.

Caz is leaning forward, his elbows on his desk, staring at his old high school ace-deuce. That was an old moniker for each other from their pretend beat-nik phase, way back, Caz remembers.

"Yea," Caz is nodding his head up and down as he says this, "What'd he say about me?"

Jimmy turns away from Caz's intense stare. Caz is hardly known for intense anything, except maybe intense drinking.

"What difference does it make, Caz?", Jimmy asks, it even sounds ridiculous to him. Caz has got him, he knows Jimmy took every piece, every shred of advice from his Dad as absolute, not maybe.

Jimmy looks at Caz and nods, yes, "All right, listen, this cannot be spoken to anyone, any-mother-fuckin-one, Caz, nobody! We'd be endangering someone else's life. Not yours and not mine, someone else's-," Jimmy says seriously, and looks to see if that's how Caz is taking it as well.

"All right," again Caz is nodding, yes, "shoot, let me have it," he says.

Jimmy exhales, "Dr. Smarts wife, Victoria, she -uh, she was having an affair, Caz. That's who killed her," Jimmy tells him.

Caz is wide-eyed and all ears too. "Who, Jimmy? Who was the affair with?", he asks. He thinks he already knows the answer! Shit! Fuck!

"You can't tell anyone, nobody Caz, or Dr. Smart is dead. I lived right there with him in Raiford for four years, where he's at right this minute," Jimmy pounds home the point, one last time, again.

The silence in the office is palpable. The two high school buddies, now grown men, are staring at each other.

"I think I know, Champ. I do, but- you tell me," Caz says.

Jimmy hesitates for just a moment before saying, "Hugh Mayor, U.S. Senator Mayor."

Caz just nods his head again, not surprised, not shocked, nothing. He raises his eye brows and gives Jimmy a tight lipped smile, or grimace, same thing.

"What do we got to do?", is all Caz says, and he can see the stress and tension literally deflate out of Jimmy. He damn sure can't blame him, shit!

They talked the rest of the morning away and Caz had lunch brought up, with Rene joining them. The talk, at least in regards to this mornings topic, was finished. Caz could now fully engage the lovely Rene with flirtation and frivolous banter, a subject he is much better suited to.

Caz told Jimmy about the money, the $1,999,000 loan to Nicole. He also mentioned his wife and that their expecting a child in, oh, 7 - 7½ months, almost as an after thought, seemingly. Trish, Patricia Vance.

Patricia Vance? Jimmy tried to place her, from school?

"Nope, she didn't go to school down here with me and you," Caz told him.

"Her name is familiar, why?", Jimmy asked.

"Well-", Caz was smiling like the cat that ate the canary.

Jimmy had to concede, "I give up," he said.

"Her Daddy's the Governor!", Caz literally crowed. Wow!

Jimmy and Caz hugged like long lost brothers when they parted. Caz is in, whatever he can do, just say so and he'll make it happen.

Jimmy is absolutely certain, positive, that Caz will not disclose their conversation to anyone. He'll update Baron and his brother by phone, Baron today if he can catch him in the office.

Joseph could be a bit more difficult to reach. He's scheduled to lead a Ranger officer qualifying and field assessment test at the Ft. Walton Beach Ranger training camp.

Its 30 days of you by yourself in the wild, with nothing but your dud weapon and ammo, your skills, and your- in soldier parlance- balls. You eat what you catch, no gunfire. That's only for the enemy. Of course, there are none of them here in the good old U.S. of A, hence the dummy ammo and weapon, but you're still toting the 8 pound M-16 and 14 pounds of dud ammo for authenticity sake. No, you hunt with your knife. Water? Well there's plenty of water. No matches, no fires period, ever, you're deep in enemy territory.

Whoever makes it out the other side, maybe they'll lead a Ranger patrol- maybe.

You fail if you're late. You have 30 days, not 30½ days, you get lost or for any reason have to activate your emergency locator beacon, you emerge without your weapon or any of your equipment, you allow Joseph or the other observer, Lt. Col. Mackey, ambush you, or set a trap you run into without first marking your discovery clearly in green day-glo dye, (you have one tiny vial, its as precious as your own blood), It will be verified whether you located and marked your trap, the one set very specifically for you.

Any failure, out of the hundreds of required duties you must accomplish during the 30 days, besides actually living through it, you fail.

You will not lead Ranger's. You may lead troops but not a Ranger troop, sorry. It is a grueling designed for failure survival course, that 80% of the junior grade lieutenants sent here to qualify fail. The same failure rate as the enlisted men who aspire to be a Ranger.

Baron is out till the following day, Joseph is out till March 19th. All Jimmy can do is wait.

Gordon is busy, very busy. Its early March, the Black Tuna Gang has been tried in state court in Miami and he testified at that trial. Now, a federal grand jury has indicted three of the members, the leaders, and Gordon is assisting the federal prosecutors in preparing the case for a federal trial some time later this year.

The state verdicts rendered are sufficient to get the gang imprisoned, but not for life. The federal indictment charges all with murder for hire, and a conviction for that offense will result in life sentences in a federal penitentiary. Life in the fed's is life, forever.

He has traced back the origins of each man in the federal

indictment. How did they come to power? By who's sanction were they allowed to operate in Miami? Who did they answer to?

In digging deep into the past of the three indicted men, Gordon has uncovered ties to the one time Boss of all Miami. Jimmy "Blue Eyes" Abaticcio, who's own ascension to power, the top spot, followed the hit on Eddie Coco in December 1968.

Almost 2 years to the day later, Blue Eyes himself was shot point blank inside a Hallandale nightclub, right under the noses, literally, of over 200 Mafiosi celebrating the New Years holiday.

Something that gordon can't sew up or account for is, why?

Coco's hit coincided with another hit in New York, the Bronx, of Philip "Philly Black" Catalanotto. It was typical Mafia style house cleaning, out with the old and in with the new. Some up and coming Mafioso wants a promotion and he don't want to wait any longer. The wait comes to an abrupt end in a hail of bullets, to the next biggest fish ahead of him. And now that job, that position, is his.

Its been going on for generations, that's the normal path of progression in the rackets, murder.

In Blue Eyes instance, Gordon can't find the thread, there isn't one. It was not a planned or sanctioned hit. In fact, in the weeks following Blue Eyes murder there was a scramble for succesion, who would replace him?

Gordon has gone cross-eyed looking for a lead, anything. There isn't one. But if there isn't, then why is he dead? That's the mystery, a Mafia Chieftain is whacked and nobody within the outfit carried it out? Under no orders from anyone?

But, there is no in house retaliation either. The Mob didn't kill Blue Eyes, Gordon is certain, so, who did?

The next question and a bigger mystery is, why? Why? What was the motive? A hit on a made man of high rank such as Blue Eyes? Who only answered to two people above him, the leader of his crime family and the Godfather of all the families.

Its a million dollar hit, not maybe, He was killed in a room full of Mafiosi. And his button man? Two Ton Tony Gallante, that's his name. The Boss has a greeting card, a Happy New Year card, for his button man, for his body guard!, in his dead hand.

Gordon actually laughs and shakes his head. Hey, you gotta want to shake that guy's hand. Sure he's a criminal, a killer, a bad man. But the man he killed was evil incarnate, and it was a very neat and tidy piece of work. You got to love the guy's style and sense of humor, Gordon actually chuckles. Its been a long day, its been long weeks of long months actually, too many.

He closes the file on his desk. There are another two dozen or so scattered all over on every piece of furniture and piled in every corner of his office.

He turns out the lights and makes his way through the deserted office, its 6:30 p.m. He's the last one here except for the two guy's emptying the trash cans and sweeping up.

He nods good night to Donnie and Lucious, the night janitors. He knows their names and they know his. They've had coffee together a couple of times the last three months.

"Calling it quits early, Mr. Rollins?", Donnie jokes.

Gordon smiles and nods, "Only till I can get a cot brought up to sleep on, Donnie, good night," Gordon answers.

Gordon gets on the elevator and down to the lobby. One good thing about the late hour? No traffic on I-95 towards home.

Jimmy had spoken to Baron by phone twice before finally reaching Joseph back at Ft. Benning.

The attorney was upset and mildly irritated that James had taken it upon himself to be candid and truthful with the Casworth gentleman. Wasn't he, uh, involved with Miss Smart?

There was no easing his attitude towards Caz. Baron would reserve further comment concerning the man until he had an opportunity to consult with both James and his older brother, Joseph. In his office, if possible.

To avoid any further complications with Caz and Nicole, Jimmy decided not to meet Caz at his office nor at the Country Club. They'd meet for a drink at a small hole in the wall. At a Big Daddy's lounge called, The Hut, right off Sunrise Blvd. and the intracoastal.

It was much safer to avoid any questioning whatsoever, from whomever, at the purpose of Caz meeting with Jimmy. They could always fall back on being old acquaintances, but better to leave it completely blank.

Jimmy, Joseph and Baron are having coffee at his offices. Its near 6:00 p.m. but still relatively light outside. Next week daylight savings time goes into effect and some of the larger construction companies will begin overtime, working through 7:00 p.m.

It won't bother Jimmy, his $15.00 an hour job is $600.00 a week, with overtime he'll bring that amount home, maybe a little better.

"So, Joseph, James, you both seem very certain that this Casworth fellow is trustworthy. Its my clients, well actually, our clients freedom at stake, possibly his life," Baron is saying, and he looks directly at Jimmy as he says the last.

Jimmy starts to protest but the old lawyer holds up his hands in a gesture of surrender before continuing, "I'm not questioning you, James, nor you," he nods to Joseph.

"Henry has absolute faith and trust in you," he looks at Jimmy, "And so do I James. Without you we'd still be muddying around with the dying statements validity, the challenge as to his guilt would not be the strong issue we have now," Baron finishes.

"Thank you, I appreciate it, Mr. Baron," Jimmy tells him.

"Listen, Caz is okay, don't worry he's with us- his wife, Trish,is the Governor's daughter! Talk about getting a head start? Great place to begin if you ask me," Joseph says, shaking his head as if in disbelief at their- good fortune? Divine providence?

"I've thought that exactly myself, its my sentiment also, Joseph. If we had one law enforcement professional on board, just one, a prosecutor perhaps, or a state police investigator, even a former retired man of that persuasion," Baron says, looking at the two brothers as if he expects one of them to magically produce such, right off the top of their heads.

"What if we did, Mr. Baron? What would that do?", Joseph asks.

"Do?! Indeed! I would file a petition to the Governor for

clemency, right now, as fast as they would set a hearing date. With your military credentials, and my own not to shabby reputation," Baron adds self deprecatingly, before continuing, "One law enforcement agent in agreement with us, that Henry is innocent, and his son-in-law's already on board, you said so yourself-," Baron finishes.

He once again is looking between the two brothers, from one to the other, as if he expects a challenge to what he's just said. Like his summation to a jury, he gets no objections here either.

The old lawyers, call it what it is, instincts, tell him that his query of just moments ago has yielded results. To say he's not surprised would be untrue, because he most certainly is, quite in fact.

The esteemed courtroom litigator, "Lord of the Court", he's fondly nicknamed because of both his name and his demeanor in front of juries, now says, "Joseph, do you care to reveal this person?" He's looking at the Lt. Colonel searchingly. Joseph seems hesitant, why?, he wonders.

Jimmy is also staring wide-eyed with astonishment at his brother.

Joseph knows someone, from many years ago, in a steaming jungle.

He now says to Baron, "I have to make a call. Can I use your phone?"

Joe Baron smiles and nods, yes, as he hands Joseph the phone.

CHAPTER TWENTY TWO

March 1977

"You can't hide your lyin eyes,

and your smiles a thin disguise."

Lyin Eyes/ The Eagles

Gordon is engrossed in the thick phone book sized state
trial transcript from the recently concluded trial of the Black
Tuna Gang in state court.

He is very displeased with what he has so far gleaned
from his review of the documents.

The state, in its zeal to obtain convictions, had offered
many of the prosecution witnesses extremely generous judicial
largesse in exchange for their testimony.

So generous in fact, that it comes very close to suborned
perjury by the state prosecution. It is so blatant that no Federal
District Court Judge will allow such testimony. It will be dis-
qualified in the upcoming federal test.

Gordon will be surprised if the state appellate courts
uphold the convictions. He feels quite certain that the trial
courts judgements/ convictions will be overturned, vacated.

It was a very sloppy job, poorly done at every phase of
the prosecution.

It makes obtaining convictions here at the Federal level
critical. It is imperative that federal prosecutors deliver guilty
verdicts on all three defendants, on the offenses charged in the
bill of indictment.

With the state judgements almost certain to be overturned,
should the prosecution fail here in Federal court, the three
criminals responsible for over a 100 murders would be back on
the street in possibly 1-2 years.

It definitely adds a sense of urgency to Gordon's present
discovery investigation. The prosecution has 90 days, from the

date the bill of indictment is rendered by the grand jury, to present to the court and defense counsel its case, preliminarily called discovery.

The clock is now ticking, each day counting against the 90 day time limitation. The federal case presented to the grand jury relied heavily on witness testimony, testimony that Gordon has just now found to be highly questionable, flawed and unusable in the upcoming discovery phase.

They could lose the case without ever having a jury empaneled, or the presentation of any evidence, if the discovery is not credible enough to warrant proceeding to trial.

It is Gordon's responsibility to compile the vast amounts of facts. The physical evidence, as well as material, expert, or eye-witness testimony, that the government will present in each particular criminal prosecution. He is the investigative arm of the U.S. Attorney.

The prosecutor in the courtroom can only present to the jury the evidence amassed against the defendants by Gordon's investigation. He has a tremendous burden in all criminal prosecutions. His investigative summation of every facet of the criminal complaint, is the bedrock that the U.S. Attorney and his assistants stand on in the arena that is the courtroom.

Their case, their successful presentation to a jury, is wholly dependent on Gordon's compilation of unimpeachable evidence.

If the courtroom litigator has the unenviable task of presentation, he must be concise and brief, but also instructive, simple yet exact. He must display brilliant oratory without

appearing pompous. He can do none without the inglorious trench
work of Gordon. The lawyer standing at the bar gives voice to,
vocalizes, the case Gordon makes. That's it in a nutshell.

Gordon closes the thick transcript, and rubs his eyes.
He's going in circles. He looks at his watch, its just after 6:00 p.m.
He's deciding whether or not to call it a day. Maybe go home and
be able to get in a quick 3 mile run on the beach before its
fully dark, or perhaps get a cup of coffee and dive right back in,
what to do?

As he sits contemplating these choices, the phone begins
to ring in his office. After 5:00 p.m. there is no switchboard,
the phone rings straight through to four locations around the
U.S. Attorneys offices, his is one of the four.

One ring- Answer it or not? If he does-, two rings, it may
forgo his having to decide the earlier options entirely, three rings-,
yes or no?, four rings- he finally answers. "U.S. Attorney's
office, Chief investigator Gordon Rollins speaking, how may I
help you?", he asks.

Gordon's answering the phone is quite a surprise to Joseph.
He takes it as one more sign of being on the side of the angels.

He now says, "Yes, sir, I'm Lt. Col. Joseph Carosa. I'm
stationed at Ft. Benning in Columbus, GA."

"Yes sir, how can I be of assistance Colonel?", Gordon asks.

"I, uh- Lt. Gordon Rollins? Flew F-4 fighters off the U.S.S
Enterprise? June 1969?", Joseph asks. There is dead silence on the
phones open line.

Joseph's known for years who the Navy fly boy was that
they pulled out of the jungle from the North Vietnamese Army.

Hell, Gordon had called everyone but the President himself trying
to locate G.I. Joe. But, it was Joseph himself who had insisted on
anonymity. He was doing his job, his duty, he didn't want any
special attention for it.

The men, boys actually, who'd been left over there
deserved all the attention. There were still over 2,000 listed as
M.I.A right now.

"Excuse me, Lt. Rollins, are you there sir?" Joseph asks,
and immediately regrets using the mans military rank. He's a
civilian now, a government lawyer.

"I'm, uh- yes, yes I am Colonel. I looked for you since,
uh-, since I got stateside," Gordon says, he's almost whispering.

"If I've reached you at a bad time, I'd be glad to call
you again when its more convenient, Mr. Rollins, or- I can give
you my ph-," Joseph is saying, but Gordon says, "No! Uh, no, no
its fine Colonel, I'm just," he laughs, "speechless," he finishes,
and they both laugh. It breaks the awkwardness they both were
feeling.

"Mr. Rollins, I-," Joseph says, but Gordon interrupts
once again, and says, "Please, call me Gordon, Colonel, I insist."

"Okay, Gordon, uh- we need to talk, this isn't purely a
social call, as you may have guessed? I managed to conceal my
identity from you for quite some time," Joseph tells him.

"You certainly did, Colonel. I ran into a brick wall
everywhere I turned. So did my Dad, he's former military, too.
Between both of us we managed to come up with exactly zero," Gordon
tells him, with a hint of admiration. Joseph had certainly went

to ground.

"Well," Joseph laughs, "You're very persistent, I'll give you that. Had the need for your assistance not arose, I never would've contacted you, or allowed the Army to disclose my identity. I did my duty in Vietnam, that's all I was doing. I didn't want, don't want any special recognition for it. The men we left behind, both the K.I.A and the M.I.A are the only ones who deserve our recognition," Joseph informs Gordon truthfully, thinking back about Weegie and Ruckus as he says the last.

"All right, yes, understood Colonel. Would you prefer we meet to discuss your- issue, or?" Gordon asks.

"Yes, if its not to much of an imposition or inconvenience? I'm at an attorney's office in Ft. Lauderdale. Is it possible for you to come here? Is that improper considering your position? We could-," Joseph is asking, but Gordon says, "No, no imposition or impropriety, give me the address, Colonel."

Joe Baron takes the phone and gives Gordon the address and exact directions to the former residential townhouse he now uses as his office.

Gordon jots down the address and says, "Give me 45 minutes, I'm leaving now."

After the connection is ended, Baron and Jimmy are staring at Joseph inquiringly. They both expect an explanation of some sort. They're not going to get it, not the long version of it anyway.

Joseph says, "A fly boy I pulled out of the jungle, maybe he'll help."

Baron and Jimmy look at one another, and then at Joseph,

before once again looking at each other.

"That's it? That's all you're going to say? You're not telling us more than that?", Jimmy asks expectantly.

Jospeh turns to him and nods, yes, before saying, "Yep, that's it."

Baron smile broadly and thinks, just when you think life holds no more surprises for you, it jumps up and bites you right on the ass.

"More coffee? Or-," he asks now.

Joseph says, "Coffee's fine, thank you."

Jimmy just nods, yes, he's scowling at his brothers obstinance.

As Gordon is driving North on the interstate, he remembers that he forgot to call Lisa and tell her he'd be late, maybe real late, he'd found G.I. Joe! Well, the soldier found him, but still. He's pondering what he'll say to the soldier, who's own modesty or not, saved his life.

Lt. Colonel Joseph Carosa, the name is familiar for some reason. Carosa, Carosa- he can't place it but he knows he's heard that name somewhere, where? As hard as he concentrates, it doesn't come, its just out of his consciousness.

At exactly 46 minutes from the moment he hung up on the lawyer, he is pulling into a Spanish styled townhouse with a red tiled roof and stucco finish.

All the lights are blazing inside. The house stands alone on the West side of the broad avenue that runs through the heart of downtown Ft. Lauderdale. Its situated on a recessed lot, without neighbors to either side.

Gordon shuts off his car and exits. As he approaches the entrance he sees, Joseph Baron, esq., Attorney At Law.

Its dark, the last traces of dusk having disappeared. As he reaches for the doorbell, the door opens, and a distinguished looking gentleman of perhaps 55 years old, in shirt sleeves with his tie loosened, extends his hand, and says, "I'm Joe Baron, thank you for coming on such short notice. Follow me." They shake hands and Gordon walks into a foyer.

The building is a huge hacienda styled two story townhome that has been converted to Baron's place of business, as a sole practitioner.

Gordon has heard of the esteemed lawyer. He's called, the Lord of the Court, he remembers all this now because the first trial Baron ever lost came about 5-6 years ago.

He was defending the rich society doctor, yes, that's it Gordon thinks, he recalls the whole episode now. It was Jill's friend, Nicole's father, a Dr. Smart. Could this meeting be in regards to that? No,- could it?

Gordon follows Baron down a long terrazzo floored hallway. The stone was used in all South Florida homes in the pre-air conditioned era of the 30's, 40's, and 50's.

The hallway terminates into a huge library that spans the entire width of the houses veranda along the back of the home. There must be 1,000's, perhaps 10's of 1,000's of volumes in this room, more than many public libraries he's certain, its very impressive.

There are two men seated in plush arm chairs, and they both rise to their feet as Gordon and the old lawyer enter the room. Gordon steps up to the Colonel, he's in dress uniform, and extends his hand, saying, "Gordon Rollins, Colonel, very pleased to finally meet with you, again, its been a long time."

Joseph smiles genuinely and shakes hands saying, "Yep, it sure has, and may I say that you're looking a hell of a lot better than the last time I saw you." Its true, what he just said to Gordon. The last time Gordon was naked from the waist down and black and blue from navel to toes.

"How are you feeling?", Joseph asks. He's surprised to see Gordon looking so well, the miracles of modern medicine.

"Fine, just fine Colonel. I uh- I want to say thank you. I know it was just your job, your duty, but please let me say it," Gordon tells him. He's waited years to be able to.

Joseph nods his head, yes, he understands. He extends his hand to Gordon this time and they shake firmly. Gordon's gripping Joseph's with both hands.

"This is my brother, James. We call him, Jimmy, and you've met Mr. Baron?", Joseph asks.

"Yes," Gordon replies. He extends his hand to Jimmy and they also shake.

"Pleased to meet you," Jimmy says.

"Gordon, may I call you, Gordon?" Baron asks, and Gordon says, "Certainly, yes."

"Do you want some coffee, or-? Lets have a drink, I think the occasion calls for it, hmm?", the old lawyer asks, looking around at all of them.

Gordon nods, yes, and says, "Sure, whatever you have is fine with me."

Joseph says, "Okay, this is a special occasion, I agree."

"James?", Baron asks, and Jimmy says, "Sure, whatever you all are having."

Baron brings out a bottle of 30 year old single malt Scotch and pours two fingers each into four tumblers. He says, "A toast, gentlemen?"

Joseph looks around at them and says, "To us, to success in what we are here for this evening."

They all touch glasses and take a swallow of the very smooth and aromatic whiskey, the old lawyer saying, "Here, here," to second Joseph's toast.

They sit in four arm chairs around a huge oak table.

"I'll get right down to business, Gordon. Its getting late and I'm sure you have a home you'd like to get to, so lets not waste time," Joseph says.

Gordon nods, yes, and Joseph looks at Baron and nods to the lawyer, giving him the floor.

Baron rises, he thinks better on his feet. Its from all the years he's spent pacing in front of juries, sometimes with a man's life, literally, hanging in the balance.

"I represent Dr. Henried Smart. He is innocent, Gordon," Baron informs, as he holds up his hand in a stopping gesture towards Gordon. He could see Gordon's surprise at that statement, and before Gordon can interrupt he wants to continue with his soliliquoy, let the young lawyer ingest the whole tragic story at one time.

"Victoria, Mrs. Smart, was- a hem, involved in an extra-marital affair, this affair was approximately 3 years in duration. I have every reason to believe that it was her lover, in this relationship, who- murdered her," here he pauses to take a sip from the tumbler of Scotch, and then he continues, "I have personally gone over every facet of the investigation conducted by Ft. Lauderdale police Lt. Arena. I've reviewed physical evidence, witness testimony, and all items seized during a search effected at the Smart residence that was authorized by warrant. Only one piece of physical evidence is out of place, that being a bottle of Dewars White Label Scotch found at the murder scene, literally, in the master bedroom where the shooting occured. Finger prints taken from the bottle do not match any of the Smarts who resided there, nor the servant staff. Further, that was the only bottle of that brand found at the home," Baron concludes.

This time his pause has purpose, to allow Gordon to ask questions, which he obliges almost instantly by asking, "Who is the lover?" Gordon looks ashen, all the color has drained from his face. Odd, Baron thinks, but he looks to Joseph and Jimmy who almost as one shake their heads, no.

"We'll get to that, Gordon, I- we, cannot disclose the identity without certain assurances from you," Baron says.

"Mr. Baron, I am a law enforcement agent. I cannot withhold any information from my superiors concerning any criminal conduct, nor offer immunity without first seeking their approval," Gordon responds. What do they know? he wonders. He may be ethically and duty bound to disclose anything they discuss here to the proper authority.

"We are not asking you to withhold any information into criminal activity that may yet occur," Baron says, citing the canon of disclosure, for any knowledge of crimes that may occur sometime in the future.

Gordon looks at each one of them in turn, contemplating his decision. The criminal activity they want to discuss has already occurred, he won't be ethically bound to disclose it. His own sense of dread is what is making him hesitant, not the men here in the room with him.

The old lawyer is a pillar of respectability in the legal community. As for the Lt. Colonel, there is no need to have any, not one iota, of reservations concerning the soldier, he is the epitome of honor. The young man, the soldiers brother, he is the only unknown quantity. But, just his familial ties to the Colonel makes his case, why not.

"Okay, I'm listening. As long as this is in regards to past conduct you have my guarantee it won't leave this room," Gordon assures them.

Baron looks at Joseph and Jimmy before going ahead with the tale. "The lover is a very powerful man, Gordon. So powerful that I fear, we all fear, that should he become aware that he is the object of an investigation, it could become very dangerous for Dr. Smart, especially where he now resides," Baron says this seriously and in hushed tones to convey the gravity of what he's just said.

Gordon is looking about the room, nervously it seems to

the old lawyer, at each of them.

Baron looks at Jimmy, and as if on cue, Jimmy now takes up the conversation.

"Gordon, I was in Raiford with Dr. Smart, for over 4 years," Jimmy says. He can see Gordon's astonishment at that fact, but he too continues quickly so the young attorney will get the entire picture in one dose.

"Dr. Smarts life is very expendable being where he is. He can be killed for a carton of cigarettes, by any one of more than 2,000 convicts, at anytime. He can be killed by, lets call it assisted suicide, that's really murder, at any time, by the guards," Jimmy is saying. He could see that Gordon was getting ready to interrupt him so he's holding up his hands and says, "Please! Let me finish, don't interrupt- hear me out."

Gordon had involuntarily reacted to Jimmy's statement involving collusion on the part of the state, or any government body, to kill a person they are entrusted with the custody and care of. Gordon is a straight arrow and he will not accept the existence of inherent evil conduct being sanctioned by agencies of the state or government.

"Whether you believe it or not, it happens all the time, Gordon. The outside world doesn't hear about it, but that doesn't mean it doesn't happen," Jimmy finishes.

Gordon makes sure the young man is finished and now he adamantly refutes what Jimmy has just told him, saying, "I don't believe that for one minute! Do you mean to tell me that the guards kill inmates? You expect me to believe such utter falsities?" He has just tacitly called Jimmy a liar.

Jimmy is not stupid, not by a long shot. He knows what this goody two shoes, Mr. straight and narrow asshole, has just called him, and he's red-hot.

Joseph sees this in the nick of time, thankfully- and before Jimmy can pounce he's standing in front of him. He's ordering him, literally, to stand down. "Don't you dare, Jimmy-, you hear me!? Don't!" Jimmy is still standing nose to nose with Joseph.

In a much milder tone, Joseph says, "Let me handle this, Jimmy. Come on, I got it," Joseph reassures and Jimmy sits back down.

"First, Gordon, you owe my brother an apology. He's not a liar, he's as much a Ranger here," Joseph points at his heart when he says here, "As I am," Joseph says, looking intensely at Gordon. Jimmy is still glaring at him, and Gordon relents.

"Okay, I'm sorry. I -uh, whew! This has been a rough couple of months for me, and this meeting here tonight-, I apologize, Jimmy," Gordon says, extending his hand to him.

Jimmy looks at Joseph, who's glaring at him now, and so he complies and shakes Gordon's outstretched hand.

Baron has been quietly observing all the interplay amongst the three men. Joseph the honorable modest warrior, young James rough and tough, brutally honest, the old lawyer thinks and smiles. And Gordon-? Gordon has something hidden, he doesn't know what it may be, but something...

Joseph now takes the floor, time to lay the cards on the table. Before Jimmy beats the guy up, Joseph thinks with amusement. It had been close.

"I'm going to cut through all the innuendo and subtlety, you in or you out Gordon?", Joseph demands.

Gordon looks at Joseph, this man saved his life, if he can help him he must. "I'm in. If I can help I will. This may be out of my league, I-," Gordon says and shakes his head. This definitely wasn't what he anticipated.

"Mrs. Smarts murderer is a U.S. Senator, Gordon," Joseph says this quietly, almost as if he fears being overheard.

Gordon is staring open-mouthed, shaking his head, no, no-

"Until Dr. Smart is safely out of Raiford this cannot be made public. Will you give me your guarantee, as one man of honor to another, as a comrade in arms, that you'll keep this in confidence? Only until we can resolve the issue of Dr. Smarts personal safety, after that-," Joseph asks with grave sincerity.

"Yes, yes- you have my solemn oath as a member of the bar, and as a fellow officer and comrade in arms," Gordon avows to Joseph.

Gordon looks totally wrung out, like he's had a very difficult time of ingesting so much controversial information in one sitting.

He stands now and shakes Joseph's hand, and then actually salutes him. He also shakes Jimmy's hand, again offering an apology. At last he clasps the old lawyer's hand, the Lord of the Court. "What do you need me to do?", he asks Baron.

Baron looks at Joseph and Jimmy, and they both nod, yes, this time. He's in.

CHAPTER TWENTY THREE

April 1977

"Do you feel like we do."

Title Song/ Peter Frampton

Gordon's investigative ability has been greatly diminished the last few weeks. It is nearing the end of the month and he's made little if any progress with the upcoming discovery conference, scheduled for the three leaders of the Black Tuna Gang's attorney's, in preparation for trial.

He hasn't been able to live and breathe the case, as he's done so often in the past with previous investigations. The reason for his uncharacteristic departure of single mindedness in regards to his profession is two fold.

One was his discovery of the identity of the man that was killed that night in December 1968 with the infamous, Eddie Coco. After an exhaustive search back through the stacks of records that he'd reviewed previously, he'd found that man was one Angelo Carosa, Joseph and James Carosa's father. Now he knows who killed Blue Eyes.

More disturbingly, by far, is his recollection of a conversation he'd had with his lovely wife, Lisa, oh lets see, shortly after they had married in June 1970. It is the content of that long ago conversation that has haunted him night and day since that night at the old lawyers office.

Lisa had told Gordon about her parents marital problems of the preceding six months, specifically, her father's infidelity to her poor, sweet, saintly mother, Cynthia. To repeat it verbatim, 'My father's betrayal of mother, of all of us, for that bitch, Victoria."

Those words have been echoing continually through his head, almost to the breaking point. He has been on automatic pilot, his physical appearance is suffering as well, he has bags under his eyes from lack of sleep, even his occasional night time jogging on the beach has done nothing to quell his anxiety and stress.

His co-workers attribute it to his dogged pursuit of perfection in his investigation, working non-stop and overtime on the Black Tuna preparations upcoming discovery presentation. If they only knew-.

He hasn't confided in anyone, not the old lawyer or Joseph and Jimmy, and certainly not his own wife, Lisa. He's kept his oath of confidence he swore to.

Something has got to give.

Joe Baron has two witnesses, known only to him, that can offer incriminating testimony against Hugh Mayor, his father-in-law. One can positively place him at the murder scene. The finger print on the Scotch, the Dewars White Label bottle found at the scene, will be the physical piece of evidence that, along with the witness testimony placing him there in Victoria's bedroom, convicts him of her murder.

Gordon is positive the print lifted from the bottle, which just happens to coincidently be Hugh's preferred brand of Scotch, will be a match. He gives a bitter laugh to himself.

If he doesn't let this out to someone, soon- it will be his undoing, literally. He's lost 15 pounds, his 6' even frame looks ghastly at 150 pounds, his suits and shirts are hanging on him like a young boy playing dress up in his Dad's clothes.

Lisa too has begun to notice and she is becoming alarmed. She's made a doctor's appointment for him and insists he keep it, or else!

Or else? Hey Lease, the doctor said I'm okie-dokie, fit as a fiddle. All I have to do is help put your father in jail for the rest of his life and viola, good as new! He again laughs bitterly.

He must make a decision one way or the other. If he goes one way he risks losing his wife and baby daughter, forever. If he goes any other way he loses himself, everything.

Everything he's ever been or stood for, stands for right now this minute, believed, lived and was ready to die for,- gone.

He is going to do something, he must, today, it ends today. He loves Lease, he loves baby Carla, she's a miniature Lisa already at 20 months. It is to them he owes his happiness and to all that is good in life, in being alive.

But, he gave his oath to the Colonel, his brother and the old lawyer. It is to them he owes his honor. He is a Navy man, an aviator, his father flew combat missions as a Marine over Guadalcanal. There is a calling even higher than love or family, or both.

It is duty, honor.

Gordon picks up the phone and calls Ft. Benning. He is put through to 2nd battalion headquarters and speaks to a Lt. Bell before Joseph quickly comes on the line. They agree to meet that evening in Ft. Lauderdale at the law offices of Joe Baron, esq.

Lisa and the baby are playing happily on the beach across from their home on Ocean Blvd. Carla loves the surf, she can play dodge the waves all day until she is totally exhausted, and falls fast asleep in a matter of seconds upon being placed in her play pen crib.

Her Mama is also exhausted from playing catch Carla all morning, and now as they enter the cool shaded house both mother and daughter are ready for a nap.

After placing Carla in her playpen crib in the living room, Lisa strips off her swimsuit and heads for the shower. She'll bathe Carla later, the poor darling is so sleepy she's cranky and fussy.

Just as Lisa is entering the bathroom the phone rings, she wraps the towel around her and goes back into the living room where she collapses onto the leather couch and picks up the phone.

"Hello, this is Lisa, how may I help you?", she says into the phone.

"Hi, Lease, its me," Gordon answers.

"Hi Sweetie! Didn't expect you to call, is everything all right?", she asks.

Gordon hasn't been eating or sleeping well and he looks terrible, he's lost weight and she's worried.

"Yes, everything is fine, Lease. I'm going to-, can you and Jill meet me, say about 5- 5:30 p.m., at Ernie's? We'll have some conch chowder and a beer. There's something we have to talk about and Jill needs to hear it too," he tells her. Ernie's is a local restaurant that is frequented by police and courthouse personel.

Lisa has to fight down her rising panic and calmly asks, "Gordon, are you all right? Did the, um-, did the doctor find something? You're beginning to worry me, are you okay?"

"Yes, I'm fine, don't worry. I promise, there's nothing wrong with me, okay?", he insists. It works, Lisa is calmed.

"Okay, I was just you know, you haven't been sleeping or eating well and I thought-," she says, leaving her last thoughts unspoken.

Gordon laughs, "The appointment isn't until May 5th, I've got that long for sure," he teases her.

"Oh, you!", she replies, feigning anger.

"How's my other baby girl?", he asks.

Lisa yawns, "Oh, excuse me," and now she laughs, "She's sleeping like her mommy needs to," she tells him.

"Okay then, night night, I'll see you at 5:00 p.m., okay?", Gordon finishes and hangs up.

What is going on?, she thinks. Why in the world does Gordon need to see me and Jill? She shakes her head and gets up and goes into the shower. She'll call Jill after she gets refreshed and awake. She yawns deeply again, being a mommy is hard work she muses. Its a tough job but somebody's got to do it, she laughs to herself and turns on the shower, cold and full blast. That'll get her moving.

Joseph called Baron right after he spoke with Gordon and they've made the arrangements for a sit-down tonight at his law offices. He asked Baron to please get a hold of Jimmy at Whiteside Construction, and the old lawyer has assured him he'll make sure James knows he needs to be there at 5:00 p.m. Baron will meet Joseph at the airport.

Joseph's flight to Ft. Lauderdale arrives at 3:55 p.m.,

from Columbus, GA via Pensacola, Florida, via Orlando, Florida. The two hour flight takes almost six due to the connecting flights needed.

He is not concerned, Gordon must come on board fully, Baron has made probes to the Governor's office, he's spoken to Vance's Chief of Staff, Archibald Henry, twice, setting the stage for an audience with the Governor.

Got to sew it all up today, they've wasted enough time- weeks- Joseph thinks, as he's packing one overnight bag for the trip South.

Gus has called Jimmy on the walkie-talkie. Jimmy is supervising the two cranes hauling buckets of concrete up to the 16th floor for the column forms they are pouring. Every bucket holds one cubic yard of concrete. One bucket is swinging out to the pour crews every minute, they'll finish in 3-4 hours tops.

"Jimmy here, Gus, what's up?" he asks.

"You got a lawyer- Baron, says to be at his office at 5:00 p.m. tonight," Gus informs him.

"Ah- you need me here, Gus? I'll get there late if-," Jimmy is saying.

"Nah, no overtime tonight, probably Wednesday and Thursday, you're good," Gus radio's back.

Tonight? Must be Gordon's pumped his ball- ah, nerve up. Its about time, Jimmy thinks.

At 4:00 p.m. Jimmy is roaring out of the ground level parking area. He'll make it to the old lawyer's in 40 minutes,

no fooling around with traffic, he'll run up the emergency vehicle
lanes and when necessary, in between the regular traffic lanes with
the backed up, stopped cars- fuck it.

Joseph is greeted at the gate by Baron. After exchanging
greetings they make their way through the airport towards Baron's
car, parked at the curb outside, illegally, right where a sign
says: No stopping, standing or parking anytime, in bright red.
Hmm, fuck it.

Gordon leaves his office early, without notifying anyone.
He wants to beat the rush hour traffic going North and by 4:00 p.m.
it'll be jammed. He races along I-95 doing 70-75 m.p.h in his
government issued Ford Fairlane, the epitome of an unmarked cop-
car. He doesn't care, fuck it.

At 4:45 p.m. all four men are at the attorney's office
just South of the courthouse and Ft. Lauderdale. They shake hands
all around and Baron, the unofficial chairman, calls the meeting
to order. They've dallied long enough, its time to proceed.

"What's your decision, Gordon? We are prepared to proceed
with a clemency petition. I have everything I need to make a very
convincing argument and I see no reason for further delay, so-
what's it going to be?" Baron asks forthrightly.

Gordon's lips move but no sound comes out. He clears his
throat and tries once again, and this time he speaks and says,
"My wife is Lisa Rollins, nee Mayor, Lisa Mayor Rollins," he says

only that to the trio, who are all shocked to silence.

"Excuse me, ahem- did I hear you correctly?", Baron asks, he is shaking his head as if to clear the cob webs, or whatever, from his ears, he couldn't have heard what he just did.

Jimmy is gaping open-mouthed. He is floored by Gordon's announcement.

Joseph is the one who finally finds his tongue and says, "By the way you look, am I correct in assuming that you haven't yet discussed this with, ah- Mrs. Rollins?"

Gordon is shaking his head, no, as he says, "No, I haven't, but I can't continue like this ah- Colonel, the last few weeks have been-." He cannot continue to speak, he has tears in his eyes and its plainly evident that the stress has finally won out.

Joseph gets up and walks over and pats Gordon gently on the shoulder. He can only imagine the pressure he's been under the last few weeks.

He looks at Baron and with raised eye-brows asks, "Can we go ahead without him?"

"Well Joseph, I- uh-," the old lawyer begins to say, but Gordon interrupts, and standing now he says, "No! No, I'm in! I have to, that's not why I asked you all to meet me here, no." Gordon is shaking his head, no, to emphasize his position. He looks at the three men who are all looking at him questioningly, each with the same identical thought, how?

Its his wife's father! What will this do to them? His marriage? They cannot ask this of him, they can't, Joseph knows that.

"Gordon- you can withdraw, we cannot ask you to do this, its to much. You've kept your oath under such extreme circumstances, that no one in this room were aware of, excepting yourself of course." He's being offered a way out by the Colonel, all he needs to do is take it, he can walk away with his dignity in tact.

"No! I am not withdrawing, Colonel. I want to bring my wife here, now. She's waiting for me at Ernie's Grill, its just a few minutes away. She has to know why I'm doing this, and-, I need," Gordon hesitates, looking from one man, to the other, to the other, and then continuing, saying, 'Your help- in telling her, her father is a murderer," he whispers the last.

They can plainly see this has taken a lot out of him, but he wants to finish it.

"Do you want me to accompany you to Mrs. Rollins?", Joseph asks.

But Gordon is shaking his head, no, and then says, "No, I'm fine. I'll be back in 15 minutes," and he heads out the door.

Lisa and Jill are seated on the 2nd floor open air patio with the baby Carla sitting in her hi-chair between them. Its quite comfortable and cool. The patio faces East, and at this hour its been in the shade for 4-5 hours already.

They are drinking iced-tea. Carla has chilled apple juice in her bottle, that she's alternately sucking a few swallows from, banging on the hi-chair and, on occasion once or twice now, she's thrown it onto the floor laughing happily at the way it bounces. The three make a very attractive little party. Many of the patron's are admiring the ladies with the adorable baby.

Lisa knows some of the admirer's from her days with the Broward State Attorney's office. A few have stopped to say hello and compliment on how beautiful her daughter is. Where is Gordon?, she thinks.

It's just past 5:30 p.m. when he arrives. He leans down and kisses first Lisa, and then his little bundle of joy personified in baby Carla, who squeals with delight and throws the bottle to the floor, to show her Daddy what a neat little trick she's learned, bouncing the bottle off the floor she laughs. He gives Jill a quick peck on the cheek and takes a seat between the two sisters, opposite the baby.

Lisa and Jill both look at him expectantly. They've discussed what the issue could possibly be that required both of their attendance here tonight. A promotion? No. A divorce? No! Definitely no, on that one. They found that choice hilarious, Gordon loves Lisa madly, and the baby. He's been fired? No! Why would Jill be needed to hear that? He's ill? He had promised he wasn't, but- if it were something very grave, wouldn't it be better if Jill were present? To console Lisa? Regretably- yes.

"Are you guy's hungary?", he asks, he's stalling, he doesn't know how to begin the task...

Lisa and Jill look at each other and both simultaneously shake their heads, no, before Lisa says, "We're curious is what we are, Gordon. Don't you have something you want to tell us? Some Earth shattering news?" She regrets the wording immediately, what if he is ill? Not a very good choice of words, she chides herself.

They are both staring at him, waiting. How do you tell the woman you love something like this? How? He doesn't know, he can't, that's why he has the three men waiting at the old lawyer's office, he couldn't do it alone.

.   "I, uh- we have to go see some people, a lawyer actually, and his associates, they can explain everything. They're only a few blocks away, come on," he says, and stands up to leave, or starts to anyway.

Lisa will not have any of it, no sir! She's been stressed out all afternoon and lets have out with it, no more games!

"No! Gordon no, I'm not going anywhere but home. You either tell me, us," she looks at Jill as she says, us, "now- or we're leaving. I don't know what the hell type of stunt this is suppose to be but I'm out, and I mean it," Lisa says with finality.

Gordon is sitting again and he tries to take her hand, but she snatches it away, and says, "I'm waiting."

"Hey, Lisa! Gordon," Jimmy says, as he approaches their table, "And, oh! Look at the baby! She's beautiful, Lisa- Hello, Jill," he says very nonchalant, like its the most natural thing in the world, running into them here, like he's just seen them days ago, instead of years, (almost 9 in fact, but hey, who's counting?).

Carla has tossed her bottle to the floor. She wants to show her trick to the nice man who just walked up, and she is squealing delightedly at its bounce.

Silence, dead eerie silence in fact, as if a ghost had just popped up at their table, at Ernie's of all places, a cop hang out.

"Uh-," that's all Gordon can make his mouth say.

Jimmy's only surprise is Jill, he didn't expect her to be here with Lisa. After 20 minutes he decided to ride over, see if there was some problem, what the hold up was.

"Can I sit down? Or-," he asks.

Jill is staring at him, gaping openly. She actually shakes her head in utter confusion before finding her tongue and mumbling, "Ah- yes! Yes, excuse us we're, uh- we weren't expecting-."

Well of course you weren't expecting me, he thinks, you all look like Boris Karloff just walked up in full mummy regalia. He has to stifle a chuckle that's threatening to boil up.

"Gordon, what is? What is going on?" Lisa asks. She is definitely floored with the sudden appearance of Jimmy Carosa, who they haven't seen in years. And the strange meeting here tonight? Its all very- odd, yes, and confusing.

Gordon looks at Jimmy. Both sisters observe this so they too look at him. He says, "Let's go have a drink, some 30 year old Scotch, at our associates place, okay? Be a lot simpler to let him explain it all."

Now that the initial shock has worn off, Jill is looking at Jimmy with eyes like sponges, absorbing every drop of him. She's completely forgotten she's suppose to hate him, isn't that what Lisa said? She doesn't hate him, not at all, she..., and as she's thinking all this he turns and looks at her. His eyes, all that emotion pouring from them, just like they used to, she remembers it like yesterday.

"Come on," Jimmy bids the group, as he stands offering his

hand to Jill, "let's go have that drink."

Jill takes his hand and- it fits!, she thinks, it fits perfectly. Lisa is looking daggers at her but Jill could not care less, she's not letting him go twice- uh, uh.

Lisa has picked up Carla and she and Gordon are going downstairs to the parking lot.

"Want to ride on the bike with me?", he asks her.

"Okay, yes," she answers. He gives her hand a squeeze at that and she squeezes right back, both of them smiling.

Jimmy now contemplates the task at hand, it will be anything but easy. The touche moment he had imagined, upon telling the snob Lisa her father is a murderer, won't happen, Jill was not part of that equation, not at all.

When they get outside he tells Gordon they'll follow them over, keeping Lisa's car in between them so they don't lose her at a red light or something. Its only about 6-7 blocks to Baron's office.

As he hands Jill her helmet, that he's unbuckled off the sissy bar on the back of the bike, he has to assist her in strapping it under her chin. She's looking up at him while he's doing this, and a flood of emotions come back to both of them. He can't help it, its almost an involuntary reflex, truly, he gives her a quick "Dear Prudence" kiss on her lips. Her eyes widen and she smiles.

When she gets on the bike behind him she wraps her arms tightly around his waist, but only after she ran her hands up and down his chest. He turns to look at her and she tries to return his quick peck of a moment ago, but their helmets clunk together and their lips come up short. They both laugh.

He tells her, "Hold on, Jill," and she thinks, I'm not letting go again.

They follow Lisa out of the parking lot, she's behind Gordon, and the little caravan heads to their meeting with destiny and fate.

PART V

KNOCKIN ON HEAVEN'S DOOR

(Epilogue)

CHAPTER TWENTY FOUR

May 1977

"Mama come take this badge off of me,
I can't use it anymore."
Knockin On Heaven's Door/ Bob Dylan

Patricia Vance Casworth is 5 months pregnant and it certainly has begun to show. Her mother, Lynn Vance, the First Lady of the state of Florida, is hosting an early lunch for a small group of ladies. They are all here for the same purpose, the Governor's expected pardon of Dr. Henried Wright Smart.

For two of the ladies it comes at great sacrifice and personal loss. The ladies are all chatting cordially and politely, and Lynn Vance is thankful for that. It could have been quite a disparate group had the ladies not been friends since childhood.

Lisa Rollins is here with her simply adorable baby, Carla. Her sister, Jill Mayor, is also in attendance, and Nicole Smart, who's father is the man Lawrence, Lynn's husband, is pardoning.

Lynn knows the entire tragic story of Dr. Smart. The Governor and she had spoken about it at length.

The ladies are here at the behest of the attorney Baron. Lisa, Jill and Nicole may be called upon to present testimony in the proceedings soon to begin at the Governor's executive offices.

Considering the circumstances with which the group is presently gathered here for, it could've been very ugly for all parties involved, it is quite much to put behind one, but...

Joe Baron is at the Governor's office with the petition for executive clemency. He is joined by Gordon Rollins, Assistant U.S. Attorney for the Southern District of Florida, Lt. Col. Joseph Carosa, a concerned citizen, his brother James Carosa, also a concerned citizen, Barnaby Casworth Jr., the son-in-law of the Honorable Lawrence Vance.

For Gordon, the irony of this date is comical. Its May 5th, he has a doctor's appointment they've forgotten to cancel. With all the recent events it was the last thing on his or Lisa's mind.

After the meeting at the old lawyer's that night, some 12 days previous, many perspectives have irrevocably changed.

Most assuredly Lisa's regarding so many aspects of her life that heretofore, she would've never thought possible. And for Jill also, so much so, about everything.

And last but not least, Nicole. The guilt ridden and contrite Nicole.

The three women will never be the same as they were before. It will be left to each individuals perception of whether the changes wrought were for better, or worse. Only time will bear the truth or falsity of each.

Contrary to what may have been the popular or favored outcome of the events of 12 days ago, it was Lisa who sat quietly, listening, accepting the old lawyer's presentation, piece by agonizing piece, calmly and analytically.

Jill was the disbeliever, her emotions refusing to accept logic, proof of the obvious incrimination of her father, the Senator. She was outraged and hostile to everyone sitting in the conference room. She had attempted a physical assault on Gordon for his perceived betrayal.

It was James who managed to finally get through to her. He used every bit of charm and persuasion to console her, to bring her to acceptance of the cold hard truths about Senator Hugh Mayor, her beloved father.

Hugh's dishonesty and lying to her mother, Lisa and herself, about everything, his entire life was one big lie, and that hurt Jill deeply. It was as bad as her realization that he was a murderer. She hated him.

And not a little girls hate, like that horrible Christmas years ago, this hatred would never heal.

Nicole had forsaken her father, abandoned him, never writing to him, not once, or visiting, ever. She had compounded her cruelty and abject indifference to his plight, by stooping to the depths of a common thief, in her callous and selfish, greed inspired attempt, to loot the Smart estate trust.

And her former lover, Caz, who is now reconciled with his wife, Trish, and is expecting the birth of their first child in September, no more hanky panky there. That's over with, for now anyway. Nicole is a formidable opponent, and very beautiful, it will be many years before this siren's song is silenced,

All she has left now is her father. She is ashamed of her behavior, truly, her doubting his innocence was the worst of it. Will he take her back? Will Henry still love his little girl? Perhaps.

At Governor Vance's office, Joe Baron, attorney for the petitioner, is pacing up and back, issuing a masterful soliloquy as to the merits of the presented petition to the Honorable Governor. He has placed all the evidence in perfect sequence, and has with him here this day all the true facts, regarding Dr. Smarts innocence of the crime he is presently imprisoned for.

He begins with the first of two written statements. The
first, that of Aranxa Vasquez, chief housekeeper at the Smart
residence, and employed over 10 years as part of the domestic staff.
She has stated in a sworn affidavit, "That on the night of Mrs.
Smarts murder, she herself observed a tall blond man, later positively
identified as Hugh Mayor, exit the master bedroom just seconds
after a sharp loud popping noise. He ran to a boat docked at the
neighboring property, the Blackwell estate. Dr. Smart persued
this man, firing two shots from a pistol at the hastily retreating
craft, before returning to the bedroom and calling for the police and
medical assistance. He then tried giving aid to his mortaly stricken
wife.

"Joe, I have a question before you proceed. Why didn't
this domestic tell the police this the night of the, uh- incident?",
the Governor asks, using the familiar Joe, they are old acquaintances.

"She is a Cuban emigre without the necessary green card
documents, at least at that time, she now possesses the needed permits.
She was concerned that she would be expelled, returned to Cuba, so
she feigned sleep to avoid being questioned by the police. The
police weren't very thorough in their interrogation, only questioning the few who volunteered to speak with them. She did this out
of fear, Governor," Baron informs him.

The Governor nods, yes, and says, "Okay, continue."

"The other statement is from a Jewel Kedd, a domestic at
the Mayor residence, and still employed there by the way," Baron
says and hands the statement to Governor Vance, who dons a pair of
reading glasses and begins to peruse the affidavit.

They are all watching him to see any reaction, hopefully not a negative one.

"Hmm-," the Governor says, and he is once again nodding, yes.

Joe Baron has gone far beyond thorough in this presentation, he is leaving nothing to chance. Since that day in August of 1971, the old lawyer has been sick morally and emotionally. He had failed, and he had failed a friend, who also happened to be innocent.

It has been a crushing burden and he's fought tooth and nail, every inch, to vindicate his old friend, Henry. He is on the doorstep now, knocking...

The Lord of the Court could never get around Victoria's last dying statement implicating Henry. From the trial jury's finding on through the appeals process, her statement carried far more weight than any of the combined evidentiary exhibits together.

Governor Vance knows all the facts. He understands completely the need for confidentiality. It is why this hearing is presided over by only him and his chief of staff, Archibald Henry, and not his full cabinet.

Baron now calls James Carosa. He is sworn in by the chief and begins his testimony. Then his brother, the Lt. Colonel Ranger battalion commander, then the Governor's son-in-law, Caz. There is no adversarial cross examination in such a hearing as this. The Governor and his designee can simply ask whatever they wish at any time during a discourse.

Now it is Gordon Rollins turn. He is sworn in and relates his knowledge in regards to this matter. The Governor has heard from the citizen witnesses, James, Joseph and Caz, but it is Gordon's

testimony that carries official weight. He is a sworn officer
of the U.S. Justice Department, a member of the bar, He talks for
two hours, even retelling the quote of Lisa's, almost 7 years before.

But the statement that gets the most attention is,"The
unindicted assailant, who in my professional opinion is the murderer,
is Senator Hugh Mayor, who happens to be, ah- my wife's father, my
father-in-law."

Both the Governor and Archibald, his chief, are taken by
complete surprise. They knew about the Senator, but they didn't
know about the family association between he and Gordon. They both
exhale loudly as they shake their heads and look at one another
in disbelief.

Baron gives them a moment to compose before continuing,
he's almost done.

"Investigator, at this juncture, do you anticipate Senator
Mayor's indictment for the murder of Victoria Smart?", he asks.

"Yes, I do. Its a certainty," Gordon replies.

"Just so we know, do you think Dr. Smart is falsely
accused? Falsely convicted? Falsely imprisoned?", Baron asks.

"Yes, I do," Gordon answers.

"One last question, would you stake your professional
reputation on it?" Baron queries.

"Yes, absolutely," Gordon says, nodding, yes.

"Governor, I ask for Henried Wright Smarts release, under
the authority vested in you, by the constitution of the great state
of Florida. What say you?", The Lord of the Court finishes with
a flourish.

"Granted! Henried Wright Smart is hereby granted executive clemency," Governor Vance orders.

He then says, "Arch, call Louie, (The Department of Corrections Secretary, Louie Wainwright), Tell him he's got 20 minutes to have Dr. Smart out the front door."

The Governor rises and shakes Baron's hand, the old lawyer has tears in his eyes. The Governor then goes around and shakes the hands of all the participants. He's actually thanking them, "for their determination is setting a grave injustice to right," he tells them.

Governor Vance then takes James to the side for a personal chat.

"James, I've attached an addendum to the clemency certificate of Dr. Smart," the Governor says, and seeing his surprise, he explains, "You've been pardoned, son."

He holds up his hand to keep Jimmy from interrupting, and says, "Its an earned gift, you're a young man, you've served your sentence. This will allow you to move forward," he tells Jimmy.

Jimmy is stunned almost speechless, but he does manage to say, "Thank you, sir! You won't regret it, you have my word."

"Good luck to you," the Governor says, and they shake hands,

The pardon, dated May 5th, 1977, effectively shields Jimmy from any and all state prosecutions, for crimes committed up to today. He's free.

Blue Eyes, the Sumter incident, all of it.

When Jimmy thanks Baron, the old lawyer is stumped.

"No, James, it is I who thanks you," he says.

"No, no, the- uh, the pardon," Jimmy says, and nods towards the Governor.

"Oh-," the old lawyer says and smile, "You're thanking the wrong man, James. You should thank him," he says, and points to Gordon.

"I've got to run, I'm driving over to Raiford to pick up Henry. We'll see you tomorrow?", Baron asks.

Jimmy nods, yes, and says, "I'll call, in the morning."

Jimmy strolls over to Gordon and offers his hand. Gordon looks at him and they shake.

"I want to thank you, for talking to the Governor for me. I appreciate it, you won't regret it, Gordon. I'm done, with everything, finished," Jimmy tells him.

"Well, are you going to make an honest woman out of Jill?", Gordon asks.

Jimmy nods and says, "Hopefully, yes. I haven't been able to see her since the night we-, at the lawyer's office."

Gordon looks at him, "Give her some time, Jimmy. She took it a lot harder than Lisa," he says, and pats Jimmy on the back. They shake hands again and part.

As Jimmy is walking away he hears Gordon calling him, he turns around and looks.

Gordon says, "Very nice piece of work, Jimmy."

Jimmy looks at him confused, but before he can ask, Gordon has made a pistol out of his right hand, and as he shoots Jimmy with it he winks at him and says, "Happy New Year."

CHAPTER TWENTY FIVE

September 1977

"Mama come put my guns in the ground,

I can't shoot them anymore."

Knockin On Heaven's Door/ Bob Dylan

Jimmy is standing with, Caz, at the nursery room glass window. Both men are staring in awe at the tiny baby boy with the blue wrist band attached, that proudly declares: Barnaby Casworth III.

Caz is bursting with pride, he almost can't believe that he's actually a father.

He and James are going down in a few minutes for the celebratory cigar, blue-banded naturally, and a good stiff drink, of black coffee- . Caz has quit drinking, its been over 3 months now. Its time to grow up, he's been a teenager for 27 years now and that's long enough, he's a proud father and a family man.

The two men are awaiting their friend, the good Dr. Smart, its almost 6:00 p.m. he should be along any minute. The three will go down together for the coffee and cigars.

It has been a very tumultuous Summer for all, much has happened. Gordon, Lisa and baby Carla have become sailor's, literally. They've bought a 42' sailing vessel, and with Gordon at the helm, are now sailing the Carribean Sea at a slow unhurried pace, they have all the time in the world.

Gordon has resigned from the U.S. Attorney's office, effective May 6th, 1977. Lisa too has ended her brief career as a state prosecutor, turning her temporary leave into a permanent one. She's Gordon's wife and Carla's Mommy, that's all the career she wants or needs.

Gordon is a sailor in heart, spirit and soul, and Lisa is the sailor's wife, Carla will have traveled the world with them by the time she is a teenager. It is an idyllic life they've decided on, God Bless.

Debbie Kamp graduated high school in June and she now is the first Kamp to attend college, she is a freshman at the University of Florida in Gainseville.

Kate is a lovely young woman of 22, and Richard Casworth is thoroughly convinced, indeed, he is smitten with the wise and womanly Kate, so much so that he convinced her to come to Princeton, NJ. with him while he earns his doctorate degree.

Hugh Mayor, the former Senator, is free on a 1 million dollar bail. He was arrested by the F.B.I at his senate office amid intense media coverage and scrutiny. He presently resides alone at the one time love nest condominium that he shared many an afternoon with Victoria at. Cynthia has filed for divorce, seeking award of all jointly held assets, including the condo.

The finger print taken from the bottle of Dewars White Label Scotch, found at the murder scene, is Hugh's. The testimony of Aranxa, the Smarts former housekeeper, along with the testimony of Jewel, the faithful Auntie Jewel to the girls and Cynthia, in support of Aranxa's testimony, will be enough to convict Hugh of Victoria's murder. His intoxication or lack thereof, will be inadmissable as speculation. The jury will hear of his bloody appearance upon return to his home later that evening.

In addition to the criminal proceedings, Henry and his daughter have filed a wrongful death civil action against Hugh Mayor. Things look very grim for the one time powerful politico.

Speaking of Henry and Nicole, the father and daughter have made amends. Nicole is all Henry has left of his beloved Victoria. Looking at Nicole now he sees his wife all those years ago, the night he first saw her. And Henry is all Nicole has too. She also has grown up and is no longer the foolish, selfish young woman she was just months ago.

The $1,999,000 checks are paid. Henry took care of it personally without the blink of an eye. He actually thanked Caz for, "Looking out for his little girl in her time of need,'" he had said.

He purchased a $400,000 penthouse condominium atop the Points of America for Nicole, and she will recieve a $25,000 quarterly dividend check, $100,000 annually, for the rest of her life. He's made it very clear that she is to live within that budget.

For himself he is undecided as yet. He's met a very attractive woman and perhaps... He smiles, yes, perhaps he'll enlist her help in choosing their(?) domicile. He presently resides in the residential portion of the old lawyer's offices.

Lt. Colonel Joseph Carosa will relinquish command of the 2nd Battalion, 101st Airborne division, at 2400 hours, December 31st, 1977. He has been designated for reassignment to the Army War College in Carlisle, PA., where he is to report by 1800 hours, January 31st, 1978. He will be 35 years of age when he completes the College of Command and becomes a full Colonel, the youngest on active duty in all branches of the armed forces.

He is marrying Captain Judy Stevens of the Criminal

Investigations Division, (CID), that same month, and they will
spend their honeymoon relocating from Ft. Benning in Columbus, GA.
to the War College in Carlisle PA.

Christy has married a great big bear of a man, a Norwegian
named, Flayvl, who is kind and gentle and loves her madly. The man
really can eat, and to Nettie's delight he consumes humongous
portions of her cooking. They continue to reside at the Carosa
home and any time Jimmy feels the need to revisit the past, whether
out of nostalgia or something deeper, it is there he goes.

After Henry's clemency hearing the ensuing days were a
confused jumble. Jimmy returned to work at the Whiteside project
and he gave Jill room to evaluate what she wanted to do.

He is certain those days at the Mayor home may just have
mirrored the days immediately following Angelo's untimely death.
Angelo's departure was complete, the healing could begin as fast
as the family could cope with and accept the loss, it still took
a long time.

With the Mayor tragedy there is no end, no closure, none
at all. It is an open festering wound for the three Mayor women.

Jimmy feels bad for all of them, Lisa too, her snobbery
a foolish affectation resulting from her cushioned, sheltered upbringing. She paid a very steep price in being rid of it.

Hugh Mayor is a monster and Jimmy feels nothing, no empathy,
for him. The man had everything, a beautiful wife and daughters
who loved him, financial means and a very good life indeed. It
wasn't enough, why? He deserves no consideration, he never gave

any so he hasn't any coming.

That doesn't mean the Mayor women. Jimmy feels they all deserve every consideration, the always correct and proper lady Cynthia most of all.

Just as Jimmy needed some time and space after Angelo, Jill needs hers now also.

And so, he waited. He saw Hugh's arrest on the television, he saw the T.V. and newspaper cameramen swarming the Mayor residence. He saw Cynthia, shielded by Gordon, Lisa and Jill making her way to the courthouse, and the same on the return trip from the court-house to the car.

The electric gates opening at the estate, the car slowly navigating through the throng camped outside, and finally the gate closing and sealing out the shouting hoard.

Thank God for that wall, he thinks, remembering the first time he visited the home and how awed he was, a walled castle he thought.

Useless? An unneeded visual accessory? An out-moded accoutrement of the rich without real purpose? Alas, not so, not at all. That wall now afforded them sanctuary.

And so he too stayed away. The one time he had phoned, the call was taken by a private security man who politely told him he would pass on, "his calling for the Miss," but she was at the moment unavailable.

The weeks passed. He brought Dr. Smart to his old home for Nettie's incomparable Italian cuisine. They went for steaks one night, got drunk another, celebrating-?, whatever.

Dr. Smarts insisting Jimmy take his offer of a loan, but Jimmy's holding to his refusal, "I don't need it, I've got a good job and I make pretty good money. If I need something I know where to come, and I know how to ask, okay?", Jimmy had told him, and Henry acceded.

Henry sent $100.00 a month to his friend, Scotty Fair, and $50.00 each to the two boys, Nelson and Skidmore, the latter nearing release soon.

Jimmy still made it to the beach during the long summer daylight hours to run 3,4 maybe 5 miles, right as the Sun would be beginning its descent into the West around 6- 6:30 p.m. His job working construction kept up his strength, the run his wind, and he would also air his thoughts out as he'd make his way up the nearly deserted shore.

Every other Sunday he took his mother to visit Angelo's grave and they'd lay fresh flowers and pray. Jimmy isn't very religious, however, he is Catholic and has beliefs. All Italians do, its that simple.

You ever see a Mafioso's funeral? Long lines of limo's, everyone in black, and the church packed full. Even the triggerman sometimes in attendance, its respect for the church, his murder was just business.

The centuries old curses the Italian mother's use, the ma' loika's?, you'll never see an Italian scoff at their validity, ever.

Some of the most hardened killers in the Mob have respect for the church. They may kill viciously and brutally, but they'll

doff their hats entering the church for the funeral. Also, no
shoes on a table or hats on a bed.

Is it their world that's the reality? Or-. Everyone has to
decide for themselves. Murderer's are some of the most polite,
cordial and respectful people you'll ever meet. While cowards are
usually the most obnoxious, rude and disrespectful of people, makes
you wonder-.

Jimmy is running the last ¼ mile back down the hard packed
sand when he see's her. She is shading her eyes with one hand and
using the other in a hitchhiking thumb out gesture.

He comes to a stop as she says, "Can I have a ride?" She
is bare foot in shorts and a bikini top.

He smiles and says, "Sure." He scoops her up and plunges
wildly into the surf with her howling laughter echoing up and down
the beach.

They are out chest deep facing each other. She is so
beautiful he can't help it so he kisses her.

"Will you take me back?", she asks.

"Jill, don't you know the answer?", he says.

"I want to hear it with my own ears, please," she playfully
insists.

He smiles, "Yes! Yes, and yes, okay?" he dutifully replies.

"You don't sound to sure, do want to think about it?" she
giggles. She's looking at him searchingly as he says, "I've thought
about nothing else since the night you rode on the bike with me to
the old lawyers."

She nods, yes, and says, "okay, I'm convinced, you may take me home now."

"Home?", he questions.

"Yes, its right there," she says, and points to a small frame house with a wrap around upper deck porch on the top floor, right across Ocean Blvd.

"It's Lisa and Gordon's, I'm house sitting until it sells. It has everything Jimmy, it just needs us, you and me, and then we're home," she says with utter finality.

Dr. Smart joins the two young men at the nursery window and they all wave at the small baby boy and head downstairs. Henry takes a puff on the stogie and starts coughing as Jimmy and Caz get a good laugh at the old Doctor's expense.

"Well the horrid things, now you know why they've been banned indoors," he wheezes. Dr. Smart and Jimmy hug good bye, as usual, while Caz shakes hands with both.

"One last thing gentlemen while I've got you both here. James, I've taken title of the beach house. The note will be held in perpetuity until the Mayor estate is settled. That could be some time- but regardless, the Rollins have been compensated and the house is now part of my trust. Whenever the Mayor estate is finalized then the note becomes due, but not until then," Dr. Smart says. He has finally been able to assist his young friend and is very pleased.

"Barnaby, if Nicole should need access to extra expense money by all means take care of it, but do not let her know I am aware of it," the Doctor instructs.

"Okay, Dr. Smart, I'll take care of it," Caz answers.

"Dr. Smart, I appreciate your help, I'll-", Jimmy begins but Henry silences him by raising his hand in a stop gesture, and says, "Understood, James, no problem, now- I must run. Mari is expecting me and I'm late already. God Bless you, James." Then Dr. Smart turns and walks away with quite a bounce in his step on the way to his car.

Marilyn and the good Doctor are engaged, both have recaptured the zest for life with each other.

Never say never, Mari, Jimmy thinks. He looks up into the star filled sky and nods, yes, definitely.

THE END.